The
BONES
OF THE EARTH

ALSO BY RACHEL DUNNE

In the Shadow of the Gods

THE BONES OF THE EARTH

A BOUND GODS NOVEL

RACHEL DUNNE

HARPER Voyager
An Imprint of HarperCollinsPublishers

THE BONES OF THE EARTH. Copyright © 2017 by Rachel Dunne. All rights reserved. Printed in the United States of America. No part of this book may be used or reproduced in any manner whatsoever without written permission except in the case of brief quotations embodied in critical articles and reviews. For information, address HarperCollins Publishers, 195 Broadway, New York, NY 10007.

HarperCollins books may be purchased for educational, business, or sales promotional use. For information, please email the Special Markets Department at SPsales@harpercollins.com.

Harper Voyager and design are trademarks of HarperCollins Publishers LLC.

FIRST EDITION

Designed by Paula Russell Szafranski

Library of Congress Cataloging-in-Publication Data has been applied for.

ISBN 978-0-06-242816-5

17 18 19 20 21   LSC   10 9 8 7 6 5 4 3 2 1

For my sister,
even though she
probably won't
ever read this

The Bones of the Earth

Prologue

Etarro's fingers scraped along the wall, loose stones crumbling away and rough spots tugging at the pads of his fingertips as he ran. The path he followed made a circle around the inside of the mountain, and he was running fast enough that the circling was starting to get to him, making his head spin worse than it already was, making it harder and harder not to throw up. If it hadn't been for the screaming, he would have stopped to catch his breath, to settle his head and his stomach. But there was the screaming, and his feet couldn't stop moving.

He ran from one pool of dull light to the next. The low-crackling torches with their blue flames were the only thing keeping the inside of Mount Raturo from being tar-black. The spaces between the torches *were* tar-black, so dark his hand against the wall was the only thing keeping him from stepping over the edge of the path and turning into a splatter on the floor of the mountain. He stopped breathing each time the wall ended in one of the hallways that branched off the central spiral, and he didn't start breathing until his fingers barked against the other side of the tunnel mouth.

There was no night or day here, but he tried to separate up the days nonetheless. The mountain had its own rhythm. It was dark, of course, but dark didn't always mean night, not inside Raturo. That was the thing with the preachers; they were nocturnal, or they liked to be, when they were out in the world. But they always slipped back into normal sleep patterns inside the mountain, resting when the sun was down. If they were sleeping now, that meant it really was night. It wouldn't be for much longer, though; the sun would poke up its fingers soon and wash away the night. He could imagine it, even over the distracting screaming: the sun touching the very top of the mountain first, so bright and warm it almost felt like he could reach up and wrap his arms about it. Avorra always scolded him when he went outside, cuffed him and told him he should know better—what if someone saw him? He almost turned around then—his twin was still sleeping; she wouldn't wake for a few hours, so no one would know if he watched the dawn.

But the screaming. He had to help, and so he kept going, down and down the finger-scraping spiral. He was almost glad no one else could hear the screaming, that it was only inside his own head. Almost. Because if anyone came walking up or down the spiral to investigate, he probably wouldn't have seen them. It wasn't any kind of comforting to think that if he ran into someone, at least he wouldn't be a lonely splatter on the mountain floor.

He'd forgotten his cloak, in the panicked waking and flight, and the cold tugged at him. It wound up along the path, riding along the insides of the mountain and nipping at his skin like a thousand tiny mouths. Avorra never minded the cold.

The preachers were always so proud of that. They'd watch her dancing around the Icefall and they'd grin, and then they'd look at Etarro, bundled miserably in furs and cloaks and blankets, and their smiles would flip. "Come, brother!" Avorra would call, sounding to all the world like an innocent girl at play. They couldn't hear the deeper tone, the warning in her voice, the threat. She'd told him once that she didn't like the cold any more than he did, but they had their parts to play.

Avorra was still sleeping now, but soon she'd wake up and see that Etarro was gone. He wouldn't know what to tell her when she asked. She never listened when he talked about the thumping, and she laughed if he brought up the voice. She would never believe the screaming—she didn't believe anything she couldn't see or touch. "You're getting too wrapped up in your part, brother," she would say. He said the words aloud, between raspy breaths, between the slaps of his feet against the ground, to try to convince himself of it.

The end of the spiral came on all sudden, his feet still trying to go down even though the floor was suddenly flat. He stubbed his toes against the ground and fell, palms and knees scraping against stone. The floor had been worn smooth by thousands of feet, but it was still rock, and it bit harder than the cold. The screaming got louder, like it was crying out in pain with him. It quieted back down when Etarro picked himself up, but it didn't fade away.

He had to pass by the arch with its big carved figures, but he kept his eyes on the floor. He could remember the first time he'd really understood what he saw. Avorra had touched the face of Sororra, the goddess who fell from the heavens without looking back. Her brother, Fratarro, did look back, and he cried and begged for mercy and reached for his Parents, and because he was looking up and not down, he didn't see the ground coming, didn't have time to hold himself together. The preachers never showed Etarro any pictures of how Fratarro would look, with his arms and legs torn off, and they never promised Etarro they knew where to find the missing limbs— they just gave vague answers when he asked, said they were sure all would be made whole again. They didn't seem to want him thinking about that part.

The way deeper was almost hidden, a small hole in the wall where the blue torchlight didn't quite reach. Etarro closed his eyes as he stepped through the opening, though there was no point to it. It would have been just as dark if he kept his eyes open. There was a difference to it, though. It was easier to walk in a darkness that was of his own making.

He knew when to open his eyes, knew where the first flickering ghostlight would be. Dirrakara had said that they must have been something of Fratarro's creation, the purest light. The preachers had been trying for years to use the little moving lights to replace the blue torches, but they hadn't had any luck. Out of the Cavern of the Falls, the ghostlights guttered and died.

Inside the big cavern, the screaming started to quiet. It didn't go away, but it faded enough to make him feel less panicked, to let Etarro think about something other than the pain that wasn't even his. He could breathe, could feel his heart slowing down. He reached up to touch one of the ghostlights, feeling the soft warmth against his palm. Not enough to make him stop shivering, or to keep his breath from frosting in the air, but enough to make him smile, even though the screaming still rattled around between his ears.

He liked to imagine Fratarro as the creator the preachers said he'd been, pulling Raturo from the earth so he could sit at its peak and shape an untouched corner of the world that could be his alone. He liked to think of Fratarro standing here, in the center of a big empty cavern, and wondering how he could make it beautiful. Even though it froze the tips of his fingers, sometimes Etarro liked to break off spines from the Icefall and shape them into castles or creatures, breathing on the broken-off ends until they melted enough to stick together. "I am Fratarro," he would say then, trying to make himself believe it. He wondered if Fratarro could be put together so easily, breathing on his arms and legs until they stuck back on his body.

He walked out to the Icefall, not to shape anything but because the voice was always loudest there. He'd told Avorra that, once; she'd made him repeat it when more of the Ventallo were around. "You can't forget the audience," she'd reminded him.

This was a calm place, a powerful place. Even though they were still so far away, Etarro always felt like they were closer here, in the Cavern of the Falls. There was a small space, almost too small for him now, between the Icefall and the stony ledge it tumbled motionlessly from. He wedged himself into the space, shivering, and let out his breath in a slow fog. "I'm here, brother," he said aloud, though he said it to the screaming in his head. The screaming didn't stop, but little by little, across the immeasurable distance between them, Etarro felt the terror slowly begin to fade, leaving behind only the pain that was too great to be held back yet. Etarro sat there, cold burning through his nose and lungs, and offered what comfort he could.

Help me, the familiar voice finally came, smaller and weaker than usual, soft behind the screaming and the sobbing. *Please. It has been too long. This is too much. Please. Find me.*

"We found your foot," he offered, though it wasn't enough. One of the Ventallo, Tenso Ocdeiro, had shown him and Avorra five glowstones that he said showed the path to glory. The broken-minded mage, Anddyr, had made the stones so the Ventallo would know when their emissaries were successful. The five stones were laid out like a crooked compass on top of the giant stone bier, and Ocdeiro had lifted Etarro up so he could press a finger to each one. Four of them were just like normal stones, cold and lifeless, but the one that was slightly north of center had a soft light to it. When Etarro had touched that one, he'd seen the gnarled roots of an enormous tree, holding something huge and black. He hadn't been able to see it as a foot, but Ocdeiro had been sure of it. He said Ebarran Septeiro would be back with it any day, and then they'd know for sure. He said the other stones would start glowing soon, too, that soon they'd have all the pieces of Fratarro. Soon they'd be able to put the poor lost god back together.

Find me, Fratarro said weakly, the same plea it always was.

Avorra had laughed at Etarro the first time, but she'd gotten scared the more he'd talked about the voice that begged to be found. She'd told him to ignore it, to never talk about it again. He hadn't, he'd been good, but it had happened once when Anddyr had come slinking into their rooms. The mage had sat quietly in the corner and watched them play with eyes that were almost hungry, but he wouldn't join them. When Etarro had heard the voice, he'd seen it roll through Anddyr as well. "You hear him, too," he'd said, and the mage's eyes had been even bigger than usual. Avorra had yelled at him for that, and then she'd started crying, sure they'd be in the sort of trouble that preachers sometimes disappeared for. Anddyr's hands had been shaking, but he'd touched the top of her head, gently, comforting, his skin pale against the darkness of Avorra's hair.

There was a crack, the sound of ice breaking. Etarro's head snapped up, and there, among the ghostlights near the entrance to the cavern, he could see them. A line of preachers was filing into the cavern, fifteen of them in their black robes, and the ghostlights picked out the red points sewn over their hearts.

Etarro thought of squeezing out from his hiding place, standing and greeting the Ventallo so they would know he was there, so they would let him go somewhere else quiet to share Fratarro's pain. Then he thought of Avorra, and how she knew every secret passage and hiding place in the mountain, and how she always said with a toothy smile, "Anything worth hiding is worth knowing." She didn't always share the things she learned. It was the having of secrets that mattered to her; the using and the doing could be saved for later. She gathered secrets around her like a shroud, or a shield. She might listen to him for once, if he had a secret to offer her. So quietly he wedged himself deeper into the crevice, and he watched through the holes and the thin places of the Icefall.

They had stopped at the edge of the frozen lake, all the Ventallo except the ones who'd gone out searching. Valrik Uniro stood before them, as always, with Illo Duero and Ildra Trera on either side. Some of the Ventallo gazed up at him with red sockets that were an empty mirror of Uniro's own missing eyes.

Many of the preachers had been desperate to follow his example in blinding themselves, though it was hard to tell whether it was because of renewed faith or the fearful following that took over in times of change. "They've all got their own parts to play," Avorra had murmured. She'd told him how she'd heard Duero and Uniro talking, how Duero had begged to keep his eyes because he was the historian, the recorder of times. She'd lowered her voice in a poor imitation of Uniro and rumbled, "In the darkness, we have no need of the past. In the darkness, there is only the now, and to write of it is to waste it." Duero still had his eyes, though, so he must have won the argument. Trera, too, still had every part of her hard, unhappy face.

"I have had a dream this night," Uniro said, his voice made louder in the big space. "Many of you know, my dreams have become sharper since I embraced the darkness." There was some murmuring of agreement among the ones who'd also blinded themselves. "It was a dream that unsettled me deeply, my brothers and sisters, for it was a dream that rang with truth even as it showed me hard choices. We stand now at the center of a crossroads, and the path forks in many directions. Which to choose? Which is right, and which is best, and which hurts the least?

"In my dream, I took each path in turn. I have seen all the endings, my brothers and sisters, and I have spent long hours thinking on what I saw at the end of each path. If it has been given to me to choose the path of the Fallen, then I must make sure I choose wisely." Uniro bowed his old head, and was silent for a long while. The silence sent a chill tiptoeing up Etarro's spine. Etarro had true-dreams, had them almost as often as he slept, and Uniro's words had had the sound of truth.

Etarro wrapped his arms tightly around himself as he shivered in his cocoon of ice. He wished he'd left when he'd had the chance. Avorra would have thrilled to be where he was, giddy with spying on the Ventallo, but Etarro only wanted to be far away from this place.

Trera's voice was gruff as she asked, "What is it to be, brother? What path will you choose for the Fallen?"

Uniro took a heavy breath, and lifted his face to her. "Tell me, dear sister. What is it we always say the Twins will do? What is their goal?"

"To pull down the Mother's Sun," she said, slightly uncertain, as though such an easy question must be a trap. "In the darkness, all are made equal."

"Precisely. And yet . . ." Uniro spread his arms wide, like he meant to embrace the Ventallo standing before him. "What are we? We are leaders. First and second and twelfth and twentieth among the Ventallo, and the Ventallo are first among the Fallen. We are rulers, when the Twins would have no rulers in the Long Night.

"If we find the Twins, if we go to them as the Ventallo, we shall surely be among the first to be struck down. I cannot bear this thought. There must be change, and it must begin with us." Uniro's empty eyes looked out over the Ventallo gathered before him, and his voice was like a deep drum. "I, Valrik Uniro, eighty-seventh leader of the Fallen, do hereby disband the Ventallo."

There were shouts and cries from some, Trera and Duero the loudest . . . but some of the Ventallo stayed silent and still, their faces smooth as ice, as if they weren't surprised at all.

They fell silent when Uniro lifted his hands again. "I feel

your concern, brothers and sisters. Change can be a frightful thing, and I can feel the anger glowing in some of you. Trust me when I say you do not wish to face the Twins as Ventallo. Trust me, for I shall lead the way along this path."

"Lead?" Trera snapped. "Who are you, to stand above the rules you would yoke us with?"

Valrik seemed to study her with his empty sockets. "Who am I?" he repeated. "I shed the name Uniro, for I am first among none. I am only a man. Yet . . . a flock has a shepherd, an army a general. Though the night sky is full of stars, still there is the moon. I am no longer Uniro, but I have seen the dark that sits at the end of some paths and the light that covers others, and I shall be the moon to show the way through the night. I shall lead, for someone must, and I shall face the judgment of the Twins when I stand before them. I will spare you all that much, at least." His old face, grizzled with long beard and longer hair, looked so sad in the glow of the dancing ghostlights. "It is time, brothers and sisters, for the first judgment."

From his hiding place, Etarro didn't see the men until they were almost behind the Ventallo. He recognized them, five of the big swordsmen Valrik had been collecting as bodyguards. Blades for the darkness, he called them. Etarro saw them before the Ventallo, who didn't even have time to turn and scream before the swords went through them. Five fell instantly, and then three more. Etarro had to bite his tongue to keep from crying out, and pressed both hands over his mouth. Only four of the Ventallo were left standing before Valrik and Duero and Trera. Only four, three blind and one sighted, among the bodies and the blood that began to spread slowly over the cold ground. They stood with their backs straight, faces tight but fearless.

Etarro had seen that look before, on new preachers fresh off the mountain—they'd already faced their death half a dozen times, and weren't afraid of it anymore.

Etarro wished he could be that fearless, but he was shaking, and there were tears warm in the corners of his eyes.

The blades looked to Valrik, who gave a small nod, as though he could see their gazes. Two of the blades stepped forward, to his sides, and gave two more bodies to the pile. Trera had time to scream and name them all traitors before her voice was cut off. Duero died as quietly as a page being torn free from a book, the sickly, surprised look never leaving his face.

Etarro wrapped his arms around his head, and shook silently. He couldn't bear to see any more, but from where he hid, there was nowhere else to look. Still, he couldn't hide his ears.

Valrik sounded almost sad as he spoke again to the fallen Ventallo. "I have judged you more kindly than the Twins would have. Even had you stood before them not as leaders but as common men and women, they would have found you wanting. May they find you more worthy in your next life than you have been in this one." He blinked and looked up from the scattered bodies, and it was like he forgot about them, easy as breathing. When he talked to the four who were left living, his voice came harder. "You have your own paths to choose. In my dream, I saw each of you walking at my side down this path . . . but you were shadows, wisps of cloud, indistinct and impermanent. I hope that you would choose to solidify your places at my side, that you will prove your faith time and again. I hope that you will not prove my judgment in you wrong, for when the Long Night comes, there will be no mercy for liars and blasphemers." Then he clapped his palms together three times, the sound loud enough to shiver the icicles hanging from the ceiling, to make the Icefall vibrate around Etarro's curled form.

Etarro wanted to keep his face hidden, to pretend he was somewhere else . . . but he thought of Avorra. If she were here, she'd have her eyes pressed against the Icefall, lips stretched back in a dog's grin. "All secrets are worth knowing," she'd say. "A secret pays better than gold." Etarro lifted his head again and pressed his forehead against the cold of the ice. Great big shivers rolled through him but he didn't look away.

A dozen preachers and half as many shaking blue-robed mages came down the tunnel at a slow pace. They went to stand next to the four survivors, in the spreading blood. No one looked down, but they were very careful not to step on the bodies, even the ones who'd blinded themselves and couldn't possibly see the sprawling limbs.

"Welcome, brothers and sisters," Valrik said softly when they stood before him. "You have been chosen, but know this: you are not Ventallo. You are not leaders among the Fallen. In the darkness, there are no kings and queens. You are guides, only. Stars in the darkness, to give our brothers and sisters enough light that they do not stumble, or fall. If you came here seeking greatness or power, leave now. You will not find them here." No one moved. Only the blood, creeping out slowly onto the frozen lake, stretching out toward Etarro where he hid. Valrik nodded his head. "Know this, too: I am Valrik, and I am not Uniro, but I will lead the Fallen to our destiny, and I will face the Twins' punishment for placing myself above you. I will bear this burden, so that no others have to. If you cannot abide this, speak now."

There was silence again, broken only by the creaking leather armor of the blades, who stood with their arms crossed at the waist, ready, waiting. No one spoke against Valrik.

"Good. Then, my brothers and sisters, there is something we must begin here, word you must spread among the flock. We have found powerful allies in our friends, the mages. But Delcerro Uniro—may his spirit rest at ease among the stars— was not wise in their deployment. The mages are spread out among us, and we keep them as servants, as assistants. They can be so much more. We must correct the mistake of my predecessor. United under one hand, our mages will be a powerful force indeed. Neira."

A woman stepped forward from the group, the hem of her robe heavy with blood. She'd been one of the ones to stand still and silent as her brothers and sisters died around her, her empty eyes fixed on Valrik. She stepped to his side now, her feet sure and her steps steady, and she lifted a small jar before her. It was the same as so many other jars in Raturo, full of the black paste called skura that made the mages . . . *helpful*. Neira held the jar like it was something holy as she said, "Our sister Dirrakara was the one to create skura, but she did not unlock all its uses. She gave us the key to binding a mage to one preacher, but . . . I'm sure you remember Gerthis."

Etarro shuddered. Gerthis had been a mage serving Serteno, one of the oldest preachers in the mountain, and old Serteno had died in his sleep. Gerthis had gone slowly mad—or more mad than all the mages were—and his screaming had echoed through Raturo for days until he'd finally died in his sleep, too. At least, that was what everyone said had happened to him.

Neira smiled faintly. "We won't have that problem again. I've found that skura is quite versatile. We can change its binding powers." She lifted her other hand with a flourish, and Etarro could hardly see what she held between her thumb and forefinger—something small like a bead, and deep-ice blue. She dropped it into the skura, and then pulled out a small knife. Valrik held his hand out to her and she pricked his thumb, letting a few drops of his blood fall into the skura jar. She stirred it all together, and then she called the mages forward to spread some of the black paste on each of their tongues.

There were a few heartbeats where nothing happened . . . and then, one by one, the mages collapsed, screaming and screeching, hurt-animal sounds that made Etarro's teeth ache. He screwed shut his eyes and clapped his hands over his ears and tried not to add his own screaming to theirs.

It felt like it went on for hours, shaking the Icefall so that he was sure it would crumble around him, fall to pieces so that they'd all see him curled there, cowardly and snooping, and the blades would come forward with their star-bright swords and his body would join the others on the cavern floor, his blood creeping along the ice . . .

The screams stopped suddenly, though the echoes were slow to fade. Etarro peeked one eye open and saw that the mages were sitting up slowly, holding or shaking their heads, groaning and muttering. He couldn't see any kind of wound that would make them scream like that, and they seemed to be fine now—or as fine as the mages ever were.

"Rise," Valrik said, and the mages got to their feet as quickly as they could. Valrik went on. "You see that they're still obedient, still helpful. They'll still aid any who ask it from them. But . . . Neira?"

The woman stepped forward to stand right in front of one

of the mages, tapped his forehead to get his attention. She pointed to one of the black-armored blades and, holding the mage's gaze with the empty pits of her own eyes, said slowly and clearly, "Kill him."

Etarro could see the panic touching the blade's face as the mage began to twist his fingers in the shapes of sigils, murmuring the spell under his breath. The spell built and built, and Etarro could feel the pressure of it behind his eyes. The blade drew his sword, and then couldn't think what to do with it, he just stood facing the mage and the glow of the killing spell building between the mage's dancing fingers. The mage made the final flourish and was halfway through throwing it at the blade when Valrik said softly, "Stop."

The mage scrambled to pull the spell back, curling into himself, frantic fingers weaving wildly. The spell shattered, knocking the mage to the ground with its force, and Etarro nearly choked as the sudden change in pressure made his nose begin to bleed.

"Kill him," Neira said again to the mage, who was sprawled and gasping, but he didn't move, didn't raise a finger to obey her, and she smiled.

"Through this process," Valrik said proudly, "they will heed my word above all others."

No one argued aloud against one man having such power, and the silence almost—*almost*—spoke clearly enough for them. But Etarro knew better than anyone that a silence was easy to ignore.

"We must bring everyone home now, all our wandering brothers and sisters," Valrik said. "We will need our full might for what is to come. Each of us has our part to play, and we must be ready. So go. Send messengers, send the faithful to find our brothers and sisters who have spread the word of the Twins far across the land. Bring them home. We must stand together, tight as family, tight as blood, for we walk a new path. Hear me when I say we step toward power, and greatness, and eternal acclaim. These are our first steps on the road to a glorious present."

They cheered him, the Ventallo who remained and those Valrik had named shepherds for the Fallen. If they were unhappy about the mages, the unhappiness faded away quickly. They praised his name, and he bade them to go forth and spread the word that all should prepare, that their time was nigh, that the faithful would be rewarded beyond their dreams and the judgment of the Twins would not be a gentle thing for the faithless.

And then they left, preachers and mages and blades walking unerringly on the icy and stone-scattered ground. The blades took a body over each of their shoulders, and then the Cavern of the Falls was empty of all but Etarro and the freezing blood.

He didn't know when the screaming in his head had stopped—sometime after the Ventallo had come, he'd been so focused on them. There was a final sob from distant Fratarro, a lament for the piece of him that had been destroyed and would never be restored, and then he piled it all behind a wall again, to keep the fear and the pain trapped. No one, not even a god, could feel so much pain and survive it. Fratarro had learned to keep his locked away. Etarro wanted to offer some last comfort, but his throat was tight and, now that he didn't have to hold them together to keep quiet, his teeth were chattering so bad he didn't think he could speak anyway. In small movements, he gingerly unwedged himself from behind the Icefall. The blood had stilled, frozen with its fingers stretching halfway across the lake. He wondered if Valrik would send someone to clean up the blood, of if he'd have it left there as a reminder, or if it was even something he'd thought about behind his sightless eyes.

He had to climb over rocks to avoid the blood, but there was no getting around the red boot prints. There was only the one way out of the cavern. He closed his eyes as he always did, and wrapped his arms around his shaking body, and tried not to think much as he left the cavern. When his mind couldn't stay still, he repeated over and over to himself, *A part to play. A part to play.*

"You have to be the people they expect you to be," Anddyr had whispered to him and Avorra, in one of the times when his pupils weren't so big that you couldn't see any color around them. "Think of it like a game. Do the things they'd want you to do, always. Even when it's just the two of you. Play the part so well that you forget it's a part. Be what they need you to be. It's the only way." And then he'd twisted up, hands grabbing at his stomach, his legs crumpling. Avorra had held his head in her lap, to keep his shaking from making his head thump against the floor, and she'd cried for him. "You have to be what they need," Anddyr had hissed, his fingers like claws around Etarro's arm. "If they don't need you, they'll kill you." Etarro had run off to find Cappo Joros, and when they'd got back Avorra was across the room, far away from where Anddyr lay shaking, and Etarro hadn't known the look in his sister's dry eyes.

Avorra had looked at him differently, after that. Her face had gone hard. He couldn't remember if they'd ever really been young, either of them, but if she ever had been, Avorra wasn't after that. "You'll have to tell them," she'd said the first time he'd heard Fratarro after what Anddyr had said. She could always tell when it happened. "It's one of the things they'll want to hear. But . . . you have to act like it's real. You can't tell them you're just pretending." There had been a question in her face, and a hope, and a need he wasn't used to seeing. She'd wanted to believe so bad. So he'd nodded and told her he'd keep pretending, just like he had been all along, but he'd pretend even better now. She'd smiled like a starving person finding food and hugged him hard, and never believed anything except the lie.

There was a part to play. Avorra loved her secrets, but Etarro held on to his, too, when he could. He didn't tell them when he heard the voice, not always, not if Avorra hadn't seen his eyes go distant. It was his small way of holding on to himself, so that he never forgot it was just a part he was playing. He thought Avorra had probably forgotten, lost inside the Avorra that had been shaped by the mountain and the Ventallo and the desperate words of a crazed man. He didn't think she would have cared, if she'd seen what Valrik had done today. He could almost hear her laugh and say, "They should have played along better."

Light finally touched his eyelids. He looked at his feet first, and there, among the big red boot prints stretching behind him like a tail, was a set of smaller, fainter prints.

As he passed by the huge arch this time, he stopped. The carving of Sororra's face was on a level with his, her mouth set, watching the ground below prepare to swallow her up with her hard eyes. Avorra used to stand here, when everyone else was sleeping, holding a torch in one hand and a piece of polished bronze in the other, her gaze flicking between Sororra's face and the mirror. It had sent chills through Etarro, the first time she'd gotten it exactly right. It didn't scare him anymore, it was just the way her face was now. It was the part she'd become.

He had to step back to see Fratarro's face, so high above. Mouth open and begging for mercy, face twisted with grief. Fratarro had just watched Patharro destroy his greatest creation, the beautiful lands to the south and the *mravigi* he'd shaped to live there. There were tears carved onto his cheeks. Etarro couldn't remember if he'd ever cried. He supposed all children cried, but he'd never been young, never been allowed to be a child.

There was a part to play, and if Etarro placed any value on his life, he would have to start playing it better. Red boot prints followed behind him as he went to find Valrik. He would stare into the places where his eyes weren't, and tell him of the screaming and the hand and how things could still be made whole.

PART ONE

It's a lucky man who knows his place in the world.

We're not all given such good fortune.

—Parro Kerrus

CHAPTER ONE

Sometimes it felt like not moving at all, like lifting your foot up and setting it down in the exact same place, over and over again and not even knowing it. There was no telling one gray swirling spot from another. Even the sounds here were faded, the snow swallowing up the hoof steps, the wind snatching at any voice. The only thing that made Rora believe they were moving were the drips of blood that trailed after 'em, sometimes tiny flecks of it and other times big splotches that grabbed at her heart and made her kick her horse faster, leaving the blood behind in the snow.

Joros, the closest thing their little band had to a leader, he'd tried half a dozen times to call a halt, to stop and sleep and eat. Rora'd just stared him down, and she guessed the other set of staring eyes—the giant white cloak she wore had a snowbear's head for a hood, and its black eyes glared above hers—well, they cowed him a little, too. It was mostly the merra, Vatri, who talked him down, though. Those two were stuck together tighter'n flies on a corpse, ever since they'd found and burned the god's hand.

At least Aro was helping much as he could, keeping his horse right at her side. Her brother was good for loyalty, that much was true. The mumbling witch, Anddyr, was sitting double behind Aro. The witch'd been pretty silent ever since the burning—still talked to himself, of course, and he'd point the direction whenever Aro asked him for it, his shaking finger jabbing into the featureless gray. Crazy as he was, Rora hoped he really knew where they were going. He'd got them to the hand in the first place, so that was a mark in his favor, but only having one choice was always harder to swallow.

She twisted around toward the horse trudging along just behind her. All the blood had spooked it at first, but now it just kept on going, one hoof in front of the other. It looked about as tired as Rora felt, ready to tip right over if it leaned too far one way. There wasn't any blood anymore to spook it, and she hoped that was more a good thing than a bad thing.

Back at the camp, near everyone'd been useless, all of them half-panicked after Scal'd collapsed and they'd seen the blood hidden by his layers of furs. The witch'd said he was tapped dry, no magic left in him until he rested, and Joros'd just glared like he wasn't used to having to mind when people under his command got hurt. The merra'd fallen on Scal's chest and wailed like a widow, most useless thing she could've possibly done, so it'd been up to Rora to put as much pressure as she could around the big gaping wound and tie him up tight. There wasn't anything better she could do there, so their best hope was getting out of the fecking North.

Aro'd surprised her by pulling a few coils of rope out of his travelsack, and even though her blood'd been pounding in her ears, Rora'd paused to lift her eyebrows at him. "Garim always said to keep some rope around," he'd said as he unwound it. There wasn't much room in her for anything but the fear right then, but maybe later, once they were safe and she knew if Scal was dead or not, maybe she could think on how her brother might be just as grown as she was.

The witch had taken the rope and not met any of their eyes when he said he knew how to tie a man to a horse. He'd done a good enough job of it, because even though Scal'd slumped farther and farther down, near curled in half now, he hadn't tipped to either side. Dried blood stretched down his side, winding down his leg and the rope wrapped around it. He'd been bleeding for so long . . . It had to be that the wound had finally just sealed itself up, stopped bleeding on its own—had to be that, because the only other thing that made sense was that he was out of blood to bleed . . .

She hadn't dared to stop, to peel back the layers of clothes and makeshift bandages—stopping would mean time, and that was one thing they didn't have. And if she checked, then she'd know for sure if he was dead or not.

She tried to tell herself he wasn't, but truth was, she'd seen lesser wounds kill people. Scal had a big gash in his side, curving around his ribs and down to his stomach so you could see bone and other pieces that weren't ever supposed to see daylight. She could remember being surprised, after Scal'd fought half the North, that he hadn't been hurt at all. Turned out he was just real good at hiding his hurts, because she hadn't had time to even try to count the other scratches and pokes all over his body before they'd packed up that bad wound and gotten moving. And since then, it'd just been moving, trying to find their way to anywhere before . . . well, before.

Sometimes, when the wind died real sudden like the last breath leaving a person's lungs, Rora could hear the merra praying soft but steady, words about warmth and the heart's fire that sounded small surrounded by so much snow. Rora'd never had much cause to thank the Parents, but she'd never cursed 'em much either. Maybe she should've done more of one or the other.

With the sky and the ground the same color, Rora didn't notice anything different at first. It wasn't until Aro called, "Rora?" that she noticed the bit of yellow licking at the clouds, a fire not quite ready to die, but having a hard time finding anything more to eat.

They stopped for the first time in what seemed like forever. It felt wrong, with Scal behind her maybe-dead. It made her twitchy. Squinting through the snow and the smoke, Rora could pick out a wooden wall, part of it burned, part of it still burning, most of it still standing as far as she could tell. "You think it's a town?" she asked. "Did we make it through the North?"

"The camp," the witch said quietly, his face pressed up against Aro's back, eyes squeezed shut. "It's burning again."

She could remember passing by the convict camp on their way farther north; part of it'd been burning then, too, a different chunk of the wooden wall. Scal hadn't wanted to go anywhere near it. Aro'd said he felt guilty, leaving the place to burn, not knowing if there was anyone hurt. Joros'd scoffed at him and said even if they were all dead, they were convicts anyway, and Aro'd bristled at that. Most of the Scum back in Mercetta, most everyone they'd known in the capital, would be judged convicts if they were ever unlucky enough to get caught. Scal had called the place Aardanel and moved away from it like he could feel the flames, even far away as they'd been.

On the way into the North, Aardanel'd been a handful of days after the last village. That meant they were more days away from any help for Scal. Rora couldn't decide if that made her want to throw up, or cry.

"How is it still burning?" Aro asked. It was a thing he was good at—asking stupid questions when he was too scared to let there be silence.

"It's not," Rora said. "It's burning *again*." The witch'd said those same damn words a moment before, but Aro couldn't let a silence stand, couldn't let smarter people take any time to think . . . But it made something rise up in Rora's throat—not puke, lucky enough, but something that tasted real close to hoping. "Better question is why would you burn a place twice, if you'd already killed everyone and got everything you wanted?"

"Because Northmen are brutal bastards." Aro glanced guiltily back at Scal, but he didn't apologize. It was true enough, and Scal sure as hells wasn't going to argue.

"Or because everyone's *not* dead," Rora said, excitement rising up along with the hope. "You keep attacking a place because you need to kill everyone before you can get to what's inside." Her fingers ached with how hard she was squeezing them around the reins. "Aro, there might be people there still. There might be help."

Aro stared with her at the burning chunk of wall, both of 'em trying to see through the fire and the smoke. "Or there might be Northmen," he said softly.

"There might. But before you wanted to go check and make sure everyone was okay, yeah? Better later'n not ever." Rora glanced over her shoulder; beyond Scal's slumped form, she could just make out Joros and the merra, far enough back that maybe they would've heard if she shouted, but probably not. Even though Joros was the head of their group, she didn't see much point in wasting time waiting for him to catch up so he could make the choice she already knew he'd make. On the way into the North, he'd wanted to stop at the camp just as bad as Aro. "Let's go see if there's anyone alive," she said. It took some persuading to get her horse to pick its feet up again, but it started dutifully forward and Rora's numb fingers pulled at Scal's horse, towing it behind.

By the time they got close, Joros and the merra had caught up, drawn by the flames. Rora could see people scurrying around the fiery wall, throwing buckets of snow. Already, the fire was beginning to die down. Even though they were still a ways off, Rora heard the clanking of chains.

They reacted fast enough, especially considering how much of a distraction the fire was. Rora and the others hadn't gotten much closer before a group split off and formed a line, and then there were some scattered *thunks*, and suddenly the ground in front of Rora had a handful of crossbow bolts in it. That made her pull up sharply, because even if those hadn't been great shots, she knew the second round'd be better.

Joros stood up in his stirrups and cupped both hands near his mouth to bellow, "Hold!"

No more bolts got fired, and after a moment, a voice came over the snows: "Your business?"

"We've a wounded man," Joros called back. "We seek shelter."

They took their time about it, huddled together and talking, and all the while Rora couldn't help glancing at Scal, at how still he was. If he was breathing, they were small breaths, so small they hardly moved him. The merra rode up next to him, placed her hand on his bowed head, and prayed for him again. Rora caught her lips moving along with the words and stopped them, clenching her jaw and praying instead that the people from the camp would fecking hurry up.

Finally they started walking forward, keeping their crossbows leveled. There were seven of 'em, which meant enough bolts for them to feel safe. They were walking so slow it made Rora want to scream, until they finally stopped and one of them called, "Where's your wounded?" Rora tugged at the reins she held, and Scal's horse plodded forward a few steps to stand even with her. Even far away as they were, she heard the low, angry hiss that rippled through the seven of them. "Northman," one finally spat.

She should've expected it. She'd been so wrapped up just in finding anywhere that she hadn't thought about how most Fiaterans would go out of their way to *not* help a Northman. The hate probably ran even deeper in the men trapped up in the North. Hells, Aro was right; it was probably Northmen who'd started their camp afire.

The crossbows were still aimed; Rora, because she was at the front with Joros, could see the one pointed right at her chest. "You'll be leaving now," one of the men said levelly.

With slow movements, to keep from spooking any of the

men, Joros reached inside his cloak and brought out a draw-string bag. He tossed it so it landed between him and the bow-man, hitting the ground with the heavy clink of coins. The man always seemed to have coinpurses ferreted away; Rora pushed that into her brain for the future, but there were other things to worry about now. "Shelter for one night," Joros said, his voice steady and certain, like he knew you couldn't argue with what he was saying. "We'll tend to the Northman—he's in no condi-tion to cause any trouble."

"Sure won't be after he's dead."

Rora saw anger flash on Joros's face, and she grimly kicked her feet out of the stirrups. He was about to do something stu-pid, which meant she was about to have to avoid a crossbow bolt. She flexed her fingers, trying to work some blood back into them so maybe she could throw one of her daggers if she had to.

"Do you have a priest here?" The merra pushed her way to the front of their group, her head held high. A fire had made a wreck of her face, but if they could look beyond the scars to notice her yellow robes, they'd know her for a priestess.

It took a while for any of them to find their voice back, to give a tentative, "Aye. We've a parro."

"You will take us to him," Vatri said, and there wasn't any room for arguing in her voice. You'd have to be dumb to argue to a priest's face in the first place, and this one's face especially. They put on a show of resistance, shuffling their feet, suddenly none of 'em wanting to be in charge, but they eventually turned and marched back to their camp, and Rora and the others fol-lowed with the merra in the lead. Anddyr scrambled off Aro's horse to retrieve the coinpurse for Joros, and then the witch-man trudged along next to them, slogging through the snow.

The fire was under control by the time they reached Aardanel, only a few small spots of flame that were almost ready to die even without the buckets of snow being thrown at them. One of the crossbowmen broke away, probably to report the situation to the others, and probably to ready everyone inside for the arrival of a Northman, too. Keeping her movements small, Rora slipped one of her daggers out of its slim sheath at her hip and snuck it up her sleeve, fingers rubbing at the broken blue stone in the hilt for comfort. The edges of the pommel stone were sharp, but it was a hard habit to break. She didn't like her odds of taking on a whole convict camp with only a few knives, but she'd be damned if she wouldn't be ready for it.

They were hard people, harder even than they'd been when they were sent here in the first place. You had to've got damned unlucky to become a convict—hells, Rora'd be judged a convict more'n a dozen times over if she ever got put before a magistrate—and for convicts, it was hanging or working. It seemed easier, to choose working. That meant living, after all. But looking at the faces of the convicts, the men and women with a cross cut into their left cheeks, some with chains strung between wrists and ankles—their eyes were deader'n hanged men's.

The children were worse.

Back in the Canals, kids ate what they could steal or earn, and that usually wasn't much. Pups—those kids who had enough skill to earn the protection of one of the packs—ate a bit better, but they still mostly got scraps. Here, you could tell there was no kind of protection, nothing to steal or earn. They had hollow eyes in hollow bodies, and each of 'em looked a step away from death.

It seemed like they had to walk through the whole camp to get to the priest, past every skinny face and all the people waiting like tinder for a spark to light them. But finally they got to the chapel, which looked just like every other building except for the sun and flame hanging above the door, and found the parro outside wringing his hands. He was small, almost swallowed by the thick furs he wore over his red cassock, and he looked like the nervous sort of man pickpockets learned to avoid, the kind that was always checking to make sure his coins were still there.

Vatri glared him into submission, and he quickly opened up the door to the chapel. It took all of them—no help from the convicts or the crossbowmen, of course—to drag Scal down off the horse and into the chapel, where it was a little warmer'n outside. There was a fire burning in a metal bowl at the center of the room, hardly big enough to give off any warmth, but it was better'n nothing. They laid Scal out near the fire, and still the parro hadn't said a word, but he started praying pretty hastily as they unwrapped the layers of bloody cloth wound around Scal. "I need water," Vatri told him, and the parro was happy enough to leave for a while.

The cloth stuck to him, the dried blood trying to use the fabric like extra skin, and when they finally peeled it back, there was fresh blood with all the dried. They cleaned away as much of it as they could, the parro muttering frantic prayers as the water he'd brought went from pink to red to brown. The big wound was starting to stitch itself up at the far edges, but it still gaped open in places. Scal had blood left in him, so that was good, but he'd already lost so much of it, which wasn't good at all. Rora didn't want to ask the merra if they were already too late. They should've stopped sooner, shouldn't've let him bleed so much, should've done something different . . .

"We'll need clean linen," Vatri said grimly to the parro. "And brandy." She paused as the priest left, and didn't meet Rora's eyes as she added, "I'll need a knife."

The blue-pommeled dagger was in her sleeve, and Rora didn't need to be told what to do with it. There was a sick feeling in her stomach as she stuck the blade into the coals of the fire.

Vatri poured half the jug of brandy over the wound. Anddyr and Aro pushed down on Scal's shoulders in case he woke up, and Rora gently pushed the edges of the wound as close together as she could. The merra prayed for what felt like too long over the knife before she pulled it from the coals, her hand wrapped with heavy cloth where she held the hilt.

Scal didn't wake when Vatri pressed the blade against his flesh, which was a blessing. For as long as it took to draw one sharp breath, she held the dagger there. The stench of burned meat followed as she pulled the knife away and pressed it down again, higher up along the wound, the dagger's tip crossing over the curled, blackened edges of the wound. Where the skin wasn't burned shut, it turned a bright pink, like a piece of meat over a fire right before the fat started boiling. Aro stumbled out the door, hand clamped over his mouth. The parro was praying, his words mixing together in a blubbery fear.

Vatri had to reheat the dagger twice more to finish sealing the wound, and then she poured the rest of the brandy over the curving black line she'd made along Scal's chest and stomach. Wordlessly she pointed at the bundle of cloth the parro had dropped, and then she walked out into the cold. Rora could hear the sound of retching.

Working together, she and Anddyr managed to get the linens wrapped around Scal, though it wasn't easy. They cleaned away all the dried blood on him to make sure there wasn't any fresh, but any other wounds he'd had were already stitching themselves together and didn't look in need of much besides a gentle cleaning. Rora glanced around once, to see where Joros'd gone to, but there was no sign of him.

The parro was surprised to see the flamedisk on Scal's bare chest, and Rora couldn't blame him. She would've guessed a Northman would care about the Parents even less than she did. But the parro prayed extra hard over Scal after he saw the flamedisk, and it sounded almost like he might've even meant the words. Rora found a wall to put her back to and finally let her eyes close, because she'd done everything she could for the Northman, even if it was already too late for him.

CHAPTER TWO

It wasn't truly dark, though to Keiro it felt darker than a night with no moon. There was no warmth in the smoldering red glow that filled the cavern, nothing to chase away the shadows that clung thick as blood. Once, so long ago now, Pelir had told him that the blinding granted the faithful a special kind of sight, a sight that was deeper than seeing. Keiro, with his one eye gone and the other that he'd been too afraid to take, had never been granted anything but the lack of depth perception. Perhaps one of the truly faithful, one who'd kept his hands steady and let the ice pierce both eyes—perhaps a man like that could have looked up and faced the baleful glow and seen deeper.

Keiro could not. He lay in a ball of fear, damp and shaking, the faded screams of Fratarro still echoing through his bones, setting his nerves aflame. It was quieter now, the screams turned to sobs turned to ragged breaths, and all rising and fading like the tide of the great wide sea, starting and stopping like the beating pattern of the world's heart. Even the gentle murmurs were gone now, the comforting undertones replaced by an intermittent raw sound like bark scraping on bark. Flesh, burned black by fire so long ago, rubbing calming circles against burned flesh.

Keiro lay, and shook, and wept for his gods.

He had no idea how much time had passed since the screaming had begun, how long he had lain in this place so deep beneath the earth listening to his gods wake and sleep and wake again to blazing pain. The *mravigi* had fled the cavern at the first scream, leaving Keiro alone with the Twins. But there finally came a gentle touch on his shoulder. He looked up into two eyes like embers, nested in the coals of a scaly black face. *"It is time for you to go,"* the creature said softly, sadly, its voice little more than a breath.

Keiro uncurled his body and on hands and knees followed after the creature, guided by the scrape of its forked tail against the floor. White scales glowed like stars among the black along its body, giving off the faintest light—enough, in the darkness, that Keiro could see the stark outlines of his hands against the ground. The *mravigi* had long been thought dead, burned up with their homeland by the righteous fire of the Parents. Yet they lived, against all hope, and they lived in great numbers. Here, they were called Starborn.

It was easier to think of the *mravigi* than to think of the Twins.

Keiro and the Starborn had almost left the chamber, the red glow of the gods' gaze starting to fade, when a husky voice called after him. "Do not think we have forgotten you."

Keiro had to turn then, and face them—the Twins, cast down by their Parents centuries ago and bound in this place for the rest of their immortal lives, sleeping and waking by the strokes of some unknowable clock. Sororra held her brother, cradling his ravaged body as he seemed to sleep. It was hard, still, to look at Fratarro. Keiro had seen drawings before, guesses at what poor Fratarro would look like with his limbs torn away, but even the most gruesome artists couldn't have prepared Keiro for what he saw. Fratarro's flesh was burned and blackened, his arms and legs little more than raw, ichorous stumps—save for the left arm, which was held in place by clumsy stitches. Worse, almost, was the wound in his chest, pierced by a black stone shard and seeping blood.

This—his punishment for daring to create something beautiful.

"We will not forget that you are the first to find us," Sororra continued, her voice pinning him immobile to the floor. "We will call for you, when we have need." She held him a moment longer, but finally she released him, looking back to her brother.

Another set of red eyes stayed on Keiro's face—Straz, first of his kind, the giant white *mravigi* that lay at the Twins' feet. There was ancient, unreadable knowledge in those eyes, a creature nearly as old as the gods he guarded. Keiro was shaking again, as he turned to follow his Starborn guide, and Straz's eyes never left his back.

He knew the journey back to the surface was a long one, through twisting tunnels barely big enough to fit his body, but his thoughts were swirling so that he hardly noticed the time pass. The first breath of open, clean air nearly knocked him back into the tunnel. For a long while, he simply sat on the side of the hill with his arms wrapped around his knees, and stared up into the stars. The Starborn sat with him, silent, its own stars gleaming softly.

"I don't know," Keiro finally said aloud, to the stars and the Starborn, "if I ever truly believed. It was always the message that mattered, and the old stories spread the message. But old stories aren't often true." He looked down to the Starborn gazing at him curiously. "I wanted to believe they were real. That there was justice to fight for, lives to redeem. I wanted to believe. But I don't know now if I ever really did."

"You would not be here," the *mravigi* said in its breathy voice, *"if you were not a true believer. Often, the heart knows more than the mind."*

Keiro looked back up at the stars, so many thoughts and words jumbled in his mind that he couldn't pull any of them out and put them to use. All of his life, Keiro had walked, and he had seen more things than any other man, seen beauty and horror and death and life and more than he could give name to, but it all paled next to this night. He had met his gods, spoken to them, proved them real. He had found the *mravigi*, a race lovingly shaped by Fratarro's hands and almost as old as mankind. He had found, finally, his redemption.

A brief, sharp pain traveled up Keiro's shin, and he cried out in surprise more than anything. A creature with dull gray scales, no bigger than his hand and almost as thin as two fingers, pulled itself onto Keiro's knee. It gazed at him with small red eyes, and it seemed to purr.

"Cazi," the Starborn at Keiro's side admonished. The smaller *mravigi* was unperturbed, leaning down to snuffle at the hair along Keiro's arm. His time in the cavern below the hill felt like a blur, but Keiro recognized the little beast's name. Cazi had greeted him with no fear, amid Keiro's shock at meeting

the Twins. *"The young are too curious,"* the Starborn said by way of apology. *"And he is especially bold."*

Carefully, Keiro lifted a hand toward Cazi. The *mravigi* didn't so much as flinch as Keiro gently stroked the ridge of its back with a fingertip. "He has wings," Keiro said wonderingly. They were small, flimsy things, thinner than paper, but they were *wings*. The old stories said Fratarro had shaped the *mravigi* for flying, that they had soared above paradise and their wings had brushed against the stars. But Keiro's guide, and all the other Starborn he had seen beneath the ground, were wingless.

"Yes," the Starborn said, though the word was so soft Keiro almost missed it. *"He has wings."*

They sat in silence for a time beneath the stars, as Cazi ventured up and down Keiro's arms, nuzzling into his hair, sniffing at the scarred socket where Keiro's right eye had been. The moon crept down, and behind it the sky began to lighten, the start of a new day like any other, though so much had changed in the night. The Starborn's white scales began to dim, until they were as dull and lightless as Cazi's scales, and finally the beast rose with a stretch.

"We must go. The sunlight is no longer ours to share." She—for Keiro had come to think of the Starborn as female, though he had no way of truly knowing—fixed her red eyes on him. *"We will come for you when we are bid. If you have need, come to this place and call my name. I will hear. I am Tseris."*

"Well met, Tseris," Keiro said formally, ashamed that he hadn't thought to ask her name sooner. "It has been an honor to meet you, truly. I . . . I hope we might speak again. I have so many questions." None of which, of course, he'd thought to ask the whole night she'd sat silent beside him. The creeping sun was kicking the cobwebs from his brain, and he was beginning to curse himself for ten kinds of a fool. "Would you—*ow!*" Keiro instinctively shook his hand, and Cazi tumbled onto the grass, his teeth tearing free from the tender webbing of Keiro's thumb. The little Starborn scrambled to his feet and disappeared into the hill, and Tseris sat watching Keiro with a tilted head as he sucked at his bleeding flesh. It was just a small wound, a half circle of tiny punctures, but it was a sharp pain still.

"All questions are answered in time, son of gods. You will find your answers, whether you seek them or not." She left him then, disappearing down the same hidden hole Cazi had gone, and left Keiro alone with the rising sun.

The sun showed half its face before Keiro finally rose to his feet. His thoughts were no clearer, questions still swirling, but sitting here would do him no good. He prayed briefly, with his back to the sun, his eye on the ground between his feet—a simple prayer, asking the Twins to keep watch over him. A simple prayer, yet heartfelt.

Yaket was waiting for him. There was an unusual seriousness to the half-blind elder's wrinkled face when he found her between the hills and the tribehome.

She held up her hand, stopping him nearly two lengths from her. "I will not ask where you have been this night," she said. "The answer isn't for me to know, or for anyone else. What has passed is for your knowing alone."

Disappointment swelled in Keiro, for he'd been dearly hoping to ask Yaket the questions he'd been too foolish to ask Tseris. There was no compromise in her face.

"There are things not meant to be spoken," she said, "lest the words taint them. Secrets too precious to share." She turned from him and walked with her slow, rolling gait back toward the tribehome.

Keiro's feet itched. The craving nearly swallowed him unbidden, the need for a road beneath his feet, a path spiraling out unending and all the world before him. He had been made for journeying, his feet and heart singing the same song, and he had been too long in this place. The tall grasses were not his home; the plainswalkers were not his people. He did not belong here.

Yet he thought of his gods, buried and bound for centuries, finally found, finally known. There was no turning from them. Keiro had walked into the trap unknowingly, and it had closed about his ankles.

He paced slowly to the tribehome, remaining well behind Yaket. The children greeted him as eagerly as they always did, for he was still a novelty here. Poret, who was sweet and who adored him, brought him half a cooked groundbird and berries on a mat of woven grass. Yaket sat across the carefully contained fire, and though her face still held its secrets, there was a smile in her eye, and a knowing.

Of all the ways to be trapped, Keiro could be glad enough it was this trap that had caught him.

The men of the tribe returned from their hunt as the sun slipped once more from the sky. They spitted birds and hares over fires, set hard nuts to cook at the edges of the coals, passed around handfuls of berries and chewy roots and skins filled with water.

With the sky darkening above them, Keiro picked the last

pieces of meat from a thin bone and set his scraps aside. All eyes turned to him, glowing at the unspoken signal.

They no longer asked for specific stories; by this point, he had already told most of their favorites, the same stories Yaket had been telling all their lives. Lately they had been asking for *new* stories, stories of the world beyond their waving grass, stories of the world that had gone by while they stayed still. Keiro had often wondered why they'd never left the Plains, why these people—so curious about the wide world, so hungry for adventure—had never gone to make their own stories. He thought, now, that he was beginning to understand why they had stayed.

The forced secrets burned inside Keiro, so fierce that it was a challenge not to shout at them: "My gods are real. I have seen them, and I have wept with them, and I know the truths of the world." But Yaket was there across the fire, her face smiling but her stern, milky eye shining with admonishment.

Keiro looked up at the stars, and the imperfect circle of the glowing moon, and when his gaze returned to the earth he lowered his ratty old eyecloth to block out the world and he began his tale.

"You know the Eremori Desert," he said, and softly the plainswalkers murmured in fear and fury. The Eremori was a short journey south through the Plains, and its hot winds and blowing sands could reach this far during the worst desert storms. "With heat as great as the sun's, the sands burn with the remembered wrath of the Parents. But it was not always so. Long ago, Eremori was a place of beauty, a land that knew love and the joy of Fratarro's shaping. Trees grew taller than twenty men, and flowers fell from their branches like curtains. Rivers sang in delight, and threw their song far over the land.

"But for all its beauty, there were no feet to walk it, no hands to mold it, no voices to join the rivers, no eyes to see the wonder that Fratarro had made. And so Fratarro, in his might and his love, shaped feet and hands and mouths and eyes, and his greatest creation rose into the sky.

"Straz, first of the *mravigi*, spread his great wings and flew, and he was like a piece of the black night sky spread against the daylight—for the world was young then, and the night sky was only an endless black, as dark as the *mravigi*'s scales. Straz soared, and Fratarro's heart soared with him. The *mravigi* touched the tops of the mighty trees, and he sang his joy with the rivers, and he loved all that Fratarro had shaped.

"Yet Straz was lonely. Fratarro grew tired from his efforts, and he did not have the strength to make a companion for Straz. He could only place a bright-stone collar around Straz's neck, the stone white and warm, and it held all of Fratarro's love. Sororra, who watched over her tired brother while he slept, did not have her brother's skill for shaping something from nothing.

"And so Straz left." Keiro dropped his voice, and he felt the plainswalkers lean in, rapt. "The bright-stone collar hung heavy around his neck, reminding him always who had given him life and love—but still he left to search for a companion.

"He flew across the land the Parents had shaped, but he found only men, and beasts that were nothing like him. The beasts fled from Straz, and the men threw pointed sticks at him, and so he left the Parents' lands behind.

"He flew higher than he had ever flown before, flying toward the sun, which glowed as warmly as his bright-stone collar. Yet the sun fled from him, drawing a dark curtain behind itself so that Straz was lost amid the deep night. He could not find his way.

"Alone, and cold without the sun's warmth, Straz curled upon himself into a tight ball, and he cradled the bright-stone at his center to hold the only warmth he had, and he wept for the love he had left behind.

"Shaped by Fratarro's own hands, Straz bore more of his creator than any had thought. Straz could shape—not mountains or men or worlds, but he had a very small piece of Fratarro's power. Just enough to pull at the edges of the bright-stone, to turn it like a glassblower and make it bigger, bigger, bigger . . . until it was big enough to hold a single, lonely *mravigi*.

"He sealed himself within the bright-stone, for he knew he could not withstand the sun's cruelty alone. With the bright-stone as his shield, bathing him in Fratarro's love, he could withstand.

"Straz slept."

It was silent, not even a breath to stir the air, and Keiro turned his face once more up to the moon. He couldn't see it behind the black eyecloth, but he knew where it hung. "The heartless sun," he went on, "drove Straz-in-stone through the sky, forcing the sleeping *mravigi* ahead of itself. The sun whipped Straz with chains of burning light, and drowned him in dark, but could not cast him down. He was held safe by the bright-stone. The sun tried, for thirty days and thirty nights, until a spear of light finally cracked open the bright-stone egg, and Straz woke with a mighty roar.

"As Straz spread his wings, they were changed: *he* was

changed. All of his night-black scales had been turned white, bleached by the sun's merciless onslaught. Straz glowed white, as bright as the sun, as bright as Fratarro's love that shone within the broken pieces of the bright-stone egg. In the light that now filled the sky, Straz could see through the night once more, and far below he saw the land he had left behind. Joy shimmered through Straz, but there was one last thing he would do: he took the shattered pieces of the bright-stone and he flung them into the sky, spread them so that never again would there be a place in the night that was not touched by some piece of Fratarro's love.

"Only one piece of the bright-stone he did not scatter. This last piece he held: the brightest piece, the piece that had lived at its very center. Straz used his small shaping powers once more, turning this last bright-stone piece until it was as big and as glowing as the egg that had sheltered him so long from the sun. He left this piece hanging in the night sky, so that the sun would always remember.

"Finally Straz could return home. He fell through the light-spotted sky back to Fratarro's side.

"Together, Fratarro and Sororra and Straz gazed up into the night at the shining moon and the flickering pieces of bright-stone scattered across the sky, and it was as beautiful as anything Fratarro had shaped on his own."

Keiro paused as the silence spun out, his heart aching. Like many of the old stories, this one ended with a reminder of what had been taken: Patharro had burned the *mravigi*, killed them for the simple crime of existing, and he'd robbed the world of their beauty. But it wasn't true . . . Somehow the *mravigi* still lived, and Keiro could not end this story with a lie, not now that he knew the truth. He paused, and the tension grew, and softly, one of the youngest children began to fuss.

He spoke again, voice low, words picking carefully through the darkness. He was a story*teller*, not a story-maker, and so the words came clumsily . . . but they rang through him with truth, with the brightness of starfire. "Straz hadn't been afraid of the sun, no matter how cruel it was . . . no matter that it was Metherra's most powerful creation. He wasn't afraid, for he knew Fratarro's love would protect him. Mighty Straz, who touched the sky and who made the moon and the stars . . . he knew that the sun was not as powerful as everyone thought. Straz had hidden within the bright-stone, sleeping, and so the sun had thought him weak—but that wasn't true, was it? Mighty Straz, who outmatched the sun . . . he knew that hiding is only waiting, that sleeping is only gathering strength. Straz knew that, with patience and with time, even the sun could be outwitted."

There was murmuring at that, confusion at the new ending, speculation already rippling through them. Keiro grinned, pleased with himself, pleased he had found a way to give them the smallest of clues to their purpose here amid the grass sea. He thought it was a thing they deserved to know, even if Yaket didn't seem to agree. When he lifted his eyecloth and looked down from the sky, across the fire Yaket's face was hard. Her blind eye, white as the moon, held no gentleness, or light.

CHAPTER THREE

It was the snows again. Swirling, biting. A dream, he knew, but the knowing did not stop the dream. The knowing only settled the fear deeper. A live thing gnawing in his guts. He did not remember anything of his first life, but he remembered well what had come after, the snows and the wandering and the fear. It was a hard thing, his first memory. A thing he did not like to remember. The dream made him live it again.

In the dream he was a child again, but he was still made for the cold. Skin hard and thick as leather. Blood flowing hot through his veins. This was a different cold, though, a deeper cold. Killing cold, they called it. The snow that grabbed at his legs when he tried to lift them. Grabbed and pulled, and the fear swelled, and then the howling swelled.

The wolves were not so far away, now. Closer, hot breath splitting the air, sharp-nailed feet flying smooth over the snow. Smelling his fear. Smelling his blood. Sleek bodies weaving through the trees behind him, thin with hunger, swift in their perfect savagery. Closer, and the tears were frozen on his cheeks. This life, so short, would end soon. Hardly a life at all. He would die, knowing nothing but the snows, biting and heartless and fierce.

The snow rose up, and drowned everything but the fear. Flakes falling all around, pieces of the world, gathered higher than his waist. He was kneeling now, too cold to cry anymore. Waiting for the wolves, waiting for the end.

"Northman!"

Somehow, he knew the word—a word that meant "fear" in any language, a word that meant "death." Louder than the heavy-falling snow. Not so loud as the fear roaring through him, but he heard it. He knew. And the men came for him, quicker than the wolves, with spears and blades sharper than teeth. With fingers faster than sharp-clawed feet, hands that grabbed and pulled. With hate swelling in their eyes.

They took him. Robbed him from the killing-cold snows, chased away the burning cold with burning fire. Stole his life, brief and bleak.

Gave him a new one. A life of warm fires and a red-robed priest whose gruff smiles felt like home.

The everflame was the first thing Scal saw when he woke. It was not what he expected. The priests said that souls of the dead were drawn to a part of the godworld that Metherra had made for the faithful. A place to peacefully spend one's death. To see again others from life, the ones who had passed before. It had always sounded a nice thing.

In the North, they did not have such beliefs. Death was death. Nothing after, save the flames to keep animals from the body.

This did not seem to be either. There was the everflame, and a roof above. Dimly, he heard praying. It hurt, tucking his elbows to push his body up. There was not supposed to be pain, after death. And then he saw the merra, her face folded and crinkled and ruined by fire. Staring into the everflame, searching for a message from the gods. A sight he had seen times beyond counting.

"I am alive." He did not ask it. He did not even mean to say it, but the words snuck croaking from his throat before he could bite them. The truth in those words hurt, more than the pain of sitting.

Vatri rushed to his side. Very gently she hugged him. "Thanks to Metherra's mercy," she murmured against his chest. "Parents be praised."

It took some convincing before she would leave him be. Finally he told her he wished to pray alone. That was a thing she could respect. She left, telling him she would return soon with food. And he was alone with the everflame.

He had not expected to wake, after the snows took him once more. He had left his fourth life, and gladly, stretching toward whatever lay beyond the snows at the doors of death. But the snows had spit him out again. Always, they took that which he had built, and gave back something different. Something worse.

It hurt, but Scal pushed himself to his feet. There was a throbbing in his side, a throbbing in his head. He had not expected to wake. Had not thought to have to face pain again. But, truly, pain had always meant little. He stood and took slow, limping steps, one hand on the wall, one on his side where bandages held tight. His travelsack sat in a corner, his sword leaning against the wall. He fell next to them, knees hitting hard on the wood floor, hard enough that his teeth clattered together around his tongue. He tasted blood. When he took his hand from his side, reaching for his sword, his fingers, too, were spotted with blood.

His second life had ended in blood. The third had been washed with blood. The fourth had been built by blood. A fifth life, now, and beginning again with blood.

It's hard, little lad, Parro Kerrus had told him long ago, voice heavy with grief as they watched a patrol return with the bodies of a new batch of convicts. They had not been more than a few hours from safety when they had been cut down. They were prisoners, criminals convicted by law, but Kerrus held that all lives were worthy. Too, there had been innocents among them. Wives. Husbands. Children, who were the hardest for Kerrus to look upon. *The Parents, in their wisdom or their folly, did not see fit to give us easy lives.*

Scal's hands were clumsy, shaking, weak. But the blade clicked free, the scabbard sliding down and away, and the sword lay naked across his legs. He did not know how he would lift it, but he would manage.

Five lives, too many for any one man to live. A life could end in blood as easily as it could begin. And then the snows would take him.

And then the snows would spit him back.

"If you need a reason not to," a soft voice said into the fire-flickering silence, "you'll make the cappo's life easier if you're dead. He hasn't earned an easy life."

Scal's shoulders slumped, and the pain flared in his side, and his fingers slid from the hilt. He had not ever cried in his fourth life. The tears poured from him now. A river of grief, for all that had been and had not been and would never be.

The floor creaked. A shoulder pressed against his. The witch-man said nothing else. Just knelt beside him in his watchful silence, and shared the little strength he had.

This new life, a fifth life, beginning in the same place his second life had begun. The second should have been a gentle life, a happy life. A priest to guide him, a friend steady at his side. It would have been good. But blood had washed it away.

All of Scal's lives had been shaded in blood. They had been shaped, too. Others' hands molding him to their own ends. They had been his lives, for he had lived them—and yet, none of those lives had ever truly belonged to him.

This new life, given unexpectedly, did not have to be the same. It could be his life, of his own choosing. Free of spilled blood.

The door opened, cold air rushing in, and there were more steps than Vatri alone. She cried out in dismay, seeing Scal out of his bedroll. Roughly she shoved Anddyr aside, muttering, "I knew I shouldn't have trusted you to watch him."

It took Vatri and the witch and the twins as well to get Scal back under covers. He saw the witch-man quietly ease his sword back into its scabbard, lean it back against the wall. He thought, perhaps, that Rora saw. She said nothing of it.

The four spread themselves around Scal. Vatri unwrapped the bandages from his middle, wrinkling her nose and spreading a poultice. Aro was at her side, passing her clean linens before she could ask. Rora, wearing Scal's old snowbear cloak, sat with her back to a wall, her eyes and the bear's on the door. The witch-man was across the room, watching Rora. The room was full of the everflame's crackle and little else.

The door swung open. Before it hit the wall Rora was in a crouch, knives half-drawn. The witch-man curled into the smallest shape he could. Joros entered, scowling.

"How long?" he demanded of Vatri.

She shook her head. "A week at least. Even if he heals fast, he won't be fit for travel for some time."

Joros snarled and stormed. They all watched him, waiting to see how his anger would end. Vatri's lips pressed tight, and Rora's.

Aro spoke, though he should have left the man to his fury. "If we could get a cart . . ."

Joros swung to him, growling, and towered over the sitting man with clenched fists. "Do you know what the bloody convicts were doing while we've been trying to save Scal's fecking life? Those idiots were *butchering* my horse," he snapped. "Do you truly think they'd give us a cart?" He swung to Vatri, jabbing a finger at her. "He *will* be ready for travel by the end of the week. I won't be stuck in this shit-hole any longer than that."

Joros had not seemed to notice he was awake, and so Scal kept his words held tight behind his teeth.

The man swore and raged, and was ignored. Finally he left, as much a storm as he had entered. The chapel seemed to let out a held breath as the door closed on his heels. Silence fell once more.

The witch-man was the first to leave. He slunk like a dog from the room, a small jar cradled in one hand. Aro followed not long after. Stretching, feigning relaxation. Wind whistled sharply through the closing door, cold air that bit. Vatri knelt before the everflame and began to pray. Against the wall, Rora looked on with hooded eyes, dark beneath the snowbear's scowl. She, too, left. Out into the wind and the snow.

"I would like to be alone." Scal's voice felt loud, in the silence of the chapel.

Vatri stared at him for a long while. Trying to read him as she read the flames, to pull out meaning and purpose. She must have found an answer. "Stay in bed," she said sternly as she rose. "There's little enough clean linen here, and I can't keep changing your bandages every few hours. I'll be back at sunrise." She stopped before the door, searching again, waiting for an answer. There was none to give. She left, and he was alone with the everflame.

There is danger in being alone, Parro Kerrus had told him long ago. He had stared into the bottle of brandy he held, and not said anything more.

Carefully Scal rose. In this new life, he would be gentle with his body. He would make it a bloodless life. Begun in blood, but it did not have to stay so. He felt the pain of his wounds, a constant thing, but the pain did not flare from being stretched too far. He moved like an old man, bent and limping, and he moved slow. Deliberate. He did not need to rush. He had until the sun returned once more.

Surprise showed in Vatri's face when she entered the chapel to find the small priest, Parro Modatho, sitting on the floor next to Scal, now upright in his makeshift bed. She did not speak, but her wide eyes narrowed in suspicion, mouth tightening. Wordlessly she handed Scal a bowl of thin porridge and knelt before the everflame. He did not think he had ever heard such aggressive prayer.

The twins entered, Aro muttering, "Gods, these people are hard to be around." His face flushed when he saw Modatho. "Sorry, Parro."

"I would speak with Joros," Scal said to no one in particular.

The women shared glances, and Aro snorted. "You and everyone else here."

"I'll see if he's busy," Rora offered.

"Tell him it is important," Scal added. Rora's hand paused on the door. She glanced at him with raised eyebrows and then nodded once, leaving. Vatri gave him a searching look, but Scal avoided her gaze.

Three returned, Rora and the witch-man and Joros. So many bodies made the chapel feel small, suffocating. Scal could remember, from a life long ago, sitting in a chapel that looked similar to this one. A deep-voiced priest and a boy whose smile split his face.

"What is it?" Joros demanded. It was the first he had looked at Scal, since he had been given back by the snows.

Scal reached beneath the blanket that covered him. The pouch was heavy, almost more than he could lift without paining the gash that ran along his side. It arced through the air, a moving shifting shape, and landed near enough to Joros's feet. A hard sound, metal against metal against the floor. More coin than Scal had ever seen in his life. More than any man needed. Slowly, clearly, Scal said, "I am no longer for hire."

From the edges of his vision he saw the others react. Vatri, clapping her hands over her scar-twisted mouth. Aro's mouth dropping open. Rora narrowing her eyes, her face a mimic of Vatri's earlier suspicion. Anddyr, with a plea in his gaze. Scal did not look at them. This new life would be one of his own shaping. He kept his eyes on Joros, and did not look away.

The man's face turned a slow red. The right side had been burned, before Scal knew him, and new skin had finally begun to grow, smooth and shiny and pink. The rest of his face became the same color, and darker. He, too, did not look away from Scal. Scal could see the possibilities flickering behind his eyes, all the ways to stretch and twist this moment.

Finally his eyes snapped away and he said to the others, "We're leaving within the hour." The door slammed behind him. Hard enough to send dust skittering down from the ceiling.

Vatri clutched at Scal's arm, nails digging in. "You can't be serious. You have to come with us!"

Scal could not look at her. His fourth life was gone, over, behind him. But it was not so easily forgotten. The memories lingered, and the feelings. "I am not Joros's man. I am not your man." He wanted to give her more. Tell her how he had been shaped by others' needs, shaped by fear of what he did not want to be. That he had never lived a life of what he *did* want to be. Because of his fourth life, he wanted to tell her all of it. But this was not his fourth life. In this life, he owed her nothing. The words were his alone, and his to keep.

Rora spoke softly to her brother and then to Anddyr, and both men slipped from the chapel. She turned her anger to Parro Modatho. The parro swallowed hard, and Scal half expected him to flee. He was not a brave man. This was his chapel, though. He cowered under Rora's gaze, but he did not leave.

"Why?" Rora asked Scal softly. Barely a question.

Scal could meet her eyes. He had known her less, yet she had understood him in a way none of the others had. There was an understanding, among those whose lives were shaped by the blood of others. "I do not owe you a reason."

"Damned if you don't!" she shouted, and the fierceness surprised him. Her fists were clenched, and her teeth. "I near died trying to save your life, and near killed myself to save it again. Don't fecking tell me I'm not owed anything."

How to tell her she had saved a different man? But looking at her, the anger and the ache, he still understood her. She was one to stand with, shoulder to shoulder, and face an enemy without fear. She would not break. Would not bend.

"I lived here, long ago," he said. Vatri's eyes widened, her hand went unconsciously to her cheek. On Scal's cheek were two lines of deep scar, making an X. The convict's cross, that would be echoed on the face of every prisoner in Aardanel. His was on the right instead of the left cheek, and had been given by a Northman instead of a magistrate. None of them had ever asked of it. Vatri, least of all, would ever ask about another's scars. "I was brought here as a child. I would have spent all my days here, had life gone as it was meant to." He paused. Hoped they would see the words so he would not have to speak them. They only stared, and the snowbear's eyes upon Rora's head stared, too. "I have not lived as the man I should have been. I will stay here, and atone. Live here, as I always should have."

"Patharro protects the penitent," Modatho intoned in his reedy voice. He clearly regretted the words as soon as they were free, when Rora's stare swung to him once more. He was a small man. He tried to become smaller.

"Bullshit," Rora said to Scal. "We've all got a pile of regrets chewing our backs, but you can't just go running off."

Scal shook his head. An unexpected sadness bloomed briefly in him. He had thought she would understand. It was not fleeing his past lives. It was trying to find the threads of the life he should have had, and knit them into something that would hold.

She yelled at him more, when he would not answer. There were no more words to give her. Already he had given her more than he had meant to.

Vatri held to his arm, silent. Her fingers like hooks that would drag him along. There was more softness in her face, but no understanding.

Aro's head poked briefly through the door. "Rora, there's trouble brewing . . ."

Her raging stopped. She stood, chest heaving, fury plain. She spat in Scal's face, and grabbed Vatri's wrist.

"I have to help them. They need me," the merra said softly, and desperation touched her words. The sound her voice took, when she looked into a fire and the flames did not spell what she wished them to. "I need you." Her clutching fingers dragged grooves in his arms as she was pulled away. Something like sadness and something like anger danced in her eyes. Perhaps the trick of reading her emotions had died with Scal's last life. "Please, don't leave me." The door closed, her voice shut out. In the place where his old lives sat like heavy stones, Scal ached. None of it mattered. He could not let it.

"You have been brave this day, child," Parro Modatho said. He was young for a parro, and awkward with authority. Not knowing the right words, or how to say them. Early as it was, his breath smelled of brandy when he leaned too close. "The Parents will surely guide you to redemption."

Scal ignored him. The parro had talked at him throughout the night, always saying five words when one would have done. Voice stumbling and uncertain, as though the parables were a thing he only half believed in. He would stand for Scal against the wardens, and that was the important thing. He could talk all he liked; a different priest's words were already laid thick in Scal's heart and mind.

He laid his head down, finally. Lulled by Modatho's babble, and the flicker of the everflame. Dimly he heard shouting from beyond the door. Voices swelling in anger, close to breaking.

Scal closed his eyes. Those were the concerns of a lost life.

CHAPTER FOUR

It was hard to even think over all the yelling, and Anddyr wanted very badly to be able to think clearly. The anger around him was near to boiling, so thick he felt he likely could have seen it even if he wasn't in the grasp of a skura-induced hallucination. He knew, if he could only think it through, that he could calm the anger, set everything to rights.

All he'd managed to do so far was clap his hands over his ears and squeeze his eyes shut, trying to block out the yelling so that perhaps his brain could get started on the problem. It hadn't worked yet, but Anddyr had never been one for giving up so easily—at least, not when he knew vaguely that his life was at stake. But it was so blasted hard to think clearly with long-legged insects crawling over his skin and piling at his feet, holding him rooted to the ground.

Cappo Joros yelled sometimes, when he was annoyed or angry or bored, but he never argued. He didn't have to; his orders were simply followed, always.

The wardens here didn't seem to know that.

He was still angry about the horses, and Anddyr couldn't

blame him for that. Both horses had been wonderful and sweet, and Anddyr had named them both Sooty, after the stuffed horse he kept tucked inside his robes. He couldn't think about the Sootys without crying, and crying wouldn't help him here. He tried to focus instead on what the cappo was shouting about, squinting through the noise and the crawling insects to find the single voice.

"... plenty of meat, clearly! I *will* have enough of it to see me out of the blasted North—and more!" The cappo had one fist clenched, shaking it in the face of a man twice as wide as he was and thick with muscle. "That's two of *my* beasts you've killed now, so I'm more than entitled to them. They're still *mine*."

The big man facing the cappo wore the blue uniform of the wardens that ran the place, but there was a chain stretched between his wrists like a convict. Anddyr tried very hard to focus on the warden-convict's face, because the chain kept coming so distractingly to life, twisting and writhing like a snake. At least the man's face didn't turn into anything it wasn't supposed to be. His mouth was hard, set, and he hadn't opened it as long as Anddyr had been watching. There was a slow storm building, and it occurred to Anddyr—a coherent thought, finally—that the storm would break, and its center was the cappo.

Good, he thought from the dark place that lurked at his center, a hidden thing of evil and malice and claws. The darkness uncurled, stretching like a shadow. *Let the storm come. Let it break him.*

A thrill of joy ran through Anddyr. He could shake his legs free of the insects and step away, melt into the crowd, and the cappo would never see him. And there wouldn't be anyone to save him. For one shining moment, Anddyr saw himself walking out the gates of Aardanel alone, free, his head high.

And then he thought of the long walk through the snows, and the twisting hunger in his belly, and Rora's face, and the brief rush of joy crumbled into biting fear.

Anddyr moved slowly through the crowd, trailing insects—not away from the cappo, but toward him. It wasn't so easy as walking away. If the storm should break, it would break over him as well.

Anddyr's fingers moved as he walked, tracing the sigils for a simple defensive spell. It was one of the earliest spells he'd learned; a master had taught it to him after watching a group of older novices pelt Anddyr with rotten fruit. "You'll earn their respect one day," the master had offered soothingly. "Boys don't like being reminded they're not the smartest creatures in the world. They like it even less from a younger boy."

"They're just jealous," Anddyr had said fiercely, proudly.

Anddyr reached the cappo's side without seeming to attract any attention. He stood at the center of a mass of people and might as well have been invisible. It would have made his younger self furious, the Anddyr he had been who'd dreamed of drawing crowds, of commanding attention. It made him wince now, both the memory and the thought of actually attracting attention. He was a shadow, a thing that slipped by unnoticed.

Quietly, lips barely moving, Anddyr released the spell. No one else took any notice, but Anddyr could sense the slight thrum in the air, the feel of live magic. He could think of no other spells to prepare—that wasn't true, but the one spell his foggy mind could always think of also made him think of blackened grass and charred bodies, and he doubted he'd ever be able to cast that one again. So he stood, hands and lips still, and waited amid the shouting and the swirling anger.

"I *will* leave," the cappo was shouting, "when you give me what's mine."

A man stepped forward from the crowd, dressed in mixed scraps of clothing that were no better than rags, though a thick fur cloak lay across his shoulders. His hands were wrapped with stained leather, and curled around the thick haft of an axe. They chopped wood here in Aardanel, penance for the prisoners and useful for the rest of the realm when it was shipped south. Anddyr didn't think the manacles around the man's wrists would at all hinder his swinging the axe. "You'll leave with what you've already got," the man rumbled, his voice like grinding stone, "or you'll leave without your arms. Man don't taste much different from horse."

Words died in the cappo's mouth, and his face paled. Anddyr watched as he seemed to notice for the first time the crowd he'd drawn, the cold anger roiling around him. Anddyr saw the moment he realized the mistake he'd made. It gave Anddyr a little joy, though it was tempered by the fact that he might very well die alongside the cappo.

Joros held his hands up in a placating gesture, but Anddyr saw that his eyes had gone hard. He never made a habit of losing, and didn't take well to it when it did happen. "Listen," the cappo said levelly, "I think we misunderstand each other . . ."

The big convict-warden who'd been facing off with Joros spat at the cappo's feet. "Heard you well enough, I think. You wanna start singing a new song?"

Anddyr wondered where the wardens were, the real wardens who didn't have crosses and manacles. Surely they'd come disperse the crowd, calm the convicts and send them back to work. With a sick sinking in his stomach, Anddyr saw that there were blue-uniformed wardens among the crowd, and they had the same hard, hateful looks as the convicts. Men weren't all that different, when it came to the simple things. There'd be no help from the wardens. It was left to Anddyr, and the cappo.

Anddyr had known from the start how this would end. There was only ever one way with the cappo.

Joros's face settled into a sneer, and his fingers flicked subtly at Anddyr in a silent command. With his stomach twisting, Anddyr began weaving a different spell, one that would hit the warden-convict first and then go jumping from man to man, leaving behind blackened and dead flesh. Anddyr had always hated that spell, even before, when he'd been himself; it was one of the cappo's favorites. "I will have all of my horses," the cappo growled, "dead and alive. I will have what's mine." Anddyr winced as the cappo drew his short sword and brought it swinging around, aiming for the axe-wielder's neck.

He might have landed the blow successfully. He had surprise on his side, and if he wasn't a master swordsman, he still knew how to use the blade well enough. He might have taken the man's head clean off, and Anddyr truly didn't know if that would have ended the matter or brought the storm crashing down.

He would never know, because two crossed daggers caught the sword and twisted it down and away. Joros swung around to face the new assailant, and his eyes narrowed at Rora. She stood ready, body loose, daggers easy in her hands, but there was a fury in her face to match the cappo's. He snarled as he wrenched his sword up and swung it again, aiming this time for Rora.

Anddyr dropped the spell, and any thought of weaving a new one. There was no thought save panic. The magic dispersed half-formed, a crackle in the air that made Anddyr's hair frizz and sent sparks dancing along the cappo's sword. Anddyr threw himself forward with a scream that might have been her name.

His chest collided with the cappo's back and the force bore them both down to the ground, breaths exploding in simultaneous *whuff*s. Dimly Anddyr saw the cappo's fingers fly open around the sword and he would have sighed with relief if he'd had any air. Rora grabbed the sword, and her eyes briefly met Anddyr's. Her expression could have been gratitude.

She didn't sheathe her daggers or the sword, but she held both hands up high, blades loose in her fingers. She was shorter even than some of the scrawny children that roamed Aardanel, but Anddyr could sense the crowd's attention shifting to her. "We'll leave," she said loudly enough to be heard by all. "Let us go peaceful and we won't give you any more trouble. We'll take the three horses. You keep what meat you need—payment, for letting us stay here. We're thankful to you for that." Anddyr didn't know how she did it with her hands full of blades, and he didn't see her fingers move, but suddenly a heavy pouch hung from her hand. She shook it, and the clink of coins was loud in the waiting silence. "We're real thankful," she said for emphasis.

Faces transformed around them, anger melting away to

greed almost too quickly to follow. They had no use for coin, so far away from the wider world, but Anddyr had learned over the years that avarice existed under any and all conditions.

"We'll let ya leave," the convict-warden said amiably. He stepped toward Rora with a smile on his face that was all teeth. "Just a misunderstandin', like he says. No trouble." He held out both hands, strung together by a heavy slithering-snake chain. "No trouble at all."

Anddyr pushed himself up to his feet, his chest aching from the tackle, and the cappo rose like a storm cloud. Rora tossed the pouch, sending it high over heads and belatedly reaching hands, but she was turning before it had even left her fingers. "Come on," she said as she brushed by Anddyr. He glanced at the cappo and hesitated a moment, but he'd already thrown the man down; if he was in trouble with the cappo, he was already in as great a trouble as was possible. He grabbed the cappo's arm and pulled.

Anddyr wove after Rora's slight form through the rank, pressing crowd, all trying desperately to go in the direction the money had gone. Panic was growing in Anddyr, the panic of fighting a river's current, knowing that in enough time, the current would win. He flailed his arms, kicked desperately, choked on the rising tide—but finally they broke free from the bodies, washed up on the empty shoreline of humanity. Rora dropped all pretense, legs pumping as she ran in the direction of the gate. Anddyr let go of the cappo's arm and raced after her, his chest pounding with a strange euphoria. He hadn't died after all.

The merra and Rora's brother were waiting at the gate, each on a horse, the merra holding a third. Anddyr was relieved to see the horses, even though two were missing from the five that had walked into Aardanel. He would mourn for them later, he promised himself, briefly touching the spot above his hip where the stuffed horse was tucked inside his robe.

Rora swung up onto the horse behind her brother, making it look the most graceful thing in the world. The cappo, his jaw set and his face holding all the storminess that had been directed at him so recently, claimed the riderless horse even though it was the Northman's. It was strange, not having the man's solid presence around. The cappo dug his heels into the horse's sides, and she nearly threw him before he wrenched her chin close to her neck. Anddyr winced in sympathy, but there was nothing he could do for the poor thing. She left Aardanel at a trot that wanted to break into a canter.

Anddyr glanced at the merra, expecting her to glare at him. Her face was blank, though, her eyes far away and troubled. There was an angry cast to her lips.

"Come *on*," Rora snapped.

Anddyr climbed carefully up behind the merra, and she didn't react or resist when he pried the reins gently from her hands. He knew this horse, he knew them all, and she wouldn't be happy about the extra weight of carrying two riders, but Anddyr understood the importance of making a quick exit. He sent the horse after Rora, through the gates of Aardanel and into the blowing snow.

CHAPTER FIVE

If there was a lesson Joros had learned in all of this, it was that no one should bother doing the right thing. It was a good enough lesson to keep him warm on the long ride out of Aardanel, along what could barely be called a goat trail but was apparently the finest road in all the North. It might even be the only road in the North, since Joros had now seen more of the North than he ever would have wanted to, and if there were any other roads they'd been thoroughy covered by snow. This footpath was the closest thing to civilization he'd seen in weeks. It almost made him want to feel joy or relief or something foolish like hope, but he had to be careful—if he let things like that start seeping through his pervading anger, there was no telling what else they might bring with them.

The others were mercifully silent, even mumbling Anddyr, and he hoped they were considering their own lessons. The merra, who normally would have been filling any stretch of travel with prayers or ham-fisted preaching, was more shaken, it seemed, by the Northman's departure even than Joros. Occasionally, as she stared relentlessly into the middle distance, her scar-seamed face almost took on a look of anger—though, with the mess of her face, one emotion looked very much like any other.

The Northman's perfidy stung, for it left Joros severely lacking in the brute muscle he'd been planning to throw at any of the Fallen that tried to get in his way. A powerful and competent killer was an asset, and the best he had now was half of each: Rora, who was competent but a weak sneakthief, and Anddyr, who was powerful but laughably far from competent. That made Joros vulnerable, made his carefully laid plans vulnerable.

The Northman also made him think of the other recent betrayal—and that one had a sharper sting. Red hair and a ready smile and the lie that she cared, the lie she told him right until the end. Dirrakara had earned his trust, vowed she was always on his side, forced *him* to care—and then betrayed him for the prospect of advancement. It was the sort of thing terrible plays were made of.

He'd gotten his storybook revenge, though, the evil witch punished, Joros triumphant. She was gone, dead, her hold on him ended. He should be elated that he'd removed such a powerful pawn, that he'd gotten revenge for the personal betrayal. He should be celebrating.

But no, instead he held on to the anger, the sting of her betrayal, because he could feel—under the triumph and the joy and the relief—*other* things lurking . . . sadness, remorse, regret. Those were emotions for weaker men, and Joros had never been able to afford to be weak. It was better to hold tight to his anger, pure and catalytic, that let him keep his sharp edge of focus.

He kept seeing her face, because it was how he reminded himself how much he hated her, and he kept telling himself how necessary it had been. Dirrakara had been one of the brightest stars among the Fallen, and killing her was a sharp blow to their power. Killing her weakened the Fallen, helped his own cause. Killing her had been what he needed to do.

It was taking on the feeling of a litany.

The sun dipped behind the trees, sending shadows creeping along the pathetic little road. The merra blinked out of her daze; something about the creeping darkness seemed to shake her senses loose. "Fire," she croaked, and the suddenness of her voice nearly sent Anddyr tumbling off the back of the horse they shared.

"We should probably stop," Rora ventured. "Don't think any of us've slept more'n a few hours the last few nights."

Joros pulled back on his horse's reins to stop it, and the rest of them took that for the sign it was. They went about setting up camp while Joros stood against a tree, staring at nothing and trying to keep ahold of his anger. Usually it was a matter of keeping his anger under control, keeping it from slipping the bit and dropping into a gallop of full-blown, incandescent rage. This was different, unexpected, and for the most part unprecedented—an anger that wanted to fizzle away into something soft and anemic.

It had been easy in Aardanel, surrounded by so much rampant stupidity. But here, with no dead horses, no pompous wardens, no traitorous Northmen . . . it was harder to feel that driving rage. He kept seeing Dirrakara's face, and it made those weak emotions stronger, made them swell, threatening to overpower. Unlike the spiraling anger that had punched his sword—repeatedly—through her chest, it was all fading into an uncomfortable, foolish sort of melancholy.

He missed her.

Despite her betrayal, despite her siding against him, despite the fact that he'd only ever intended for her to be a useful tool, a means to his end, a pretty if idealistic pawn . . . despite all of it, he missed her.

When it came down to it, he supposed her betrayal hadn't been her own fault—she'd fully bought in to the story the Fallen spewed, hitched her hopes to the seemingly hopeless. So when Valrik . . .

Ah. Now there was a stone against which he could sharpen his anger.

Valrik Uniro, the pompous leader of the Fallen, was either a world-class charlatan or the terrifying sort of zealot who deeply believed his own lies. That Valrik had stabbed out his own eyes, like a common drudging preacher, meant he *had* to be one of the two. And Dirrakara, blind to reason, had always trusted him—she'd seemed to regard Valrik as something of a father figure, though Joros had never seen him act anything like paternal.

Valrik had never made a secret of his distaste for Joros, and Valrik's rise to power had changed everything. It had spelled the end of Joros's power among the Fallen. Oh, he could have spent the rest of his days doing menial tasks for the new Uniro, letting Valrik take credit for Joros's achievements . . . But in the moment, when Valrik had taken away Joros's crowning achievement and dismissed him like a servant, the only reasonable choice had been to disavow the Fallen and instead vow to salt the earth in their plans.

He'd aligned himself with the Parents, because they were the only other option, and so he'd thrown his support whole-heartedly behind them. He was trying to do the right thing. He was going to save the world.

But it would be really fecking nice if anyone else could be bothered enough to help him. No matter how many plans he made, how many contingencies he thought through, inevitably one of the idiots stomped through and buggered everything.

Joros had never been the type to give up, and he wasn't so broken now that his will would crumble like shattered stone. There were always choices, always a new tack to take. And now . . . now he had even more reason. He would continue to fight the Fallen, to abort their plans at every turn . . . and he would destroy Valrik, for what he'd done to Joros, and for what he'd forced Dirrakara to do to Joros. And he'd be damned if he was going to let anything stop him.

His temper had always held everything else in check—it swept over the weaker emotions, made him sharp and vicious, made him into the perfect weapon to cut through any who dared stand in his way. He could hold on to that honing an-ger, so long as he didn't think of Dirrakara's face. If she drifted through his mind, he vowed to instead think of Valrik, the bas-tard who would pay for all he'd done.

It was a darkly comforting decision, and he went to help the merra throw wood into the growing fire.

They had brought no food with them from Aardanel; all they had to eat were some berries Aro found and a bark And-dyr swore was safe for eating. Joros swallowed one foul berry at a time, choking them down like those weaker emotions, and let the pitiful meal further hone the weapon of his anger. In the sky, two red points stared at him—Sororra's Eyes, and they burned into Joros like a judgment.

No one broke the silence until both the sun and the berries were gone, the crack of the fire loud in the darkness. Finally Rora asked, "Where is it we're going, then?"

"To destroy the other pieces of Fratarro's body," the merra said immediately, staring into the flames as she was wont to do. She looked intensely focused on whatever she thought she saw there; Joros was genuinely surprised she was paying attention to anything else.

Rora's eyes flicked to her, then returned to Joros. She didn't say anything; she clearly knew the value of a silence that needed filling. Much as he hated to admit it, Rora was his best chance now at any kind of success. In all his planning, there was no path to victory that wasn't littered with at least a few bodies . . . and with the Northman gone, Rora was the only willing killer Joros had left.

There was a trick to roping in followers, and Joros had learned it well in his years among the Fallen. He'd led the Shadowseekers, a specialized group of preachers who, more often than not, had been unknowingly buoying Joros along in his rise through the ranks. The trick was to give enough information that they felt important, trusted, vital . . . give them enough back-patting that they wouldn't start asking the questions he *didn't* want to answer. For Joros, who'd been raised in a family of petty squabblers that hoarded secrets like coins, it was a delicate balance: share enough knowledge to stop the questions, and retain enough to keep the others from thinking they could start making their own plans. He said, "The Twins are tied together—*bound* together, if you will—at their very core. One cannot exist without the other, and if one is weakened, the other is made weak as well. Destroy one twin, and you destroy them both. Simple enough." He even tried a smile—Twins' bones, but it had been a long time since he'd had to charm someone. "Anddyr can trace the locations of four other limbs. If we can prevent them from ever piecing Fratarro back together, we can prevent the Twins from rising."

She thought on that a while, before finally asking, "But your old friends, they're looking for these pieces, too?"

"They are."

"So I suppose putting Fratarro back together would make him strong again, and that'd make Sororra strong, yeah? That's what they're trying to do?"

"That's a piece of it," Joros said. Reluctant as he was to admit it, she was hard to stop once she began chewing on a puzzle, and seemed to have a knack for solving problems—those could be useful qualities in a follower, if cultivated properly. "The Twins need to be restored to power *and* freed."

"So everyone knows how to get 'em back to power," Rora mused. "Do the Fallen know how to free them?" She narrowed her eyes at him. "Do *you*?"

"I believe the leaders of the Fallen know of a way to free the Twins, provided Fratarro is pieced back together, and provided they have a pair of mortal twins."

That jostled the merra to attention, her head swinging up to look at him sharply. "You 'believe'?" she repeated. She was close enough that she could reach out to touch the two patches of red sewn over Joros's heart, and her fingers felt like fire even through his black robe, like a bellows into the furnace of his anger. She didn't seem to notice the flare in his eyes. "You were one of the Ventallo, weren't you? Shouldn't you *know*?"

"The Ventallo are very careful with their secrets," Joros snapped. "Only Uniro holds the entirety of the Fallen's knowledge."

"What do they need twins for?" Aro asked, breaking his silence.

Joros could have throttled him for that question. It had been easy enough, until now, to keep Rora and Aro pacified with vague promises of possibilities and plans that might never come to fruition . . . but now he was left with those last-gasp plans, and running out of room to avoid giving the twins uncomfortable answers. Still, there was plenty of room between an outright lie and the complete truth—plenty of room, even, between the complete truth and *enough* of the truth.

"Mortal vessels," Joros said, and both twins stared at him blankly. Joros pinched the bridge of his nose. "Even if Fratarro is made whole, the Twins' bodies are too damaged to be of any real use to them. I believe that the solution, and the course of action the Ventallo plan to follow, is to give the Twins human bodies to inhabit, human twins to act as their hosts."

Rora and Aro exchanged looks, a whole conversation passing silently between them. Joros scrambled to think how he could keep them from leaving if they turned uncooperative, nudged Anddyr with his boot to ready the mage for any containing he needed to do . . .

"So that's what we're for, yeah?" Rora asked.

"If we get to the point where I need you to play host to the Twins, then everything else has gone horribly wrong."

"But that's why you brought us along. Why you *need* us."

Joros popped his jaw, wading carefully through the layers of truth. "Yes. But it would only be for a short time. Only long enough for Anddyr to fight the Twins on more equal footing."

"Right," she said, and stared down at her hands. When she looked back up, there was a sharpness in her eyes. "Right. So this is the big secret. Doesn't seem like too good a secret, if you could figure it out."

"There are likely other components I don't know. A ritual. I can guess at the shape of their plan, but I don't know the details."

"But you said there's only the one man, this Uniro, who does know all of it? Just one man who knows how to bring back the Twins?"

"Possibly. No more than five others know the whole of it, I would guess." Joros's thoughts were skipping ahead, the same thoughts he could see flickering behind Rora's eyes.

"So no more'n five people knowing this one secret . . . and I'm guessing all of 'em live nice and convenient in this big mountain you keep talking about, yeah?"

They reached the same conclusion within moments of each other, eyes locked in understanding.

Vatri looked between them, a frown making deeper creases in her fire-scarred face. "What? What are you thinking?"

"It'd be easier," Rora said, "than hunting all around, trying t'find the pieces and burn 'em and fighting any of the preachers who found 'em first."

"What would be?" the merra demanded.

Joros almost smiled. "Killing the Ventallo."

In the silence that followed, Anddyr resumed his typical mumbling, the ravings of a madman.

Vatri's mouth hung open in shock. "You're talking of murder," the merra finally said. "Cold-blooded murder."

"Blood's plenty warm," Rora said. The women had reached a strange sort of peace after trying to persuade the Northman to stay with them, but it seemed that time had passed. They glared at each other with renewed animosity.

"We're talking about keeping the Twins bound," Joros said levelly. "That's your wish, too, is it not?"

The merra shook her head, not in denial, but as though the movement could jar the words into making better sense. "You know where to find Fratarro's limbs. You said destroying them will keep the Twins from their powers."

"And I believe it would, provided we could find the limbs first, which is far from a guarantee. The hand we found was fairly far-flung, and if my . . . former colleague was able to track it down, others have had just as much time to find the other limbs. For all I know, the rest have been found."

"You could find out." Vatri reached her hand toward the pouch at Joros's hip. It held the sliced-off toe from one of Fratarro's legs, which Joros had stolen from the Ventallo on his departure as a key of sorts, a way for Anddyr to search for the god after Valrik had stolen the seekstones from them. She was wise enough to pull her hand back before touching the pouch. "Like calls to like, you said. Anddyr could search for the other pieces, see if they've been found yet."

"He could," Joros agreed, and made no move to give Anddyr the pouch.

"It'd still be a lot of hunting around," Rora said, "even if none of the other pieces've been found. That's a lot of time."

Vatri spat toward Rora, her spittle fizzling in the fire. "Eager to kill, are you?"

"Eager to be away from you. To get my life back." Rora suddenly yelped in surprise, loud enough that fear quickly swallowed them all, until Joros's searching eyes finally found the reason: Anddyr crouched near Rora, clutching at her arm, his face twisted in the throes of the drug that kept him docile.

"Raturo never sleeps," the mage hissed desperately. "It knows, it always knows . . ."

Joros reached between Rora and the fire to swat at Anddyr until the mage crept away, taking his mumbling to the edge of the firelight's circle. Rora rubbed absently at her arm where the mage had grabbed her, staring after his curled form. "I take it he's met your old friends, then?"

"Anddyr has been my servant for many years."

Vatri spat again, making the flames dance. "It seems like following you around doesn't do anyone much good."

Joros felt his teeth grinding, forced them to stop. "I'll remind you again," he said tightly, "that I didn't ask you to be here. You're welcome to return to your Northman. I can promise we won't miss you."

"I'm here to do the Parents' bidding," the merra said with a glare. "We have the same goal, shocking as that may be, so I'll see this through to the end. But I can't condone murder."

"It really doesn't matter what you can or can't condone."

"Five people?" The soft voice sounded like Rora's, but it came from the other side of the fire. Her twin alternated between never speaking and speaking too much, no middle ground for that one. He was staring into the flames with the same intensity as the merra when she searched for the future. "Out of how many of these leaders?"

"There are twenty of the Ventallo," Joros said.

"Not counting you?"

"I'm very certain I've been replaced by this point."

"Then not counting the ones out looking for limbs."

"Yes. There will be fifteen of the Ventallo inside Raturo."

Aro's eyes finally lifted to meet his sister's over the flickering tips of the fire. "Fifteen isn't all that much more than five."

Rora was looking at him, thoughts racing behind her eyes once more. "If we're talking of killing—" Vatri spat, and Rora threw her a brief glare "—the thing is to not leave loose ends. If we kill the five who know the most secrets, that still leaves plenty of others to try to find those secrets again. But if we kill everyone who even knows the secrets exist . . ."

"You truly are shaped in the Twins' image," Vatri growled.

Rora's hands turned to fists at her sides, and Joros thought he saw a flash of metal in one of them. "I've spent my whole life hiding from *your* people, who'd kill me without even thinking, just for what my face looks like. I bet you'd take a knife to me, too, if I gave you half a chance. How's that any less murder?"

"Abomination, twisting my words—"

"How many babies've you killed, huh? Is it less murder if they only get in three breaths before you throw 'em in a river?"

"I've *never*—"

"Does it count if they don't even cry before you kill 'em?"

"Enough!" Joros said, raising his voice over both of theirs. They fell into sulky silence, glaring over the fire.

Aro slid closer to his sister, put an arm around her. Joros saw that flash of metal again, from one hand to another and away. Together the twins looked at the merra, their faces like a mirror, one hard and one soft. Unbidden, Joros thought of the great archway within Mount Raturo, stern Sororra's face all angles and anger, Fratarro's made with kinder lines. He thought, too, of another set of twins who'd shaped their faces to match those on the arch.

"I would've expected you'd be happier about the thought of breaking up the Fallen," Aro said softly across the fire. There wasn't sympathy in his eyes, but there was less hate than in his sister's. "Get rid of all your enemies, and you can spend the rest of your days singing praises to the Parents without a care in the world."

"The Parents do not condone murder."

Rora snorted. "Unless it's their own kids, hey?"

"They have enough love in their hearts that they could not bring themselves to exterminate even the most vile of creatures."

That brought a laugh from Rora. "It'd be nice if they passed that love on to their followers."

"Enough," Joros said again, rubbing his hands over his face. When he dropped them, he looked to the merra. "This is my mission. We will do as I see fit, and I promise you, murder is not the darkest thought to cross my mind. If you will not keep your mouth closed, then leave. We don't need you here."

She returned his glare. They'd reached their own sort of accord, after burning Fratarro's hand, a peace borne by joint purpose. Already, though, that accord had frayed, shattered. That didn't particularly bother Joros, but he could see *her* hurt lurking behind the eyes that were too pretty for her ugly face. That didn't particularly bother him either. "I'm not leaving," she said, soft but firm.

"Then have the decency to remain silent."

She was wise enough to take that advice, turning her face to the flames.

It was Aro, again, who broke the silence, speaking directly to his sister. "Fifteen's too many for you alone."

Rora barked a laugh. "What, are you gonna help?"

"No. But I know who can."

Her head snapped up, and there was something on the edge of fear in her voice. "No."

Aro turned away from her, leaning toward Joros, face earnest and the words tumbling out. "We lived in Mercetta, *below* Mercetta, I guess—"

"Shut your fecking face, Aro!"

"—and we know people. Plenty of people, fists and knives—"

"Aro, stop!" She grappled at him, trying to cover his mouth—or, possibly, to punch him. It was hard to tell.

"—people who are real good at killing for the right amount of coin."

Rora shoved him down into the snow, surged to her feet. "Damnit, Aro!" She stomped in a tight circle, her anger hotter than the fire.

Joros watched it all with a raised eyebrow, waiting as Aro sat back up and Rora pushed him over again, waiting until Rora's cursing had run its course. When her anger had burned down to coals, Joros said, "We'll turn toward Mercetta in the morning."

"Like hells we will!"

"We will," Joros said, regarding her calmly. "Your brother's right. You alone can only do so much, and Anddyr is . . . unreliable. If you have skilled contacts—"

"We don't, not ones that'd do us any favors anyway. They'd just as like—"

"Quiet," Joros snapped. "I understand difficult pasts. But you are under my protection and, more importantly, in my employ. If you wish for either to remain true, you will bring me to these 'fists and knives' you know, and help me persuade them to our cause. Do you understand me?"

Her hands clenched and unclenched at her sides. He saw her realize there weren't many options, and her shoulders slumped ever so slightly. "Yeah, cappo," she said, dropping down to the ground—not too near her brother, and certainly not near the merra, who was smirking. "I understand."

"Good." Joros wrapped his cloak tight around himself and lay back, staring up at the stars winking in the night sky. He was confident that this night had shattered any closeness that had formed in their little group. That was as it should be. In times of war—and if it wasn't war yet, it certainly would be soon enough—trust was a luxury that none could afford.

CHAPTER SIX

The grass rose like a wavering wall, surrounding Keiro on all sides, shielding him from the world and the world from him. It had even swallowed the path his careful feet had borne, stalks springing back upright as though they had never been touched. Sitting with his knees drawn up to his chest, with only the green-brown of the grass and the sky stretching blue above, Keiro could feel as though he truly were separated from everything, lost among the rippling Plains.

Teeth closed over the smallest toe on his right foot, and Keiro grinned down at the lithe gray form wrapping itself around his ankle. Cazi always found him, no matter how far he walked into the grass, no matter how high the stalks reached. The *mravigi* chirped at him, too young for speech, though Keiro thought he conveyed himself well enough. Keiro stretched his hand down and Cazi scampered into his palm, small still but growing so that he was almost too big for Keiro to hold in one hand now, almost too heavy to lift. He placed the little beast on his shoulder, claws pricking Keiro's scalp as the Starborn stretched his snout farther toward the disk of the sky. His tiny wings, nearly translucent, fluttered in the air.

Keiro hadn't seen any other *mravigi* as young as Cazi; he'd glimpsed some that were larger, though not yet full grown, but they had been as wingless as all the other Starborn he'd seen. Cazi seemed to be an anomaly among them. He would ask Tseris more about it, if she ever came to speak to him again.

Day after day he'd spent wandering the rolling hills, so incongruous in the flat Plains, but any *mravigi* braving the daylight scattered before Keiro could get close enough to them. He had called Tseris's name, as she had bid him, but the only response he ever received was young Cazi twining around his ankles. The *mravigi* would not speak to him, and his gods had not summoned him, and he felt a stranger again among the plainswalkers.

Easier, by far, to walk. To follow the beckoning of an open space, to see how long it would take Cazi to hunt him down. Walking made his heart feel light, kept his doubts at bay. Always, though, his feet led him back to the tribehome, where the children would beg him for a story as their parents watched from the sides of their eyes. Cazi never followed him there, always disappearing back into the grass sea before Keiro's feet touched the flattened stalks of the tribehome.

Later, he and Cazi would part. For now, though, the day was new, and there was an itching in Keiro's feet.

He stood, Cazi rocking on his shoulder but keeping his balance. The *mravigi* pulled himself onto the very top of Keiro's head with claws like needles, long tail winding around Keiro's neck as he stretched himself forward like the prow of a ship.

Cazi seemed to love the faint rush of air against his scaly face as Keiro walked. It made Keiro smile—such a little thing, and so easy, to give so much joy.

It had been some days since last he had wandered over the hills, and so Keiro set off in that direction, the prick of tiny *mravigi* claws in his scalp as comforting as the hard ground beneath his feet, and the air in his face a simple joy worth savoring.

The hills were desolate as always, the grass rolling like waves up and down the hummocks of land. Keiro wondered what tale Yaket had spun to keep her plainswalkers from ever wandering onto the hills, for none of them ever came close to the gentle slopes. Occasionally Keiro caught a blur of black, usually followed by a chirp from Cazi, as some other Starborn scurried out of sight.

"Tseris," Keiro called quietly. Even a whisper would carry over the hills. "I am here. I would speak with you." Cazi trilled, as though trying to echo Keiro's words, but there was no other response.

Keiro had counted the days as they spun by, and he knew it had been almost a full moon-turn since he had emerged from beneath the largest hill, since he had met his gods. He was a patient man, but every man had his limits, and Keiro was near overflowing with questions. There was an aching in him that he could not give words to—it was in the place where a soft-voiced undercurrent had run always, a voice whispering into the void: *Find me.* The voice was gone now, for Keiro had found him, found poor lost Fratarro, but the need still thrummed in him. Each passing day that his gods did not summon him was like a stone in his soul.

Keiro held his hand up near his head, and Cazi obediently

stepped into it. Keiro brought the Starborn to eye level, his one eye staring into the two small red ones. "Cazi," Keiro said in a whisper that even the grasses might not catch, "can you show me the way inside the hill?"

There was a glimmer in the *mravigi*'s eyes, and then he was off, leaping from Keiro's palm with his stunted wings flailing. Cazi landed with a puff of dirt, but seemed unharmed and scampered away, the forked tip of his gray tail disappearing in the grass sea. He sang as he ran, or Keiro would call it singing, the Starborn's tiny voice rising and falling in a melodic warble. With a grin splitting his face, Keiro raced after the sound.

It wasn't the same place that Keiro had first been led beneath the hills; this hole was smaller, more overgrown, a place that looked more forgotten than hidden. Cazi sat at the edge, practically glowing with pride. Keiro crouched down, measuring the hole with his eyes, trying to decide if his shoulders would fit through. "Do you know how to get to the Twins?" Cazi's answering chirp sounded of confidence, and so Keiro reached into the opening, feeling around with his hands. It seemed a sloping tunnel, rather than a hole like he had fallen through the last time. "After you," Keiro said, and Cazi slipped into the darkness. Taking a bracing breath, Keiro followed him.

Keiro had to squirm along on his belly for the first stretch, shifting arms and hips and knees to inch forward, trying very desperately not to think of how small the space was. The tunnel finally widened as it angled downward, enough that Keiro could crawl on his hands and knees with Cazi scurrying just ahead. A thrill ran through Keiro as they went, something made of rebellion and excitement both.

That thrill was snuffed in the sudden glow of red eyes.

Keiro nearly ran headfirst into the Starborn. Its scattered white scales like stars began to glow, giving the dark tunnel a dim illumination. Cazi was trying very hard to become a shadow beneath Keiro. *"Godson,"* the Starborn said, and he recognized Tseris's voice, as well as the reproach in it. *"I would have come for you, had you waited."*

"Forgive me," Keiro said quickly, wanting very badly not to anger the only *mravigi* besides Cazi who would come near him. "It's only . . . I *have* been waiting. I've called your name, as you told me, and . . . I thought perhaps it was a test." The lie sounded lame to his own ears, and he flushed a deeper red.

"I told you to call for me if you had need. You have questions aplenty, but that is not a need."

Keiro could read beyond her words easily enough—it *had* been a test, one of his patience, and he had failed it spectacularly. "Forgive me," he said again, and this time followed it with no justification.

"You are forgiven," Tseris said easily. *"Though I would ask one thing of you in return."* She leaned forward, nearly touching her rounded snout to Keiro's nose. *"Leave Cazi be. It is not good, for either of you, to be so close."*

It took a few moments for Keiro to find any words, and the first that came were, again, "Forgive me. I . . . feel alone here, sometimes. Cazi is a good companion."

"I understand." And there was indeed knowing in her eyes, and a deeper sadness than Keiro could ever know, the sadness of centuries. *"Still. I would ask this of you."*

Keiro bowed his head, lifted one fist to press it against his brow. "I will do as you ask." As a show of good faith, he reached down to nudge Cazi forward into the glowing circle of

Tseris's scales, though the little Starborn's confused trill came near to breaking his heart.

Tseris inclined her head and reached out one long-clawed foot to scoop Cazi closer to her. *"Thank you, Godson. Follow me. I will take you to them."* She turned smoothly in the tunnel, narrow as it was, body flowing like dark water. Cazi moved ahead of her, low to the ground, the joy gone from his quick steps.

The great cavern where Sororra and Fratarro lay imprisoned was full of the soft sounds of breathing and bodies brushing, the glow of a thousand stars as *mravigi* moved throughout the open space. Keiro followed Tseris through the darkness, to the end of the cavern where his gods sat sleeping. Bound at the wrist and ankle by mighty chains that were sunk deep into the stone floor, Sororra seemed somehow to ring with watchfulness, as though she weren't really sleeping—merely waiting, patient as a summer storm. But she *was* sleeping, her eyes closed and her breaths so shallow they made almost no sound or movement. Next to her, Fratarro reclined—though such a word implied comfort, and there was no rest in the lines of the god's body. Even in sleep stiffness was written into him, and rigidity, and an everlasting pain that made Keiro want to weep. Fratarro, with his limbs torn away, was held up only by the sharp spike of stone that pierced him through his chest, binding him as surely as Sororra's manacles. Straz, their ever-present guardian, lay curled before them, white-scaled sides like a bellows as he slept deeply. Keiro wondered briefly if Straz's sleep was tied to the Twins', drawn down with them by whatever divine sleep kept them subdued.

"They will wake soon," Tseris murmured, as though too loud a voice would wake them early. *"It is a gift, that they can wake at all."*

Keiro kept his own voice low. "They haven't always been like this?"

"No, Godson. Only for a short while, in the great measure of time. Only since Fratarro's arm was restored to him. Before that, they slept—restless sleep, angry sleep, but still only sleep. With Fratarro's arm, they gained back a portion of their stolen power."

It made Keiro's heart swell with a strange, unfamiliar hope. He had told Tseris before that he'd never truly thought the Twins could be freed . . . but here was proof, not only of their existence, but that their powers could be returned to them.

Chains shifted, the heavy sound of metal brushing stone, and Sororra's eyes opened slowly. She looked to her brother first, waiting until his eyes had opened as well, and her chains clanked as she reached to grip his shoulder with one hand. The smile they shared carried more layers of depth than Keiro could hope to count, and he felt an intruder, watching it.

Tseris stepped aside, leaving Keiro to approach the Twins alone. He did so with his head bowed, and dropped to his knees when he stood before them. He only knew that they had turned to him by the red glow that washed over him. "Forgive me my impatience," he said, the apology tumbling out. "I am eager to serve you, honored Twins."

"You will," Sororra said, and in her voice was the harsh promise of the desert. "You are the first of the faithful to find us. That is a thing we will not forget."

"There is great purpose for you, Keiro," said Fratarro, who could smile through his pain, smile with an endless love.

Sororra lifted a hand, the gesture speaking of caution. Her eyes, red on black, bored into Keiro. "The future is not written in stone. It is a changing thing, and even we cannot grasp the full breadth of it. There are many threads pulling at you, and they do not all lead to greatness."

"The choices are yours to make," Fratarro said earnestly, though his sister's eyes still held Keiro pinned. "That was my Father's gift to mankind, and I will not gainsay it. The path to greatness lies before you, Keiro Godson."

"There are other paths. Many paths into many futures, and we cannot see where all of them will end."

They fell silent, and Keiro felt very much a child as he cleared his throat. "I have spent my whole life choosing paths, honored Twins. It . . . it seems to me as though my path has always been leading me to you."

Fratarro's smile was like the sun breaking through clouds, but Sororra's face remained passive. It was she who spoke again, and there was something dangerous in her voice. "You heard our summons as you left the desert, did you not?"

Keiro felt his face flush. He had turned away from the Twins only once in his life, after he had escaped the killing sands of the Eremori Desert only to feel a reverberating call pulling him back into the desert's heat. The thought of likely meeting his own death there had been a stronger deterrent than his will to serve the Twins. "I . . . I feared my death, merciful Sororra—"

Her sharp laugh cut him off. "Brother, have I ever been called 'merciful'?"

"I do not think you have."

"You doubted us, preacher. Our powers may be broken, but they are not entirely gone. Yet you doubted that we would keep you safe."

"My other arm lies buried in the desert's sands," Fratarro said softly.

"I would have had you bring my brother a gift, as proof of your faith."

The flush faded from Keiro's face, and he suddenly felt very cold in this place beneath the earth. He could find no words to defend himself, held under two red gazes, and the slow movements of the *mravigi* were unspeakably loud. He had quailed at venturing back into the Eremori Desert, but now he would gladly take its sands beneath his feet once more and its breath burning through his lungs.

Finally Fratarro broke the silence, his smile coming again, though it was lined at the corners with sadness. "It is no matter. The past is done, and there are paths yet to walk. Others will find my limbs for me."

"If you would serve us," Sororra said, "you must learn to trust us."

"I will," Keiro said vehemently, pressing his fist to his brow. "I do. And I swear, I will never disobey you again."

"Then you must bring the faithful to us."

Keiro's thoughts whirled; he had been banished from Mount Raturo, from all of Fiatera, but he would face the wrath of the Fallen to do the Twins' bidding. He would not lose faith in them a second time. "I will leave tonight, go gather the Fallen—"

"No," Sororra said, stern and implacable. "We may yet have need of you here."

"But . . . forgive me, I have no means of contacting the others, of telling them you've finally been found . . ."

"A test, Keiro," Fratarro said with a gentle smile. "We have waited long centuries here in our prison. We can wait a while longer, to see what kind of man you are."

Keiro knelt, with his head bowed low, staring at his clasped hands. "As you wish, honored Twins. I . . . I will do my best."

"Thank you, Keiro."

"You may go now." Sororra waved a hand in dismissal. "We will summon you, if we need to speak with you again." That was a message Keiro could read clearly enough.

He rose and backed away slowly, keeping his head bowed, until he nearly tripped over Tseris. She led him in silence through wider tunnels, and they emerged together near the summit of the largest hill that swelled among the Plains.

Before she could leave him, disappearing once more into the ground, Keiro blurted, "Tseris? May I ask you one question?"

"I will grant you a second one." It took him a moment to realize the glimmer in her red eyes was something like laughter.

"Why does Cazi have wings? All the old stories say the *mravigi* could fly, but none of the rest of you have them."

The laughter vanished faster than a falling stone. She shook her wedge-shaped head. *"Do not trouble yourself with Cazi."*

"I only wonder . . ."

"You wonder too much. Mankind was not given the secrets of the world. Some things you are meant not to know." And she was gone, the forked tip of her tail the last he saw as she returned to the earth.

Keiro walked alone through the hills, and the long grass. The sun hung in the sky, low and bright, stretching his shadow out ahead of him. How to summon the Fallen to this place where none of them had ever walked before? Even if he could think of a way, Keiro doubted they'd listen to him; he was banished, apostate, condemned to death if he ever returned to Fiatera. The Twins had set a test for him, but it felt like one he was doomed to fail from the start.

With nowhere else to go, his feet led him back to the tribe-home. The women were there, and the children, working together to tend fires, strip the skin from roots, crush the tough seeds that made a strangely sweet paste. Keiro sat at the edge of the tramped-down circle where the tribe lived, the grasses tickling his back, welcome among the tribe but not truly one of them. He often caught Poret staring, but she had kept her distance since Yaket had pulled her aside some weeks ago. None of them had been cold, not even Yaket with her disapproving stare, but there had been a shifting, a gentle rebuff, a punishment for ignoring the elder's request to keep the truth from them. He doubted Yaket had told them the reason behind the shunning, but she wouldn't need to—they were her tribe, and her word was law. It stung, some, the rebuke in this place where he'd finally felt a sense of belonging after so many wandering years.

He could spend the day wallowing, or he could turn his mind to the problem at hand. *The past is done, and there are paths yet to walk.* Fratarro had spoken truly. There was no point in letting his mind gnaw on memories like a dog with a bone.

Keiro almost smiled to himself—he was a man very much given to examining the past, his memories worn smooth as river stones, chewed down to shards of bone. But perhaps he could change that, become more worthy of the trust his gods had placed in him. He could be better, so that the next time the desert called to him, he wouldn't think of his fear, of the heat so great it made his sweat steam on his skin. He could keep the past behind him, so that it did not cloud his vision as he walked forward.

One of the women placed a mat of food in his lap, startling Keiro badly; he hadn't noticed the plainswalker men return, or the sun set. He shook away his reverie and took his meal closer to the central fire, closer to the rest of the tribe. He joined their conversations, laughed at the stories the men told, gave Poret a gentle smile when he felt her watching him.

Sororra had used her powers to shape men's minds—it was the crime for which the Parents held her in greatest contempt, her twisting of minds until the people were unrecognizable, virtual monsters. She had instilled thoughts and feelings into her chosen people, along with no suspicion that those thoughts and feelings were not their own—a certainty that those alone were the proper way of things. Though Keiro didn't have the powers of a god, and would not want them, words held their own power. There was a thought, slowly sprouting at the back of Keiro's mind, that he might begin to shape the plainswalkers to his cause.

The children begged him for a story, as they did each night, and Keiro gave them a bright smile. He held up a hand to cut off their pleas for their favorite tales, and he said into the waiting silence, "Listen well, children, for tonight I will tell you a new story." The adults leaned forward as eagerly as the children, their eyes bright as the stars sparkling overhead. Keiro reached up to touch the black eyecloth that was tied always over his brow, easy to lower when he needed to preach—but he stopped and lowered his hand instead, left his eyes uncovered, the good one and the one that was gone. There was a rightness to it. The plainswalkers noted it, and a murmur rippled through them. They fell silent, though, when Keiro opened his mouth once more. "You know of the *mravigi*. They are Fratarro's proudest creation, creatures of such beauty that Patharro could not contain his jealousy at the sight of them. The Father cast them from the sky with angry fire, and he smiled as he watched them burn. Smiled as he destroyed the truest things the world had known."

It was unwontedly dark of Keiro, and he could see the unrest in the plainswalkers. He saw suspicion on Yaket's face, and he looked beyond her. "Patharro sent his fire to destroy all that Fratarro had created . . . but fire cannot burn deep into the earth. Fratarro shaped his children well, gave them long claws and mighty shoulders and slim bodies that could twist through the earth as easily as the sky. Patharro sent his fire, but the *mravigi* fled before it like the moon before the sun, and they dug themselves deep into the earth where the fire could not touch them. They hid, and they lived."

The shock went through them, eyes widening, mouths hanging, skin paling. It seemed as though they hardly breathed. He didn't look at Yaket; he could picture how the anger would twist her face, clear eye and blind eye both narrowed around the brightness of her fury.

"This is as true a story as all those I have told you," Keiro said, voice low and urgent. "The *mravigi* live, and they live here. Has Yaket told you of the Starborn, who live in the hills she has forbidden you from walking?" He thought, perhaps, he heard Yaket's voice raised to silence him, but she was drowned out by cries of affirmation, the plainswalkers raising their voices in surprise and joy. "You have lived near them all your lives, without ever seeing them. They are one and the same, the *mra-vigi* and the Starborn. Fratarro's finest creations. They live." The plainswalkers were weeping, and Keiro grinned like a fool, and he did not look at Yaket.

There was pain in his back, in his shoulder, and the plainswalkers cried out once more. The small weight settled onto his shoulder with a soft trill. Cazi was there, like a fallen star, his scales the faint glow of metal cooling after being pulled from the forge.

"They live," Keiro said again, and the plainswalkers surged forward, and Cazi stretched his head to the stars and sang a high sound of joy.

CHAPTER SEVEN

Parro Modatho liked to talk. Liked more that he had an audience that had no choice but to listen. Eagerly he said Scal was a child of the Parents and would receive all the aid a priest could provide. He said it often, like a thing he did not want Scal to forget. Said it most often to Scal's back, when Scal tried to block out the parro's constant voice. It did not seem like any of the wardens or convicts chose to keep the parro's company. Scal could begin to guess why.

Modatho said it would be months for Scal to recover, months before he could do more than sit and sip broth. Scal did not argue with him, but after three weeks—once he could throw the bowl of flavorless broth without it pulling at his side—Scal began the painful process of standing.

Sitting came first, his wound a line of dull fire along his side. He slid to the wall and pressed his back against the wood, the cold of it seeping in quick. He gathered his feet beneath him, gripped the sill of the window to his right. Pushed with his legs, pulled with his hand, and slowly his back scraped up the wall. Modatho fretted, fluttering his hands, pacing. He had tried, at first, to push Scal back down, but even hurt and weak, Scal was stronger. Modatho kept his distance now but hovered, bothersome as a fly.

Scal stood, and set one foot forward. He felt like a newborn horse, shaky-legged and weak. The second step was harder, pulling at the fire-sealed wound, stretching torn muscle. The first foot, again. He did not hold to the wall. He did not clutch at Modatho. He limped, but he walked alone.

When he stepped outside, he felt the cold against his skin, but it did not reach him. He was of the North, and his blood flowed hot through him. When last he had stood in Aardanel, it had been a place of death and blood and fire. Now, close to a decade since last he had walked down the streets, it was rebuilt in the image of the place it had been before. The same orderly and organized living quarters, the same wide streets. As he walked forward, slow and halting, it felt, almost, as though the years fell away from him. Dropped, and sank into the snow and the ice.

Almost, but it was not so. There were too many aches in Scal, too many reminders of his cruel third life and his bloody fourth. The past could not be so easily cast aside. Scal, though, had never turned from a thing for it being difficult.

There's only forward, little lad, Parro Kerrus had said. *A man who looks too long at the past is a man who's lost.*

The Chief Warden's cabin was in the same place it had been when Scal was young. He knocked, with Modatho urging him not to, and opened the door without waiting for an answer. Eddin, who had been Chief Warden longer than Scal had lived in Aardanel, had been a tall man with a long face. Kind eyes that had seen too much. He had had a way of making a man feel taller, when he spoke. But he had died, when Iveran first sacked Aardanel. The desk was the same that his had been, but the man behind it was not. Short and fat. Pig's eyes amid folds of skin. Heavy breaths that, even sitting, wheezed through a half-open mouth. He looked angry to be interrupted, angrier to see Scal. "What's this?" His voice came out thick, nasal. Modatho had said his name was Temren.

"Chief Warden," Scal said, and bowed at the waist, though it sent fire up his side. "I wish to stay here as a ward. I will work, in trade for food and a place to sleep."

"Why?" Temren demanded, mistrust heavy in his voice.

"I lived here for a time, as a child. This place was good to me. Good for me."

Modatho stepped forward, hands wringing within the sleeves of his red cassock. "He is penitent, sir. The Parents demand we turn away no man who will serve."

"More dog than man," Temren said, and spat on the floor.

"I stand for him," Modatho said, with as much firmness as he could. It was not much, but he was the second priest to stand surety for Scal in Aardanel. That was not a small thing. A string of guilt snaked along Scal's side, with the pain from his wound.

Temren looked Scal up and down, and his distaste was plain. Scal kept his face blank, a mask. The Chief Warden snorted, and turned to Modatho. "I don't care what pets you keep. But if he's well enough to move around, keep him hobbled and chained."

Scal knew the slow boil that began in his stomach, recognized it for what it was. He fought to keep his anger down. This was a new life, and he would not spoil it so soon. "I belong to no man," Scal said, low and calm. "I will work. I will atone. I will not wear chains."

"It's chains or death, Northman. Your choice."

He would not be the man he had been. There was a better man he could be, a man who could stand to be shamed. *All men are worthy of being heard*, Kerrus had told him, but another man, one that Scal had killed, had told him that the minds of small men did not matter. Kerrus had been right in most things, but not in all. "I will wear chains if I am given a place of my own to stay." He wished to be a better man, and remaining in Modatho's constant presence would threaten to undo him. Too, he did not want another priest trying to guide and shape him. The words of a long-dead priest still echoed through Scal, and that was the only priest he would listen to.

Temren snorted again. "This ain't a negotiation. If you want to stay here, you'll stay as a prisoner. You've already got the convict's cross, even if it is fecked up. You'll wear chains so you don't kill my boys, and you'll stay with the parro so my boys don't kill you. Now get out of my sight."

Scal's hands tightened at his sides. He thought, for a moment, how easy it would be to put a knife in Temren's throat. Even wounded as he was, Scal knew he would move faster than the Chief Warden. But he had no knife, no weapon at all. His weapons were in the chapel, with the rest of his belongings. More, he was not the kind of man who would do such a thing. Not anymore. He spread his fingers, loosened them from their fists. *A wise man knows when to turn from a fight*, whispered Kerrus in his mind, and so Scal turned from Temren. Stepping outside, Modatho at his heels, it seemed as though he felt the cold more than he had before.

Modatho would not meet his gaze as they stood outside Temren's door. Softly, the parro said, "We will have to get you chained. The Chief Warden doesn't tolerate disobedience."

Silently, Scal thought that Modatho did not know the first thing of disobedience. He did not say so. Nodded instead, and followed the parro to the smithy.

The smith had chains between his own wrists and a cross in his cheek, just as much a prisoner as any other. Scal wondered if he had ever struck off his own chains. If the thought had even crossed his mind. *Some men*, Parro Kerrus had said solemnly, *grow too comfortable to the things that bind them.* The smith fixed manacles around Scal's wrists, others around his ankles. Gave the heavy key to Modatho. Sheepish, the parro turned away, slipped the key into one of the many pockets hidden in his cassock. As though Scal could not find it if he truly wanted to. The chains felt heavy, short enough that he could not spread his arms wider than his shoulders. Could not step in more than a shuffle.

Scal was tired, his hurts settling in like a blizzard. This day had not gone as he had hoped, and he wished to sleep, to pray. To think of how he could still be the man he wished to be. He moved slow, limping and shuffling both. Modatho stayed ever at his side. Eyes cast to the ground, and Scal could not guess his thoughts. The irons at his wrists and ankles were like hard and heavy ice, and the cold of them reached Scal as it usually did not. He clanked as he walked, and even the warm shame of it could not burn away the chill.

Modatho, for once, had little to say. He left Scal alone in the chapel, to the quiet and the cold and the flickering of the ever-flame. Scal knelt before the flame, and he clanked as he reached one hand up to hold the flamedisk around his neck. The tip of the other pendant that hung there pierced his palm, the sharp snowbear claw. It was only another pain to add to the mix. Kerrus had told him, *There is danger in being alone.* The priest had not been right in all things, but he had been right in most.

After a time, Scal went to his belongings. In his second life, he had lived in Kerrus's hut, had a bed of his own and a small chest to hold his few belongings. He had fewer things now than he had as a boy. They were a man's needful things, instead of a boy's squirreled treasures. If the chapel was to be his home, he would make it so.

He left his sword in the corner, and his knives. He was no longer a man who needed them. The sight of them made him sad. Sick. He put his back to them, facing the everflame as he went through his travelsack.

Only one thing was not as he expected. There was a stone, green and glimmering in the everflame's light, and Scal's sight twisted when he touched it. He saw another man's hands, holding the reins of a horse. He saw, ahead, the back of a head, brown hair cut short. Rora's hair.

The witch-man had carried many stones like this one. He had called them seekstones, said they guided him. Holding it, Scal could feel the tug, as though his mind were trying to flee away from his flesh. South.

There is a danger in being alone.

Scal put the stone back into his travelsack. It held the remains of a past life. A life he would sooner forget.

He ached, and the chains sent the ache deeper. Still. Scal had set out to be the man he should have been, and he had always been taught that obstacles were tests from the Parents to see a man's true character. Cold and pain were things that Scal could handle.

"You'll kill yourself," Modatho said, standing before the chapel's door. "I'm supposed to be your protector. I can't let you do this."

Scal reached out to put one hand on Modatho's shoulder. Pushed. Sent the parro stumbling sideways. He walked slow and limping from the chapel before Modatho could find his balance.

The new day was bright and crisp. Ice crystals shining like stars on the ground, glinting in the air. The world was like a new thing, reborn. It would have been beautiful, save for the loud noises Scal's chains made as he walked.

They were gathering before the gate, wardens in blue and prisoners in fur and rags. The group was all men, strong and hard with muscle, and chains between most of their wrists. The wardens carried crossbows, and short swords at their hips. There was a sledge piled high with axes, four others that were empty. The men glared at Scal's slow approach, the wardens shifting their grips on the crossbows. None spoke to him. Since they did not tell him to leave, Scal followed them through the gates from Aardanel. Two convicts pulled each of the sledges, thick ropes slung over their shoulders. The sledge runners whispered over the crust of snow. Gentle, soothing.

The group of convicts and wardens passed through forest so thick the sledges could hardly pass, and barren fields of ugly stumps, and spaces where new trees were beginning to stretch their faces to the sun.

Aardanel was a place for criminals who chose labor over death. They labored in the thick forest, long days of cutting trees and chopping wood that would be sent south. Warming the homes of people who did not know what true cold was. People who had homes, and lives, and hope. There would always be convicts, and there would always be need for firewood. In Aardanel, they thought to the future.

They stopped in a rough clearing amid proud old trees. There was a pile of new-felled trunks, another pile already stripped of their branches. The convicts formed a line to receive axes from the wardens. The other wardens standing with crossbows raised and set, eyes sharp. Scal joined the line. None of the convicts would stand too close to him. When Scal reached the sledge with the axes, the two wardens there glared at him. One tossed the axe instead, and the convict behind Scal caught it in a clank of chains. The line flowed around him, parting like a river around a stone. Sneering convicts collecting axes from glaring wardens. Moving slow—even if he did not ache, he was wise enough to move slow—Scal leaned down to pull an axe from the pile, the wooden haft cold beneath his fingers. A single sound flowed through the clearing, a whisper of cloth as all the wardens turned as one. Their readied crossbows pointing at Scal. He held the axe loosely at his side and chose a tree, his footsteps loud in the waiting silence. He could still feel the bolts trained on his back as he lifted both arms with the axe, chains clanking near his ear, muscles bunching.

The swing near tore him in two.

He stood gasping, black and red warring in his vision. Frozen like a waterfall in winter, not moving for fear of breaking.

Not able even to move. Already broken. Only one clear thought made it through the pain, found root in the swirling horror. *This, perhaps, is what dying feels like.*

Scal's fingers were still wrapped around the cold haft of the axe. It may have been the only thing that had kept him from collapsing. He twisted his body, pulled his arms back. What little piece of the blade had sunk into the tree came free, and he could feel the warmth of blood begin to trickle down his side. He had looked at the wound, long and wicked, curving around ribs and stomach. Modatho had said Vatri had been the one to close it with fire and steel. She had done good work. He had hoped the seal would hold.

No matter. Parro Kerrus had told him, *A true penitent will do whatever the Parents may ask.* Scal did not know if this was a thing the Parents had asked him to do. If this was the kind of penance they would ask of anyone. He did not claim to hear the Parents, as Vatri had. He only knew that this was a thing that felt right.

He felled the tree, by the end of the day. It was not so impressive a thing—there were other convicts who felled a dozen trees in the same time. But for Scal, whose right side was stiff with frozen blood, it seemed a miracle. He nearly fell with the tree, blackness taking bites from the edges of his vision and exhaustion making him feel heavy, thick. His hands around the axe were swollen, blistered, bloody. Other hands, he did not know whose, took the axe from him. He followed, when the whole group of them turned back toward Aardanel. Sledges piled high with chopped wood, hauled by strong men with the ropes over their shoulders. Scal followed, and his right boot squelched on the snow, soaked through with blood.

Somehow he made it to the chapel. Modatho was waiting there, his broad face tight with worry. Inside, Scal knelt before the everflame. He nearly tipped forward into the flames, but as he swayed back he almost thought he heard a whispering. More than the sound of flames dancing on coals. No words that he could make out, but insistent. He leaned forward again, one shaking hand stretching toward the fire.

"Idiot!" Modatho snarled, grabbing Scal's shoulder. The touch was light, but it was enough to send him tipping. Scal did fall then, sideways, with a crash like the tree he had felled.

"I am sorry," he said aloud. Mumbled it, and did not know who he said it to.

Scal slept through half the next day. He blamed Modatho for it in part, for he suspected the parro kept more than prayer-herbs in his satchel. Modatho had put a neat line of stitches down his side, though, and so he could not be too upset. The stitches held better, when Scal returned to the clearing to cut down another tree. The parro still had to stitch him up again after, but Scal did not bleed so much, and he did not faint.

Twice more he went to chop wood with the convicts who glared, the wardens who kept their crossbows pointed at his heart. Twice more Modatho repaired the damage, clucking and scolding and praying each time. Scal felt stronger with each day, and at night, when he lay staring at the everflame before sleep took him, he could hear the fire whispering at the edges again. He thought perhaps it was the Parents' approval. At those times, he understood Vatri better than he had before. Understood the call to lean closer to the flames, until his skin felt stretched tight over his face, until his eyes watered so badly it seemed as though nothing could wet their dryness. He missed her. But he was not the same man who had known her.

Two days, he had been given for his redemption. They were happier days than he had thought to hope for. Filled with peace, of a sort, and hope. He was grateful for them, when the world crashed down around him.

It was the screaming that woke him. Not the screaming of Fiateran words in Fiateran voices, for those were not uncommon things in Aardanel. No, it was the war cries that woke him. The shouting of Northmen beyond counting.

Scal rolled to his knees. Ignored the ache in his side, for it was a small thing. His fingers reached for the space at his side where his sword usually slept, but they returned empty. Toes curling, legs stretching, and he crossed the room in three strides to the corner, where his sword sat propped. He would run into the night with his sword raised, and cut down any who stood before him. They would die, for being too unlucky, for being too foolish to run. He would wash his blade in blood, and though he would not enjoy it, that would not stop him. He did not fear his death, for when it finally found him, he would welcome an end to the bloodshed.

He reached for the sword, the tool of all his bloody lives, and he felt fingers crawling over him. His old lives, reaching out to grasp at him, to pull him back. To make him less, to make him worse.

His fingers fell to his side, and he stared at the sword. His arm felt too light. As though there were a piece of himself missing. And his chest hurt, in a deep and nameless place, where the hands of his past trailed their cold and bloody fingers over his skin.

He thought of the Northmen swarming around him. Blades bared, jabbing, his flesh splitting before them. No escape, no quarter. His death surging forward, borne aloft by Northern war cries. And himself, swordless and alone, facing them with open arms.

It was a thing he had not felt before, a heaviness deep in his belly. He did not know better, and so he named it fear.

Scal wrapped the fear around himself, colder than iron chains. He sat, his eyes stuck to the sword, and he listened to the screams, and he fought to draw breath.

Modatho burst into the chapel from his hut, wild with fear. "It's Iveran!" he gasped. Scal knew that was not right, he had killed the man himself, but the fear in him knew no reason. The parro crashed into a table that held candles and herbs, toppled it over. He scrabbled at the floor, pushing aside scattered candles. The scent of herbs sharp in the air. The screams grew louder, Fiateran fear and Northern anger, and Modatho flung open a door into the floor. Stray candles rolled, tumbled over the lip into the hole.

Clutching his travelsack, what little he owned in the world, Scal hurried across the floor. Modatho disappeared through the hole, wide eyes peering up at Scal from the darkness. Scal glanced to the corner where his sword leaned, and his knives. Glanced only. The sword had nearly meant his death, each time he held it. He dropped into the cellar with Modatho, who hauled at a rope to bring the door thumping into place.

Darkness swallowed them. The parro's heavy breaths echoed in the small space, and it sounded almost like sobbing. Before, Scal would have scoffed, thought less of the man. Now he understood. The fear howled in him as well.

Scal tried to keep his breaths even. To keep his mind calm. He crouched, fingers questing blindly into his travelsack. He found the square of carved wood, the tinderbox that was as precious as life on the road. Moving carefully in the darkness, he set the tinder, a hank of shredded rope, carefully nearby. The steel striker he bent around his knuckles. The jagged piece of flint in his other hand, thumb pressing a piece of charred cloth near the sharp edge, held tight enough to keep his shaking hand still. "Candle," Scal said into the darkness. It was the only word he could manage. Modatho did not answer, save for a small surprised hiccup in his breathing.

Scal struck the steel down at his flint. Missed, and bruised some of his fingers. Tried again and hit, sparks leaping into the air, dying fast. Modatho gasped, and Scal heard him scrabbling on the ground. Another try and the cloth caught an ember, glowing, precious. Scal dropped the steel, a loud sound in the quiet space, and his fingers searched quickly for the tinder. He brought the two together, spark and tinder, folded them carefully together, and gave them his breath. A slow, angry flare of red with each blown breath, the ember stubborn. It caught, finally, in a rush, flame swallowing quickly the food it had been offered. Modatho lurched into the sudden light, eyes wide, a candle thrust forward. Their shaking hands met, flame to wick, and when Scal dropped the tinder to the floor to save his fingers, the candle held.

"Thank you," Modatho whispered, staring at the flame like a man starved. In the faint light, Scal searched the floor for another candle, lit it from Modatho's. Found a corner to put his back to, tried to make the thump of his heart calmer. Listened. It was quiet in the cellar, the world shut out. Or silenced already.

They did not sleep. Did not speak. Sat through the silence as the candles and their fear ate up the air in the room. Scal wished to be doing anything, wished for a blade in his hand, and hated himself for it. When he thought of facing a Northman, that wish quailed. He hated himself for that as well. He had hated his fourth life, hated the man he had been. At least, though, he had known himself. Known how to think, how to act, how to feel. He knew nothing about the man he now was.

There were footsteps above like thunder, and they set Scal's blood pounding. He did not know if it was with thrill or with fear. Voices, speaking words he could not hear though he understood the sound of them. A laugh, like a bear's. Clattering, and more thunder, and then more silence.

Time passed slow as dripping wax. Slow as learning to breathe normally once more.

"We should . . ." Modatho's voice was a croak, sneaking into the silence like a rabbit fearing the wolf. "We should . . . go see."

Scal met his eyes across their candles. He was right. "Unchain me," Scal said quietly. He was half sure he would find his death out there. He would like to die a free man at least. Modatho did not answer right away. Finally he reached within his cassock, pulled out the heavy key. It landed loud at Scal's side. Soon the manacles took its place, the chain coiling in a whisper. Some little bit of the fear fell away with the iron.

Scal left first. The ladder complained under his weight, but it held. He pushed the door up by slow measures. Enough to listen through. Enough to peek through. Enough to see through. Enough to climb through.

It was no louder without than it had been within the cellar. Quieter, even, without shallow breaths echoing. The chapel was a ruin, the door hanging from one hinge, silently shuddering. Powerless against the cold blowing wind. Tables turned, herbs and bowls scattered, the floor torn open where Modatho had thought Scal did not see he hid away precious coins. In the center of the room, the everflame bowl lay upside down, its stand broken. Its flame extinguished. In the corner where Scal's sword had leaned, and his knives—nothing. That did not hurt so much as the dead everflame. He walked carefully through the ransacked chapel. As though ungentle feet would do more damage than had already been done. Out through the hanging, swinging door.

Outside . . . outside he was a boy again. The streets ran red. The bodies lay scattered. Limbs torn. Wardens and convicts alike, no discretion. Occasionally, the white fletching of an arrow bright against darkening blood. Carrion birds already gathering for the feast. No different than when he was a boy, save that he did not feel anger now. Only fear.

Modatho prayed and wept, and Scal left him to it. He needed to be gone from this place. He walked carefully through the streets. Stepping over bodies, around blood. Still his breeches soaked red halfway to the knee. He reached the gate, opened wide, and all the North spread out before him. White and open. Clean.

He ran. Legs churning, feet catching on ice and roots, falling. Rising again, and running. He did not think he would ever stop. He hoped the snows would take him. Perhaps they would not give him another life and he could finally, finally, stop.

CHAPTER EIGHT

Rora hadn't expected it to feel like coming home. She'd never hated Mercetta, but she'd never loved the city either—it was just the only place she'd lived, until she'd had to run from it. But the familiar streets, the buildings all crowded together, the reek of fish from the East Market, the hard-eyed sneers that passed for greetings—it put a strange feeling in her chest. She could tell Aro felt it, too. He was smiling, which was something she hadn't seen in too long. He'd never said anything when she'd dragged him out of the city, but she knew if it'd been up to him, they wouldn't't've ever left. He might've told Joros about the Canals just for a reason to come back.

She almost ducked down an alley at the first brown-coated city guard they saw, until she remembered she looked respectable enough that she fit right in with the East Quarter crowd, and anyway, ducking into alleys wasn't so easy on horseback. Aro got twitchy about it, too, but he was more used than she was to moving around topside like a real person. Part of what he'd done for the Dogshead was pretending not to be Scum, and he'd got good enough at it. He was leading them to a tavern, a place he'd been to plenty on Dogshead's business.

Rora'd been careful not to talk to Aro about it, but she hoped he had the same plan she did. They'd leave Joros and his witch and the merra in the tavern, saying they were going off to find muscle, and then they could disappear. Rora'd even stay in Mercetta, if that's what Aro wanted; they could take up with a different pack for protection, or maybe they could try to be respectable people with all the coin they had from Joros. Rora didn't know the first thing about being respectable, but she'd try her hand at that sooner than going back to Whitedog Pack. In the Canals, you could get killed for a lot less than abandoning your pack. Rora wasn't about to test her luck, and since Joros was set on them getting their "old friends" to be his new muscle, the only choice they had was to leave him.

The tavern was a big place, just before the market square really started. There was a hanging sign out front with letters on it she couldn't read, but it had a picture of a spitted boar. She could bet merchants filled the place up after market, buying each other drinks with the money they'd fleeced off honest folk. Halfway between midday and sundown, the place looked pretty empty.

A few stableboys took their horses, all being very careful not to look at the merra's burned face. Joros, looking pretty happy that his own burned-but-healing face wasn't getting any notice next to the merra's, threw the stableboys a few copper sests each, and they caught the coins well enough even with their hands full of reins. It almost made Rora smile. Kids anywhere weren't much different'n pups, who were just kids with some skills and some Scum to back 'em up.

"Right," she said, turning to Joros. "We'll go see who we can dig up, and meet you back here. Second bell after sundown?"

Joros nodded, and there was something in his face she didn't like. "If you're sure that's enough time. We wouldn't want to rush you. I'm sure Aro and I can find plenty of conversation to fill the time."

Rora went cold all over. "Aro'll be with me. I need him for—"

"Do you know what 'collateral' means, Rora?"

She didn't, but she could guess well enough. In her head, she kicked herself for not thinking that Joros'd guess their plan. Aro looked as sick as she felt, but he had the easy end of this new deal. He didn't have to go face the pack that'd view 'em as traitors.

"Right," she said again, harder. "Then I'll be back at sunup."

Joros smiled, a tight thing that pulled weird at the burned side of his face, and it made her want to hit something. Instead she leaned down and tugged off her boots; they were well-made, and she wanted to wear them again without the canal-rot getting to 'em. She shoved the boots into Joros's arms, making his smug look turn to a surprised one, and covered that up with the heavy white bear cloak. He came out of the fur sputtering, just in time for Rora to throw her tunic at him, too. It was nice and clean enough that it'd be like asking to get robbed. Her loose shirt kept her daggers covered, and her coinpurse, and that was the important thing. She didn't say a thing more to any of them, not even Aro, just turned and stalked off. The packed dirt under her toes made it feel like she'd never even left.

It was strange walking through the crowds of Mercetta in daylight. As a knife, she'd mostly gone topside at night, if she'd had to go topside at all. Walking through all those people with her back straight and her eyes up ahead felt like one of the most unnatural things she'd done in her life, and that counted burning a god's hand. She even felt fingers reaching for her purse once—a clumsy try, but it just added to feeling like a real person here. That was a dangerous sort of feeling.

Rora took herself down to South Quarter, where the nice houses of East fell apart to shacks and crumbling old buildings and refuse filling the streets. The people there were refuse, too, hard faces and thin limbs and sharp edges. Rora at least fit in better, with no shoes and the simple shirt and her own face hard as rocks. She ducked into a tavern, one that didn't make an effort at writing out its name, just a slab of wood with a rough painting of a black knife on it. She sat near the middle of the room and drank slow from a chipped mug, and listened to the news of the low city flow around her. It wasn't too heartening.

Sounded like the Blackhands'd gotten the war they'd been looking for, and it'd even started to boil up from the Canals into the city proper. Folk didn't go out after dark, not unless they wanted their bodies to send a message when the sun came up. The businesses that scraped by in South were getting looted or burned if they sold to the wrong customers, and a lot of 'em had stopped selling at all, scared they couldn't tell the wrong people from the right people. No one topside knew what things looked like down in the Canals—they never did—but most guesses were pretty grim. Knowing the Canals and the Scum as she did, Rora thought even the darkest guess she heard was probably putting a heavy shine on the truth.

When she'd heard all she cared to, sat still for as long as she could stand it, Rora went back out to the streets. She chose her place carefully, twisting through foul-smelling alleys until she found an old sewer grate, half-covered by trash. She hadn't seen anyone watching, but she made the hand signs for "pack" and "safe" and "help," just in case. The grate was heavy, but it slid away from its grooves, showing a pit dark as a cloudy night.

Shit choices, but there was some shit you could stand, and some you couldn't. Rora sat at the edge of the hole and found the footholds, slid down into darkness, and pulled the grate back over above her head. The sound of it settling back echoed down the hole, setting her teeth on edge.

She'd taken this path down to the Canals more times than she could count, and dozens of others like it through her life as a pup and a knife, but it felt different this time. She felt like she was trespassing—like she didn't belong here anymore.

No one was waiting for her at the bottom, which made her think maybe the hand signs'd worked; just in case, she made them again, for if there was anyone hiding in the shadows weighing how easy a target she looked. The paths were familiar, faded white smudges that maybe looked like dogs dotting the walls. She kept making the signs as she walked, "pack" and "safe" and "help." No one came to stop her, and that was wrong. Even when she'd been a knife, one of the eyes would've come forward by now, just to make sure she really was herself. Now, she was as good as a stranger, and still no one stopped her.

She stepped around the corner into Whitedog Den, the place where the pack lived and cooked and slept, and it was empty. Not a body, not a breath. A big open space, and not a sign that anyone'd ever lived there except the dogs chalked onto the walls.

Rora's footsteps were louder than the water whispering through the canal to her left as she walked through the Den, bare feet loud on the muddy ground. Her fingers found her dagger, her first one, the one with the smashed blue stone on its hilt. She held it down at her side, even though it didn't do anything to stop the quick thumping of her heart.

A while back, when she'd still been a knife and Aro'd still been as close to the Dogshead as a son, Rora'd sat whispering with her brother, sharing fears. "I don't know why the Black-hands have decided we're their worst enemies," Aro'd said, eyes honest and voice scared, "but if it comes to a war . . . Rora, I'm not sure we'd win."

At the far end of the Den, a spike was driven into the ground, set before the way that led deep into the pack's territory. There'd always been a dog's head stuck on top of that spike, just to remind anyone who got close enough where they were and that Whitedogs were as bloody bastards as the rest of the Scum. The head was down to a skull now, just a few strips of old flesh that rats hadn't gotten to yet. It hadn't been changed in a long while.

Rora stepped around it, palm slippery with sweat around the hilt of her dagger. She didn't bother making the hand signs anymore. It was all she could do to keep walking, to keep her feet from breaking into a run. She didn't even know which way she'd run, whether she'd race forward looking for whatever was left of her pack or if she'd run back, run away so she didn't have to know what'd happened. She just kept on going, step by step, and the dagger shook at her side.

Her feet knew the way; she'd walked it hundreds and hundreds of times. The second left, with the canal water splashing up against her ankles, and the next right, footsteps echoing on the brick that made up this stretch of floor, and then a long walk down a hall with high walls, feeling like they were crushing her in so she couldn't breathe. The chamber at the hall's end was a circle, three other paths leading off it, and the left one would take her to the Dogshead's chamber. She stood in the center of the circle room, her heartbeat and her breath both too loud, and she almost missed it. She would've if she'd been any less edgy, but her ears were straining for any sort of sound. She heard the soft footsteps and spun to face the right tunnel, saw a man with a rusty knife rushing toward her. Rora brought up her dagger, scrambled for the other one, shouted, "I'm Whitedog! I'm pack!" Then there was a dagger at her throat, from the person she hadn't heard behind her, and a hand slapping the screams back into her mouth. Pain shot through her, a shallow fiery line of it across her neck, and panic chased after the pain.

"So the bird's come back to its nest, hey?" a voice hissed in her ear. "Where'd you migrate to, Sparrow?"

Rora went still, not trying to fight against the arms around her anymore. She opened her fingers and let both daggers drop to the ground with loud clatters, held up her hands so her attackers could see they were empty. The man who'd rushed at her from the right hall sneered, leaned down to scoop up her daggers. She knew his face, but couldn't think up his name. He was Whitedog; at least she knew that much. Or he'd at least been Whitedog last time she'd seen him.

There were others, footsteps moving over stone, low voices, flickers at the edges of her eyes, but the knife to her throat didn't give Rora much room for looking around. The pressure of the blade disappeared suddenly from her throat, and the arms let her go—but her own arms were grabbed real quick, two sets of hands holding hard enough it felt like they meant to crush her bones through her skin. The one who'd been holding her stepped around the two bruisers now doing that job, stepped into Rora's sight.

"Tare," Rora gasped, half relief and half terror.

"In the flesh," Tare said with a mocking smirk Rora knew so well, but there was none of the usual warmth in her voice. "Despite all efforts."

"You have to let me explain—"

"Oh, you'll explain plenty," Tare interrupted. She held her dagger out to the side, let its edge flash. Rora's blood was on the other edge, where it'd pressed against her neck. "You'll tell me everything."

Rora's heart was beating like a bird at the bars of its cage, and a choking sob jumped out of her mouth. "Tare, it's not—"

"Shut up," Tare said, and one of the fists holding Rora let go of her arm for a second to thump his knuckles into the side of her head. It left Rora's eyes fuzzy and her thoughts spinning like seedpods in a wind. The fists started marching forward, and Rora couldn't get her feet working in time. They held her up by her arms, her bare feet dragging along the ground, leaving behind the skin off the tops. A few times she tried to get her feet under herself to walk, but it seemed like the fists were making sure she couldn't.

She knew the way they were taking her, down the left hall from the circle chamber, over a careful bridge, a quick right, pausing before a door. The only door in the Canals.

The waterfall room was loud, water roaring down in a sheet to disappear past the floor. There wasn't anyone in the room, but Rora'd bet anything the Dogshead was watching from beyond the waterfall. The fists threw Rora down into a chair, tied her arms. They were smart about it, not just tying her wrists behind her, but lashing her forearms to the rungs, too, and tying her ankles to the chair legs for good measure. Rora kept her eyes on Tare, who was leaning against the big desk, studying Rora's daggers. When the fists had her tied up, they left Rora and Tare alone.

"Tell me," Tare said, balancing the point of Rora's broken-stone dagger on one finger, "why I shouldn't kill you."

Rora was too panicky to think proper, and the thump to the head hadn't helped, so she blurted the first thing to pop into her head. "It's a longer story than you want to hear."

Tare smiled a little, shook her head. "You're still funny. And stupid. You get two sentences to convince me." She flipped Rora's dagger into the air, caught it by the hilt. "Or else I start cutting until I find some answers I like."

Rora squeezed her eyes shut, tried to shake her thoughts into working. "Someone was gonna come after me'n Falcon." She was proud of herself, remembering to use the name Aro'd given himself in the Canals. "Running was the only choice we had."

Tare shrugged. "Not convinced." She moved faster'n a snake, darting forward, one hand in Rora's hair yanking her head back and the other pointing the dagger at Rora's eye.

"We're twins!" Rora shouted, and the dagger stopped moving forward. Rora couldn't help staring at its tip, glinting right above her eye, and she babbled out all the words that jumped up in her head. "We're twins and they would've killed us, and I couldn't bring them down on you—they're scary fecking bastards. You probably would've killed us, too, if you found out, and all I could think of was to run. I'm sorry, Tare, I didn't mean to leave the pack—I was just scared." The words stopped vomiting out, and it was just Rora staring at the dagger's tip and praying harder'n she ever had before that Tare's hand stayed steady.

Tare's hand tightened in Rora's hair, used it to turn her eyes away from the dagger. Tare's face was more open now than it'd been this whole time, but there was still a hardness there, and the dagger still stayed near Rora's head, ready to strike. "Where is it you've been since you left?"

A hysterical laugh bubbled up out of Rora's mouth before she could swallow it. "I've been north, all the way North."

"Got anything to prove that?"

"I've got four people can tell you about it, and Falcon's one of 'em."

"That sounds more like a trap than proof."

"I've got the coin of the man who paid us to go with him."

Tare raised an eyebrow at that, leaned over to cut away Rora's coinpurse with two neat slices. She lifted it up, made an appreciative noise at its weight. She tossed it onto the desk so it landed next to Rora's other dagger. "You can get coin from anywhere. Now *I've* got a bag of coin that don't prove shit. Anything else?"

"I didn't bring anything with me."

Tare shrugged again. "They should've given you a better lie before they sent you back." She lifted the dagger again, pointed it back toward Rora's eye.

"Who?" Rora asked quickly, the panic rising up again. "Tare, whoever you think sent me here, I promise you're wrong."

"Dead girls will tell any lies."

"I came back because I need your help. The man who hired me wants to hire more knives, he's got a job—"

Tare snorted. "Right, we follow you to this man, and then all your Blackhands friends jump us."

"Blackhands friends?" Rora repeated, and then the realization hit and that crazy laugh came out again. "You think I ran off to the Blackhands! Tare, gods no, Tare, I'd never, I hate those bastards as much as anyone." The dagger was still moving toward her, and Rora took a chance—fixed her eyes on Tare instead of the dagger, said as calm as she could, "I didn't think you thought so little of me. I run off for a while, and you just assume I'm screwing pigs now?"

Tare laughed at that. "Still funny," she said again, smiling, and then she brought the dagger down sharp and sudden— through the air next to Rora's head. Relief flooded through her, right up until the moment Tare dangled Rora's ear in front of her face. That was when the pain hit, and Rora howled with it.

Tare dropped the ear into Rora's lap, a smear of blood across her breeches, and she could feel more blood flowing down the side of her neck. It wouldn't kill her, wounds to the head just bled a lot, but it felt like enough blood that it'd all leak out of her soon enough, and it hurt like a bloody hell. She struggled against the ropes on her arms like getting out of them would let her run away from the pain, thrashed as much as she could, howled until the screams broke on the way out, and then all her straining muscles gave up at once. She went limp and hang-headed, staring down at her own ear in her lap as her body shook. "Tare," she sobbed, not knowing what she was begging for.

"You never could take any pain." Tare's feet stood next to

her own, and the older woman crouched down. She slipped the dagger under Rora's chin, used its point to lift her head up until their eyes met. "Even if I wasn't already going to kill you," she said, and she almost sounded sad about it, "I'd have to kill you anyway if you're a twin. Either way—" and she poked the dagger's tip up into the soft triangle of flesh under Rora's chin, pulling out another scream "—it'll go easier for you if you tell me the truth."

"I am," Rora whimpered. "I swear it, Tare. I wouldn't lie to you."

"Time was, I could believe that."

"Please. Let me go get Ar—Falcon. I'll get him and the man who hired us. They'll tell you."

"Right, I'm just gonna let you go. I'm sure you'd promise to come right back, hey?" She tapped the dagger against Rora's lips, leaving a smear of her own blood. "Should I cut out your lying tongue first, or cut off your ugly fecking nose?"

"Where is Falcon?" a soft voice asked, and Tare's head swung around. With the dagger so close, Rora didn't dare move, but she knew that voice. "I'd like to see my boy again."

"Sharra," Tare said, standing real fast, and with the dagger gone Rora could lift her head to watch. Sharra Dogshead stood before the waterfall, wrapped up in a soaked-through cloak, bent over like a crone. She looked older'n Rora'd ever seen her, and Tare was quick to block her from Rora's sight.

The waterfall was loud, but Rora's nerves were singing and her ears—*ear*, she corrected herself, and she almost laughed again—strained to catch any sound. She could hear them, though it hardly sounded like more'n whispers. "I'll finish with her," Tare was saying.

"What if she's telling the truth?" the Dogshead asked.

"She's not."

"She's one of ours. We should be certain."

"Sharra, I know you want to think the best of the boy—"

"Do not talk to me like I'm a child. I know Falcon, and I've told you—he would never go over to the Blackhands, not even for his sister. There's more to this, Tare."

"It's too great a risk. It could be a trap, and even if it's not, the streets are full of trouble."

"We will not sit here like children afraid of the dark. We still hold power enough, and this is a small thing."

"Or it could be big, and we'll all wind up dead."

"I am still packhead here, Tare."

Tare's mouth was tight when she turned back to Rora, looked like her anger was ready to spill out. She still held Rora's dagger in one hand, and Rora flinched away when Tare leaned in close. She held the dagger between their faces, her eyes hard. "Where's your brother?" she demanded.

"Just off East Market," Rora said quickly, relief flooding her again. "Big tavern, the sign's got a pig on it. He's with the world's ugliest merra, a tall man, and a bastard with a burned face. I can take you—"

Tare's fist cut the rest of her words off and left her jaw aching. Rora heard the door open, low voices. She glanced over at the Dogshead, who stood where she'd been, not moving, her face pale and sad and old. They didn't speak, either of 'em. The door closed and Tare stalked back into view, wiped the dagger clean on Rora's breeches as she went by, then sat on the edge of the desk to slowly sharpen the blade's edge. She held Rora's eyes while she did it, just waiting, all of 'em waiting.

The energy was leaking out of Rora, leaving her weak and aching, and the blood dripping from what was left of her ear was the loudest sound. "Please," she said softly, half expected to get hit for even opening her mouth, "what happened here? Where's the pack?"

"Dead, mostly," Tare growled. "Probably have you to blame for most of them, yeah?"

"I'm not with—"

"Garim's dead," Tare went on. "Your friends drug him into an alley and cut him up slow. Peeled his face right off. They figured they were clever, him being the face and all. But I'm sure you knew that already."

She hadn't, of course, and it made her stomach churn. "Tare . . ."

"You pointed them right to enough of us that we had to abandon the Den—can't hold that big a space with just a handful of fists. We're real cozy now. I guess being hunted will do that. You've really brought us all closer together—wouldn't you say, Sharra?" The Dogshead didn't answer, but Tare didn't seem to expect one. "You've cut us down piece by piece, so I have to think your new masters are pretty happy with you. So why'd they send you back here? What'd you do that made them send you here to die?"

Rora couldn't find any words, couldn't meet that anger with anything. She just shook her head, looked down from the murder in Tare's eyes. She startled real bad when a knife thunked into the floor between her feet. It was Rora's second dagger, plainer than the one with the big stone, but still strong and sharp. "I gave that to you," Tare snarled. "Put that knife right in your hand. How many of our people have you killed with it since then?"

"Enough, Tare," the Dogshead said quietly. "We'll have answers soon enough."

"Or we'll have more dead fists to thank her for."

The silence hunkered down again, just the sounds of water falling and whetstone sliding along the edge of the knife. Rora stared down at the dagger between her feet, but she couldn't even muster up the effort to think of how to get it in her hand. Her head was spinning again, maybe from blood loss, maybe from hurt, maybe because she didn't want to let her mind land on anything specific and have to think about what was happening.

She didn't hear the door open—might've passed out for a little while—but when she felt the arms around her, her first thought was that it'd be Tare again, with the knife to her throat. She tried to jerk back, but the chair held her still, so she thrashed as much as she could until she finally heard the words, "Rora, Rora, you're okay, it's me, you're okay." She fixed her eyes on Aro's face and a choked sort of sob worked its way out of her throat. He pressed something to the side of her head, against the bloody space where her ear wasn't anymore, and then he held her face down against his shoulder. She hated crying almost more than anything else, but she couldn't stop the tears. It was a sick sort of thing, but if she was gonna die here, she was glad at least she wouldn't die alone.

"What in all the hells were you thinking?" Aro demanded, his voice heated over the top of her head.

"You're not the one here to ask questions," Tare snarled back.

"You let her do this?" Aro asked, and Rora knew he was talking to the Dogshead now. "I thought you kept your wild dogs on shorter chains."

"Things have changed, my boy," the Dogshead said, and there was some disapproval in her voice when she added, "since you left."

"Where is it you've been?" Tare asked.

"We went to the North, got hired on by him to look for some stupid thing in the snows."

Rora lifted her head up, met Tare's angry gaze. "See?"

Tare laughed. "Two people telling the same lie doesn't make it truth."

A new voice got added to the mix, Joros sounding like he was talking through clenched teeth. "I would request that you release her immediately. We'll be on our way."

Tare snorted loud and mocked a courtly curtsey toward where Rora guessed Joros was standing. "Awful fine words. Are you some disgraced lordling, or just an actor paid to play one?"

"Leave him out of it," Aro snapped. "This is between us." He stood up, his arms sliding from around Rora and leaving her feeling cold. He stepped forward, toward the Dogshead, and his eyes didn't leave her even though Tare stepped between them. "Why?" he demanded.

Rora could see the sad smile on the Dogshead's face. "I would ask you the same, my boy. Why?"

"My sister needed me. Family comes before anything."

"Pack is family," Tare said.

"Blood is deeper."

Softly, the Dogshead said, "Your twin needed you."

That startled Aro—she saw the surprise of it run through him—but it didn't shake him. "Yes," he said. "My twin needed me."

"Tell me your tale, Falcon. Tell me all of it." The Dogshead still looked old, but her eyes'd gotten sharper, keen like the edge of a blade. "I'll pass judgment after that."

"Untie Rora, and I'll tell you everything."

Tare bristled at that, but Sharra put a hand on her arm. "I don't think so," the Dogshead said carefully. "She's a wild dog, too, and you can't trust wild dogs to keep from each other's throats."

It took Aro a while to answer, but his voice was soft when he did. "You shouldn't be standing so long."

That put a smile on the Dogshead, and she gave a small nod, gestured toward the waterfall behind her. "Shall we talk?" Aro glanced back at Rora, then pointedly at Tare. "Your sister is under my protection. Tare won't do any more damage, will you?"

Tare shrugged and spread her hands, and her grin was like an animal baring its teeth. "I'm perfectly harmless."

"Still funny," Rora muttered, and the glare Tare shot her had daggers in it.

"Joros comes with us," Aro said, and it seemed like he'd picked up all the sense that'd leaked out of Rora's head.

There was real alarm in Tare's voice: "Sharra—"

"Enough, Tare. I am not some frail old woman. It's a fair trade." Tare tried to argue more, but the Dogshead just held a hand in her face until she stopped speaking. "Sit. Stay. Be nice.

I'll return with my judgment." She turned and walked through the waterfall, and Aro waited for Joros to step forward before they followed together.

The quiet settled over the room again, and Rora hadn't even known the others had been brought along, too, until the heavy warmth of the bear cloak draped over her arms. She felt a touch on her shoulder, gentle like it'd break her. "Does it hurt?" the witch asked softly.

Rora almost laughed at the ridiculousness of it all. "Yeah," she said, "it hurts." After a second, his fingers brushed over the stump of her ear, and she flinched at the touch until she felt the coolness that spread out from his fingers. It helped with that hurt at least. "Thank you," she said, and she meant it. His touch lingered for a moment longer, and then he was gone, his muttering quieter than the waterfall.

Tare was staring at her from across the room, toying with Rora's dagger again. She stalked forward, the dagger twirling and dancing in her fingers. "Rora," she sneered. "Is that your real name, then?"

Rora looked back at her and wanted to be angry for what Tare'd done, wanted to hate the older woman for it, but all she could feel was sad and hurt. Everything else'd drained out of her like blood. "I loved you," Rora whispered. "I never would've betrayed you. Honest word. You were the closest thing I had to family, next to Aro, and he's the only thing in the world could've made me leave." The dagger stopped its twirling. "I know I did wrong by you, by the pack, but I'd never've done anything to hurt you."

Tare's face went strange, and she didn't try talking anymore. That was probably good. Rora let her head hang, chin against her chest, and closed her eyes. The heavy smell of the bear cloak stuck in her nose, fur tickling against her cheek, and she thought of Scal just before her mind refused to think of anything else anymore.

Next thing she knew was hands on her wrists, gently rubbing to get the blood flowing again. Aro pulled her up, practically holding all her weight with an arm around her. "You're okay," he said, like saying it made it true. "You're safe."

Around him she saw Joros handing the Dogshead two of those coin-filled pouches he always seemed to have. "Two nights from now," he said. "West Gate."

"We'll be there," the Dogshead said, "all of us," and the anger was in Tare's eyes again.

CHAPTER NINE

They no longer gathered in the tribehome as the sun sank beneath the waving grasses of the Plains. Instead many of the plainswalkers would find Keiro where he stood at the edge of the hills, and they would sit before him, watching the sun fade away, listening as he wove tales that had never before been heard. He told them of what the Twins' long imprisonment must have been like, the unending years of pain and fear and heartbreak and loneliness. *And the anger, too, the anger could not be forgotten or forgiven.* More importantly, he told tales of what life would be like once the Twins were freed. Each night, he looked into one of the plainswalkers' eyes, chose a man or woman he had come to know so well these last months, and he spun a tale of their future, bright and happy and successful under the Twins' rule. He didn't know where the inspiration for these tales came from, for he had never been called a particularly creative man; but there was a new certainty in his mind, a shining surety that the words he spoke were true.

Poret had been the first, following Keiro to the hills one night and shyly apologizing for her distance. He'd forgiven her easily, knowing her allegiance lay with Yaket first, and they'd sat together, shoulder to shoulder, watching the sun paint the hills in blues and reds. Cazi—who seemed rarely to leave Keiro's side no matter how he tried to keep his promise to Tseris—had sniffed at Poret's fingers, climbed her arm, and burrowed happily into the long hair tumbling over her shoulders. "Tell me a story," she'd said, leaning her head against Keiro's shoulder. With the certainty murmuring from the back of his mind, he'd told her how she would grow strong under the Twins' rule, how she would be a mighty night-hunter and win the trust of a Starborn of her own, and they would be a fearsome team when the sun was gone from the sky. "Will there be a man to share my nights with as well?" she'd asked slyly. He'd told her there would be, though the certainty had told him also that it wouldn't be him. He'd put on a smile for her. Things would be as they would be.

She'd found him again the next night, and brought a few others with her. They'd prayed together, Keiro with his back to the setting sun and Cazi perched on his shoulder, the others scattered in a half circle before him. A young hunter, Keten, was the first to speak. "If the Twins have been here since they were struck down, why haven't they reached out to us before? We've been faithful to them for centuries."

"I don't claim to know the minds of the gods," Keiro said, spreading his hands, "but I would say they *have* reached out. That you even know of the Twins speaks to that—if one of your ancient ancestors hadn't found or been summoned by the Twins, you wouldn't know their names, their stories, their history. Perhaps they haven't extended a hand to each one of you, but I don't doubt they know of your faithfulness."

"But why you?" Keten asked, and Keiro could read beyond the words to the pain beneath.

"Truly?" Keiro smiled wanly. "I don't know. I don't know why the Twins brought my wandering old feet here, when there are so many of you faithful and strong. But I *believe* that though the Twins may have guided me here, it was not to find them. It was to find you, all of you. I would never have found the Twins without first finding you."

"Did Yaket know the Twins were here?" Keten asked, and there was a quiet demand in his voice, the faint tones of betrayal.

Keiro wouldn't lie; it wasn't in him to. "I believe she did, or that she suspected it."

"Then why didn't she tell us?"

"We all have a part to play, Keten. Yaket's part was to keep the faith bright in your hearts. She did her part well, and I don't know if any more was asked of her than that."

"*Knowing* would have made our faith stronger. She could have told us."

"She could have," Keiro agreed. It was his own question as much as Keten's. If Yaket had known the Twins were beneath the hill, why hadn't she told any of her people?

More of the plainswalkers came each night, questions eager on their tongues, hungry for the new stories he offered. He answered their questions, and filled their minds with bright futures, and there was a lightness in his chest. His whole life had been wandering, and it felt as though he had finally found what he hadn't even known he'd been searching for.

He returned to the tribehome one night, more than half the tribe around him, to find Yaket standing in their path. Keiro stopped before her and waved the others on, splitting around him and Yaket like a forking river. He watched the elder's eyes, the one milky white, hard as a stone; the other was not so much kinder.

"You should stop this," Yaket finally said, after they had been alone for some time.

Keiro shook his head. "This is why I was brought here."

"You were not *brought here*," Yaket said, and there was real anger rising in her voice. "You were cast out of your home and happened to stumble on the only place where you wouldn't be despised."

The words cut, coming from her. Not so long ago, she had welcomed him like a lost son, treating him as equal to any of the tribe. She'd pressed a finger below Keiro's missing eye, touched her own half blindness, and smiled like it was a secret they shared. "You're not wrong," he said sadly, and he managed a smile. "I've truly been walking the Twins' path, haven't I?"

She didn't seem to catch his meaning right away, but her anger flared when she did. "You are a child. You know nothing of the way this world works. I have been trusted with this secret since before your parents whelped you. You know it a day, and you sing it out to the world."

"It's not like that, Yaket," Keiro entreated. He would like to have her on his side once more, to win back her respect and kindness. There was that whispering certainty in the back of his mind, too, that told him if he could win Yaket, he would win the whole tribe. "I'm sure the secret of the Twins sang out in you as well, and it could have been no easy thing to keep your lips closed around it. That is the choice you made, to hold them secret, to keep them from your people. But I . . . I wasn't meant to keep this secret. I was meant to share it, to sing it to the world. It's why I was brought here. Yes," he said, gentle and firm as her face began to twist, *"brought here.* I have felt the Twins' call all my life. I have only recently learned to listen to it. Please, Yaket." He stretched a hand out to her. "We are not meant to be enemies. The world is changing, and we, both of us, we've been blessed with the chance to lead that change. We've both been chosen. Can't we put aside our pride?"

She ignored the hand he held out to her. "I hear you've been telling new stories out in the long grass. Perhaps it is time you heard a new story for yourself." She sat, old legs folding gracefully beneath her, and stared up at Keiro until he sat on the ground before her. "This is the first story I was told after I was chosen as elder. I was a young woman then, proud and foolish. 'Elder' is not a title given in age. It is a title to tell others that I keep the old knowledge, that I hold the secrets of generations. This is the first story I was told after I met the Twins." Keiro opened his mouth, but she glared him to silence.

"You will have seen that Fratarro has one arm. It is the best we have been able to do for him, in all the long years.

"We used to have chiefs, in the old days. One of them was named Pelen, and four centuries ago, he led the tribe to a faraway place, where the waters flowed clear and the trees grew tall and birds flew in more colors than they had known to exist. They said it was a piece of Fratarro's creation that even Patharro had not found, a small part of paradise undestroyed. They found Fratarro's arm at the bottom of a deep pool, and though it had been centuries since it was burned and torn, they said his arm still smoldered with the fires that had scorched it.

"They pulled the arm from the lake, all the men of the tribe, with ropes woven from beautiful flowering vines. They wrapped it with one hundred layers of lake grass to keep it from burning in the sun, and they pulled it across the ground with the vine-ropes whose flowers withered and died. It took them a year and more to return to the Plains with the arm, and they presented it to sleeping Fratarro, the greatest gift to give a broken god.

"But they were not done. The men went back out, hunting day upon day until they found a boar taller than a man. They chased the boar for thirty days, always at its heels, until, in the blackness of a no-moon night, the beast fell to their spears. Pelen put his spear through the boar's heart. The men returned with its tusks, white as stars and sharper than stone.

"The women of the tribe plucked grass from the earth, plucked half the grass from the Plains. They shredded the grass to the thinnest fibers, no thicker than a strand of hair, and they wove the strands together until they had a long rope of it, delicate as a spider's web and brighter than sunlight.

"The whole tribe carved the boar's tusks until they were slim and sharp and as long as a man's arm, and they carved a hole in the base of each. These they took to the Twins, along with the rope that was thinner than a blade's edge, and together they sewed Fratarro's arm in place. Fratarro screamed throughout, and he bled a river, but at the end of it, he had his arm back. A portion of the Twins' power was restored, and we rejoiced."

Yaket fixed Keiro with her one eye, hard and unforgiving.

"All stories have an end. Can you guess this one, Godson?" Somehow she made an insult of the name he'd been given. "There is a cost for any good deed done. There is a price to power.

"Sororra was reviled by the Parents for using her power to shape the minds of men. This is the power that was restored to her when Fratarro's arm was attached, when the Twins first woke from their long slumber. She touched Pelen's mind, the chief of the tribe, and she sought to use him to find the rest of her brother's limbs. It had been long centuries, though, since she had last used her power. She forgot that it took a gentle touch. When she went to shape his mind, she twisted too hard.

"That night, Pelen went from grass mat to grass mat, and he carried in his hand the bone needle, quiet as a final breath and sharper than hate. He killed most of the tribe in silence before one, dying, cried out. It would have taken more than ten men to subdue him, but there were not ten men left. Those who remained to stand against Pelen fought him, and they died for their bravery. It was a woman, quiet and cunning, who found the second bone needle. In the darkness, she stepped through the fray, and she slipped the needle between Pelen's ribs and into his heart.

"She was the first elder, but we do not know her name. There are some secrets that are meant to be forgotten, that are meant to lie unknown. When I go to join the stars, my name will not be remembered here. I will pass from this world, but I will have done the best thing there is. I will have kept the secrets that need keeping." Her gaze was sharp on Keiro again, and sad. "There is a line, thin as spider's thread, between believing and knowing. You say I chose to hold these secrets, to keep the knowing from my own people. That is not so. It was never a choice—this is the way things must be. When we helped the Twins, it nearly destroyed my people. Death was our only reward. Those few who remained vowed that they would stay, for they believed still in the message the Twins sang . . . but they vowed, too, that they would stay only as guardians. Keepers of knowledge, keepers of faith. We would guard the Twins from those who would do them harm, but we would not . . . *could* not . . . raise our hands in their aid. I believe it is why you . . . why you were *brought* here. You were brought here to do what I will not.

"My people are too few. It is better this way. Better that they do not know what lies in the hills. They have good hearts, and they are strong in their faith. They would want to help, if they knew." Her hands clutched at each other in her lap, as though she were trying to hold on to something that kept slipping away. "Things that are known gain the power to rule us. Things that are known cannot be escaped. Do you understand me?"

Keiro bowed his head, and sat in silence before her. Her words had the flavor of truth, and he understood that her sharing this tale was its own kind of trust, that her honesty was an offering. Yet there was the certainty in his mind. *The Twins were not a thing to be kept secret. Their names and their existence should be shouted from one end of the world to the other.* He heard the caution Yaket preached, but he could not follow it. "Thank you, Yaket," he said softly. "Truly, thank you. It . . . it is good to know some small piece of the history that lies here. I would like to hear more of your stories, if you would tell them to me."

She smiled at him, and it almost broke Keiro. "I will tell you all the stories I have in me, so long as you stop telling your own."

He looked away from her again as he said, "Is there not space in the world for both our tales?"

She would speak to him no more, after that. She simply rose and walked back to the tribehome, looking older than she usually did. When Keiro followed her after a time, he found his way blocked by two of the bigger tribesmen. They were still much smaller than he, for the plainswalkers had been shaped to hide among the tall grass, but Keiro knew these two, knew they were strong and skilled fighters. He knew, too, that they were endlessly loyal to Yaket.

"There is no place for you here this night," one of them said. The other handed Keiro his rolled grass mat, which was an unexpected kindness. Wordlessly, Keiro bowed at the waist and turned toward the hills once more.

Poret caught him up quickly, panting as she tugged at his arm. "It's not right," the woman snarled, anger as bright as her eyes. "Yaket is jealous of you. It's not right!"

Keiro shook his head, held her by the shoulders, and smiled down at her. "Yaket is doing as she sees best. I cannot fault her for it—she has many years of wisdom, more than the two of us together. We simply see things in a different way." He turned her around, gave her a gentle push. "Go back. Sleep. This is a night for quiet thinking."

"You're not leaving, are you?" she asked, suspicion and fear fighting in her voice.

"No. I'm where I'm meant to be."

He went to the hills, for they were as comforting a place as any, and laid his grass mat upon the ridge of a hill. He lay staring up at the stars and the red points of Sororra's Eyes and the moon that hung near-full overhead, and before he fell asleep a small scaled body curled into the hollow between his shoulder and neck.

Keiro awoke to teeth in his ear, and batted Cazi away. The *mravigi* instead bit at Keiro's finger, insistent. Grumbling some, Keiro sat up, rubbing sleep from his eyes. It was still night, the moon low in the sky but bright, lining the hills with white fire. "What do you want, little beast?" Keiro muttered sleepily, but he saw it even before Cazi perched on his knee with a chirp.

Dark figures moved across a valley between two hills, but these were not the shape of star-flecked *mravigi*. They were man-shaped, and tall, shrouded in black. Keiro caught his breath, heart stilling for a moment. There was a certainty in him not born from the confident whispering, but born from his own history, his own life.

Keiro rose, fear and joy warring in him, and made his own slow way across the hills. Cazi sat on his shoulder, long tail draped over the back of Keiro's neck, his nostrils flaring. During the walk, pinpricks worked their way down his back, his legs, Cazi fading into the night. The men took notice of Keiro's approach, and he saw the flash of steel in the moonlight. Keiro held his hands open at his sides, though they would see soon enough he was naked as a newborn, nowhere to hide a weapon on him. "Greetings, brothers," he called out, loud enough they would hear but not loud enough to disturb the night overmuch. *"Chellani baric."* He hoped they would recognize the preachers' greeting at least, and their bearings did seem to grow more relaxed.

"Your name, brother?" one of them called out.

"I am called Keiro," he said simply, hoping—a small hope—that they would not know him as apostate.

"And how have you come to be here, Keiro?"

"I've led a wandering life. My feet have taken me to stranger places than this. I had not thought to see any brothers here."

The man who had been speaking stepped forward, past the two with their swords drawn and one with his empty hands raised before him, and the speaker lowered his heavy hood. "I'm on a mission from the gods themselves, brother. I am Saval Tredeiro, and I believe that one of Fratarro's limbs lies in these hills."

CHAPTER TEN

He wasn't happy about it, but Joros paid for a chirurgeon to tend to Rora. He'd taken plenty of coin from Raturo's stores before he'd left the place behind, as much as he could carry without sounding like a knight clattering around in too-big armor, but his various purses were growing much lighter than he was happy with. Still, Aro insisted that his sister deserved more than a raving lunatic to poke at her damaged face—no matter that Anddyr's ministrations had already taken care of most of the damage—and Joros, if nothing else, needed to keep the twins from revolting. The Northman's betrayal remained a thorn in his side, and he'd be damned before he'd let these two slip from him as well. This new plan, much as he liked it, still had plenty of room for falling apart. He would need Rora and Aro with him if everything went to shit.

The chirurgeon was little help, smearing something that smelled foul on the open wound of what had been Rora's ear. It made her scream and thrash, so that Anddyr and Aro had to hold her down while the chirurgeon poured a sickly green liquid down her throat. That put her to sleep quick enough, and the man said it would help with her pain as well. He wrapped a bandage around her head and demanded an exorbitant sum from Joros, who promised to track the chirurgeon down and do unspeakable things to him if he caught the slightest sign of infection—at that price, Joros thought the man should have been able to grow her ear back—and the chirurgeon left under a hail of insults.

Joros left the mage and the brother to fret over Rora in the room he'd bought with more of his dwindling money, and went down to the taproom to buy himself a well-deserved drink. Unfortunately, the merra was at the bar as well. She seemed to have no trouble showing her face in public, which surprised him to no end. He ignored her, ordering a jug of what passed for wine in Mercetta and retreating to a corner table. She followed him, and his glare didn't scare her off.

"A gaggle of children and cripples aren't going to help us," she said.

Joros nearly laughed at her—her hypocrisy stunned him sometimes. It sounded like Whitedog Pack certainly had its share of children and cripples injured in whatever little war they'd been fighting, but he'd seen more than enough useful, strong-bodied Scum during his brief journey through the Canals. "I'm glad you've at least come around to the idea of killing."

She made a quick hushing motion. "I haven't," she hissed. "Far from it. I'm hoping reason will prevail, but regardless, towing along children and cripples will only slow us down."

"It's truly wonderful to see the embodiment of the Parents' love and mercy."

She had a look to her, sometimes, of a cat whose fur had been vigorously rubbed the wrong way. "The Parents have set me a mission. I can't afford to be distracted from it, or slowed down. Neither can you, if anything you say is to be believed."

"What makes you think it is?"

"I'm hoping you'll prove to be a better man than you've been so far."

"That's the difference between us," Joros said, and sipped the foul wine. "Aside from your ugly face, that is. You do a great deal of *hoping*. I *plan*."

"Then you have a plan for these 'Scum'?"

"My plans, and their existence or lack thereof, are my own. Now leave me be. This wine is like enough to make me vomit on its own. I don't need your face to help." She had a stubborn streak in her, and Joros could see her inclination was to stay just to spite him; he'd discovered through experience, though, that pointing out the wreck of her face often enough would drive her to leave, or at least lapse into silence. Mockery was a powerful tool against those prone to shame, and Joros wasn't above using any tool. He was ready to point out how well his own facial burns were healing, but she left without needing another insult. Triumphant, Joros sipped the horrible wine while he pondered what he was going to do with all the children and cripples he'd just saddled himself with.

They were, relatively speaking, a small price to pay for the score of fighters and the dozen skilled killers the woman charmingly called the Dogshead had promised him. Cripples had a tendency to die when confronted with anything more difficult than limping around, and children were easy enough to foist off if they proved less than useful. He didn't think either would please the Dogshead too much, since she seemed to believe Joros could take them to a place where they'd be able to live out their miserable days in peace. True, she believed it because it was what he'd promised her, but really, people should stop taking him at his word. A man with a light coinpurse was apt to say anything to get what he needed.

There were so many threads to hold. He needed to get rid of the Scum who weren't useful, but in a way that wouldn't anger the ones who were useful; he needed to get all of them into Raturo, learn what they could about anything that had transpired while Joros had been gone, kill the Ventallo, and get back out. He also needed to assume even this plan would fail, since the majority had so far; he needed to be prepared for the ever-more-desperate plans that would follow, which largely involved keeping Rora and Aro both alive and on his side. For all his words to the merra, he had little idea how to weave those threads together into something that wouldn't fray and fall apart. For all his bravado, he was leaning just as much on hope. He just wasn't stupid enough to let anyone else know that.

Rora slept for much of the next day, and they had to shake her awake once shadows started creeping through the streets of Mercetta. Anddyr pronounced that she was healing well enough to travel, which was good, since she was going to be traveling regardless.

She spoke little, eyes wide and vacant as they bundled her out to the waiting horses. It was an expression more befitting her brother, and Joros was somewhat disappointed that a little torture was all it had taken to break her. He'd rather enjoyed having one other person around who could manage to rub two thoughts together. Still, he didn't need her for her mind. She could sleep all she liked, drool on herself, rip her hair out and scream obscenities—so long as she lived.

"I'll ride with her," Aro said softly. He didn't seem to be taking well to being the twin in charge.

His sister stirred when he tried to lift her up onto his horse. "We're going to meet Whitedog, yeah?" she asked, her voice even rougher than usual.

"Yeah," Aro said.

"I'll ride on my own." She moved as if she were wading through chest-high water, but she walked to her own horse and mounted by herself, after a few false starts. Joros gave her a small nod. He'd heard somewhere that a good leader acknowledged bravery. That had always felt to him like stupid triteness, but it didn't hurt to welcome back a shade of the woman. Maybe there was more than the shade lurking behind the bags under her eyes.

They passed from East Quarter to West by way of North, where Joros had to bribe their way through. North Quarter was the nicest part of the blasted city, where all the richest merchants and nobles lived in the shadow of the ugly castle King Cordano hid inside. They didn't pass anywhere near the royal residence, staying close to the city walls, and they finally passed into West Quarter as the pinks and purples were fading from the sky. West seemed to be rapidly sinking into the disreputability of South, the buildings in shambles and the people staring with as little welcome as those from North Quarter.

There were a handful of cloaked people lurking near the gate, just out of the circle of light cast by the guards' lanterns. Aro held his hand up and rode toward them alone, Joros waiting with the others in front of a crack-faced building. Glancing back, he saw Rora looking after her brother with hard eyes.

Aro waved them forward after a few minutes of talking, and Joros led his little band to the gate. Wheels creaked behind him, two big carts full of children and cripples, pulled by the well-muscled sort of men the twins seemed to call "fists." Others followed on foot, keeping close to the carts. The gate guards, looking bored, hardly spared any of them a glance. They passed beneath the stone wall in silence, Joros and his hired help and their human baggage.

The silence held even outside the walls, save for the squeaking of a loose wheel on one of the carts. For all the money he'd given them, Joros would have expected they'd equip themselves better. He was sure they'd spent most of it on foolish things—like the torches they lit once the light of the city was behind them. Stupid as it was, it saved Anddyr from having to make his floating lights, which likely would have just terrified the Scum anyway.

Aro was the first to break the silence; though he whispered, any sound carried on a quiet night. He was riding next to the first cart, his horse plodding slow to keep pace, and he spoke to a figure wrapped in layers of cloaks. "This is really all that's left?"

Joros didn't hear an answer, but Aro's whisper came again—"I'm sorry"—before his horse moved ahead.

The boy kept moving through their little crowd, circling from person to person. He seemed to know most of them, and had a soft word even for the ones he didn't know. His careful whispering, still loud amid the silence, was grating, but Joros supposed the boy could waste his time as he chose. Aro rode next to the particularly unfriendly woman who'd cut off Rora's ear, and Joros heard him whisper, "Talk to her." He rode up next to his sister, whispered, "Talk to her." Still, no one else spoke, save Anddyr, whose incessant mumbling counted for less than nothing.

The road was as straight and logical as a drunkard's path, and Joros might have insisted on a more direct route by cutting through the fields and forests if it wasn't for the damned carts. The fists, for all their strength, were having enough trouble with the shallow ruts in the road. The squeaking wheel sounded as though it was like to fall apart without any more provocation. He'd intended to ride until a few hours after the sun showed its face, after they'd gotten a good distance from the city, but he was going to strangle someone if he had to listen to that wheel any more.

The lands they were riding through weren't so very far from his family's estate, though the place hardly deserved the title—a sad collection of old buildings ringed by a crumbling wall. If they kept going, they'd likely pass it in the night, the shadows hiding him from any eyes that might recognize a face that had been gone for over two decades. With the mood he was in, though, he wasn't entirely sure he could be trusted not to snatch one of those torches and set the whole place afire. He called a halt, to put a stop to the horrid squeaking. He would spend the night sleeping and breathing—a brief flash of memory put a delicate hand on his chest, a gentle voice whispering for him to count his breaths, soft lips brushing his cheek, but he pushed that memory viciously aside. He'd vowed not to think of her, after all. He would sleep through the night without a care in his heart, and when they rode past his former home to-morrow, he would hold his head high and not look at it.

There was a half-collapsed barn a distance from the road, and it took longer than it should have to get the carts through the field. Joros was impressed by the strength of the fists at least; he was pleased with the new muscle he'd bought, even if they spent his coin on foolish things.

They sent the children out looking for things to burn, and when they had a decent pile built under the section of barn that wasn't collapsed, Anddyr set a spark to it. In the sudden bright-ness, Joros saw most of the Scum make warding signs over their chests. The ignorant were always suspicious of things they couldn't comprehend; Joros imagined these Scum spent a great deal of time wrapped in suspicion.

There were too many of them to gather around the one fire, so they started two smaller fires apart from the main one. Most of the Scum divided themselves between the new fires, but the apparent leaders gathered around the first with Joros and his companions. There was the one they called Dogshead, with whom he and Aro had negotiated this whole affair, a woman who carried her years heavily; there was the one who'd taken Rora's ear, who didn't look like she could manage a smile even with a knife to her throat; there was a short man so packed with muscle he looked as wide as three normal men; a handful of others whose drawn faces spoke of hard lives and made them indistinguishable. Pieces of conversation drifted from the other fires, but around theirs, the silence held.

"A story?" one voice called out, hesitant and hopeful. "Haven't heard a story in a long while."

Joros wrinkled his nose—he'd always gone out of his way to avoid the storytelling tradition many of the Fallen seemed to embrace so eagerly—but there were excited murmurs from all the fires. The one who spoke first, though, surprised Joros.

"I've got a story," Rora said, her voice rough from too little use and probably a bit of a fever. Still, it carried in the openness of the barn, and an eager hush fell. She didn't look up from the fire, looking eerily like the burned merra with the flames carving dancing shadows on her face. "It's about a bird, who lives in a big tree with all the other birds and has a pretty good life, so far as birds go. She's got lots of bird friends, and a good bird family. She's happy, right? But one night she wakes up and she sees a cat prowling around the tree, and it's scrawny and hungry-looking and the bird just knows that cat would do anything to make a meal out of all her friends and all her family. There's no time to think up any good plan, there isn't even time to wake up the other birds. The bird's so scared all she can think to do is fly off and hope the cat follows her instead, and hope she can lose the cat later on. And the bird hates herself for it, but it feels like the right thing, and she knows she's kept the cat away from her bird family. And then she goes back to the big tree and finds out a different cat came while she was gone and ate up a bunch of the other birds, and the ones who're left think she's a coward for running from the cat, but they're wrong about all of it." Her eyes were still on the flames, and the silence stretched out behind her words.

From one of the other fires, a child muttered, "Kinda a shit story, innit?" and a laugh burst out of Joros.

"It was a fine story," the Dogshead said reproachfully, glaring over her shoulder toward the child, then favoring Joros with her glare as well, and finally swinging it to the ear-cutter at her side. Joros nor the other two seemed particularly affected by the glare, and the latter was staring into the fire as intently as Rora. "Let's have another, hey?"

The other stories told were little better than Rora's, though mercifully just as short. The mood in the barn was too bleak for any kind of proper storytelling, and the fists were soon arguing about who would take first watch. It was easy enough to lose them all in slumber.

There was still a twitch in Joros's eye when they rode out again, the sun on their shoulders. He'd had Anddyr magic up a fix for that damned wheel, and the silence was marvelous—it was the location that made him edgy. Slow as they were moving, still they were quickly approaching his family's estate. Joros wanted both to flee and to destroy his old home, and complicated emotions were one of the things he hated most. All things should burn as pure as the fire of a good anger.

And then it was there, just off the twisting road, an overgrown lane leading to the rotted-out gate. No matter his resolution the previous night, he couldn't help looking.

Truly, the place didn't look much different than it had when Joros had left—yet it was, the walls slightly more crumbled, the buildings slightly more decrepit. It showed clear signs of having been ignored for a good stretch of time, and that drew Joros to a halt before the splinters of the gate. His father had never been particularly concerned with appearances, but he'd never been outright neglectful.

"Cappo?" Anddyr asked softly at his elbow.

Weeds sprouted between the cobbles beyond the gate, and a stubborn tree had even begun to push its way up through the stones. The roof of the stable was completely collapsed, patches of rotting thatch clinging to the edges of the supports. The door to the main house hung off one hinge, and more than one of the windows were shattered. "They're gone," Joros said in amazement, though he didn't mean to say the words aloud. It was a relief and a disappointment both.

Joros turned his horse around to face the two carts full of staring faces, all the others scattered at the sides of the cart. He swept one arm toward the broken gate. "Your new home," he said. "As promised." The satisfaction of threads twining together was small, but it wasn't nothing.

The children swarmed over the sides of the cart and raced through the gate, scattering, small voices shouting out snippets of wonder. The fists and the knives and the various others went more slowly, but there was just as much curiosity in their faces. Only the Dogshead remained, and her sour-faced second.

"A nice place you've found for us," the ear-cutter sneered.

The Dogshead fixed him with a critical eye. "There won't be any angry landowners coming to turn us out, will there?"

Joros shook his head. "It's mine," he said, because there was no one to tell him it wasn't.

CHAPTER ELEVEN

The act of lighting a fire on the hills felt wrong—and even more wrong was that it would be one of the Ventallo to suggest it. Saval Tredeiro must have read the hesitation in Keiro's face, for he waved a dismissive hand. "It's been a long journey, brother, and I'm tired and hungry. Allow me this one little blasphemy, won't you?" He'd winked at Keiro as though they were conspirators—and they truly were, Keiro supposed, since he stood by and let Saval's attendants light the fire built of twigs and grass stalks. After a moment's hesitation, Keiro showed them how to bundle and tie the stalks together to burn slower and longer than the sparse handfuls of grass.

Keiro could feel Saval's eyes on him, and tried to keep his face toward the ground, to keep the fire's shadows on the left side of his face as he wound together grass stalks. "Have you been here a while, then?" Saval asked.

"A few months," Keiro said.

Saval whistled in surprise, or perhaps appreciation. "That's quite a while to live in desolation. What's kept you here, brother?" His words were light, but there was a shrewdness in them.

Keiro shrugged with a casualness he didn't feel. There was still the impulse in him to sing out the news of the Twins, but there was another sense, an instinct perhaps awoken by Yaket's story, that urged him to caution. The certainty in him was quiet, faded. "I have found an unexpected home here. The plainswalkers live quiet lives, and I've found that to be what I need most."

Saval snorted. "Insect-eaters. Yes, I imagine they're quite simple."

Keiro's hands tightened briefly around the grass stalks, crinkling them between his fingers, and there was a strange, cold feeling in his stomach. "They're good people," he said.

"Oh, I'm sure they are," Saval said, waving a dismissive hand. "Much as I may not understand it, I can't fault a man for seeking simple pleasures with savages. But tell me—" and he leaned in, close to the fire, as though they were conspirators "—do these savages have any interesting secrets to tell?"

Keiro kept his hands moving, his eye down. Among the Fallen, the Ventallo were law itself, presumed embodiments of the gods' wills. A Ventallo was obeyed without question, and given complete honesty. Yet, Keiro found himself wondering if these unspoken laws still applied to an apostate such as himself. "Nothing of note," he said. The lie burned a little on its way out, but not much more than would have a lie about the food he'd eaten yesterday. Keiro had been a long time gone from the Fallen, his life grown distant from the rigid strictures that told him to hear the Ventallo as though they were the Twins. Keiro had heard the Twins, and Saval Tredeiro sounded nothing like them.

"Tell me anyway. Time has a way of twisting things. Even small matters may have great import."

If Saval wished to hear of savages, Keiro would tell him of savages. "They hunt birds. They weave grass. They like listening to the old stories. As I said, they're simple folk." The last came out harder than he had meant it to, but Saval took no notice. Still, Keiro tried to turn the direction of the conversation before the Ventallo noticed his banked anger. "You said you think a piece of Fratarro lies here?"

Leaning back, Saval said, "I did say that. I'd hoped a brother found in distant places might be more help in finding it."

"Why would you think to find Fratarro here?" Keiro asked, ignoring the jibe. "There's nothing here."

"Where better to hide something? 'To the far horizons,' we say, and if the world doesn't end here, well, then I'll eat one of those foul-looking birds too stupid to live anywhere else." One of Saval's attendants chuckled at that, and they shared smirks.

Keiro stared at Saval. There was that certainty in his mind again, the whispering. *He should tell this man, tell all the world, sing the joys of the Twins loud and free.* The certainty almost drowned his caution; the truth almost came spilling from his lips. If it hadn't been Saval Tredeiro, if a different Ventallo had found him, Keiro might not have swallowed the words. "I do not think you will find a piece of Fratarro here," he said instead, and the words were not a lie—but so very close to one. He didn't think the *mravigi* would show Saval into their tunnels, and even if they did, Fratarro was Fratarro and not a piece of himself.

"No?" Saval asked with one raised eyebrow, and Keiro was sure he would have said more, but he was stopped by a dark shape moving through the grass, one of his attendants yelping in surprise.

The shadow cast itself perfectly across Saval's face, two wings drawn in darkness beneath his eyes. Cazi, perched before the fire on his back legs, front paws clawing at the air as his wings flapped for balance, let out a shrill, high scream.

That threw them into an uproar. One of the attendants prostrated himself, another lurched forward to grab at Cazi, and Saval stared with open mouth. Keiro wouldn't have thought he could look any more surprised, but he managed it when Cazi scurried around the fire, scrambling onto Keiro's knee and up his side, to the shoulder where he usually sat. Keiro reached up to run a finger over the ridge between Cazi's eyes, a familiar, calming gesture for the both of them. Of course the little beast would have the worst timing.

"What is that?" one of the attendants asked, the one who had lunged after Cazi before thinking to question what he was.

"The savages here call them Starborn."

"Legend made flesh," Saval said, with the first real reverence Keiro had heard from him. He had almost guessed the man a false believer.

Keiro tried to shrug Cazi from his shoulder, but the *mravigi* dug in his claws and refused to budge. "A unique lizard, to be sure," Keiro demurred.

The sudden, sharp laugh rolled through the grasses. "I wouldn't have guessed you had any sense of humor, brother." Saval rose, knelt next to Keiro, and reached with slow fingers to touch Cazi's head. "Starborn, you said? Well, the savages aren't wrong!" There was wonder in his voice, genuine awe. Cazi leaned into his hand. "Where did you come from, young one?"

"I've been to the Eremori Desert," Keiro said, "and the sands breed strange creatures. I know what you think this is." He reached up a hand and Cazi slithered into his palm, obedient. "But he is only a lizard, twisted somehow by the distant touch of Patharro's fire. I feed him, and he follows me. There is no magic to him." The lie tasted bitter on his tongue, and Cazi turned an affronted eye to him, but Keiro didn't want to trust this man, this stranger come seeking secrets beyond his worth.

"You're wrong about that," Saval said with easy confidence, wonder still touching the edges of his words. "I can't blame you for it. I hardly believe it myself." It seemed hard for him to look away from Cazi, but he did it, fixing his gaze instead on Keiro. The fire was full in his face. "Say it," the Ventallo said, voice soft with promise—of anger, of violence, of fury. "You know what that is. Say it, brother."

Keiro looked down, unable to hold the intensity in Saval's gaze. *There was no sense in hiding anymore, in lying.* There was that strange certainty that he shouldn't have bothered trying to lie in the first place. He ran a finger down the ridge of scales along Cazi's back, noting how the scales had grown darker of late, a gray that was almost black. *"Mravigi,"* Keiro said, hardly more than a whisper.

"That's right!" There was a fierceness in the grin that crossed Saval's face. "How did you find him?"

"He found me," Keiro said. "Two lonely creatures meeting in these hills."

Saval's eyes held no compromise, nor his voice. "Tell me the truth of it, brother."

Keiro stared down at the top of Cazi's head, and wanted nothing more than to keep his lips closed around the truth, but a realization struck him. The Twins had set him a test—and here before him was the key.

Keiro lifted his hand to shoulder height, and Cazi flowed smoothly onto his usual perch. Keiro rose to his feet, and he made himself meet Saval's eyes as he said, "Come with me."

They followed him, all four, across the hills. Cazi's tail flicked directions against Keiro's shoulder, a subtle guide. It awed the others more, when Keiro led them unerringly to the hole in the ground. It was not one he had used before—the hills were peppered with entrances, as plentiful and hidden as the doors into Mount Raturo—but Keiro slid over its lip with an easy confidence he didn't truly feel.

It impressed him, some, that Saval was the first to follow—a man who would send others into danger first was no kind of leader. He didn't want to give the man any respect, not even grudging respect . . . and yet. He turned away, dropping down to hands and knees, and didn't wait for the others as he began the long crawl.

Cazi's scales gave off a dull glow, just enough for Keiro to see his hands lift from the ground, set back down on another piece of ground. It was nothing like the star-flecked light of the older *mravigi*, but it suitably dazzled Saval and his attendants, following with scrapes and muffled curses. To their credit—or, perhaps, to their remorse—they asked no questions, and gave no complaint. They felt the life-pulse of the earth, the throbbing heartbeat that threaded throughout the tunnels—felt it, and fell silent in its wake.

The great central chamber was wide and dim, the starlight

scales of the *mravigi* scattered sparsely. There was a red glow, fainter than stars, at the far end of the chamber. Keiro could feel it like a call, the thrumming of the Starborn making him buoyant, carrying him up and along toward that red glow, and quiet, hesitant footsteps traced his path.

They were awake and waiting, the Twins—Fratarro as relaxed as he could be, Sororra looking like a coiled snake waiting to strike. Keiro went to one knee before them with a fist pressed to his forehead, close enough he could have reached out to touch the white scales of silent Straz. Saval and his attendants fell over themselves to make obeisance, blathering astonished words that would have held little meaning even if they'd been audible. What was audible was the snap of their jaws closing when Sororra raised a hand.

"Welcome, faithful followers," she said, and her voice was no less icy than when she had first greeted Keiro.

Fratarro grinned, though, as if he showed all the joy she never did. "Bear witness to the first steps of our return."

They babbled again, a jarring chorus of prayers and vows and wonder. When Keiro lifted his face, he saw that Fratarro's eyes were fixed not on the newcomers, but on Keiro himself. It was a look that did not need words to ask what Keiro would do next.

He rose, smoothly and confidently, as though anger and fear and disappointment weren't making war of his guts. Rose, and placed himself sideways between the Twins and Saval—a barrier, a bridge. "You've seen the truth of it, brother," he said to Saval. "Now go. Return to Raturo. Tell the Ventallo—tell everyone. Tell them what you've seen, and bring them here." Saval's attendants stared at him with awe, and the man himself had something like respect in his eyes. Keiro didn't want his respect; he just wanted Saval to leave, to fill the purpose that had surely led his feet here. "Go. Bring them all. We'll begin a new age—together, we'll carry the Long Night."

"Go," Fratarro echoed, and Keiro could see his eyelids beginning to droop. He didn't think the Twins would want these newcomers to see their weakness.

"Go," Sororra said, implacable as stone. "We have waited too long already."

Keiro ushered them from the chamber quickly, though they all craned around to look back over their shoulders, eyes wide on their fallen gods. Cazi, a pale streak on the dark ground, led them to a near tunnel, the sooner to hide the somnolent Twins from sight.

They talked among themselves as they crawled for the surface, low voices echoing through the tunnel, ringing loud as shouts. They talked still beneath the light of the moon and the spinning stars, as Keiro led them far from the tunnel's mouth, so that they would not try to find it once more. They only stopped talking when Keiro's feet fell still and he turned to face them. "You will go?"

Saval grinned at him, teeth white as a slice of the moon. "Of course, brother! Of course. How could we not go and spread their glory to the far corners of the earth?"

"Raturo will be far enough," Keiro said tiredly. He was pleased to have found a way to do as the Twins had asked—alert the Fallen, without himself bringing them that news—but he would be happier when Saval and his men were gone. He left them, then, though he set Cazi to keep a watch, to alert him if they tried to find their way back to the Twins. Because he was barred from the tribehome, he found a hill of his own, far from where Saval and his attendants still raised their voices in loud wonder, far enough away that he could lie on his back and let the moon fill his eye, and sleep in peace.

Cazi was waiting when he woke, greeting him with an insistent chirp—nothing urgent enough to wake Keiro, but pressing nonetheless. Keiro followed the *mravigi* over the gentle hills, valleys wet with dew where the sun's light had not yet reached.

He shouldn't have been surprised, really, but it was easier for a man to look into the past than to guess at all the futures that stretched out from a single point. Keiro could look back and call himself ten kinds of fool, could berate himself for sleeping, for leaving at all, could slap a hand to his forehead and think, *Of course.* The past wrote a clear path.

Grinning at him over the tips of a morning fire, Saval said, "I didn't say we'd *all* go."

PART TWO

Sororra was patient. She had learned that greater reward came to those who waited, and so she knew well the value in planting the seed of a plan and waiting for it to bloom.

—from The Tale of Sororra and the Golden Rose

CHAPTER TWELVE

Pain rippled through Anddyr again, pulled another moan from his lips, and that in turn brought a hand thumping against his skull. "Shut up, witch," the fist said for the hundredth time. Anddyr could only look at the edges of him, at the ill-fitting black robe that had belonged to a now-dead man. Anddyr's own black robe had been stolen, too, and Anddyr hated the way the color felt against his skin, hated the memory of the farmer and his family that the robes had come from. They had been preachers, but relatively innocent ones. Folk who worked the land, took a simple pleasure in a good harvest, pride in well-raised cattle. They were preachers still, though, and that was the only distinction that mattered to the cappo. "If we leave them alive," he'd said, "they'll get to the mountain just after we do and raise the alarm."

"They're innocents!" the merra had shouted at him, twisted face twisted more with fury.

"They're preachers," the cappo had said calmly. "That should be crime enough for you." She'd argued with him more, but he'd had his way in the end. He always did. They'd taken clothes and coin, the farmers' wagons, provisions for themselves, and enough tribute to not raise suspicion. The merra had fallen into a silence of loathing and anger.

Anddyr tried to keep his distance from the fist, sitting as close as he could to the end of the wagon bench. It was a small bench, though, and his arm brushed against the fist's occasionally. Where they touched sent screaming shivers through Anddyr's flesh.

"Wait," Anddyr told himself softly, the mantra he'd been repeating since they left, Cappo Joros's words but Anddyr's voice. "You have to wait. It has to be perfect. You have to wait." The skura hunger chewed at him, though, gnawing his intestines. He'd seen bodies at the Academy, part of his education, all manner of corpses and all the things that sat beneath their skin. He'd seen a man savaged by wolves, his stomach ripped open, the pieces of him scattered and shredded. That's how Anddyr felt, just without the gaping wound—but he could feel the wolves inside him, tearing apart his vital bits. "You have to wait. It won't be so much longer than usual. But you have to wait."

Anddyr made the mistake of looking up again, and a muffled scream earned him another thump. He could almost forget, if he wasn't looking. Children always covered their eyes and pretended a thing didn't exist if they couldn't see it—and it *worked*, that was the thing, and Anddyr had been staring at his hands to not stare at it, and so he'd forgotten about it, because a thing unseen was not truly a thing at all. But now he'd seen it again, and so it was real, and it cackled at him as its tendrils reached for him like black smoke.

Mount Raturo shouldered aside the sun, pressed back the

sky, crushed down the trees, swallowed the world—its shadow reaching out to swallow *him* . . .

"Enough," the fist growled. He twisted around, called softly to another fist in one of the other wagons: "Be ready if the crazy fecking bastard makes everything go ass-up."

"I'm waiting," Anddyr told him sullenly, looking down at his hands again, making the horrible *thing* disappear by looking away from it. One of the pockets of his stolen robe was heavy with a small jar, so heavy he could hardly breathe over its beckoning call. But he couldn't have any yet, he had to wait, and it couldn't be much longer because the *thing* had been so close when he'd seen it, and it had been horribly real for a moment.

The wagon rocked to a halt, and bile bubbled up Anddyr's throat. He didn't want to, but the cappo's commands slithered through him like snakes, filling his arms and legs, making him move. He stepped down from the wagon, walking hunched over on unsteady legs—and paused beside the mule pulling the cart, resting his hand on her neck. He decided she looked like a Sooty. It was a good name, even if she wasn't quite a horse, and he reached into his robe to pull out the stuffed Sooty, her namesake, to show her, to let them talk—

"*Go*, damnit," the fist snarled, startling Anddyr forward, and he made the mistake of looking up again.

He hadn't really seen the mountain from outside before—not in daylight anyway. He'd only seen it in the night, that one blessed night when he'd left the place behind, a darker shape against the dark sky. When he'd first come to Raturo—*been brought*, more accurately—it had been with a burlap sack over his head. He'd seen the mountain's twisty insides for eight years, learned all the secrets it held in dark corners and fissures and forgotten places. This, though, was the first time he'd truly seen anything of its outsides.

Horror pulled his eyes up farther, but no matter how far back he craned his neck, he couldn't see the top of it—just the wall of its face stretching endlessly before him, swirling with blues and reds and blacks, like a giant pulsing bruise. It made him feel sicker, looking at it, the anger of it shimmering like the air on a hot day, and he wanted nothing more than to hide beneath one of the wagons.

"Witch," the fist rumbled.

Anddyr stumbled forward and reached out, hands flat against Raturo's cold stone, and sent a pulse of power skittering into the mountain. He didn't know how it was done normally, what old blood magics had been bastardized to let the simple farm folk come calling with tribute, but he knew the magical signal that rippled through Raturo, and that he could mimic.

Anddyr returned to the wagon and clambered back into the narrow space that was his on the bench. He could feel the fist staring at him. Anddyr wanted to say that he'd done it right, he knew he had, and the fist just had to wait. The words stayed behind his teeth, too frightened to slither out toward the fist.

After a time the stone door opened, a great pit spreading like a maw, wide enough to drive two wagons through side by side. They went singly, though, the mules—brave Sooty leading them—twitching their ears, the fists hunching their shoulders, Anddyr curling around the ball of need in his gut as they slipped down Raturo's gullet.

There was a preacher waiting within the darkness, an old man with his eyes plucked from his face and two mouse-faced initiates. "Name and purpose?" the old man asked.

"Kelnen," Anddyr supplied. It was the name the farmer had told them, before the cappo had put his sword into the man's chest. "Beef and potatoes, for tribute." Inside the sleeves of his robe, Anddyr's fingers began to weave, moving slow as worms in a rainstorm, his mind fractured between magic and need and fear. The spell eked out of him, a deflection of attention; the preacher and his initiates wouldn't wonder why none of the farmers looked familiar, wouldn't pry any deeper. An attendant made a mark in his ledger, and waved the wagons forward. Anddyr made fists of his fingers to keep them from shaking, straightened them back out to be ready for another spell, got lost in the jarring sway of the wagon over the pitted floor.

In the wide cold storeroom where the walls leaked ice and words made gentle clouds, Anddyr stepped to the side as the fists unloaded the wagons, moving his fingers again in familiar sigils. The crates were carefully stacked, the burlap sacks set gently down, and the attendants counted each but failed to check any of them. The head of the fists was given a jangling pouch, the wagons were turned with the mules—sweet Sooty leaving him first—straining for light, the no-eyed man and the initiates left, and Anddyr stood unseen.

His fingers scrabbled at the lid of the first crate, prying against the nails loose-set into their homes to free its occupant. Rora was like the sun rising, like cool water against the twisting in his gut. She was real and true, no matter what else his eyes might show him.

"Ten fecking hells," Rora spat as she climbed from the crate, twisting her back, bones popping.

"I'm sorry," Anddyr said, keeping his voice low. There was

no telling if there were any preachers outside the room, and if there were he certainly didn't want to attract their attention. "They went as fast as they could . . ."

She shook her head slightly, eyes not on him. "Help me open the rest of these." As she turned away Anddyr saw the smooth patch of skin her hair didn't hide. He'd done as much as he could to heal it, but his magic couldn't regrow flesh, couldn't hide the unprotected hole of her ear. He still remembered when they'd found her, tied and bleeding, and she'd leaned into his hand as he'd eased her pain.

There were twenty crates in total that they'd brought in, and half of them were subtly marked, their lids held in place loosely enough that they could be pried open with fingers. Ten of those who Rora called "knives" climbed quietly from the open crates, slim and silent as the blades they were named after, mostly men but a few women as hard-faced as Rora.

One of the crates held more black robes, taken from the farmer and his family. As the knives drew robes over their sharp bodies, Anddyr wedged himself into a corner and finally pulled the jar from his robe. He'd waited so long that the wolves had eaten so much of his insides. But it was timed, all so carefully timed, not a second to spare or waste, and the skura tasted so sweet on his tongue. It shuddered through him, suffusing him, melting along his veins and nerves, sending the wolves howling in fear, and it slowly tacked together the fragmented pieces of his sanity. The skura sat as heavy in him as it always did, like weights dragging at his limbs, like handfuls of mud in his stomach, the filthy aftertaste of dirt and iron that would linger on his tongue for hours—but it made him whole once more. The heaviness and the aftertaste were fair prices for his sanity . . . no matter how fleeting it would be.

Though, truly, he almost wished for the sweet, simple madness—any hallucination his mind could conjure up couldn't be worse than the knowledge that he'd once more stepped inside Mount Raturo.

A preacher stepped before him, startling Anddyr badly—until he realized how short the preacher was, and how loose the robe hung off her frame. It was just Rora, the robe's hood drawn low, showing only her deep frown. "Are you ready?" she asked.

"I have to be," Anddyr muttered, levering himself to his feet. She didn't offer him a hand.

All of them wrapped in dark robes, hoods hiding their faces, they stepped from the cold storage room. Anddyr, the only one who knew Raturo's circling paths, led the way, and his hands drew in the air once more, wrapping them in a cloak of the magical kind. It would send eyes sliding away, keep any watchers from focusing on them. It wouldn't hide any sounds they made, though, and it wouldn't stop anyone who was suspicious or persistent from seeing through the cloaking.

The lowest floors of Raturo were seldom traveled, frequented only by servants and workers—preachers who were so only in name. They passed less than a handful on their way and none took notice of them, though Anddyr was sure the shaking of his hands would rattle loudly in the stone passages, that the black-robed servants would sniff out his fear.

He took them to another storage room, smaller, closer to Raturo main, but thick with dust, dripping with cobwebs. "Stay here," he told the knives. "I have to go search out . . . how best to do this."

They all looked at him with the same suspicion, eyes shining like coins, but it was Rora who spoke. "I'll go with you," she said, and the mistrust in her words cut worse than blades.

The women of Whitedog Pack had argued long into the night. Tare, who Anddyr hated with the unshakable strength of stone, had refused to leave her master unprotected, but also hadn't wanted to let Rora lead the knives. "Goat's dead, yeah?" Rora had said. She had been clouded and strange for a long time after leaving Mercetta, but the strangeness had faded from her eyes when her brother had unwound the bandages from her head and she'd touched the smooth skin where her ear had been. She'd gone hard, after that, brittle as untested steel. "Have you picked another hilt, then?"

"There hasn't been time," the one called Dogshead had said, voice old and sad.

"Right. Then I'm hilt now."

More arguing, but it had come down to no other choices. None of the other knives save Tare were fit to lead, and Tare wouldn't leave the Dogshead. Rora had the cappo's clear favor as well, and so the Dogshead named her hilt, which seemed to be the leader of the knives—"Such quaint names," the cappo had sneered. They'd parted with glares, Tare and Rora, but Rora had ridden out from the cappo's estate with her head held high, proudly showing her missing ear.

Anddyr couldn't meet her eyes, but he shook his head with as much firmness as he could muster. "You'll get in the way," he told Rora, and it wasn't entirely a lie. He reached into a pocket, held a seekstone out to her flat in his hand. She took it, the tips of her fingers barely brushing his palm. "You can watch me. Make sure I'm not betraying you. I'll return as soon as I know how to proceed. Please, stay here." He cast off the cloaking from around them, leaving it over himself—and over Rora, who he half expected would follow him.

He moved farther up through the halls of Raturo, walking as quickly as he dared. So little time, and so much to be done . . . but his heart rode choking-high in his throat. He reminded himself again and again that no one would see him, that he was as hidden as he could be, and even if someone *did* see through his cloaking, all they would see was another black-robed preacher, as inconspicuous as anything. He was safe, he was safe, he was safe.

Anddyr passed through Raturo's heart, the wide chamber with its path spiraling almost up to the mountain's peak, and stepped between the horrible carved faces of the Twins, through the arch into the Ventallo chamber beyond. The room was empty, and that meant no one to hear him fight with the door behind Uniro's chair. Cappo Joros had had a key to this room . . . but Anddyr had destroyed it, after they'd realized it could be used to track Joros. The door wouldn't budge, no matter how much magic he threw into it—that door had been crafted long and long ago, when the preachers had known a darker magic, had powers mercifully lost to time. Anddyr didn't know its secrets, and so he couldn't open it. His hands shook and his gut twisted as he briefly rested his forehead against the door.

"Destroy the leg," the cappo had said, the command unbending. "It will make them weaker, and that will make us stronger."

Anddyr had known this might happen, that he'd have to find a different way to get to Fratarro's leg. He'd need a key from one of the other Ventallo, but those weren't easy to come by. He could wait until after Rora and the knives had . . . done what they'd come to do, take a key off one of the Ventallo then, and hope there was enough time to burn the leg and get out before anyone discovered the Ventallo were no more. Since the only other option was trying to take a key from a living Ventallo and hoping no one discovered the destroyed leg before the knives could do their work, he supposed the leg would have to wait. It was disobeying the cappo, in a way, but what could he do? There was no way around it. Still, it started the slow roiling in his stomach, the small evasion combined with the burning, trembling horror of being back inside Raturo. It was too soon, but a small wolf began to chew at his insides.

"Learn everything you can," the cappo had said. "We need to know their plans, need to know where they stand."

So Anddyr wasted no time in leaving the Ventallo chamber, walking beneath the arch of the Twins but able to avoid seeing their faces, mercifully. He moved slowly through the halls, his feet tracing familiar paths—it was something he had done often for the cappo, when they'd lived here. Cappo Joros had been a Shadowseeker—the *head* Shadowseeker—a gatherer of secrets and useful things. Joros's chamber here had been lined with all manner of miscellany—anything that might someday prove useful, many things that looked so innocent until the cappo smiled and gave voice to the secrets they held. Secrets could be better than coins, more powerful than kings. Anddyr had known each of the mishmashed items, known their uses and their secrets, for they practically shouted to him when he was deep in his madness. Anddyr was one of them after all, just another useful thing, and the cappo would never discard something he might use later. Even the burn-faced merra might be a useful thing, and so he hadn't driven her away.

His feet walked the same paths they'd walked for years, unseen and listening, a wide loop that took him past the circular meeting rooms, the sleeping quarters of the always-gossiping initiates, the canteen, the deep pools where warm water bubbled from the center of the world. There was bustle everywhere he went, more preachers than he had ever seen within Raturo, and everywhere he heard the same murmurs: *The time draws near. Time to leave. Time to free the Twins. Time to sink the sun.*

With each step, each overheard conversation, each unfamiliar face—Anddyr's gut made another twist, the wolf took another bite. He hoped no one saw through his cloaking, because he wasn't able to hide the terrible way his hands shook.

He had learned what there was to know. The Fallen had found more limbs, and they had called back the wandering preachers who spread the word of the Twins, and they were preparing their next move.

"After all that," the cappo had said grimly, "you need to find Etarro." He'd repeated his instructions, another easy mantra for Anddyr's weak mind to remember: "Burn the leg. Learn their secrets. Kill the boy."

He knew most of the places Etarro would hide, knew the boy's mind as well as his own. The wolf grew and grew within him, spawned mates and pups, all of them gnawing at him. He walked invisible past the preachers, so many of them, and he was sure they would see him, hear the roaring of his guts, the mewling hunger of his need. His shaking hand reached into his robe, drew out the stuffed horse Etarro had given him, held it tight against his chest like a talisman.

Kill the boy.

Anddyr didn't remember stopping, but he recognized the door he stood before. How could he not? The mountain, evil and unchosen, had nonetheless been his home for years. He knew its secret places, and so of course he knew the faces it would show the world. There was a voice from beyond the door, and it called his name.

There was no one else around, no one walking this deep hall. No one to see the door creak open, close again.

Shelves lined the walls, shelf after shelf after shelf, and though there was a blue haze over all of it, and though the walls pulsed with breath and laughter, there was no doubting his eyes here. Even in the throes of deepest delusion, he would trust this sight. He walked slowly between the shelves, fingers reaching out in wonder, pulling back so as not to taint them. Not until the very end of the chamber did he let himself take one, cradling it in both his hands, holding it like a new-hatched bird fallen from the nest. One of the thousands of skura jars that sat in storage, waiting to enslave, waiting to enrapture.

He wanted to put it back. Anddyr would swear that until his last breath left him. But the hunger in him was howling now, tasting the smell of release. The world shrank, paring off all the pieces that didn't matter, everything that wasn't the little jar cupped in his palm. It was too soon, much too soon, but the fear-born wolves tore at him, and he couldn't bear it.

There was a small space between the last shelf and the wall, a space that a determined man could wedge himself into. Hidden from sight, should anyone walk into the chamber, Anddyr dropped his cloaking and twisted open the lid with shaking fingers. He knew better than to try to hold a spell during his dosing—once, he'd thought to heal some of his wounds while the skura took him, but he'd returned to himself to find an entirely different spell raining fire around him. Anddyr had learned that lesson well. Naked of magic, he reached one finger only into the jar, the black paste sucking at his fingertip, and brought it to his mouth.

The ecstasy of it washed over him like a wave, his tangled innards unknotting, the wolves dissipating, his shaking hands stopping. The world that had narrowed to the jar in his palm now exploded, expanded, spiraled away into shades of blue. Anddyr sagged against the wall, mind and body slack, holding to the moment for as long as he could, for the real world was a thing he was not yet ready to face. But it turned wrong, half-way through the euphoria, like not tasting the rot in an apple until after the third bite. His stomach turned sour and throbbing, the taste of mud thicker in his mouth than usual, and he could feel worms writhing slowly down his throat. When his sight cleared of the blue haze, he still felt heavy and stupid, and birds wheeled slowly against the far wall—nothing at all like the clarity that usually followed a dose of skura. The gnawing need was gone, but worms and bile fought now in his belly.

There had been a few times where he had taken his dose too soon—but not many, for they had left him feeling sluggish and fuzzy. But this . . . this felt like poison crawling through him. This must be the effect of skura unmixed with the cappo's blood.

Plain skura, unbonded, waiting for a few drops of blood to activate all its properties—those that enslaved as well as those that restored sanity, both sides of the so-heavy coin. It sat in his gut, boiling and bleeding, and a weak whimper of a sob burst out of Anddyr—he wished for the wolves back.

"Anddyr," a soft voice said, and Anddyr's foggy eyes tracked the sound. He shouldn't have been surprised, and yet he was—he could blame it on his slow-moving mind, weak and useless. Etarro knelt before him, Raturo's own boy-twin, and his face was painted with sadness. "You shouldn't have come back."

"I had no choice," Anddyr murmured, barely lifting his head to meet the boy's gaze.

"You always have a choice." Etarro took the jar from him, put its lid back in place, set the jar on a near shelf. He took Anddyr's limp hand in both his own, held it gently just as he held Anddyr's eyes. The touch felt like ice, searing cold. "Tell me why you're here, Anddyr."

"You know." The boy always knew, knew far more than he should.

"Tell me anyway."

"To burn the leg. To kill the Ventallo." He blinked, slowly, the boy's face fading from focus, swimming back. "To kill you."

Etarro bowed his head, looking at their entwined hands. "You always have a choice, Anddyr." His fingers slipped from around the mage's as he rose, taller than when Anddyr had last seen him, close to man-grown. "Valrik and the others gather in the Cavern of the Falls each night. There's a place, within the Icefall, where a man can hide."

The boy left him then, moving on quiet feet. Anddyr's head lolled so he could follow Etarro with his eyes. The boy left him alone, with the pieces of his fractured mind drifting together and falling apart, the world and all its problems closing around him like teeth. This was wrong, all wrong; he should have . . . He should not have taken the skura, he had ruined the careful timing, perhaps ruined everything with his weakness.

He imagined Rora, back in the storage room, holding the seekstone he'd given her and watching with disappointment, disgust.

Slowly he rolled to his knees, clinging to the shelf for support, his limbs practically useless. He dragged himself to his feet, stumbled forward a few steps, crashed into one of the shelves. A jar fell, shattered on the floor, skura oozing from it like mud. Anddyr left a pile of sour vomit next to it before lurching toward the door. His stomach was twisting again, though not with the skura-hunger, but with something deeper.

CHAPTER THIRTEEN

R ora sat with her back to a wall, the cold of it seeping into her bones, and held her dagger in one hand, the round little stone in the other. She hated those rocks, the ones that made her head twist and her eyes not her own; she didn't trust 'em, not since she'd found out strangers had been using them to look through her eyes for most of her life. Curiosity was a powerful thing, though, and even she'd admit the stones could be damned useful, sometimes.

The one the witch'd given her, so far it didn't seem too useful, or even interesting enough to make up for that. The witch had wandered around for a while, but now he was just sitting in another storeroom. She'd felt dirty, spying on him, but that guilt was dripping away with how boring he was being. She tapped the point of her dagger against the stone, restless, impatient.

The other knives were scattered around the room Anddyr'd put them in, small groups talking in low voices, sharpening blades, three of 'em tossing dice across one of the black robes to keep the rolls muffled. Rora watched them, and they made her throat hurt.

When she'd been young, after they'd found a home with Whitedog Pack and Aro'd been all a-bubble with the things the Dogshead was teaching him, Rora'd felt a poke of jealousy that'd made her say, "I'm going to be hilt one day. I'm going to lead all the knives." She'd glowed with the pride of those words, knowing deep in her stupid little bones they were true.

But Aro'd frowned at her and said, "You're better at taking orders than giving 'em, Rora. Everyone says." She'd cursed at him and shoved him hard, spun away before she could see the surprise on his face when he landed on the ground. She'd gone to prove him wrong instead, rounding up a handful of other pups, most of 'em younger'n her but already taller, but they didn't have real jobs like she did. They were just pups, maybe good enough to be feet or fingers someday, but none of them were like *her*. She'd waved her dagger in their faces, the bright sharp knife with its shining blue stone, and she'd told 'em about this place in Blackhands territory, where they left some small treasures and didn't even guard them much. She'd told 'em how a few small and sneaky pups could make names for themselves, and get the attention they deserved. She'd grinned at the light in their eyes that *she'd* put there.

Pups went missing all the time. It was a hard life in the Canals, and things went wrong. Pups got picked up by guards or other packs or worse. No one really thought much of it, when a few pups disappeared. No one asked where they'd gone to. No one went looking for a few small mud-pile graves, scraped together with hands and tears. And no one even wondered when

Rora started telling other people she didn't ever want to be the hilt, didn't ever want to lead. "I'm better at taking orders anyway," she'd always said, making a smile, and no one ever saw that it didn't touch her eyes.

And now here she was, hilt anyway. Leading two handfuls of knives in spite of everything, and the responsibility sat on her like a stone.

They were some of the best knives Whitedog Pack had left, even if that wasn't saying too much. Most of 'em she recognized, young faces from the knifeden. Maybe *young* wasn't quite right, since most of them were probably as old as or older'n Rora, but none of 'em had been knives as long as she had. None of them had been raised to it, born to it. So they were new faces, fresh-made knives, all bright-eyed and glow-skinned that they weren't fingers anymore, or fists. She tried to remember them that way, how she'd seen them in the knifeden before she left, before everything happened . . . to her and to them. But it was hard to picture them happy when their faces now were so skinny, their eyes haunted. It was as hard as trying to use her own eyes when she held the damn seekstone, twisting and straining, and not really working. Some of the knives she didn't know at all, couldn't pull their faces from her memory, and when it came down to it, she hadn't been gone all that long. When your best fighters kept getting killed, though, you had to replace 'em somehow.

"Lanthe," she called softly, and he lifted his head from the dice, came ambling over. He had the same sort of grace all knives did, loose easy movements that some people compared to dancers, but Rora didn't know anything about dancing.

Some people said knife work was its own kind of dancing, and maybe that was true.

"Yeah?" Lanthe asked, hunkering down next to her. He was close enough to her age, and he'd probably been a knife longest of all the knives she'd been given to lead. Still meant he hadn't been knifing much more'n a year before she'd left, but it didn't take too long after your first contract to start thinking how a knife had to think.

"What d'you think of this contract?"

"Truth?" Lanthe asked, raising an eyebrow.

"Truth."

He sucked at his teeth, stared out over the other knives with her. "Seems a little stupid, going in somewhere dangerous with only one crazy bastard who knows anything about the place."

"But you're still here."

"I go where the Dogshead tells me to." He met her eyes, and she couldn't quite read what was in them. "I do what the hilt tells me to."

Rora tapped her dagger against the seekstone, staring out over the knives, staring through the witch's eyes at the dark storeroom. "What happened?" she asked softly. "While I was gone?"

"A lot."

"Lanthe."

"Rora," he said sharp, using her real name and not the name he would've known her by before, setting her apart. "I tell you true, you don't want to hear half of it."

And he was right. She didn't want to hear how many of her old friends—her old near-family—had died, or all the ways they'd been killed. Didn't want to start thinking about how many of 'em she could've saved if she'd been around, or how much they must've hated her, thinking she was doing the killing. But they were still here, all these knives, listening to her, all because the Dogshead had traded them for a few pouches of Joros's gold. Maybe they were only here to make a show of it, just waiting to get her and Anddyr in the same room so they could stick knives between their ribs, sneak back out the mountain to tell Joros they'd tried, done what they could, but Rora and his witch had died in the trying. They could go back to their pack, richer'n they'd ever been before, and they could try to make something good out of what was left. It wouldn't surprise her, really. It was something she could see Tare doing.

"Go," Rora said, waving her hand back toward the dicing, and Lanthe left without another word. He'd been knife longest here, next to her—if Tare'd given orders to put a dagger in her heart, she probably would've given them to Lanthe.

Stupid as it was, she wished she'd brought the snowbear cloak with her. It wouldn't be doing any good back at the old crumbling-down estate, and she could do with a little warmth.

For the last few weeks—ever since the Canals and she'd lost her ear and everything had gone to shit—it'd felt like walking out of the sunlight into a pitch-dark room: your eyes panicked and couldn't pull anything out of the black. It was just you standing there with your breath in your throat and wondering if you were the only one there, wondering if you'd start seeing things before or after a knife was swinging toward you. It'd felt to Rora like she was just stumbling around that dark room, bumping and tripping over things she couldn't see, her hands stretched out looking for *something* but not sure she'd recognize it even if she grabbed it. Finally she felt like her eyes were soaking in the dark, seeing the gray lines of the things in the room—and she didn't like the shapes of the things she was starting to see.

She'd wanted to leave Aro back at that old crumbling house with the rest of the pack, where he'd be safe and out of the way, but Joros'd insisted he come with. "If this fails," he'd said, piling a threat on top of a threat, "you and your brother may very well be my last hope at keeping the Twins bound. If you fail in this, there won't be any time to waste on fetching him—we'll need to move immediately."

Even if she did hate having her brother put closer to danger, Joros's words were almost some kind of reassuring. If he needed her and Aro as bad as it sounded, she felt like he'd at least *try* to make sure Aro stayed safe. But Joros told the knives how dangerous the mountain was, and how they'd be killed right away if any of the preachers got a sniff of 'em, and then he said that Rora needed to go in with 'em. Aro was important enough to bring along, but seemed like Rora wasn't so important that he couldn't risk her life. That made her five kinds of suspicious, and when she'd asked him about it, he'd just ground his teeth and said he wished he had any other option. Didn't really do much for helping with the suspicion.

Joros'd been whispering to his witch a lot before they'd come to the mountain—and sure, those two were always whispering, but it'd felt . . . *different* this time. She'd seen how much they looked at her when they whispered, and she couldn't count high enough to say how many times Joros had told her she'd be fine, Anddyr'd take care of her.

There were pieces that just didn't fit together right.

Something caught her eye—well, not exactly, but something in what the seekstone let her see got her attention. There was someone else with the witch. It was too dark to make him out clear, no matter how much she squinted or how hard she pressed the stone against her palm, but the witch wasn't alone . . . and there was no way to spin that to mean anything good. Either he was found and about to be dead . . . or he was meeting with someone on purpose. Maybe someone Joros'd told him to meet, someone he'd known back when he lived in this cold fecking place . . .

She hated the seekstones, but now she was cursing whoever'd made them for not making 'em better—what use was seeing out of someone's eyes if you couldn't hear what their traitor lips were saying?

The other person didn't stay long, getting up and leaving the miserable witch alone again, and Anddyr picked himself up not too long after. Rora tucked the seekstone into a pocket and tucked her anger away, too, let it sit at a simmer. Boiling anger didn't do much good, unless what you wanted to do was get a lot of people killed.

She went and crouched down next to Lanthe and the others throwing dice, and she spoke quiet—talking just to him, but loud enough the other dicers could hear, loud enough everyone in the storeroom could probably hear if they were listening close . . . and she was sure they were all listening. She said, "You see anything go strange with the witch—not his usual strange, mind, but bad strange—if you see anything . . . don't ask permission first. Just do what needs doing. Hear?"

She gave him a hard eye, and he gave it back to her, but

there was maybe something like respect in his look—or at least something less like he thought she was stupid. "I hear," he said.

She wasn't a kid anymore. She'd learned plenty since the last time she'd tried to lead, and she'd make sure this time didn't end with bodies dead and buried.

The door to the storeroom opened, and there were a dozen daggers ready to be thrown. One *did* get thrown, zipping through the air and then clattering to the ground like it'd hit a wall, even though it'd only hit the air in front of the witch's face. Still, it was only Anddyr, and Anddyr was alone, so the daggers got put away, and the knives all made a sudden point of not looking at the witch. Knives were good sneaks, the best in Mercetta, but most times they were shit at being sly.

The witch didn't even seem to notice them, which was all to the good. He stood a little hunched over, one arm wrapped around his belly, and when he did start walking he moved slow and jerky like he didn't quite know what he was doing. That was good, too—it let her catch him by surprise when she asked, "Who was it you were talking to?"

He gave her a big-eyed blink, his face pale and shadowed, but he sharpened a bit when she stuck her hand between them, the seekstone sitting on her palm. "Oh," he said softly. He reached out like he'd take the stone from her, pulled his hand back. "There are some here who are . . . not as loyal as the Ventallo would hope."

"The who?"

"The Ventallo. The . . . packheads of the Fallen."

She didn't let it show how surprised she was that he'd put it in a way she could understand—hells, he was probably talking down to her with it. She put her anger away again, put the seekstone away, too. He didn't try to stop her keeping it. "So who was it?" she asked again.

"Someone I knew from before. Someone . . . good."

Rora didn't like that pause, but there was only so much pushing she could do. Joros'd probably ordered the witch not to tell her anything, and she knew he wouldn't, couldn't, go against an order like that. She wouldn't get anything useful out of him, and that set her teeth to grinding.

She didn't like any of this, not a piece of it. If it'd been just her, maybe she would've left, quietly snuck out the way she'd come in, gone back to face things she could at least see the shape of. But it wasn't just her. There were all the knives, following her but just looking for some weak point they could stick her. Maybe staying wasn't the smart thing to do, but running before there was any danger was the coward thing, and knives weren't cowards. Knives knew when to run, but it wasn't till after there was blood. They wouldn't respect her for trying to keep them safe, and they wouldn't follow her after it. They'd tell Tare, too, and Tare'd smile that smile she had, the one with hate behind it, the one Rora'd seen before but never had aimed at her. And Joros would be furious she hadn't even tried, would maybe do worse than whatever he had planned inside the mountain, but Aro would put his arm around her and tell her it was okay, he understood, he was glad she was smart and safe . . .

No.

There came a point when things would happen however they were supposed to happen, and the best you could do was be ready. She knew her knives were ready, each of them sharp and hungry, and she knew where to put a blade to stop things from going to shit.

"Right," she said, the word coming out heavier than she'd planned. She asked the witch, "You got a plan, then?"

He nodded, looking like tears might come pouring out of him any second, and that didn't put any kind of confidence in her. "The Ventallo meet every night . . . all of them. They gather in one place, so we can . . ."

"Kill them," she finished when his voice stopped, his throat working like the words'd got stuck. He nodded, looking sicker. "How long?"

"A few hours until they gather. We'll need time to hide in the chamber, but we don't want to be too early."

"Right," she said again, and turned away from him. Let him prepare however he was going to; Rora put her back to a wall and got out her daggers. They were already sharp, sharp as fear and hate, but it wouldn't do 'em any harm. The sound of whetstone along the blade was a familiar old comfort, but it didn't do anything for the way her heart was pounding. She had the taste of Canal mud in her mouth, and the memory of her weak little hands scraping away mud to push down small bodies, to hide 'em away where no one could see how bad she'd done, how wrong everything'd gone.

CHAPTER FOURTEEN

The road spread before Scal like a pale arm reaching. Layered with snow and with ice, crystals cracking beneath his boots, each step like bones crunching. He had been walking through the long snows and the long nights and the days like punishments, the sun rebuking him for his cowardice. He could almost feel the Parents glaring with their displeasure as his slow feet took him south. Once, he had told Vatri he did not think the Parents would waste their time, to focus on one mortal. If he had been wrong about that, he did not know how she was able to bear their attention.

Behind him Modatho prayed. Each prayer a gasp. A sob. The snows had given him to Scal, the parro finding him somehow after the long race through the cold, away from Aardanel. Scal had not thought the parro would live. Not thought he would keep pace. Not thought much, truly. Scal's feet were heavy with guilt and with grief, snow grinding beneath his heels. He barely had thought enough to keep himself living, and walking. He still was not sure that he should be trying.

Scal found himself wishing that one of them would fall.

Truly, it did not matter who. Yet Modatho was still there, following slow. Praying. Desperate as they walked, more desperate when the sun fell. Some men clung to life, clutched it hard. Too scared it might slip away. Some men feared what might come after.

"Parents be praised," Modatho rasped all sudden, and the fear was melted from his voice. Scal lifted his eyes from the snow covering the ground. Ribbons, red and yellow, were hung against the sky, dancing in the wind.

A village. Scal knew it, even from the distance. Berring. Fiatera's last extended finger before the wild North laid claim to the land. He had been there before, in his fourth life, stood at the village's outer edge and stared back into the cold breath of the snows that had birthed him. Before Joros had made him, he had never dared step into the village. It had not been cowardice. It was not cowardice to be afraid of a thing worth fearing.

The ribbons flew, and the sound of song reached them over the ice. That made it midwinter, or near to it. The year's longest night, and all across Fiatera the people would be celebrating. Centuries ago, it had been on the longest night that the Parents had cast down their headstrong children. The day was remembered and celebrated. And, too, the people of Fiatera showed their own strength: they fought back against the lowering dark, shining their lights through the long night.

Modatho broke into a ragged run. Slower, Scal followed.

Berring was in the midst of celebration when they stepped between the first of the few huts. Modatho led, his hands clutched over his chest, around the flamedisk hung there. Joy swelled when the villagers caught sight of the parro. The celebration reached out a hand to draw him in, cheering and prayers of thanks. They would not likely have a true priest here. Only an old man or woman who was good at telling the old stories. The few dozen families of Berring were grateful beyond telling for a priest, and on solstice night no less.

After a time they saw Scal, and their joy dimmed. They would be used to seeing Northmen. It was not a thing they could avoid, living at the edge of the snow. But mistrust ran strong as a current beneath ice. It was a current he had swum wide around before, for Scal had heard tales. Berring was not kind to Northmen, who so often raided their homes. Berring was certainly not kind to a single Northman, and Scal, too, bore the convict's cross, though on the wrong cheek.

"My friend has brought me safely here!" Modatho rasped. Generous, in his salvation. "He's a true follower of the Parents, and surely blessed by their hand for his actions! He—he is the brother of my heart!"

The village swelled once more, voices raised, cheering. They surged forward, mouths wide, eyes bright with fire. Instinct put Scal's hand to his shoulder, but there was no sword there. The villagers swallowed him, bearing him forward with happy hands. Their joy was a ringing between his ears. Their smiles caught on his face, and stuck.

Food, enough to fill the hungry nights wandering the snows. Enough to fill all the hungry nights of all his lives. Drink, to make his head light and his laughter ring. Prayer, long prayer and heartfelt, Modatho leading with tears bright on his cold-red cheeks and all the other voices rising to join. Lanterns burned, and candles, and children ran with twists of blazing straw until the flames tickled their fingers, screeching with delight as they dropped the fire to melt hollows into the snow. They sang all the longest night, among dancing points of light like fallen stars.

Scal had sought to make something different of his fifth life, to let it begin where the second had ended. To wipe away the stains of his hard third life, his bloody fourth. To be a good man, who followed the whispered words of a dead priest. Who let himself be guided by the Parents' fire and not the cold ice. To be the kind of man to bring a smile to that dead priest's face. To accept absolution from the forgiving Parents and live his life in their hands. To be more than the man he had been made into.

He had thought that working in Aardanel for the rest of his days would be the way. It was what his life would have been, if not for Iveran. It was the life he should have had. But that was not a true thing. He would have left Aardanel with Brennon when they were old enough. Walked slow through the snows and the ice, with nothing but themselves. Stumbled into Berring and been greeted by the villagers. Feasted, and drunk, and celebrated the new lives they had bought for themselves, paid with strife and toil and bravery.

Scal looked at Modatho, who had stood at his side as Scal sought to remake the paths of his missed and wasted lives. He had named Scal "brother." Always the snows took, without mercy, but for all they took they gave in equal measure.

At length the sun beat back the darkness, reaching light like spears through the black. There was a great cheer, tired but triumphant. They had seen the night through. Lived the long dark and come out its other side. A woman touched Scal's arm, and her child put his small hand into Scal's. They led him to their home, where her husband was building up a fire. Scal slept on the hearth, wrapped around himself, warm for the first time in a very long time.

When the village woke again there was more celebrating. Three days, in the middle of winter, given over to rejoicing in the Parents' triumph over the Twins. On this, the last of three days, there was a frenzy to the air. When the sun rose again, things would be as they had been before, and Scal did not need to be told that life in Berring was not easy. So they took joy while joy could be taken, and Scal with them. He sang, in a voice that was not suited to it, and prayed, and carried shrieking children on his broad shoulders. They fit there better than his sword ever had.

It was during a prayer led by a joyous Modatho, all others on their knees with heads bent and fists pressed to foreheads, that a weight slammed against Scal's shoulder. He tumbled to the packed snow, surprised. He was a large man, and not easy to move. Not even caught unawares.

The Northman loomed over him. Big and blond and braided, like looking into a mirror. Wrapped in brown furs, sword at his hip. His face twisted, in anger and in disgust. "You shame us all," he spat in the Northern tongue.

"What is this?" Modatho asked in his reedy voice.

"Peace," Scal said softly to the Northman. He did not recognize the man, did not know what offense he could have given. "I have no quarrel with you."

"You mix with heathens. You sully your blood." His glare found its way to Scal's cheek where his beard was pale and thin around the old cross-scar. His eyes went wide, his teeth baring. "*You*. You killed Iveran Snowwalker?" His hand went to his hip, fingers to a leather-bound hilt.

"Peace!" Scal said louder, and it felt that it was his thundering heart the Northman wrapped his fingers around.

"No peace for you, kin-killer," the Northman said. His sword came free, sharp and shining. There was death written in its edges. The arc of it through the air spoke of blood.

Scal stayed on his knees, and though fear flowed cold through him, he looked away from the blade. He had lived and died enough lives that another ending was not a thing to fear. Perhaps this would be the last ending. He had felt joy, here in Berring, and love. They were good things. Things a man could remember, after his last life was gone.

He had spent all this life running from who he had been made. Running from the threat of blood, but it had found him yet. *Inevitable.* It was a good word. He did not know who had spoken it, a priest with a soft smile or a bear-faced man. It was fitting, still, that his last life should end in blood, and in the song of steel.

The last thing you do, lad, Parro Kerrus had said, *will speak for all your life*. It was good, that his last act should be prayer. Perhaps it was enough. Scal bowed his head, bared the back of his neck for the falling blade.

He heard the whisper of it falling, sharp enough to slice the air itself. The whisper seemed to carry another familiar voice. The voice of winter, the voice of a snowbear's grin. That other man, all sharp angles and hard as ice, his last words had been, *Must this be how we end?* It had been a chance, in its own way, to step from the blood, to step from the bright steel-song. A chance, refused. The falling blade seemed to whisper, too, words spoken before that man had died. Words spoken to a boy, full of anger and sadness, a boy who had no place in the world. *While there is breath in you*, it whispered, *you will not stop fighting*.

Scal twisted his body. The sword planted its tip in the hard earth, and Scal rose, mountain-tall, to face the other Northman. Their eyes met. No time for fear, or for surprise. Scal struck with his fist, a careful hit, and holding the weight of years.

The Northman fell heavy as stone. He clutched at his throat briefly, eyes bulging and mouth gaping. After that, he did not move.

Silence filled Berring, a silence deeper for all the song and prayer and joy that had come before. All staring at Scal, and at the other unmoving Northman. Scal let his fingers release from their fist at his side. It did not release the shame that was rising in him. It did not stop the tide of hatred. For himself, for the man who had made him this way, for the claws of the past he could not loose.

"Murderer," a voice said softly into the silence. There were murmurs of agreement.

A hand reached gently for his arm. Stopped, at the last moment. Modatho would not meet his eyes. "You should leave," the parro said. Softly, but loud enough that all the others heard. There was a place, in Berring, for a priest.

Scal turned, silent, alone, and walked into the snows once more. Sparse snows, the True North left behind at the other end of Berring. Soft snows, that took nothing and gave nothing in return.

It was a long road from Berring, and lonely. Scal walked it with shoulders hunched, and when he slept, he simply lay down at the side of the road. There was no one to challenge him, and his fear was gone. His past lives had been full of the red-blinding anger that washed his sight like blood. He had thought fear to be the thing to fight the anger—a man who ran was a man who did not fight. A coward did not know anger.

But the fear had been like another man's cloak. He could wear it, but it did not fit. He left it in Berring, beside the North-man's body.

The red anger had not risen to replace it. Nothing had. He walked, and he felt nothing, like a limb gone dead to the cold.

He sometimes saw villages on the horizon, the white-dusted road snaking toward their centers. He left the road then. Sank his boots into the deeper snow, drew a wide arc with his footprints. He would find the road again, when the town was at his back.

There was a day when feet joined his own. Four of them, toes splayed wide atop the snow. The dog nosed at Scal's hip, where he carried the half-charred remains of a rabbit he had trapped. Scal offered the dog a piece of the meat, and she stayed by his side, crunching thin bones between her jaws. Her tail waved the air, tongue hanging from one side of her mouth. Scal had not liked dogs, since a pack of them had once tried to eat him. Still. That had been another life. In this life, perhaps, he could like dogs.

She lay near him at the side of the road when he stopped to sleep, and when he rose with the sun, the dog, too, rose with a mighty stretch and trotted once more at his side. Tulli, he called her; it meant "dog" in the Northern tongue. He had never been good at naming things, but a companion deserved a name. Tulli raced down a hare of her own, and Scal stood patiently by for the dog to finish her meal. Again they slept at the side of the road, but the sun's next rising showed no sign of Tulli. Scal waited for two hours. The dog did not return. Finally Scal rose, began walking once more down the lonely road. He could not get anyone to stay with him. Not even a dog.

He thought of Vatri, who had found him and followed him, refused to leave even when he had offered her no kindness. She had stayed until he had not minded, until he had grown used to her, until she had understood him better than he had thought someone could, and he her. And she, too, had left him. He had driven her away, but still, she had left.

His hand dug into his near-empty travelsack, fingers roving, brushing. His sight flickered, layered with the vision of another man. Rock and darkness all around, and the steady pull. *South.* He turned the seekstone in his hands, watched through the witch's eyes. Watched, and could not help but think of them. The witch, and Rora, and Joros. Vatri. They would have made him someone he was not.

But Scal, in his fifth life, was no one. His hands were not made for shaping, and there was an emptiness inside him.

The road grew wider, and more populous. The villages closer together, and bigger. The cold less, though not by much. Winter still held its hand closed firmly around Fiatera. Scal kept his head down, and skirted wider around the villages, and slept farther from the edge of the road.

He chose a stand of trees as the sun slipped away, pink shadows reaching across the sky and the snowy ground. It would shelter him from wind and sight. The copse was thick, wild for as small as it was, two dozen tangled trees fighting for the same patch of ground. The branches nearly shut out the light of the setting sun, and so he did not see them until he was upon them. It did not help that they wore black robes, dark as night themselves.

"Greetings, brother," said one of the three, in a low voice that was not welcoming. "I think you've found somewhere you don't want to be."

CHAPTER FIFTEEN

It felt strange to Joros, to be sitting still and doing nothing besides staring into a fire. He'd had so little time for relaxation since well before he'd left Mount Raturo that trying to relax now felt unnatural. He had the overwhelming sense that there was something he should be doing, something vital, and the fact that he *couldn't* do anything made his hands twitch.

Relaxing was far more stressful than it should have been. True, some of it may have been due to a lingering unease caused by building a fire in the shadow of Mount Raturo— not, perhaps, the smartest suggestion to ever pass his lips. He would never admit it, but in his long years within dark Raturo, he'd forgotten the simple comfort of a light against the pressing darkness. This being the first time in nearly a decade that Anddyr had been out of his reach, that little comfort helped. He'd never admit to that aloud either.

Still, he couldn't shake the edginess. He couldn't do anything until Rora returned with his damned mage, and he couldn't trust that Anddyr would do anything besides cock it all up—there was nothing more Joros could do to help them at this point. They would succeed or die without him doing anything, and that was the proper way to keep one's hands clean, but it made him feel as useful as pissing on a forest fire. He hadn't relaxed in years because he hated this kind of stillness—hated it now, especially, because not keeping his mind occupied made him think of red hair and a soft breath in his ear . . . Dangerous thoughts.

He'd tried whittling earlier, borrowing a dagger from one of the fists. That was something one of his brothers—he couldn't remember which one anymore—had tried to teach him, back before Joros had stopped trying to fit in with his family. He'd turned a stick into a sharper stick, and that had filled all of an hour.

The uselessness was frustrating to an incalculable degree, and the frustration made him want to go *do* something with his wasted energy—but each time he thought of what else he could be doing, it simply drove home the fact that he *couldn't* do anything. The most useful thing he could do was be right here to celebrate the triumph or clean up the failure when Rora and Anddyr returned, and the waiting was what made him feel so damned useless. It was a self-propelling cycle of irritation, and one he couldn't seem to divert.

One of the fists had pulled out a deck of cards, and they'd sat around playing some sort of bluffing game Joros had never seen before. He'd watched them play and that had actually done wonders for shutting down his mind—it gave him something to focus on, a clear objective. Once he'd learned all their tics, he'd asked to play; it had taken them a few seconds to get over their surprise, but they'd shuffled around to make room for him in the circle. In retrospect, he probably should have lost a few rounds, or at least given them some of their coins back after two of the fists stormed into the trees. But he'd won fair and—well, he'd won, and that was how gambling worked. It wasn't his fault they were shit liars.

It would be different, so different, if he still had his network of Shadowseekers, but they'd been taken from him, too. All of his tools had been stripped away, leaving him only the maddening mage, the almost-smart twins, and a series of human shields. He could get by fine without any help—he always had—but it certainly limited his options.

What rankled most was that he was so out of options that the crux of this particular plan was Anddyr, of all people. If that wasn't a sign of how far he'd fallen, then Joros would eat his boots.

Joros wouldn't lower himself to pacing, and so his only option was to stare sullenly into the fire, which did nothing to improve his mood. Didn't worsen it either—just a flat level of annoyed anxiety that made him want to scream if it wouldn't have brought the Fallen crashing down around his ears.

Aro was busy trying to make friends with the fists on guard duty, some of whom sounded like they *had* been his friends, in whatever checkered past the twins had come from. The fists weren't having any of it, though. Aro didn't seem to understand why, but Joros couldn't blame the fists. It was harder to contemplate killing someone if there was too much of a friendly air.

"All my people'd better come back," Tare, the ear-cutter, had said to Joros, jabbing a finger into his chest. He'd thought about snapping her finger off for her, but she looked like the kind of woman who would give back twice as much as she was given. She'd made sure Joros was near when she'd said to the leader of the fists: "If every last knife doesn't come out of that mountain, you kill the boy."

Joros had neglected to tell Rora that part; she dealt with stress poorly enough as it was. If one of the knives was fool-ish enough to get himself killed inside Raturo, by the time it became an issue Anddyr would be back with all of his protec-tive spells, rendering the fists and their command a nonissue. Still, it was somewhat pathetic to see Aro so doggedly trying to engage with them.

He offered at every turn to help gather wood, to skin the rabbit whose skull a fist had smashed with an impressively ac-curate rock-throw, to join the few looking for fresh water, to walk the donkeys so they stayed limber, even to help dig a la-trine. Mostly they answered him with silent shakes of the head, which seemed to hurt him more than an outright rebuff would have. Rora had once compared her brother to a kicked dog; Joros couldn't deny the accuracy of that.

There was nothing Joros could do but wait. It would be easier if he could just accept that. He leaned back, resting on his elbows, staring up as embers crackled among the stars. He forced his jaw to loosen, his fingers to open. For a moment, the embers seemed to dance in familiar shapes against the dark sky, cascading red hair and an eager smile. He'd been avoiding thinking of her so that he could stay focused, stay sharp . . . and here he was with nothing to focus on, nothing he needed to be sharp for.

He watched the embers dance against the stars, twining and twisting into a familiar smile, familiar curves. He didn't allow *too* much to come bubbling up—he wasn't a fool—but he did feel a rumble of sadness, a frisson of remorse. Regret for everything that could have been. Good to know, in a way, that he could feel this without it undoing him; that he could still think of her without dissolving into a puddle of grief or a tower of rage.

It was, surprisingly, a good moment, silent and peaceful and calm, and so of course the merra would ruin it.

"What's after this?" she asked. Joros looked down and found her horrific face staring at him through the fire—jarring, after the dancing embers. "What happens after you've killed all your brothers and sisters?"

He swallowed his regret quick enough. No more time for indulgence—there were other things he could waste his time on, in this endless waiting. "I'll finally be free of you, for one."

She didn't react to that at all—Joros supposed he'd been growing a little lax with his insults. "You'll just walk away?" she pressed. "Go back to a normal life as, what, some nameless merchant? A farmer?" Her laughter was almost as ugly as her face. "What will you do, once you've won?"

"What do you care? Once the Ventallo are dead, there will be no more Fallen to defeat, no more reason for you to follow me."

"Once the Ventallo are dead, there will be hundreds of people suddenly with no leaders. It would be the perfect time for an opportunistic man, conveniently positioned, to step in."

Joros was very careful not to show any reaction to that beyond a single raised eyebrow, though internally he was calling her every kind of foul name he could think of. "You think I want to lead the people I've turned my back on? The ones I've betrayed?" There was an art to making the truth sound an utterly ridiculous thing—it was in the tone, in a carefully raised eyebrow. "Why in all the hells would I be working so hard to destroy them if I wanted to lead them?"

"You're not destroying them," she said, undeterred. "You're just removing the ones who stand in your way."

"You're a fool. You do remember we burned Fratarro's hand together? That it was *me* who found it, *me* who wanted to burn it?"

"Oh, I believe you want to see the Twins kept bound. I do believe that. Who would you lead if they were freed?" She made a broad motion, taking in herself and glum Aro and the fists with their silent disinterest. "Us?" That laugh again, setting Joros's teeth to grinding. "No. If the Twins stay bound, the Fallen will still need leaders. If you kill everyone who stands in your way, everyone who knows better, why wouldn't they let you lead them? And you're smart enough to get others to do all the work for you, to keep your hands clean."

"You've an impressive imagination, I'll give you that. It's a dangerous combination with a mistrustful personality. No wonder the Northman was so protective of you. You're like a child bashing its head against everything to test what's the hardest."

That silenced her for a while; it seemed she didn't like being reminded of the traitorous Northman. He'd have to remember to mention Scal more often.

"You didn't see what happened in the North," she said softly. Joros almost didn't bother straining to hear her low voice, but, truthfully, he was bored. More, she was the sort of person who would consider an argument won if she got no response. "You didn't see what I did. Boy." Joros heard the scuffle as Aro startled nearby, clearly not prepared for the merra's attention. "You saw what happened to the Northmen."

"I was too far away to see anything," Aro muttered.

"You saw me call out, and you saw how the Parents answered my call. Every last one of the Northmen fell beneath the Parents' fire."

"Fell asleep," Aro said. "You said you made 'em all sleep."

"I lied."

Aro turned a little paler, the firelight making his face pink, and he wouldn't meet the merra's gaze.

"Do you have a point?" Joros asked, voice radiating boredom.

"You see the scars on my face and think me cursed, but you have it wrong. I've been blessed by the Parents, and when I call on them, they answer."

"I'm sure they do," Joros drawled, and one of the fists snorted in laughter.

Her eyes narrowed at him, the scarred ridges twisting down. Her lips moved, though if she said anything aloud, Joros didn't hear it. The sudden flare of the fire drowned out any other comment he might have made. The flames flared with an audible roar, as though some invisible giant had leaned down to blow a gust of breath at the fire, rising three times their previous height, tongues leaping out to flick at Joros and the fists. There were plenty of curses in the face of the sudden heat, and a few shouts, and every one of them scrambled back from the fire—save the merra, who stayed where she sat, smirking.

Slowly the fire shrank back to a normal size, crackling angrily, its fingers still reaching out as though searching for something to grab hold of. The hobbled donkeys huffed restlessly, woken and uncertain. The fists edged back closer to the fire, suspicious but clearly more scared by the thought of sitting outside its circle of light. Joros had no such fear, and it seemed Aro didn't either—the two of them remained where they'd fled from the fire's reach, at the edge of warmth, the edge of darkness.

Into the silence that lingered, Vatri spoke her words softly. "If I find that you've been using us solely for your own ends, I swear by the Divine Mother and Almighty Father that I will bring all their power to bear, and I will destroy you. Doubt me if you like. Test me if you must. But I so swear."

She was stubborn beyond telling, and there was no doubt in Joros that she meant every word. Worse, it seemed she wasn't entirely crazy or bluffing, and he'd been assuming both. Still, there was an old saying that a clever man could make a powerful enemy into a powerful ally—that was the mind-set with which he'd handled Anddyr, until he'd realized the mage was powerful enough, but a fool otherwise. "And if you're wrong?" Joros asked over the fire. "If I'm truly fighting for the greater good, with no motive other than seeing the Twins never rise?"

"Then I will bring the Parents' power to bear in support of your cause. Truly, I hope that's how this will end."

"I hope it ends tonight," Joros said softly, thinking of Anddyr and Rora and the knives within Raturo. If all went well, they would bring an end to this, and the merra could take herself and her disconcerting powers very far away.

No one else seemed much interested in talking, the fists silently curling onto their sides to sleep, a few staying awake to keep a watch. Joros left them to it, and he noticed that he was not the only one to sleep farther away from the fire, and farther away from the merra.

CHAPTER SIXTEEN

Rora'd always hated the cold. In the Canals, she'd seen more people than she could count who'd lost fingers or toes in the winter, swelling and turning black and then just falling off. By the falling-off point, they said it didn't even hurt anymore. Winter meant falling asleep and just not waking up again sometimes. The different packs in the Canals were usually fighting, but once dirty snow started falling from above and the slow-moving canal water froze over, all the fighting stopped.

Going through the North, where the ground turned to ice and even breathing hurt, that'd been like ten winters at once, and she'd been glad to leave it behind. It'd still been winter when they got back to Fiatera, but it'd almost felt warm after the North. She'd thought then that she'd be safe from ever feeling a cold like that again, hadn't thought anything could come close to it.

She'd been wrong about that. The shaking witch'd taken them to a place that was colder'n winter and near all made of ice.

"The Cavern of the Falls," Anddyr whispered over his

shoulder, said it like it was a holy place. It probably was—the preachers thought the whole mountain was holy, so anything inside it was probably given the same treatment. It was pretty enough, but it took more'n pretty to impress Rora, and the bone-deep cold was already a dozen marks against the place.

The witch stopped at the edge of the frozen-over lake, hugging himself tight as his whole body shook. He was probably more than cold; Rora'd seen lartha addicts in Mercetta get the same sort of shakes when they were wanting a fix. He'd been acting funny since he'd come back from his little scouting mission, and that'd got Rora nervous. Joros had promised his witch would know when to dose himself, but the timing felt off to Rora. She kept her eyes fixed on Anddyr, and wondered who he'd been talking to in that dark storeroom, and what they might've planned.

Back in the Canals, back when she'd really been part of a pack and not just forced her way back in, she'd learned plenty about trust. You had to trust that the packhead was giving good orders, trust that the face and arm and hand were passing on the orders right, trust that everyone else in the pack would do their jobs right. You had to have trust in a pack, or everything would fall apart.

Joros'd gathered together a group of people, but they weren't pack, not really. It was easy to think they were, because she'd spent most of her life in packs and it was how her thinking worked. But they weren't pack, because it was no kind of pack that couldn't trust the packhead, and you'd have to be stupid to trust Joros. The witch was Joros's pet, and that meant he couldn't be trusted either. So Rora kept her eyes on the witch, and kept her senses sharp.

"You should find somewhere comfortable," the witch said. You didn't have to speak too loud, in a place so big and empty. All the ice shone words back just like light. "We may be here a while. It's hard to tell when night comes . . ."

Rora made a gesture with one hand, and the ten knives scattered out around her. They moved careful, stepping soft over the ice, going around stones instead of over them. Knives learned to move without messing anything up. They were even careful not to touch any of the little ghostlights that floated in the cavern, twisting their bodies away if one of the wisps drifted close.

Rora stayed where she was, watching the witch as he watched the frozen waterfall. He didn't seem like the kind of man who could keep a secret too well, but who knew what kinds of magics he wove when his fingers twitched. He could've cast some spell to make her trust him. Still . . . She walked up behind him, careful to make enough noise it wouldn't surprise him—she'd seen what he could do with his finger-waving. She stood next to him, shivering, wishing for the heavy white bear cloak she'd left behind. The cloak was big enough for her to drown in, but it made her feel bigger, too, and the snarling bear head was good and scary. You needed extra weapons, sometimes.

"Shouldn't you be hiding, too?" she asked the witch. He had his crazy eyes on, the ones that darted and danced, and he was shaking. She'd seen the madness take him often enough now that she could see it tugging him down, pulling him deep.

"I will." His head twitched in a way that might have been a nod toward the waterfall. He always had trouble looking at her. "There's a fissure in the ice." His eyes flicked to her. "A hole, a place to hide, a pocket. I . . . should stay out of your way. I have to stay out of the way, stay quiet, stay hidden."

That was a thing he did, in the madness: repeat whatever orders he'd been given, and she could guess who'd told him to keep back. Stay away from the bloodshed, where she couldn't blame him if he was too far away to help in time. "You can hide with me. Just stay back when it all starts."

"I'll need a lot of power to keep all of you hidden. I can't waste it on cloaking myself, too. And if they see me first . . ."

'Course he'd have an excuse ready. "You could sit behind a rock. There's plenty of 'em."

"Then I wouldn't be able to see what was happening." One of his hands reached out, fingers stretching for the ice, then pulled back quick like he'd been burned. He looked down to his feet, but, short as she was, Rora could still see his eyes, and their centers were getting huge. "I don't blame you for not trusting me."

There wasn't too much to say to that, so Rora shrugged. "Should I?"

He looked at her—for a little while at least, and then his wide eyes started flickering around. "I don't know," he said real quiet, and then flinched away from her. "You should go. Hide. I'll keep you all cloaked, but . . . hidden is better. Hidden is better." He didn't let her answer that, just started taking quick steps along the frozen lake. There wasn't much else for Rora to do besides take his advice, and hope he kept his word. If he didn't, she had a dagger that was balanced for throwing, and a hand that wouldn't hesitate.

The knives'd scattered themselves out pretty well, and Rora

picked a place close to the center of the chamber, near the edge of the ice-lake. She crouched down, staying on the balls of her feet so she could get up quiet when she had to. It didn't take long for her leg muscles to begin to burn, to get stiff with the cold. She pulled out both her daggers, kept her fingers flexing around their hilts so they wouldn't freeze up. When she peeked her eyes over the top of the rock, she couldn't see the witch, but she could see pieces of the knives poking out from their hiding places. The witch said his spell was like throwing a big blanket over all of them—they could still see each other under the blanket, but no one outside the blanket would see them. Seemed a stupid way to explain it, since anyone with half an eye would see a dozen people-sized lumps under a blanket. But it'd worked so far, at least. She just had to trust he'd actually cast the damn spell, and wasn't leaving them sticking out like lumps.

They waited longer'n Rora would've liked, to the point where even she was starting to get twitchy, and the other knives weren't any better off. They all heard the voices, though—couldn't miss 'em, rolling down the tunnel entrance and bouncing around the chamber, turning a few normal voices into a sound like charging animals, words crashing into each other.

"—word from Dayra—"

". . . on her way back already?"

"—had to drain half the lake to—"

". . . missive from the Masters of the Academy."

"You don't think they'd ever turn on us in force?"

"They're too old, too cowardly. Like women locked up in their . . ."

"—anything from Saval? He's been silent as—"

". . . heard it was terrible. Monsters and horrors . . ."

"—boy told me I'd never see again. What does he think blind is?"

"He just likes to think of himself as a prophet . . ."

"—wasn't wrong about Dirrakara."

The floating wisps didn't give off much light on their own, but the ice made up for it, catching the light and throwing it back doubled, and there was no end to the ice. A little light became enough to see by, so Rora could see 'em clear as day, the sixteen who stepped into the chamber. It was one more'n Joros'd expected, but one more wouldn't make much difference. As they walked closer to the lake, she could see that they all had, every one of 'em, red and puckered pits where their eyes should've been.

They stopped near the lake, about five lengths from where Rora was crouched, and they stood gathered in a loose group, though one of them was clearly their head. It was creepy, the way all their empty eyes fixed on him. He was just like Joros'd described him: "An old man, tall, with a beard halfway down his chest. He's the . . . head, you'd call him. The leader." Joros's eyes'd gotten hard then. "If you do nothing else—make sure *he* dies." Rora'd told the other knives early on to pick other targets, that she'd deal with the head. That was how it should be, leader against leader, with the worthy one surviving. True, it wasn't much of a fair fight, her against a blind old man, but her time in the Canals'd taught Rora not to question whose throat her blade was pointed toward. If your head told you to kill someone, you killed 'em. Simple.

"Brothers and sisters," the head said, his voice carrying real nice through the cavern, "many of you have already heard the news. Sister Dayra has found another piece of blessed Fratarro. A leg, to go with the foot Brother Ebarran has returned to us." A few of the others touched one of the men on his shoulders, and Rora couldn't figure out how they knew which one was the right man, or where he was. "She will return to us soon. Our success grows by the day."

Rora took as deep a breath as she could without making any noise. There was no reason to delay it now that all the heads of the black-robes were here. Even with her leg muscles gone cold and stiff, she rose in a smooth motion, but she paused soon as she was standing straight, froze and waited. She didn't really expect them to see her, what with having no eyes and all, but still—it was a relief when the head just kept on talking. "Soon, brothers and sisters, we shall be able to restore them to their full power."

As Rora took careful, quiet steps around her hiding-rock, one of the other black-robes called out, "How? You keep saying *what* we'll do, brother, but never *how*."

Rora near snorted; 'course they'd start talking about their plans soon as she showed up. Joros'd probably strangle a few people to be able to hear this sort of talk, but he'd strangle people for a lot less, and anyway, she wasn't here for spying. Out of the corners of her eyes, she could see the other knives standing up, stepping out from their hiding spots, moving quiet and slow and unseen across the ice. The head turned to the black-robe who'd spoken, and his voice was deeper when he said, "You must have faith, brother. I have said it before. The Twins have entrusted me with the secret of their freedom, and it is a secret that sits heavily upon me. I would not burden any others with it." That almost pulled a snort out of Rora, too—those words near dripped horseshit, but at least it wasn't anything worth strangling over.

It wasn't easy to do—Rora and the knives placing themselves near enough to the black-robes to strike, but not so close that they'd know before the strike. Rora'd known a blind man in the Canals who said he could hear the air move different when there was a body near enough, and he'd had the skill with a knife to prove it. Still, set two men at him from different directions, and he went down easier'n most. Maybe blindness made you better at hearing, but it didn't make you better at fighting—that was fact.

The black-robes were clustered together, mostly, with some empty spaces between their bodies that Rora might've been able to slip into, if she'd felt stupid enough to try. Instead she stood herself behind the head black-robe, one dagger pointed at his kidney, the other waiting, waiting until her other knives were in place. Then she lifted her second dagger, the one with the shattered blue stone in its hilt, and saw the other knives raise their daggers as well. None of 'em made a sound about it, but they all brought their daggers down at the same time.

Rora's, instead of sinking into the head black-robe's neck, clattered against metal and went skittering down the blade of a sword as the black-robe lurched sideways. The shock of that hit Rora harder than the fist to her jaw. She stumbled back, managed to get her feet steady and her knives up to face the huge man stepping out from a space between black-robed bodies, a space she'd thought'd been empty. His face was smooth and hard and had no emotions, and he held his sword angled up across his body.

Fecking witch . . . she knew she never should've trusted Anddyr.

Her knives were making noises now, and they weren't any good kind of noise. They were fighting noises, dying noises. The swordsman was stepping forward slow enough Rora could flick her eyes quick, see more giant men just like him facing off against her people. Cutting through her people, spreading their blood on the icy floor. Then the man was in front of her, and the only way to fight a swordsman when all you had was daggers was to get in close and do it fast.

She darted to one side and he swung his sword over to block her before he recognized it was a feint. The recognition lit only after one dagger sliced through his belly, but he got an elbow in the way of her second dagger before she could put it in his neck. She twisted away, dragging the one dagger along with her so that when she ended up behind him, she'd also opened up half his stomach for him.

Bastard was too stupid to know he was dead on his feet. He twisted to follow her, the top half of him sliding around faster than the bottom half, and his sword arm flying out wild. Rora dropped to the ground, rolling under the blade and slicing a dagger across the backs of his ankles while she was down there. That put him down, and no matter how long it took him to realize he was dead, he wouldn't be coming after her anymore.

Back up to her feet, and Rora only saw three of her knives. Well, three left standing; there were plenty on the ground. A few of the black-robes were dying with 'em, and some of the big swordsmen, too—that was good, but there weren't enough of 'em dead. Two of the knives were fighting together, smart-mouthed Lanthe and a girl he'd been dicing with, backs pressed against each other, fending off three men. There were two more who'd cornered the other knife, a youngster she hadn't even recognized, but he must've done well enough for himself to not be dead yet. She started forward to help him, and then she saw the black-robes.

They were standing near the ice-lake, except the three who were busy dying. They were clustered together again, and it seemed like the eyes they didn't have were fixed on the fighting. The head black-robe stood at the front of 'em, and the bastard was smiling.

If you do nothing else—make sure he dies.

She could do that.

Rora stumbled across the floor, the ice more slippery with blood, but she had a clear shot on him, nothing in her way. She threw her dagger and it bounced off the empty air in front of the head black-robe's face. She kept going forward, the other dagger held ready to sink into his neck like it should've from the start.

Something hit her chest. It felt like being hit with half a tree, knocking the air out of her even before her back touched the ground. She lay there, mouth wide open but nothing else moving, her whole body putting all its efforts toward trying to breathe. And that was before she even felt the burning. It was like someone walked up and set a coal down at the center of her chest. She didn't have any breath to scream out the pain of it. There was a wailing in her ears, getting louder with each moment she couldn't draw in air. The ghostlights were dancing above her, and other-colored spots joined them before shadows started creeping in at the edges of her sight.

One of the swordsmen stuck his face above hers, blocking out the ghostlights, and she saw him lift his weapon.

Something let go in her chest, and she hauled in a messy, desperate breath. It gave her enough strength to screw her eyes shut—there was a kind of bravery, one she didn't have, to watch a man kill you.

The wailing leaked slowly out of her ears as her lungs filled up, and under it she heard the head black-robe say, "Hold, Cerren. We want to keep her. She's a twin." That killing blow never fell, but a cold ball of fear lodged in her belly under the burning pain in her chest.

CHAPTER SEVENTEEN

When it became clear that Saval and his one remaining attendant weren't going anywhere, Keiro took them to meet the plainswalkers. No one barred his entrance to the tribe-home, and even though disappointment and anger still lurked behind Yaket's eye, it was full, too, of curiosity.

Saval, to his credit, handled it well. He was of the Ventallo, a leader of men, and his mind was both quick and sharp. He stood among the staring plainswalkers, shorter than he by half a length, and gave them a winning smile. "Greetings, brothers and sisters!" he said. "It is truly a wondrous miracle to find the faithful here. I am Saval Tredeiro, Thirteenth among the Fallen, and I speak for the Twins."

Elsewhere, that line likely would have brought awe, made the men respect him and the women fawn over him. It was not a lie; among the faithful, the Ventallo were considered to speak the will of the Twins. It was only that the plainswalkers knew Keiro, knew that he truly gave voice to the Bound Gods, and that was a greater truth than Saval's. The plainswalkers stood in silence, long enough to make plain their doubt, and then they surged forward with questions dripping from their lips. The novelty of a preacher like Keiro might have worn off, but a Ventallo was not quite the same as a preacher.

Keiro stepped through them, leaving Saval and his near-silent attendant to the attention that Saval seemed to crave. Keiro stepped toward Yaket, who stood resolute as her tribe burst in a flurry of excitement. "May we speak?" Keiro asked her. She inclined her head and, wordless, turned into the grass.

They sat secluded, facing each other as they had two nights previous, and there was more tension in the silence than there had ever before been between them. Keiro could hardly meet her eye, and instead he spoke to his clasped hands. "I only wanted to warn you . . . change is coming, and perhaps soon. Saval is only the first. Soon enough, all the Fallen will come here, and . . . and they'll be freed, Yaket. We'll free the Twins."

When her silence held, Keiro glanced up at her. She, too, stared down at her hands, and she, too, spoke to them. "I am an old woman. When I was young, when the knowing shone bright in me as it does in you . . . I dreamed of that day. That *night*, I suppose, the Long Night. When the Twins would rise, and face the Parents as equals, tear the sign of their tyranny from the sky and judge all equally. It was a good dream, and I was sure I would see it come true. Now . . . now I am old, and I am scared." She looked up then, and their eyes met. "My people are good people, but . . . are they good enough? I worry that not all of them are. Should the Twins rise, and look into the hearts of my people, I fear not all of them will walk away from the meeting. You're young still . . . I don't expect you to understand. But it grows harder, with age, to think that the greater good is worth more than the lives of those I love."

Keiro thought, unexpectedly, of Algi, the woman who had left him to walk a path of her own. A pagan, she would likely be struck down should the Twins be freed to pull the sun from the sky. "Faith is easier," he said softly, "when the stories are only stories. I do not think there is any stopping this, Yaket—even if . . . even if we wanted to." *He didn't want to*, of course—that would be blasphemy, heresy. Keiro was not such a fool to ever speak something like that aloud. "This is beyond any of us. We can only have faith in the justice and wisdom of the Twins." Keiro touched two fingers beneath the empty space where once he'd had an eye, their gesture of shared understanding. "We two," he said, "we know." She mimicked the gesture, and though there was no less sadness in her eye, there was a small smile upon her lips.

They walked together from the grass, a strange peace made once more, a deeper understanding strung through the space between them.

A large crowd was still gathered around Saval, listening to him tell a story. Others had moved away to cook or clean or otherwise tend to the tribe's needs, but Keiro could see even these listening with half an ear. The only one not enthralled was Saval's attendant, sitting away from the crowd and methodically shredding stalks of grass. With a small frown, Keiro left Yaket to her tribe and went instead to crouch next to the man.

"I don't believe I learned your name," he said softly, so as not to disturb the story.

The man muttered something under his breath before saying, louder, "Nerrin." His voice had a touch of music to it, and when he turned, very briefly, to look fully at Keiro, he was shocked to see a woman's soft features. The attendant had spoken so little that he—*she*—hadn't drawn any attention to herself . . . not even enough for a proper glance, it seemed. Keiro looked at her now with enough intensity to make up for the oversight.

She had the look of the Highlands about her: tall, black-haired, sharp-featured. It was strange to see a Highlander in black robes; they tended to be as passionate about their one God as Fiaterans were about the Parents or the Twins, depending on who you asked. "You're a long way from home, Nerrin."

"I go where the cappo goes." A strange shudder rippled through her, despite the heat. Her pupils were so wide that he could hardly see any color around them.

Frowning, Keiro reached out a hand to touch her shoulder. "Are you all right?"

She flinched away, another shudder rolling through her. "Forgive me. I . . . I'm not feeling myself." She got to her feet, something that seemed to take more effort from her than it should have, and went stumbling away into the grass.

Keiro was not the sort of man to go prying into others' lives . . . but something about Nerrin tickled a faint memory, and left a heavy taste lingering in the back of his throat. He rose, and quietly followed the woman through the grass stalks.

Nerrin was kneeling amid the grass, her back to Keiro, oblivious to his approach. As Keiro watched, great convulsions shook her, and a clench-toothed scream broke the silence of the grass. She crumpled as though her bones had turned to water, and lay trembling upon the ground. Watching with hanging jaw, Keiro saw a small jar roll from her loose fingers.

The near-forgotten memory flickered through Keiro's mind: a madman, or a man driven mad, clutching to a preacher's robes as she held a little jar just like that one. That was after the madman . . . the mage . . . had struck down his own father with a bolt of fire.

Keiro knelt by Nerrin's side, reached out slowly to cradle the woman's shaking head. "What has been done to you?" Keiro asked, half curiosity and half horror.

"I go where the cappo goes." The same words she'd said before, bursting from her mouth as though from long habit, the cadence of a mantra. When her eyes opened, peering up at Keiro with vague confusion, they no longer looked so crazed as they had before.

"Nerrin . . . what are you?"

"I am the cappo's loyal servant." These words, too, had the sound of rote, though they were said almost tiredly, as if they were a thing that weighed her down.

"You're a mage?"

"Yes." Nerrin pushed herself away from Keiro, up to sitting, one hand held against her head.

Keiro reached for the little earthenware jar, careful not to touch any of the black muck within it. "And this . . . ?"

Nerrin's eyes went wide, and she snatched the jar from Keiro's hand, looking ready to spit like a cat. She quickly calmed herself, one hand finding the jar's discarded lid and pressing it into place, making the jar disappear within her robe. "A private matter."

There was a heaviness in Keiro's heart. "Nerrin, I have been away from Raturo, away from Fiatera, for a long while. I do not claim to know how things have changed since my leaving. But . . . I have seen your like before. A mage who was, I believe, twisted against his will. I don't know why. But . . . if you—"

Nerrin held up a hand to halt Keiro. "I am the cappo's loyal servant." She spoke the words firmly, but her eyes . . . Keiro did not know her well enough to read her, but in any person he did know well, he would have said there was pleading in those eyes. Nerrin would say no more; she merely rose, and walked from Keiro, leaving him alone in the grass.

Keiro's heart ached for the woman, ached with not knowing the truth or how to help, ached with a dull anger that *something* was being done to mages . . . and, beneath those whirling emotions, rang a single clear thought: *a mage would be a useful thing indeed.*

Keiro couldn't stop thinking of Nerrin—or, more accurately, he couldn't stop wondering how long it would be before she became as twisted as the last mage he had seen. If Saval—brash, thoughtless Saval—had brought danger to the plainswalkers, Keiro vowed the man would pay for it. Keiro was not a violent man, but he was protective, and the plainswalkers were as close to him as family—he would not see them come to any harm.

Dark thoughts, for a dark night. Keiro sat amid the grass, staring at the hanging stars, Sororra's Eyes staring back from their place above the horizon. He wondered how much she saw through them, or if that was only an old legend. All the half-believed legends had been proven true, so far. Why not this one, too? Keiro raised his hand in a sardonic salute, a humorless smile plastered on his face—and regretted it immediately, burying his head in his arms.

He felt useless. If Saval was here, one of the Ventallo, what need would the Twins have of him anymore? With Yaket keeping her tribe from aiding the Twins, Keiro had been the gods' best—their *only*—hope for freedom, but a much better hope had been dropped right into their laps. Saval could bring all the Fallen, unlike an apostate. Saval had proven himself enough to be raised to Ventallo. Saval had the aid of a mage . . .

For the first time in years, Keiro's feet did not itch with the need to walk. He had found a home, a purpose, happiness. He didn't want to leave it all, but it was growing more and more apparent that he was not needed, did not belong. He might need to take up his walking ways again soon, and the thought held little appeal.

Keiro lifted his head, stared back into Sororra's Eyes. So be it. He would leave, if that was the way things were to be . . . but he would not leave the tribe in danger. There was that ringing certainty in him: *the mage must be dealt with.* He stood, and his steps were firm as he walked back to the tribehome.

They were sleeping, save for the shift of sentries who nodded to Keiro as he passed. He moved carefully through the tribe, feet quiet with practice, and stopped next to one of the dark-shrouded forms. Nerrin flinched when he touched her shoulder, eyes snapping wide, panic written briefly through them. Keiro held open his empty hands and the panic faded, replaced with confusion. "Will you walk with me?" he asked her, keeping his voice low so as not to wake the others, so as not to disturb Saval, who slept a few lengths away.

Nerrin half sat, her gaze flickering between Keiro and distant Saval. "I . . . I shouldn't . . ."

"There are a few hours left in the night. We'll be back before he even wakes." Still she hesitated, speaking so softly to herself that he couldn't hear the words. "Please, Nerrin. I would like to know you better."

After a last, long look at Saval, she placed her hand into Keiro's, let him pull her to her feet. Relieved, he led her back into the grass.

They walked in silence at first—or relative silence, for Nerrin's muttering grew more pronounced, though Keiro still couldn't make out any of the words. He waited until they were a good distance from the tribehome, where they couldn't be heard or stumbled upon, and then he sat, motioning for Nerrin to join him. She crumpled like he'd pulled out her lynchpin, but her long limbs arranged themselves into a position that didn't exactly look uncomfortable, so he let be. Above the waving grass-tips, Sororra's Eyes watched them, a reddish cast to the starlit night.

"I spent a good deal of time in the Highlands," Keiro told her. "You were born there, yes? You have the look of a full Highlander."

"Yes," she said, nothing more. Her eyes were fixed on him as unwaveringly as Sororra's Eyes, which was a touch unsettling.

"Where were you born? I may have passed through your village."

"Sertorat, near the Montevellese border."

"I don't think I know it—I never did make it too near to Montevelle. Will you tell me about it?"

Her descriptions were at first stilted, flat, as though she were reading from a page she was translating at the same time. But with more encouragement and gentle prodding, her words began to flow more freely, more naturally, and her eyes lost some of their unsettling hyperfocus. It was as he'd hoped: getting her talking made her seem more like a person than a puppet. There was nothing spectacular about her village or her life before going to learn at the Academy, but the longer she talked of it, the more passion filled her voice, the more memories made her eyes light. Keiro prodded her with every question he could think of—anything to keep her talking.

"You had *five* cats?"

"It wasn't intentional! They just kept showing up at our door, and my mother had a soft heart for them. Though it might have been because I kept leaving food out at night . . ."

"Climbing the tree was how you broke your leg?"

"No, climbing the tree was how I broke my *arm*—the leg happened when I was running home to tell mother about my arm and tripped over a rock."

"And your sister, you said she was older than you—did you look up to her?"

"Oh, of course. She was only a year older, but Neira was always much smarter, much more responsible, much more *driven*. She was the one who dreamed about being a mage, about getting into the Academy—I only wanted it because she did, because I wanted to be like her." Nerrin sighed. "My power showed sooner and stronger than hers did . . . I think she resented me for that. When it was clear that it was time to take me to the Academy for testing, my parents insisted Neira come, too—it was a long trip from our home to the Academy, and they didn't want to make it again in a month or a year or however long until Neira's power inevitably rose. So we went to the Academy, together in everything. The masters accepted me right away—with the way my power was manifesting, it was clear I had the potential. But Neira . . . They said her power would never grow, that she was already as strong as she would ever be . . . and it wasn't enough, not even close. She'd never be a mage." Nerrin folded her arms atop her knees, rested her chin on top of them, and stared into the grass, seeing a different time, a different place. "That alone broke her heart, but that wasn't the end of it. She didn't have enough power to join the Academy, but she had enough power to be dangerous, if she was left as she was. It happens more often than the masters would like to admit."

When she paused, seemed like she wouldn't go on, Keiro prompted gently, "What does?"

"They had to lock off her power. Sever her consciousness from it, essentially. She'd never be able to access her power, and it would never be able to manifest. It was to keep her safe, to keep everyone safe. An untrained mage is an incredibly dangerous thing." That last had the sound of something she'd been taught to recite, someone else's words using her mouth. "It broke her, I think. I don't know. I never saw her after that. I think she would have run away sooner, before they'd locked her off, but they didn't give her any time. They told her what had to be done and then they did it, didn't give her any time to run or argue or process. It was just . . . over. And she ran off, and I never heard from her again, and I don't think my parents did either . . . though it's been years since I talked to them . . ."

Keiro's heart was loud in his own ears. He'd been circling so carefully toward this moment, loosening her tongue with inconsequential things so that she wouldn't think to stop talking when he asked the real questions. "You haven't talked to them since you were taken to Raturo?" He was guessing, but it felt an even better guess after all that she'd told him—Nerrin had loved her life, loved her home. He didn't think she would have left it by choice.

"No," she said softly. "Not since then."

"When were you taken?"

"Three years ago. I was going home to see them . . . my parents . . . I'd finished my training two years earlier and I'd decided to go back to Sertorat, to stay there, to make a life. But on the road . . . they . . . they . . ." Her hands were wrapped around her elbows, but Keiro could see how they shook, see the tightness in her knuckles.

Keiro ached, but was also certain he couldn't stop. *Not now, not when he was so close to knowing. He needed to know what Saval was doing, what all the Fallen were doing to mages to twist their minds, and why.* If he knew what had been done to her, maybe he could help her . . .

Nerrin dropped her face into her arms, but not before he saw the tears in her eyes. Even thinking of it brought her to tears—how much worse would it hurt her, if he forced her to speak of it? How much more of a monster was he willing to be? *It would be for the best, though, for the greater good, if he pressed her just a little further—there was no knowing how much her knowledge might help, and her pain would fade after time.* Hurting her now, briefly, might help Keiro learn how to free the Twins, might tell him the Fallen's plans, might make him useful once more . . .

His own voice shook, as badly as the hand he rested on Nerrin's shoulder. "I'm sorry," he said, and she leaned against him when he put his arms around her. Keiro held her as she wept and muttered, and he said nothing more. No more questions. *It was a foolish moment of weakness* . . . but Keiro couldn't bring himself to press her further. He held her until her madness turned him into a monster in her eyes, and then he simply sat as close as she would let him until the vision passed.

He was still unneeded, and this night had taught him nothing to make him useful. Nothing had changed. Nothing *would* change, if he were to leave the Plains—their lives would carry on as though he had never been there, never mattered.

Keiro stood, and he held his hand down to Nerrin. "Will you come with me?" he asked. She stared at his hand for a very long time before carefully placing her fingers inside his.

There was a place among the waving grass sea, an irregular circle of shorter grass and flowering plants that, during the day, was a beautiful sight. At night, the flowers closed their petals and the place swam with shadow, and it looked like nothing special, nothing to draw a traveler. Poret had first brought him here, her eyes shining.

Keiro stopped at the edge of the clearing, and with Nerrin at his side, her fingers clutched tightly around his, he swept out his other arm, ran it across the tops of the hip-high plants. It started slowly: dim blue lights winking to life, growing brighter, multiplying. Butterflies rose like scattered clouds, disturbed from their resting places, and the edges of their wings glowed blue.

Keiro watched Nerrin, watched wonder and uncertainty war on her face. "Is this . . ." She reached her hand out toward one of the fluttering insects, curled her fingers back before she touched it. "Is this real?"

"This is real, Nerrin," Keiro said softly, gently. He released her fingers and, with both hands held out at his sides, he walked into the clearing. The plants tickled against his legs and his palms, and the butterflies rose around him in a glowing squall. Grinning, he turned back to face Nerrin, butterflies swirling between them.

Her first step was hesitant, as though she thought she was stepping into a pool of fire. Maybe that *was* what she thought, what she saw. But she did take a careful step, and where the butterflies had begun to settle, they rose once more, brushing against her so that they drew a breathy cry from her mouth. Another step, her hands reaching before her, and another. Through the swirling blue, Keiro thought he saw one of the butterflies land on her outstretched hand, saw joy spread over her face. Her steps grew more certain, and then she was running, hands and feet stirring the glowing insects, and she ran laughing through the cloud of them.

Watching Nerrin run through the butterflies, Keiro made a decision. Maybe the Twins and the tribe didn't need him, now that they had Saval; maybe Keiro truly was an outcast who didn't belong. But at least he wasn't alone in that. Nerrin was just as far from her home, farther even, and had suffered worse than Keiro. He didn't know if there was a way to help her, or if he would ever learn the secret of her madness, but this he could do: make her life here a little less bleak, a little less frightening. It was a small thing, but it wasn't nothing. It was enough to make it worth staying.

CHAPTER EIGHTEEN

S cal stood before the three black-robed preachers. They stared at him in the rising dark, and he stared back.

He had never quarreled with preachers before. In his long traveling he had crossed paths with some, but they had left him in peace. He had returned the same courtesy to them. True, they were a threat to the Parents—but a vague one, a distant one. As great a threat as the horse-worshipers beyond the longest river. Only a threat in that they believed different things, but they were, when it came to it, people as any others. Traveling with Joros had only proved to Scal that a preacher was not a thing to fear.

Scal spread his hands to show they were empty. "Peace to you. I mean no harm."

The preacher who had spoken laughed, a sound of surprise and suspicion mixed. "Big man like you could do plenty of harm with a finger, but I wager there may be more of me than there is of you. What's your name, brother?"

"I am Scal. I . . . I have been traveling a long time."

"Alone?" one of the others asked. A woman, gray hair and nervous eyes. "The road isn't safe for a man alone."

The first man laughed again, his broad belly shaking. "For us, maybe—but look at him! Man like that has nothing in the world to fear."

"Then wouldn't it be wise for us to fear him?"

The broad man fixed his gaze on the youngest of the preachers, a boy with splotchy skin and hair bright as fire. "What say you, Herrit? Is it wiser to fear a stranger in the night, or welcome all company?"

The boy glanced nervously to Scal, who was beginning to step slowly backward, hoping to move back through the trees. More disconcerted by their talk and their regard, than their presence.

The boy said, "In the night, all men are strangers, their faces hidden." His voice broke, the voice of near manhood. "In the night, we should greet every man as though he were a brother . . . for he may be."

"Good, Herrit!" the broad man said, eyes near to disappearing as his skin folded around a grin. He turned back to Scal, made motion to the empty space at his side. "Forgive us, brother. A mentor must take every opportunity to teach. Join us, please. I don't doubt the open road holds no fear for you, but the nights grow cold. We have no fire to share—" that pulled soft laughter "—but we make for good company."

Scal halted and, after the passing of a few beats, stepped forward to take the place at the broad man's side. Their eyes all were on him. Curious, and somewhat fearful despite their words. Still, they had spoken true. Scal was a man who had nothing to fear, and there was a comfort in the nearness of bodies. In the soft sound of breathing that was not only his.

"I am Berno," the broad man said. "Herrit is the mouse there, squeaking on occasion. Zenora, of course, is our bodyguard."

"Har har, fat man," the old woman said. Her hands shook, wrinkled skin and bones like birds, but she made an obscene gesture at Berno clear enough.

"You said your name was Scal?" Berno asked, and when he nodded the broad man went on carefully, "You seem to be . . . a long way from home."

"I have been traveling a long time."

"Yes, you did say that . . . What brings you to the warmlands?"

Scal looked to his feet, to avoid their staring. "There is nowhere else for me."

"Berno, leave him be," the woman Zenora chided. "Strangers in the night may wish to *stay* strangers."

Berno huffed out a heavy breath. "Twins' bones, woman, I'm only being friendly! A man decides to sit with strangers, he must expect curiosity. I don't doubt he's just as many questions for us!"

"Which, you'll note, *he's* polite enough to keep behind his teeth."

They bickered, with the familiarity of those who had long traveled together. It put him in mind, almost, of Joros and Vatri, but their bickering had held a sharper edge. Not the gentle jabs of old friends, but words meant to cut. Voices honed by danger and mistrust.

The boy scooted closer to Scal, and beneath the sound of the other two squabbling, he asked, "You're a Northman?"

Scal nodded.

"Is it really true you fear nothing?"

"I do not know if it is so for all Northmen," Scal said.

Herrit's eyes were wide in his face, a green that was striking beneath his red hair. His mouth was as wide, and his lips barely moved as he breathed, "How?"

Scal did not answer right away, trying to find the words. Trying to decide if they were words to be shared. "My death waits for me in the true snows," he finally said. "Only they can take me. The only thing a man should fear is death. There are no snows here, and so I have nothing to fear."

"Only death?" Berno interrupted. He had ceased his quibbling with Zenora, had leaned in to hear the end of Scal's words. "A wise man fears more than death, m'boy!"

"There's snow here," Herrit said. His brow was wrinkled, confusion plain.

"Not true snow. Not killing snow."

Berno huffed. "Herrit." The boy's back snapped straight. Eyes darting to fix on the broad man. "What fears should all men have?"

The boy sucked on his lip, brow wrinkling again, though this time with deep thought. Unexpectedly, Scal was reminded of himself. He and a boy named Brennon had sat at Parro Kerrus's feet and answered his questions. *Philosophy*, the priest had said. *Morality. Ethics. Just because the world has abandoned us, that doesn't mean we should all turn savage.* Brennon had always been better at those lessons. Perhaps it was the taint of Scal's blood. Perhaps simply that words came less swift to his tongue. Most often, he had listened to them as they argued a point. Sat in the warmth of the everflame, wrapped by voices sometimes raised, though never in anger. Strong wills, quick minds. Scal did not realize, until that moment, how much he had missed those debates.

"A smart man," said Herrit, "should fear sharp things."

"Explain," Berno prompted.

"It's an animal thing. All animals fear the sharp-clawed predator, and what are men if not animals? What are men with weapons if not sharp-clawed predators?"

Zenora snorted. "There are sharp things that are not weapons, boy. Hunger can be a sharp thing. Disappointment. Love can be the sharpest thing there is."

"Men should fear the abstract," Berno muttered.

Herrit's face turned a red as deep as his hair. "All men should fear love, surely. But it's a different fear. A sharp weapon means a threat, pain, death. Love is . . . a gentler thing, a well-laid trap."

"Says the boy." Zenora laughed, and Berno joined her. The boy's flush deepened, shoulders brushing his ears, eyes fixed to the ground. Zenora waved a hand at him, still chuckling. "Come, boy, enlighten us. What else should a man fear?"

A small silence fell as the sun dropped from the sky. The copse darkened, barely enough to make out faces, eyes. Still, Scal saw Herrit's jaw jut forward, and there was defiance wound through his next words. "The dark."

The two preachers stiffened. Shrouded in the thing the boy had named, their faces were hidden but disquiet was written in the dimly seen lines of their bodies. Softly, Berno asked, "How's that?"

"Anything can hide in the dark," Herrit said, and the strains of his voice wove around the lowering night. "It gives shelter to all manner of things, good and bad, and with no light there's no way to tell the difference. How could a man not fear it?" His silence fell again, a thing of shadows and spiders. "But that's the thing. In the dark, everything but that fear is stripped away. We're reduced to simple things, easy to understand. We're all made equal."

After a long while, Berno muttered, "Remind me to send you to Tressein when we get back."

"You did well, boy," Zenora said. There was something like tenderness in her voice. Scal had not known her for long, but the tone seemed not to fit her well. "Now, to sleep with you. Unless . . ." Her voice dropped, low and dangerous. A growl, almost. "Unless you fear the dark?"

Berno laughed, a sound loud enough to wake birds. He laughed over their angry chatter, and after a time, Zenora joined him. Menace gone from her voice, eyes flashing in starlight. Herrit's laugh took a hesitant step from his mouth, quickly retreated. In the darkness, though they could not see it, Scal felt the corners of his mouth turn up.

Amid the muttering of birds and lingering chuckles, Scal lay upon the ground. It was cold beneath his cheek, but it did not touch him. He fell asleep to the soft sounds of breathing, and slept more soundly than he had since before Berring. Before Aardanel. Before the killing-cold North, before wandering Fiatera with his sword, before Valastaastad, the village that floated on a cliff of ice. He slept as well as he had slept on the warped wooden floor of Parro Kerrus's small hut, with a warm fire and a thin blanket and snores to shake the walls.

They woke with the sun, and the black-clad preachers moved with the silent surety of routine. The boy fetching wood, the woman stacking tinder and twigs, the man filling a dented pot with water from a half-empty skin.

Scal sat in silence, watching them. He should rise. Leave. This was not a place he belonged. These were not people for him. There was a flamedisk hung around his neck, and they wore robes of black. After a time, he did rise. Joined Herrit, filling his arms full of wood.

The preachers made a simple porridge, thick and lumpy. Filled their bowls and, without words, handed the dented pot to Scal. There was porridge still—some burned to the bottom, and not much of it left, but none of them had taken much. Had given up some of their own portion, that he might have some. Scal's throat was thick as he ate. The porridge, of course.

After they had all finished, quiet scraping and chewing and heavy swallowing, Berno was the first to break the silence. "Where are you bound, m'boy?" His eyes were honest, fixed on Scal with blue intensity.

Scal shook his head, lifted his shoulders. "I do not know."

"Well, we're headed south. If you've any business in that direction, you're welcome to travel with us." Berno smiled, a grin broad as his belly. "I know *you've* nothing to fear, but the boy, here . . . well, I don't doubt having the company of a big bear of a man would put his mind at ease."

Scal's throat grew thick again, and this time he did not have the excuse of the porridge. He looked down at his hands, clasped in his lap. Softly, he said, "I have nothing to give."

Fingers touched his knee. Next to his, Zenora's hand was

small as a broken-winged bird before a cat. Scal had big hands, strong hands. A killer's hands. Stained with old blood, stained so deep they would never be clean.

When she spoke, there was that strange soft note in Zenora's voice once more. "We're not asking for anything."

There was a freedom in those words. They did not want to shape him to their own will, to make him something he was not. They did not want him to be anything. They saw him, silent and serious, and did not mind the shadows in his eyes, the deep stains on his hands. He simply *was*, and that was the only thing that mattered.

"Yes," Scal said. "I am going south."

They walked from the copse, and Scal trailed in their wake. Before they left the winter-growing trees behind, Scal opened his fingers and let the thing he held fall to the ground. Swallowed by brush, swallowed by snow. The witch's sight faded from his eyes as the seekstone left his fingers. He would go south, but not because of any pull. Not because of any need. He would go south because it was a thing he, and he alone, had chosen to do.

CHAPTER NINETEEN

The bars of Rora's cell were so cold they stung, the one time she touched them, and when she yanked back her hands she left skin stuck to the metal. After that she didn't go near the bars, curling up on the ground and holding her blood-spotted hands against her chest. She didn't think she'd ever be warm again.

Rora figured it must've been Anddyr. The first time she'd seen him, he'd made an invisible wall around her and Aro, one that'd turned back thrown things just like her dagger had been turned back from the black-robes. Since then, she'd seen him call up fire with a wave of his fingers and roast a whole village with a finger-wave not too much different, so she didn't expect it'd be much harder for the witch to make the fiery pain that'd burned through her chest. If the witch'd had time to make cahoots with the black-robes, she bet that was plenty damn time for him to tell 'em all about how she was a twin, which made at least two betrayals. The number changed the angrier she got.

She'd known she shouldn't trust him, but that was the trouble of thinking like pack. You didn't betray pack, not ever, that was why Tare'd cut off her ear and still hated her. Pack was everything, but Joros and the witch weren't her pack. Easy to forget that, but it was true. Still, the betrayal stung.

If she ever got out of the mountain, ever got warm again, she made a promise to herself: she'd use her warmed-up hands to wrap around Joros's throat. She wasn't one for killing with her bare hands, but if anyone'd earned it, it was him. The witch she'd give a quick knife in the eye, so he didn't have time to wiggle his fingers to stop her. Those were the warmest thoughts she could think up, in the long, cold dark while they kept her waiting.

Those were better thoughts than the ones about the knives. For a little while, she'd had a real pack again, even if she'd forced her way into it. She'd had a pack, and she'd got enough trust to lead some of 'em, and then she'd gotten 'em killed. Hadn't been hilt more'n two weeks, and the first real leading she'd done had ended in death. She tried not to think about it, because the sad and the guilt would drown her if she let them.

She'd spent time in cells before—never too long, that was the good thing about having a pack—and she'd figured out it was mostly just waiting. Waiting for the stomp of iron-shod boots and a jailer to swing open the door, waiting for the whisper of feet and the louder whisper of metal tools scraping in the lock, waiting for a door or a hole to open where it didn't look like there should be one, waiting for any way to get past the bars 'cause once you weren't locked in, the rest was easy as a blade. All you had to do was wait long enough for an opportunity to throw yourself at.

But this was different, near as different as you could get. They'd left her in the dark, darker than any place she'd ever been before, dark as somewhere that'd never once seen a touch of fire. That was enough to make her twitch, but the quiet was maybe worse. No other prisoners, no jailers in a faraway room, no drip of water in a damp place. There wasn't even the soft scritch of rat-feet—it was too cold for rodents. After a while her stomach started filling the quiet—mumbles at first, like something huge being shook awake and grumping about it, then rolling roars that near pulled scared screams out of Rora before she realized it was her and not monsters in the dark. No one came to check on her, no one came to feed her, no loose bricks fell away on a tunnel just big enough a small person could wriggle through, no opportunities to escape.

Then the eyeless black-robes came.

One of 'em carried a torch, though she couldn't imagine how the light could make much difference to them. After so long in the dark, it burned at Rora's eyes, made it look like she was weeping like an old woman—still, she'd take it, for the way it pushed back the blanket of shadows.

One of them stepped forward, smooth and confident for all she had no eyes to see, and stuck her arms between the bars. She was holding a small basket of food and a jug of water, and Rora couldn't decide which she wanted more. She wasn't stupid, though. She stayed where she was, curled up, shielding her eyes with one hand. The black-robe set down the food and drink inside the bars and stepped back to the others, the line of five of them, all with no eyes on their faces and red Eyes sewn onto their chests.

The first one to speak was the old man, the one Joros'd wanted her to kill more'n any other. He held the torch, and even if she hadn't already known he was the head black-robe, everything about him said "packhead." "Tell me your name, child."

"I'm not a child," Rora croaked at him, even knowing it was something a kid would say.

"As you say. Your name?"

"Tare," she said, because it was the first name she thought of that wasn't her own.

"Didn't your mother teach you not to lie?"

"Never had a mother."

Another old black-robe stepped forward, the pits of her eyes new-made and crusted with pus. "Where is your brother?"

"Never had one of those either." The light, small as it was, was making her feel a little braver, or at least a little less scared. "You should just let me go or kill me, 'cause I don't see this ending any other way."

The head black-robe rumbled out a laugh. "Then you've a poor imagination, child."

He turned away from her, him with the torch held above his head, and the rest of 'em turned, too. The shadows crept back in, starting at the edges of her cell but creeping fast, near ready to swallow her up. "Wait!" She didn't mean to call out, wouldn't've if she'd thought about it, but the word exploded out of her as the light took her little bit of bravery away with it. One of 'em stopped, a woman, the holes in her face staring at Rora as the torch kept going, pulling the shadows behind it. Rora held her breath, staring back at the eyeless woman until the light was gone, and there was no telling if she was alone or if the black-robe had turned and gone up the tunnel, too . . . In the cold and the quiet and the dark, she could pretend the chattering of her teeth was just from the cold.

If there'd been any light, she could've waited it out, knowing her eyes'd adjust eventually, knowing she'd be able to see if there was a darker shape in all the dark, if the woman was still there. But there wasn't any light, and her eyes wouldn't ever be able to see through that kind of dark. So she waited long as she could, but her voice burst out of her again: "What d'you want?" She managed to keep her voice low so it wouldn't crack, made it a little like a snarl so it sounded less scared. Then she held her breath, to see if there was anyone there to answer.

A light swelled like a stick just catching fire, slow and growing, not enough to make her eyes burn like the torch, but still plenty enough to surprise her. The light kept growing, brightening the cell piece by piece—showing the hand the fire was sitting in and boiling black smoke, sending light crawling up the black-robed woman's face and making dark pits out of her empty eyes. She was right at the bars, her face boxed in by the metal, her arm on Rora's side of the cell as she held the glowing, strange fire. Rora shrank back from her, shrank back from the black smoke sneaking across the floor toward her feet. "I want you," the woman said, and a small smile touched her lips. "I am the shadows, and I know your name. *Rora.*"

Instinct put Rora's hand to her belt, grabbing for any of the daggers that weren't there. Her heart was flying around in her chest, and there was a rushing in her ears that sounded like *To the ends of the earth* . . .

"Oh, don't worry." The woman was whispering, but her voice still cut through Rora. "Your secrets are safe with me. A shadow can hide so very much."

"Who are you?" Rora demanded, and it did come out shaking this time.

"I am Neira. My name, freely given. We are not the enemy, Rora—or, at least, not all of us are. You, of all people, should know that a shadow is a thief's finest friend."

"I'm not a thief." It was the only one of those she could think to answer, and the lie came easy—any good thief learned early on you had to be able to say that with a straight face.

"No?" Neira's other hand stuck through the bars, and in her weird hand-light, Rora could see she was holding a dagger, Rora's dagger, the one with the big broken gem in its hilt. There was fresh blood along the edge of the blade, shining like a line of jewels.

It'd been so long ago that Rora'd stopped thinking of it as stolen; the dagger'd been hers near as far back as her memory went, or at least as far back as she wanted to remember things. But she supposed she had stolen it, taken it after she'd pushed it into a man's heart. Her first kill, her first dagger, her first taste of what power and fear and blood could do. She thought about leaping forward, grabbing for the dagger, wrapping her fingers around the blade if she had to . . . but she didn't really want to move, or maybe couldn't. Sometimes those were the same thing.

"What was his name." It wasn't a question; it was just like a hand in the middle of your back, pushing you through a crowd.

Near whispering, too, she said back, "Nadaro."

"Just so. Remember the shadows, Rora."

A big shiver rolled through Rora, the cold shaking her and ripping her eyes away from the empty holes in Neira's face. She'd forgot about the black smoke boiling out of Neira's hand, creeping across the floor of the cell and snaking around Rora's ankles . . . she'd forgot about it, and in the time she hadn't been looking at it, it'd started snaking up her body—over her hands and up her arms, around and around her chest, circling around her throat, crawling over her face, between her lips, sneaking careful down her throat—

Rora lashed out, even though there wasn't much you could do to fight against smoke, scrambled up to her feet spitting like smoke was something you could spit out. Neira was just watching her, her hands steady holding the weird flame, holding Rora's stolen dagger. Rora was careful not to look at her empty eyes, stared at the woman's chin instead. "What are you?" she asked.

Neira smiled, all sad innocence. "I am the shadows. I am the unsleeping dark, and I know your name." Her head tilted to the side, the pits of her eyes staring at Rora, and Rora had to keep herself from staring back, from getting lost again. "I think we will meet again, Rora, sister of Aro. I hope you will remember how far a shadow can stretch." Neira closed her fingers, and the light died a sudden death.

Rora held her breath again, didn't start breathing until she heard footsteps moving away, gone. She slid slowly back down to the floor, feeling only the cold, no smoke twisting over her skin. She pressed one hand against her throat, wondering if she'd feel the smoke there, or if it'd already worked its way to her stomach or lungs, or if she'd just imagined it all . . .

It seemed like more time had passed than it actually had, probably because her heart had done more thumping in the last few minutes than it had in the hour before. But she remembered one of the black-robes setting a basket inside the bars, and even if her stomach was full of smoke, it didn't seem like smoke did a lot to stop the hungry twisting in her belly. Trapped in a cell, there were more important things to think about than one of the crazies in this mad place.

She crawled along the floor, her hands and knees gone so numb she didn't feel the cold, or the press of stone. Her head bumped into the cell bars first, and then she groped around until her bloodless hands bumped against the water jug. It tipped over with a sound like glass breaking in another room, but it was just ice snapping as the water flooded over the floor. She lost most of it, and what she did drink sat in her belly like a lump and really did make her shiver, so hard it made her muscles hurt. The basket held some bread and some cheese hard enough she could barely bite into it, but it wasn't frozen, and that was enough to make her insides feel a little warmer.

Next thing she did was piss into the empty water jug, which was no easy thing in the dark, but it was better than dirtying a corner when she didn't know how long she'd be stuck in the cell. That was what she set out to fix after that, though—getting out.

They'd put a cloth napkin in the food basket, which was nice of them, but stupid. She wrapped it around one of her hands, the right one that'd never been as good since she'd broken the arm as a kid. When it came down to it, she'd rather save her left hand, the good hand. She stuck her wrapped-up hand through the cell bars, groped around with it. All the movement'd started to warm her hands up some, made her skin prickle with the blood rushing back, but her hand froze right back up again the longer she held it against the bars. Felt as useful as a dead fish at the end of her arm. Finally she thumped it against something wider than an iron bar, and she knew she was probably lying to herself, but she thought her numb fingers felt the shape of a keyhole.

After that she spent a long while breathing on her hands and sticking them under her arms—anything to get 'em warm again, so she could actually make her fingers move. It hurt like a bloody hell when they warmed up, and Tare'd been right when she'd said Rora was a baby about pain, but there was nothing else in the cold and dark and lonely to do besides wait until she could make a fist and straighten her fingers back out, each little movement like a hundred needles.

She started ripping up the basket, which was made of wove-together rope but came apart easy enough. She got a few good pieces of it, a mix of long and short and thin and fat, trusting her fingers on the sizes. She dipped each of 'em into the piss-jug, letting 'em soak for a bit before she laid them out on the ground. Then it was more warming her hands up while she waited until the piss had frozen the rope into straight, hard pieces. She wrapped her hand with the napkin, the left hand this time, leaving enough of her fingers out that they could move easy enough. Then she took her makeshift lock picks to the cell door.

It didn't work great, and not only because Rora'd never been great with picks. Even though her hand felt half-froze, there was enough warmth in her fingers to start to melt the frozen piss in the rope-pieces, making them go all soggy and useless as she was jamming 'em into the keyhole. A good pick was a lot more than something hard to poke a lock with, and she didn't really expect it'd work, but it felt better than doing nothing.

She tried it a few more times, soaking and freezing and picking and unfreezing, but it didn't do much good. When she saw light start to touch the floor of the tunnel, sending the shadows slinking back, she quickly hid her rope-pieces against one of the corners—they might be useless so far, but she wasn't the kind of person to give anything up.

She waited near the bars until the torch appeared, with the black-robes under it. Neira wasn't there this time, which Rora counted a blessing. But there were two extra people this time, and they shook her, a little, once the light-tears cleared from her eyes enough to let her really see them. She'd never seen twins before, save looking at herself and Aro in dirty canal water.

"She looks like you," the girl sneered to her brother, and even though Rora's short hair made her look more like a boy, she didn't really think she looked like either of 'em. These twins looked pretty young, a handful or so years younger'n Rora, probably, and they had the soft faces of kids who ate pretty well and got cleaned often and always slept long enough. Those kinds of things put less of an edge on a face, and Rora knew hers had plenty of edges.

"She looks like herself," the boy said softly. Seemed like he was careful to keep his voice a whisper in such a quiet place. His face looked young enough, but there was more age in his eyes than in near anyone else she'd ever seen. It was like the head black-robe, old as he was, had cut out his own eyes and stuck 'em on the boy's face.

"You see," the old man said, the torch above his head making dark pits in his face, "that there are more choices than leaving or death."

"If it's a choice," Rora said, "I'll take leaving, thanks."

"You can choose to bend," the head black-robe said, "or to break."

The boy was staring at Rora, and his gaze made her skin crawl for no reason she could name. Still quiet, he said, "She won't bend, not ever."

"Then she'll break. Such is the way of things. You'll want to watch her, Etarro. You'll see that fighting only puts you in a worse position at the end."

Rora snorted. "Etarro, yeah? Watch who you trust instead." She thought of the witch, how he'd practically told her not to trust him and she'd just ignored that good advice. "You can't trust anyone but yourself."

The boy blinked at her. "Not even your twin?"

She thought of sweet, simple Aro, and blinked back at the boy. "No one but yourself."

"Where is your brother?" the black-robe interrupted.

Like she would just tell him that kind of thing. "Why don't you tell me where that lying traitor is?" Rora demanded. Let him think she'd trade Aro's life for Anddyr's. She wouldn't mind if the black-robes brought the witch down to parade in front of her—she could probably reach through the bars and get her hands around his neck. At the least, swearing at the witch would make her feel better.

The head black-robe raised his eyebrows, which looked all sorts of creepy with no eyes under them. "You've fought? Have you parted ways?" His hands reached out and, even without eyes, he rested them perfectly on the little twins' shoulders. "It doesn't do for twins to be separated."

She was careful not to let anything show on her face

when she realized the black-robe thought she'd been talking about her brother when she'd said "lying bastard." One of the things Rora could do best was keep a straight face. Back in the knifeden, what felt like a whole life ago now, no one'd ever liked to play cards with her because—she guessed—it was hard to play against someone you couldn't read. "Better that he's not here," she said.

The boy, Etarro, tilted his head at her, and she got that crawling feeling again. His eyes, whole and blue, were almost worse than the empty eye sockets of the black-robes. "He's hiding," the boy said. "Hidden is better. He doesn't blame you for not trusting him. You should listen to him, though, when he finds you."

Rora was watching him close enough that, even in the little light, she saw the old black-robe's hand tighten on the boy's shoulder, saw him wince. "You shouldn't waste your words on her, Etarro. She's not worthy of them. Not yet."

The boy's words'd put a shudder in Rora, because she was pretty sure she remembered the last person who'd spoken about hiding, and it hadn't been Aro. Still, she didn't let the boy or the black-robe see that those words had had any effect on her. She threw on bravado like armor. "So you keep pet twins, hey?" she asked the head black-robe, and she spat onto the floor. It froze right away. "How well have you trained 'em? They know any tricks?"

The girl bared her teeth at Rora, was stupid enough to step close to the bars. "Let me in there and I'll show her a trick."

"You mustn't let yourself anger so easily. The weak will always try to twist the minds of the strong."

Rora laughed at that. "You know he's just using you, don't

you?" The girl snarled, so Rora turned to the boy. "You're a tool to him, that's all. How long, you think, before he decides he doesn't need you anymore?" The boy just blinked at her with his too-old eyes. "Bet that's why I'm here, isn't it? A replacement for when the two of you aren't so useful anymore."

That was when the rest of the black-robes herded the twins away, leaving only the head black-robe. "Tell me where your brother is," he said.

"Not likely."

One of the black-robes had left a basket near the old man's feet, a basket like the one Rora'd tore up, only bigger. He reached down into it and pulled up a heavy quilt, so thick and warm-looking it made Rora feel the cold all over again. "Tell me where your brother is."

"You think I'd trade him for a blanket?" she scoffed.

The head black-robe shrugged. "I think, in time, you'll realize being somewhere warm with him is better than freezing to death alone." He shook the blanket at her. "I spoke to you of options. You've seen now that you're not my only option— you would merely be a convenience. I do not need you. Tell me where your brother is, and I vow you'll both be kept in comfort and health."

Rora'd had her share of promises made and broken, and she wasn't stupid enough to let in another promise that just begged for breaking. So she stayed quiet, glaring out at the black-robe, and let the silence stretch and stretch. It'd bend, or it'd break.

The quilt slipped from the black-robe's hand, making a heavy puddle on the floor. "Freeze, then." He turned, leaving the blanket well out of arm's reach, and he took his torch and left her again, to the cold and dark and quiet.

She still tried to get the quilt, even knowing it was out of reach, pressing the folded napkin between her face and the metal bars as she swept her fingers out along the floor. She tried until the cold bars put a bone-deep ache into her shoulder, and after she gave up she just sat for a while and tried not to think too much about freezing.

She was in the middle of jabbing her rope-pieces into the lock again when she heard a sound. It was soft, but in the ghost-quiet dungeon, any noise was loud. She went still, listening hard as the sound kept on going, a scraping like dragging a body over the ground, and her heartbeat was near loud enough to drown it out.

Rora scooted slowly back to the far wall of her cell, and all the while the scraping kept going, kept getting louder and closer. Whatever it was, maybe it could be scared off . . . She let out the loudest yell she could, wordless and made half of fear, but it was sudden and loud and she near scared the piss out of herself with it. There was a yelp, a scrabble, a thump, and then only the sound of breathing—not running away, not leaving. Something that got scared, but was too stupid to run from fear.

"Who's there?" Rora demanded, 'cause animals usually had more sense than people.

More moving sounds, and then the scraping started up again, still getting closer. "One of you," a voice said, and she recognized it.

"Boy?" she asked. What was it the black-robe had called him? "Etarro."

"Yes," the boy said. She heard a heavy sound of fabric, probably him wrapping himself up with the quilt. Snide little bastard. "Rora."

That put the chill right in her. "What?" she asked, hoping she didn't sound as surprised as she felt.

"He talks about you. Whispers your name when he sleeps."

"The witch?" Anger was enough to warm her a bit, to make the surprise leak away in a trickle. "You tell him to come say my name to my face."

"You'll kill him."

"You're damn right I will."

"Then I won't let him come here. Not yet."

Rora snorted. "What, are you his new master?"

"Life binds people together unexpectedly. He and I are bound—not master and servant, but equal parts of a whole."

"How old are you?" Rora asked after a pause. The kid spoke a lot like Joros, all big words and measured paces and a tone like each sound he gave you was a gift you should be thankful for.

"Fourteen in three full moons."

And there he was, talking like a kid, counting down the days until he was one step closer to grown up. The kid was damned weird, no doubt about that. "How long since they brought you here?"

"We were born here. The mountain itself raised us as surely as any other hand."

"Gods above, so they've been twisting you your whole life. You need to get away from this place."

"We'll leave soon enough."

"Let me out of here, and I'll show you what a real life is like. I never much had the chance to be a kid, but I bet I could still show you better'n what you've been doing. I'll even let the witch live. Just get us out of here."

There was silence for a while, long enough she thought maybe the boy'd slipped away somehow while she'd been talking. "You told me not to trust anyone."

"Yeah, I did. No one but yourself. So be truthful with yourself, that's the most important thing. You can't really be happy here."

That quiet again, and maybe he had the thoughts to back up his big words. "Will you be truthful with me, Rora?"

"Sure, kid. I've got no reason to lie." She'd tell him anything he needed to hear to get him to let her out.

"Tell me the honest truth, and I'll let you go. I'll even go with you. Just tell me the truth." Another pause, and she could hear the chattering of his teeth, maybe the sound of his bones clacking together under his skin. When he spoke again, he sounded a lot more like a kid than he had so far—a kid with a big, scary question that was eating away at him. "Do you ever hear them?"

"Hear who?" You had to step careful around kids with big scary questions—Aro'd had his share of them, and a wrong word was like enough to break a kid.

"The Twins."

For the first time, Rora was glad for the dark—she didn't think she could've kept a straight face for that, no matter how hard she tried. "Do you?"

"You said you'd answer my question."

She wished Aro was here—he was better with people than she was, and he always seemed to know the right thing to say. He usually told the truth, but he could lie well if he had to, and he always knew when he had to. He'd know what to say— hells, he'd probably understand the kid, make him feel safe and not so alone so that whatever answer he gave, the truth or a lie, wouldn't matter so much.

"I do," she said.

There was a sigh, loud in the empty dark. "The truth is important, Rora," he said quietly. "You should learn when to give it, but you *need* to learn when you hear it."

"The truth doesn't matter as much when you're slowly freezing to death."

"You won't die, so long as you hear the truth when it's given."

His footsteps left then, whispering across the floor and disappearing up the tunnel. The kid spoke too old, and too mysterious. There'd been a man in the Canals, who'd got hit on the head so his eyes went funny, one pupil small as a knifetip and the other so big you couldn't see any color around it. He'd started talking like the kid, spewing up nonsense, his talking going in circles, using bigger words'n most anyone else knew, words he'd never used before in his life. They'd all started listening to his nonsense, though, after he babbled something about Firren with black eyes and hair like snakes. They'd found Firren drowned, her long hair caught and tied up in canal weeds, and two fat leeches on her eyes. They'd all *definitely* listened after he said rats' claws were enough to kill a dog, because then some spy from Rat Pack that'd been hiding in Whitedog had gone on a stabbing spree before sneaking back to his masters. The Far-eye, they'd called the man, and if he ever looked right at you with his mismatched eyes, you damned well listened. He'd only looked at Rora once, but he'd said something about shadows, and that was enough for her.

"Hear the truth," she muttered, but that was less helpful than rat-claws or snake-hair. She went back to the cell lock with her shitty picks, but on the way there she stumbled over something. Big and soft and still with a little warmth to it. Somehow, the kid'd gotten the quilt through the cell bars.

CHAPTER TWENTY

Tears had frozen to Anddyr's cheeks, heavy lines that drew his skin tight. His tears came away in fractured pieces when he scrubbed at his cheeks, falling like a sparkling storm onto his black robe. Breath came hard through his nose, and he found snot frozen on his upper lip. He was disgusting, an utter mess.

He peered through the sheet of ice before him, thick enough to distort the chamber beyond, but still offering a good enough view of the place. It was clearly empty. That was wrong . . . he knew that much, though his mind and memory were slow coming back from the skura-haze. There was something important he needed to be doing, something he needed to have his full awareness for. It was all about the timing; Cappo Joros had said that again and again . . . the timing was vital. They'd carefully planned Anddyr's dosing of skura, so that he could shrug away his madness and be coherent for . . . whatever it was. He squinted through the ice, knowing there should be people out there. If he could just see someone, he knew that would spark his memory. Here he was, coherent and ready to act, needing only to be pointed in the proper direction. Why in God's name was his head so damned fuzzy? It usually took a moment or two for his mind to readjust, to get a good grasp on sanity, but memory was proving more elusive than usual. It must be the timing . . . yes, the cappo had told him it was all about the timing, that he'd have to be strong and fight against the madness, so that he could be ready when the time came.

But he hadn't . . . no, he'd been weak, and he'd stolen skura, scrabbled too soon after sanity and poisoned himself in the process. That had thrown the timing off . . .

Memory hit him then, like a fist to the gut.

The Cavern of the Falls, Rora and her doubt and all the hidden knives. He'd gone to shelter behind the Icefall, tucking himself out of the way so he wouldn't ruin the surprise . . . and so Rora wouldn't see him descend deeper into madness. It had clawed at him, the rising skura-hunger and insidious insanity that came with it, and the deeper twisting scream of the un-bonded skura inside him—but all he'd needed to do was hold a cloaking for a while, keeping Rora and the knives hidden until the moment was right. He could cast a cloaking without thinking, which was good, since rational thought leaked away quickly. He'd sat behind the ice, wedged uncomfortably in the small space Etarro had told him about, and he'd waited as the madness took bigger bites out of him. It was all the timing . . .

"You'll have to be sane once the killing starts," the cappo had said. "You'll have to be ready to do anything to help—distract the Ventallo, freeze a few feet, give one of the knives a boost of speed. You'll need to be ready for anything, and you'll need your wits about you. It has to be timed just right."

Skura was a thing of habit, an unshakable regularity. He

always waited the same amount of time between his doses, the hours trickling by. And so he'd waited, because his stolen dose had been his last, and when madness had ahold of his mind, there was no room for reasoning or logic or bravery. He'd waited, lost in madness, watching impassively as the knives were slaughtered by the hidden swordsmen he hadn't seen, hadn't thought to look for. He'd watched through a blue haze of madness and stupidity as the carefully laid plans fell to pieces. Watched the Ventallo walk away, alive. Watched Rora hurt, defeated, captured. All because of him . . .

He only got himself half-unwedged from his hiding place before his stomach burst out of his mouth. It left a foul taste, the skura much less pleasant coming back up than it had been going down. He was glad the cavern was empty, glad there was no one to witness his shame as he hung half-stuck behind the Icefall, covered in sour vomit, fighting to draw in air without retching.

It was all wrong. He should have gone quietly mad, hidden behind the Icefall, and then swept in with confidence and sanity to save the day, to save Rora. It would have worked, if he hadn't been so weak, if his fear of the cappo's orders—*Burn the leg. Learn their secrets. Kill the boy.*—hadn't twisted his stomach, twisted his mind. He'd been weak, and he'd ruined the timing, ruined everything. Because of him, Rora had been taken . . .

"There is no one," he told himself softly, "in all the world, worse than you."

Anddyr had freed his head from the space behind the Icefall, one arm and half his chest—enough that he could probably pull himself free of the icy cage. Ignoring the sick-smell surrounding him, the pain in his side where the ice held him tight, the way his breath scraped into his lungs and bubbled out his nose . . . he deserved those things, and worse. He ignored them, and pressed his body back into the ice, back into the prison he deserved. It would be easier if he just died. He would never have to feel the shame of facing Rora . . . of learning what they'd done to her . . . if they'd even let her live . . . He curled into the small, pathetic thing that he was, cocooned by the ice. The tears froze once more on his cheeks, sharp, cold lines. He left them there this time, as they hardened and drew his face tight like a mask.

He would have startled more, at the touch on his shoulder, if the ice cage had left him any room for startling. As it was, he scraped his forehead and cheek trying to turn his head enough to see out the opening of his hiding spot.

The fire-demon standing there would have startled him doubly, but again, not enough room for a proper startle. Or maybe there was, and he'd just gone so numb with cold he couldn't feel his body jerking in surprise.

Regardless, the demon took its very human hand off of Anddyr's shoulder and knelt down. Anddyr wondered if the fire-demon would melt away all the ice before burning Anddyr up, and that thought was almost enough to make him cry. The ice was so pretty. "Anddyr." There were only the pale ghost-lights, more flickering shadow than light, but they were enough for him to see the fire swirl away to reveal a boy beneath, a boy whose face he knew.

"Etarro," he croaked, the letters dropping from his mouth like larvae. A shiver rolled through Anddyr, as much as it could with no real room for movement. He would have thought his eyes too clogged with ice to allow any more tears, but they burst out of him, warm against his cold, cold cheeks. "I failed."

The hand touched his shoulder again, stayed there this time. He could feel the flesh shifting and bubbling atop his, but he couldn't flinch away. "You did," Etarro said softly. "Why did you fail, Anddyr?"

"Because I'm weak."

"Weak is what others call us. We should never say it of ourselves." Fires burned in the boy's eyes, glowing embers that made the tears on Anddyr's cheeks steam away. "You can be strong, Anddyr. I can see it in you. Do you believe that?"

Anddyr shook his head, the ice scraping away more of his skin. "No."

Etarro bowed his head, rested his cheek next to his hand on Anddyr's shoulder. It burned, where he touched, burned away the cold that the ice had clawed into Anddyr. "That makes me sad."

They sat together for a while, both their bodies shaking, Etarro's form wavering between his own and the fire-demon, burning-hot until the flames faded into the boy and the cold drew back in, a deeper burn.

"Anddyr," the boy said, "what do you want from the world?" Anddyr only shook his head, the ice shaving away at his chin. "There must be something. Everybody wants something. Don't think, just say it."

"Rora," he said.

Etarro lifted his head, ember-eyes piercing. He nodded slowly. "Do you want to be free? Free of all of this?"

Anddyr could remember, long ago, that the cappo had asked him a similar question. Then, he'd had only a vague memory of what "free" had meant, riding on horseback through the mountains, weaving spells for noblemen's children, feted at any town he graced with his presence. It had been like looking at those memories through a hole the size of a needle's point, enough to grasp the shape, the sense of them, but not able to reach out and touch them. Now . . . now the word fell like a stone into an empty well, echoing hollowly all the way down. "I don't know."

"Do you want to go back to Cappo Joros?"

Even pressed tight by the ice, Anddyr found enough room to shudder. "I am the cappo's loyal servant." Quick words, deeply engrained.

"He scares me, too," the boy whispered. He looked away, looked somewhere Anddyr couldn't follow. "If you were free," he said, "you could be with Rora."

Anddyr's tongue swept around his dry mouth, darting like a snake to lick at his lips. "I . . ."

Etarro's eyes swung back to him, burning so bright Anddyr had to squint to see the boy's face around the light. "What, Anddyr?"

"I . . . would like to be free."

The boy smiled, a soft thing, though the light fell from his eyes. "That's good, Anddyr. I can help. Do you have your skura?"

Of course he did; he knew exactly where it was, and there was enough space for one hand to find the jar, pull it free, lift it to his mouth. With the world bubbling and shifting shape, the edges of his sight writhing with monsters made of shadow and blood, it was a challenge to instead twist his arm around and give Etarro the jar.

"You'll still have to go back to Cappo Joros," the boy said as he twisted open the lid of the jar. The scent of the skura sent a river running from Anddyr's mouth, made the ice encasing him pulse like a quick-beating heart. "Anddyr," Etarro said, soft and stern, and Anddyr tore his eyes from the jar. "You'll have to go back, but it will be different. You won't belong to him anymore. You'll be free." The boy reached out, his hand shaking in the cold, and pressed his fingers to Anddyr's cheek. "But free is something you have to fight for. Are you ready to fight, Anddyr?"

"Yes," Anddyr said, his gaze drifting back to the jar.

Etarro pulled an icicle free from Anddyr's prison, slim and sharp. Then he pressed down so it bit him, snake-like, teeth sinking into the pad of the boy's thumb, fangs pulling back bloody. Etarro chewed his lip, a wince and a single whimper. He held his thumb above the skura jar, blood gathering, swelling, dropping. Anddyr counted five drops before the boy stuck his thumb in his mouth, looking more a child than he had even when he'd been younger. He dropped something else into the skura, a thing like a bead, solid but no larger than a drop of blood, and the blue of a summer sky. It fell into the skura and was swallowed by the black paste, no trace of its warm blue left. With the icicle, Etarro stirred blood and bead into the skura. An ignominious moan slipped past Anddyr's lips at the scent of it, nearly made him start clawing his way free from the ice. He'd been resolved to let himself freeze to death for the shame of his failure, but now, awakened and restored, his mind was complaining that it had been much too long since his last dose, the air was reaching heavy down his throat, suffocating . . .

Etarro held the icicle out to him, its point glistening with the black paste, and Anddyr latched on to it like a babe to a teat. The sweetness of it flowed through him, suffusing him with warmth, his eyes glossing over . . . and then a rock dropped into his stomach, and a second slammed into the outside of his stomach as if trying to join with the one within. A scream erupted out of him—or would have, if it weren't for the icicle sealing his lips together. The sound that did emerge from him was more choked-cat than scream, and died quickly in the face of the pain in his midsection.

It stopped as suddenly as it had begun, the pounding rocks fading away to leave nothing more than a faint ache in his belly, and the icicle melted away under the warmth of his lips. It allowed Anddyr to open his mouth, his eyes finding Etarro in the light-speckled darkness, and croak, "What did you do?"

"I'm helping you," the boy said.

Anddyr met the boy's eyes, held them with his own, and refused to look away. His mind was sharp, sharp as it ever was after a dose of skura. "What did you do?" he asked again.

Etarro looked away, fidgeting with the skura jar in his hands. "I've been watching. I've seen how they . . . enthrall . . . your people. Mages. I've watched, and I've seen how it works." He met Anddyr's eyes, a trace of defiance flashing. "You belong to me now."

"I thought you said I'd be free." Anddyr could hear the petulance in his own voice, the whine of a disappointed child.

"No, Anddyr. I said you'd have to fight to be free. I've given you the tools. Now fight." Etarro stood, slipping the skura jar into his own pocket.

Anddyr wailed a wordless protest, and Etarro raised a single eyebrow at him. Over the surging panic brought on by his empty skura jar pocket, the best Anddyr could manage was, "I need it!"

The boy gave a dispassionate shrug. "You can't have it. You have a choice to make now, Anddyr. You can leave here and fight to get back some sort of life, and the fighting will be horrible and painful and the hardest thing you've ever done. You can go crawl your way to a new master and spend the rest of your life as a miserable slave. You can stay here, and die a slow death that's every bit as painful and miserable. It's your choice. This is your life now, Anddyr, and yours alone."

Anddyr felt like there were worms in his stomach, twisting with the sick fear of not having his skura, writhing with the hatred of wanting it so badly. "You . . . you could tell me to stop. You said I'm yours now. You could command me to stop taking it."

Etarro looked so sad that it made Anddyr hate himself more than he already did. "That wouldn't be real, Anddyr. I can't *give* you your freedom, no one can. You have to choose to fight for it, if that's what you want. You have to choose to be a better person. I think you can do it, but I won't make you." The boy's eyes went distant suddenly, that familiar, far-off look he got when something from the future flickered before his vision, or when a god spoke in his mind. As he refocused, coming back from whatever he'd seen, a sound between a sigh and a whimper left him. Ghostlights danced around his face, their eerie light making him look something less than human. "I'm so sorry, Anddyr," he said. "There is one thing you have to do. When the time comes, you have to try, no matter what happens, no matter how it looks. You still have to try. And when you do . . . I'll forgive you. You need to remember that, And-dyr. I'll forgive the choice you have to make." He did turn then and faded through the ghostlights, leaving Anddyr alone once more, wedged uncomfortably behind the Icefall, his mind clear enough for a spark of anger to take root.

Anddyr fought against the ice caging him, twisted his shoulders, tried to find something with his free hand that he could grab for leverage, scraping off more of his face on the ice. If he could get out, he could chase after Etarro, demand answers, take his skura back . . .

Fear hit him then, a crippling thing. He'd only had the one jar of skura, and oh, he was sane enough for the moment, but that would pass and quicker than he'd like . . . and then he'd be left a mad, drooling mess, with no way even to relieve that, and then . . .

He'd once heard a commoner tell the tale of a man who'd gone so crazy he'd died, but that was utter foolishness, as silly as dying of a broken heart. Madness wouldn't kill a man. It would, though, make a man do foolish things, and foolish things were apt to get anyone killed.

Anddyr started to fight again, putting all his long muscles to the task of freeing himself from the cubby behind the Ice-fall. He pulled, he twisted, he pushed; he lost more skin than a flaying. His hands grew so cold from gripping at ice that he became convinced his fingers would snap off and he wouldn't even notice.

There was no way to track time in the Cavern of the Falls. He could convince himself the ghostlights moved in some sort of pattern, that when two drifted across each other's path in a certain way, that meant an hour had passed; that the spiraling movements of one meant another hour had gone by; that when one fought with the enormous bird that swooped into the cavern, it had been an hour more; that when each ghostlight exploded into a shower of fiery flowers, it meant he was going to die there, trapped behind the Icefall. When the ghostlights began talking to him, giggling and whispering of his death, it began not to seem so silly that a man could die of madness.

There was pain—pain like he had never known before. The sort of pain that ground his bones to dust, that sliced slowly into flesh, that twisted him away piece by piece until there was nothing left but a fiery, throbbing pain, the core of his being, the sum of his parts.

There was laughter that echoed around his skull, around the cavern, around the world. It set his teeth on edge, ground them down to gums; made him bash his head against the surrounding ice as hard as he could, hard enough to fill his ears with blood instead of laughter, hard enough to batter a hole through hair and skin and bone and crush his brain to pulp, hard enough the ice shattered around him and fell in a sharp wave, heavy and drowning and slow as a single drop of blood.

The Icefall was gone, or he was gone. He lay on the floor of the cavern, flat and still as stone, and the ghostlights winked down at him.

Free.

The word whispered under the laughter, and it tasted of clean breath, of warm flowers, of gentle-spoken promises. It shuddered through him, setting his nerves alight, mixing with the pain at his core to create something steady and sharp.

Now fight.

He flew apart, flinging all the pieces of himself, scattering in all directions as they said their Fratarro had. When his limbs sped back into place, stitching themselves together, making him whole once more, he was standing. His feet against the ground were heavy and solid and feelingless as ice.

He ran. *My choice.*

His vision swirled with blue and white, painting the shadows, illuminating the monsters that lurked there. The colors clouded his sight, sending him careening into walls. He fell, scraped his knees and hands, got up and ran more, crashed into more hard stone.

Now fight.

He could feel his fingers twitching, guided by some dim and whining part of his mind, a part of him that was barely himself, or maybe he was no longer his own self. His fingers twisted, and light blossomed around him, and a tingling shuddered over his skin. The whimpery piece said he was hidden now from the lurking monsters. The running piece, the color-swirling piece, the crashing piece, didn't care.

Through the colors, through the blood dripping over his eyes and falling like snow, he saw a face. The face of dreams, the face of kindness, the face of love. He would find her. Find her, and save her, and they'd be free together. He would prove himself worthy of her smile. He would be better than he had been.

My choice.

Something hard pressed into his head, scraped along the length of his body. The whimpery piece said it served him right—a blind-running fool was bound to crash into a wall eventually. The blue veil parted, and the white, falling away from his eyes in a wash of blood. His head hit the floor, bounced with a wet squelch. Even the red faded away.

Free . . .

CHAPTER TWENTY-ONE

It was still colder'n death, but the blanket helped. Rora gave up on picking the lock—not really giving up, she told herself, just taking a break from it—and instead sat for a while with the quilt wrapped around herself. It still held some of the boy's warmth, and it caught up what little warmth she had left and held it gentle, like a pile of kindling just before it takes the spark, and Rora's bones finally started to thaw. She even slept for a bit, her body heavy with cold and tired, her mind heavy with the things she didn't want to think about.

One thing Rora'd learned, though, was that good things never last.

The head black-robe had said he didn't need her, and maybe there was some truth in that, but there was some lie in it, too. She wasn't too surprised that when light began to creep down the tunnel, it was the head black-robe and his cronies come calling again. Maybe he didn't *need* her, but he'd talked about options, and having more'n one was never bad.

"Welcome back," Rora said, warmth making her cockier than she maybe should've been.

Even though the head black-robe didn't have any eyes, his brows knitted up like he was narrowing them at her. He said something to one of the other black-robes, too quiet for Rora to hear, but it sent the man scurrying back up the tunnel. To Rora, he said, "I came to see if you'd like to be reunited with your brother."

That sent a chill back into her, sure enough. "What?"

"Your brother. Surely you haven't forgotten him already?"

"Don't know what you mean," Rora said, even though she could suddenly hear her heartbeat. There was no way they could've got Aro . . . was there? Hells, it'd be just like him to get impatient and get some stupid idea in his head to come rescue her . . .

The head black-robe waved a hand. "No matter. Clearly you're tired of the topic."

Curse the man to the bloodiest of all the hells. She couldn't ask about Aro without admitting she had a brother, and even if the black-robe already thought he knew that, admitting it would be giving him power. It was a special kind of torture, being smart enough to know when you were being played, but not smart enough to figure out how to get around it.

"I feel we should get to know each other better," the black-robe said, a shadow of a smirk on his face. "You are our guest after all. Why don't you tell me your name?"

"Because I'm not stupid," Rora spat. Not *that* stupid at least. She half suspected that Neira'd already told him her name, and he was just playing some kind of power game. If that was true, Rora sure as hells wasn't going to let him win at it.

"Come, now. What harm is there in a name?"

"What's *your* name?" The blanket's warmth felt a little bit like armor.

He didn't answer right away, and she was about to call him a hypocrite, which was a great word she'd picked up somewhere. Aro, probably; he always had big words that surprised her when he trotted 'em out. She didn't get the chance to use it, though, since the head black-robe did give her an answer: "My name is Valrik."

Usually, she would've snorted and called him a liar, maybe gotten to use her big word after all. But a thought poked at the back of her mind. *You won't die, so long as you hear the truth when it's given.* The far-eye back in the Canals, he'd never bothered muttering predictions about stupid things like people telling little lies—or maybe he had, just no one'd ever taken notice of the small stuff. The little twin had told her to listen for truth, but it couldn't really matter if she believed the black-robe's name or not. Still, it was enough to keep her words in her mouth—and maybe that was a good thing, considering he might actually know something about Aro.

"And your name?" the black-robe poked.

If they had Aro, Rora knew her brother wouldn't be able to keep his mouth shut—that just wasn't one of his skills, especially not if he was threatened at all. If it was between bending or breaking, Aro'd bend in whatever direction he needed to. More, he'd lived with the name Falcon for near to a decade, but he'd always been forgetting it. He wouldn't know better than to give his own name, and she didn't think her own would be far behind. So if this black-robe didn't know her name, that meant they *didn't* have Aro. Then again . . . he'd been different since they'd left Mercetta the first time. He'd been just a little tougher, a little smarter. Maybe he'd learned when to keep his mouth shut. "Shouldn't you know it?" Rora asked the black-robe. "Someone told me a long time ago that the shadows knew my name."

That shut him up for a while, and Rora smiled inside her cocoon of warmth. She didn't think he had Aro, and she could stand anything, so long as her brother stayed safe.

She'd forgot about the black-robe who'd scurried off at the start, but she remembered him when he came back down the tunnel with a few friends. The friends were of the ice-faced variety, some of the swordsmen who'd popped up out of nowhere in the Icefall room and killed all her knives. Anger warmed her up even more, so that she would've felt downright cozy if it wasn't for the rabid-dog fury near boiling over.

"I'd like my blanket back," the head black-robe said quietly as the swordsmen split around him, heavy steps coming toward the door of the cell.

Under the blanket, Rora coiled her body like a snake, ready to spring. She said, "Then come take it."

A key flashed, clicked in the lock. Two of the swordsmen stayed in the doorway, their big bodies overfilling the opening, and the third took steps toward Rora, one hand stretched out toward her. She let him come, waited till he bent down to snatch the blanket from her shoulders, and then she burst. She flung herself forward and sideways around him, and her trailing leg thunked into his ankle hard enough she maybe heard bones breaking—ankles were soft things, when you got down to it. She got her feet under her quick and, holding the blanket tight in one fist, took two long leap-steps toward the door. Her hand flew out, the blanket soaring like a net and hitting one of the swordsmen square in the face. She got a foot planted, a knee bent, and with her muscles nice and warmed up from the blanket, she jumped. Small as she was, she still got high enough to get an arm around the swordsman who didn't have his head covered, driving her shoulder right into his neck. He made a nice gurgle as he fell backward. Rora got her arm free of him before his back hit the ground, came up in a half crouch on his chest, and grinned up at the black-robes who were the only thing left between her and freedom. She got her feet under her, put her head down, and ran for all she was worth.

Good things never last.

The blanket got caught up in her legs, thrown by one of the swordsmen who then landed on top of her as she went down swearing. He was twice her size and weighed five times as much, and there wasn't much you could do to fight against that. She spat and kicked and scratched, but he got an arm around her neck, and that was pretty much the end of it.

She ended up in the cell again, back pressed to the cold floor as air and eyes came back to her. By the time she got to sitting, the swordsmen'd locked the door again, and taken the blanket out with them.

The head black-robe shook his head at her. "That was . . . ill-advised."

Rora rolled her tongue around inside her mouth, tasting blood where she must've bit her tongue or cheek; she gathered up a gob of blood and spat it toward him, but it spattered against one of the cell bars. She couldn't even get that right.

"We don't have to be enemies, you know," the black-robe said. "You would be treated very well here. A suite of rooms all to yourself, servants to tend your every need, warm meals whenever you should want them. You're a twin. Fated, some would say, to be here. You belong with us—you only need to stop fighting that simple fact."

Rora sat silent, nursing her hurts.

"I'm sure you've heard plenty about the Fallen. We're deemed evil, horrible people bent on destroying the world. But we are people, the same as those who live outside these high stone walls. We have ambitions, dreams, fears. We make mistakes, and we celebrate our triumphs. We are not the monsters we have been painted."

Rora ran her tongue over her teeth, found one that wiggled when she pressed on it, tasted more blood. She felt double cold, after being reminded what warmth felt like and having it taken away.

The head black-robe stepped up to the cell bars, which would've been a stupid thing if Rora'd been able to muster up any more fight. Behind bars and a locked door, facing a handful of black-robes and three big swordsmen who probably wanted her blood, trying anything else would be pretty stupid. The black-robe stuck his arm between the bars, and another basket dangled from his fingers, just like the one that'd been full of food the first time, the one she'd shredded.

"So you'll let me freeze," Rora said, spacing out the words, "but make sure I die fat?"

"You have not yet earned a blanket."

Rora snorted. "What, do I have to slaughter a few goats first?"

The head black-robe set the basket down on the floor of her cell. "We make fearsome enemies," he said as he stepped back, "but valuable allies. You'll be sure to let me know when you'd like to see your brother." Then they left, the whole lot of 'em, taking the light with them. It was easier to believe, in the cold quiet, that maybe they did have Aro . . .

No, if they had her brother, they could've brought him down, paraded him in front of her. They had to be bluffing, and she could face down a bluff. She just had to keep herself from thinking about her brother stuck in a cell like this, cold and whimpering and wondering where she was, when she'd save him . . .

She just had to not think about it, and the best way to stop thinking was to do something else.

There was strong, and then there was stupid. Rora could pretend she wasn't hungry, that she was amazing enough of a person she didn't need food to live. That would be stupid, though. So she crawled on hands and knees until she found the food basket, more bread and cheese, but it had taste and put a comfortable feeling in her belly, and that was really all you should ask of food.

It was an honest surprise when light came creeping down the tunnel again before she'd even finished the crust of bread. "Miss me already?" she called out around a full mouth. It was just the head black-robe and more of his ice-faced friends, none of the other black-robes. That didn't feel like a good sign. Then she saw the littler body in with the swordsmen—the boy-twin, Etarro. He was pale to start with, but it didn't seem like there was any color on his face now. Just fear.

"There are rules here," the head black-robe said, and his voice was hard, though there wasn't any meanness in it. If anything, there was a touch of sad lurking under the words. "We are a society like any other. When a rule is broken, punishment is given. Etarro." He knelt before the boy, his old knees popping, and put a hand on the boy's shoulder. "Do you know what you have done wrong?"

The fear was still in the kid's face, but you wouldn't know it from the calm way he spoke. "I did what I believed to be right."

"And that, sometimes, is the wrong thing to do."

Rora still didn't quite understand what was happening, not until after the swordsmen had already pushed the boy forward, unlocked the door to her cell, pushed him in. It was only when they were locking the door back up, with the boy on her side of it, that warm anger flared up in her again. "Right," she called to the black-robe, "I see how much it helps to be your friend!"

The old man spread his hands. "Justice is not always kind. The right path is not always easy to walk. Life is a heavy thing, made of complex emotions and difficult choices. That is the way of things. Etarro made a choice, for which he knew the risks, and he must now face the consequences."

The kid stood there shivering and pale, but it almost seemed like the fear had melted off his face, and Rora suddenly understood. It was a trick, and the kid was in on it. "So you think if you leave him here with me for a while, he'll convince me everything's roses and sunshine with you lot? Few minutes of talking with the kid and I'll just give everything up?"

All the old man gave her was a shrug, and then he turned away, the swordsmen with him. He stopped, just as the shadows from the leaving torch started to creep back over Rora, and he said to the man with the light, "Leave them the torch. We're not monsters after all." There was a bracket on the wall that the torch fit into, close enough to drive the shadows from the cell but far enough away there was no hope of reaching it. It was a weird kindness, and one she didn't trust. They did leave after that, going up the tunnel in darkness. She didn't think it bothered 'em too much.

Somehow, after all the time alone in the dark, being in the light with another person almost felt worse, and that was a twisty sort of feeling. Made her hate the damn black-robe even more, for messing with her thoughts. She sat against the wall, just watching the boy who hadn't moved from near the door, standing there with his skinny arms wrapped around himself. He was dressed for the cold better'n she was, but he was already shivering hard, just staring out at the torch.

"Kid?" Rora called soft. Her voice sounded strange—it was different, talking to someone who was trapped just like she was.

"The torch won't last more than an hour." It wasn't much more'n a whisper, but the room had that way of making every sound loud.

Rora couldn't think up much of a reply to that, so she tried, "The dark isn't so bad."

"It is."

"They'll probably be back for you before the torch dies. Hells, they'll probably be back for you in minutes, when they realize their plan isn't going to work."

"Rora," he said, still calm and quiet, but the word sounded deeper, somehow. "Do you remember what I told you before?"

You won't die, so long as you hear the truth when it's given.
"Yeah."

"I'm not part of any plan Valrik has for you. I won't tell

you to stay here. You should run from here, as far and as fast as you can."

There was quiet again, as Rora tried to think of what to say to that. Kid had a way of dropping his words like stones into a calm pool, and the only thing you could do was wait until the ripples died. "That's my plan," she finally said. "Getting to the running's the hard part, though."

"You'll get the chance." He finally turned to face her, big blue eyes like flecks of ice in his pale face. "When it comes . . . remember your brother."

She had to focus on breathing normal. "Do you know, is he in here?"

"No."

"No he isn't, or no you don't know?"

"No," he just said again.

A growl snuck between her teeth. "Lot of help you are."

The boy walked to lean his back against the wall across from her, so they were sitting staring at each other, both curled into tight balls. Didn't say anything, just watched her with those too-old eyes.

"You a far-eye?" she asked. She hadn't meant to, but the light made her want to fill the room with words. In the dark, you could hide, stay secret and quiet.

The boy tilted his head at that, and it almost seemed like he smiled. "I've never heard it called that."

"But you are?"

"I . . . see more than what most people see."

"Oh, so you're just a grifter."

"What?"

"You read people. Make good guesses at their fears and

dreams and all the things that make 'em up, and then you throw on a good voice and spout important-sounding nonsense. It's a good trick, a good way to fleece people."

The smile had faded fast from his face while she'd been talking, till he looked almost pained. "It's not like that."

"'Course it's not. But I don't blame you for it—my life's been made up of fleecing. We all do what we have to to get by."

The boy looked down at his knees. "You're not how I thought you'd be."

"Yeah, well, there's few enough twins wandering around, have to make sure we're different. Otherwise I might end up going with the wrong brother."

He laughed at that, a laugh like she hadn't heard from anyone in a long time, and for the space of a laugh, he looked like a kid—happy, fearless, young. A corner of Rora's mouth tilted up at him. There was silence again, but it wasn't the kind of silence that begged for filling.

"Tell me about your brother?" He asked it timid as a mouse, but his eyes still looked young, and they were full of the curiosity that poured out of kids.

Rora sharpened her eyes at him, remembering her suspicions—that the black-robe had just left the kid here to pry for information, that the kid was trying to twist her thoughts. She could already feel it happening . . . But the boy knew her name, and he hadn't given it to the black-robe. When she'd been a kid, Rora'd never been above a good fleecing . . . but that didn't mean all kids were like she'd been. Etarro, even with his far-eyes, he looked innocent as anything. Still, any kid who'd known a hard life learned the right faces to make to get something . . .

"I know trust comes hard to our kind," the boy said, and then a big shiver rolled through him, the sudden breath out through his chattering teeth making a cloud in front of his face.

A few years ago, when Aro'd been younger than this boy, before either of 'em had really made much of themselves with Whitedog, a hard winter had hit Mercetta sooner'n anyone'd expected. Most everyone had been caught unprepared, so that even a lot of people topside had died, and it'd been even worse in the Canals. People'd frozen to the ground, frozen into the canals, so that anywhere you walked, staring eyes in white faces followed you. They'd survived it somehow, she and Aro, but they'd spent it curled together for warmth and still shivered through it all, bone-deep shaking that made your muscles ache. Just one of the reasons she hated the cold so much.

But the kid, Etarro, he was shivering just the way she'd been all those years ago . . . the same way Aro'd shivered inside her arms.

Rora held out an arm. "C'mere," she said quietly.

The boy didn't stand right away—he wasn't wrong, about the trust thing. But he did stand, and he put his back to the wall next to her, and he curled under her arm. He didn't have much warmth to him—hells, he felt cold as the stone floor, half-ice— but Rora didn't need more warmth. She'd survive this cold; she'd survived all the other cold places that'd come before it.

"My brother," she said to the top of the boy's head, "is a good kid. He . . . he still believes the world's a good place, no matter how much it shows him it isn't. Sometimes I wish I could be more like that . . . but most of the time, I wish he was smarter about things, wish he could see how the world really is."

"Wish you didn't have to take care of him so much," the

boy said softly into her side, and Rora didn't answer that. That wasn't something she'd ever say . . . "My sister's the same. She's the strong one, she always has been. They say when we were babies, she slept from sunrise to sunset, a perfect little nocturnal thing right from the start. I cried a lot. When I was a baby, I mean. I always wished I could be strong like her, not scared of anything, even if she's not exactly . . ."

"Warm?" Rora suggested into the pause, but he didn't answer. Maybe that was something he'd never say out loud either. After a while, she said, "You told me to run from this place . . . why haven't you? Why're you still here?"

"I'm needed here."

"Something you've *seen*, huh?"

"Yes, but . . . not how you mean. Avorra needs me. We keep each other balanced. Without me, she'd tip. Without me . . . she'd mean nothing."

That made Rora go quiet, 'cause it gave voice to something real similar she'd never had words for. She'd spent all her life taking care of Aro, keeping him safe, fixing his messes, cleaning up after the stupid shit he did . . . but when it came down to it, she wasn't taking care of him for his own sake. She was taking care of him because she needed him . . . because, without him, she'd tip into something not human.

In the silence that fell between 'em, a silence of cold truths and dark fear, the damn torch ran out of room to burn and the whole cell went black.

CHAPTER TWENTY-TWO

Keiro spent much of his time walking across the plains and the hills, his only companion young Cazi trilling in his ear. The tribe remained enthralled by Saval, which left a sour taste in Keiro's mouth; the man had even seemed to win over Yaket, and the two would frequently sit together trading stories. Each day felt like a reminder that Keiro was no longer necessary, that there was no place for him here. Even Nerrin was often barred from him, Saval preferring to keep her at his side. "You never know when she'll be needed," Saval had said with the sort of smile that made Keiro's hands curl into fists. He hated those violent feelings, and so he tried to avoid them—which meant avoiding Saval, and Nerrin by extension. He could sneak her away some nights, show her all the beautiful surprises the Plains had to offer. It was good, when he could put a smile on Nerrin's face, when he could chase away her fears and her madness for a short time. But too often, when he tried to wake her in the deep night, she would startle awake from some nightmare and grow trapped in her own madness, convinced Keiro was a horror of some sort, and he would have to leave before her terror woke the whole tribe.

It was easier to stay away from the tribehome, to leave them to their stories and their new preacher and the mysterious mage. He always expected to hear footsteps following—Poret's or Yaket's or Nerrin's. But no one ever followed after him. Always, though, there was Cazi. The young *mravigi* always found him, flowing smoothly through the grass to twine his body around Keiro's ankles. The little beast had a way of lightening Keiro's mood, no matter how dim. He hooked his claws into Keiro's leg and hauled his slim body up to Keiro's shoulder. The *mravigi*'s claws, once small but kitten-sharp, had grown with the rest of his body and now had more power to puncture. Balanced carefully on Keiro's shoulder, both front and back claws gripping to keep from falling, Cazi was as large as Keiro's head. It made Keiro proud, and slightly sad, to see the *mravigi* growing so quickly, his scales darkening to gray.

He continued on to the hills, idly hoping he might find Tseris and discuss Saval with her. If not, though, the hills had something of a curative property for Keiro's mind and heart. Whether it was the palpable traces of his faith made real, or the simple fact that the hills had been so little touched by humanity, he couldn't deny they'd become, perhaps, his favorite of the many places his feet had taken him.

At the edge of the hills, Cazi's significant weight abruptly launched itself from Keiro's shoulder. That was nothing unusual—the *mravigi* was constantly spotting mice in the grass, or wanting to stretch his legs, or taken by sudden fancy that required his presence on the ground. What *was* unusual was that Cazi didn't land on the ground. His wings, which had grown in proportion to the rest of his body, snapped out sharply and caught at the faint wind that rustled the grasses. He dipped, nearly going snout-first into the dirt, but two frantic flaps of his wings righted him. As his snout pointed instead toward the sky, wings flapping with determination, one small red eye met Keiro's, and it was full of triumph. Cazi's mouth opened as he rose, wings beating, and a high scream of joy ripped from his throat.

The ground dug into Keiro's knees; he didn't remember falling, but he knelt, watching with his hands clutched over his mouth. A delirious laugh made it past his lips. Cazi, the only winged *mravigi*, some miracle Keiro hadn't been able to crack—*flying!* The first Starborn to touch the sky since Patharro had wrought their destruction.

The little *mravigi* was clumsy at first, dipping crazily through the air, nearly plummeting a few times—but his wings, his beautiful wings, always righted him, catching the air and sending him soaring. He grew more graceful in a short time, his form drawing circles in the air, looping and spinning, plummeting a-purpose with wings folded tight to his sides only to snap out at the last instant, skimming just above the waving grass.

In all his life, in all his wandering, in all the marvelous things he had seen, Keiro had counted seeing the *mravigi* sing together on the full-moon nights as the most wondrous thing he had ever seen. But this . . . seeing Cazi fly topped that tenfold.

He was so enthralled with watching Cazi that he didn't see the other *mravigi* until they had already surrounded him. It startled Keiro badly, and another laugh burst from him. "Tseris!" he said, recognizing her among the half dozen who stood with uptilted eyes, watching Cazi soar. "Oh, Tseris, do you see him?"

"*I see him,*" she said softly, her red gaze never leaving his distant shape.

Cazi eventually returned to the earth, trying ungracefully to land on Keiro's shoulder, his wing-flaps stirring up clouds of dust. He eventually gave up on it and fell instead into Keiro's waiting arms. Keiro hugged the Starborn tight, laughter bubbling through him, and Cazi replied with a series of excited trills. Keiro pressed his forehead against the rough scales of Cazi's head, feeling how the *mravigi* vibrated with joy.

"*Come with us, Godson,*" Tseris said. "*There is a thing that must be done.*"

They walked, Keiro at the center of the ring of Starborn. Cazi struggled from his arms, launching himself into the air once more to glide above their heads. Keiro watched him with a broad smile, but the other *mravigi* seemed to be pointedly ignoring the young one's antics.

When they came to a tunnel into the earth, Cazi was reluctant to leave the sky, needing to be coaxed by Keiro and, finally, by a few unwontedly harsh words from Tseris. He made a sad chirrup as they filed into the earth, Keiro and the Starborn. There was plenty of room for Cazi to fit in through the tunnel, for he was still small, not yet close to full grown, but he walked with his wings folded tightly against his sides, as though newly worried about damaging them.

There were more Starborn gathered in the main cavern, more than Keiro usually saw at once. He guessed they had burrows beneath the earth, down the many branching tunnels they'd dug through the years, places they could stay safe and hidden. Aside from Cazi and Tseris, the other Starborn had shown no interest in Keiro, had even outright avoided him at times. He harbored no anger for that—he must be the first human they had seen in centuries, and so their distrust and uncertainty were more than understandable. Now, though, they gathered in a mass, like a sky full of glowing stars . . . as many of them as there had been on the first night Keiro had met his gods. The chamber was loud with the dry scraping sound of scaled bodies moving against each other, with the low cacophony of countless voices whispering. Beneath that, there was something strange in the air.

The *mravigi* parted before Keiro and Cazi and their escorts, Tseris leading the way through the murmurs and the baleful eyes, to the far end of the chamber where Sororra and Fratarro sat, the great white Starborn lying before them. Red eyes watched their approach, the Twins awake and even Fratarro looking somber, and Straz, first of the *mravigi*, showing all his centuries in his eyes. Cazi quailed before their regard, or perhaps he, too, could sense the strangeness that hung in the cavern. Keiro leaned down to scoop up the young creature, cradling him against his chest. It seemed to bolster Cazi's courage, and it bolstered Keiro's as well.

They stopped before Straz, before the Twins, and the other *mravigi* faded back so that it was only Tseris and Keiro, with Cazi in arms. As Keiro knelt, the silence that fell was sudden, and absolute.

"Forgive me," Tseris said to him, quietly and full of grief. *"There is a thing that must be done. Already, we have waited too long. It . . . it will be harder, now. Still."* Her eyes met Keiro's, soft and sad. *"It is a thing you should see."* She stood then, her

weight shifting to her back legs and long tail lashing for balance, and her powerful jaws wrapped carefully around Cazi's neck. The young *mravigi* gave a startled scream as he was lifted from Keiro's arms, and Keiro made a move to snatch him back, but something stopped his limbs like a puppet with cut strings. When he looked up, Sororra's eyes were on him, hard and uncompromising, and his own stillness was written in them.

The goddess held out a hand, broad as Keiro's chest, and Tseris set Cazi down in her blackened palm. Her fingers held the *mravigi* tight, but careful, holding only tight enough that he could not flee. He tried, of course, for he was a fighter, and loathsome of being restrained. Keiro couldn't say why, but there was a heaviness in his chest that made breathing hard.

Sororra lifted her hand, bringing Cazi close to her face. "He is big," she said softly, her chains clanking as her other hand lifted to tilt up the young Starborn's chin. In the quiet of the cavern, Keiro could hear Cazi whimper.

Tseris, returned to Keiro's side, bowed her head. "*I was moved to wait. The fault is mine.*"

Sororra glanced to her brother. "It seems . . . unkind. He has known the air."

Fratarro's cheeks were wet with tears. "It is as it must be. We cannot draw our Parents' sight. Do it. It will be hard, but it will not grow easier with waiting."

"As you say." Sororra lowered her hand, bringing Cazi even with mighty Straz's head. It felt as though her other hand were wrapped around Keiro's chest, and his heart was like thunder in his ears. His jaw was clenched too tight to let out the scream that burst within him.

"*Forgive me,*" Tseris said again, to Keiro alone. Softer, a whisper wound in grief and regret, she said, *"I did warn you to stay away from him. To spare you this."*

Sororra's hand shifted, tightened. In the light of red eyes and the starlight glow of a hundred *mravigi*, Keiro saw, emerging above her curled fingers, Cazi's wings, stretched and frantically fluttering. In an instant he saw them no more, Straz leaning forward over Sororra's hand, and there was the smallest, saddest snap.

The unseen hand released Keiro's chest and he fell to his knees, a wrenching gasp of a sob tearing from his throat. When he found air once more, he released it in a cry of anguish, and another voice, high and sweet, screamed with him in agony.

"Forgive me," Tseris whispered.

Straz lowered his great head, two points of gray sticking from his muzzle. Within Sororra's curled hand, a small form thrashed, screaming the mindless terror of an animal in pain. Cazi's scales had grown darker, but he was still lighter than black, light enough that Keiro could see blood pouring over his scales from the places where his wings had thrust so proudly.

Sororra lifted both hands and, with the empty one, touched a finger to the ichorous stump where Fratarro's arm had been torn away. "Shh," she murmured, the sound nearly lost in the screaming. "Shh, little one. Almost over." Her finger came away wet, a deeper black than her burned flesh. She ran her finger across Cazi's back, over the raw wounds where his wings had been bitten off. "There now. Shh."

In time, the high screams faded. From where he knelt, and with tears blurring his sight, Keiro could see no change, but he could imagine how well a god's blood could heal flesh. Sororra set her hand to the ground, opened her fingers. Cazi fled from her palm, skittered past Straz, came to rest against Keiro's knees. Keiro hugged the young *mravigi* tight, weeping unabashed, joy that he lived still, sorrow at what had been taken from him.

"Why?" Keiro asked heavily, his head pressed to Cazi's. Asked it of Tseris, of Straz, of Sororra and Fratarro both, of all the watching Starborn. Asked it of the world itself, the oldest question, ever unanswerable.

Fratarro's voice was as thick with grief as Keiro's. "It is the only way they may live. If my Father knew he had not killed them all . . ."

"His hatred is boundless," Sororra said. "He would hunt them to the end of the earth, if he knew there were any left to hunt."

"*Usually,*" Tseris said, "*we do it before the young have tasted the sky. It is easier when they do not know what they have lost.*"

Keiro shook his head, wordless, anger and anguish battling. He wanted to deny it, deny the necessity, say that Cazi would have been careful to go unseen in his flight . . . but he knew those were lies. He had watched Cazi fly. Watched him climb so high into the sky he was little more than a speck, high enough to be seen half the world away . . . high enough, certainly, to be seen by eyes watching the world from above. The young were careless, reckless. This was the only way . . . the only way to keep him safe. *There was no other choice.*

When Keiro lifted his head from Cazi's, he saw that Sororra's eyes were fixed intently on him, and that Fratarro's were fixed to the ground. "They have left us no choice," Sororra said earnestly. "It is one of the many crimes for which they will pay."

Keiro ran one hand gently over Cazi's back. His scales

were still damp with blood, but his shoulders were smooth, the scales unbroken, no sign left of the wings that had borne him into the sky—not even a trace of a wound, to remember that they had been there.

"You will help us, Godson," Fratarro said with unexpected fierceness. "Avenge Cazi, and all the others before him, all my children who have suffered mutilation for the sake of petty jealousy. Bring the Fallen, so that we may rise."

"I will," Keiro said, throat still thick, hand sticky with drying blood, cradling the trembling young Starborn against his chest. "For Cazi."

CHAPTER TWENTY-THREE

Darkness had a way of sharpening you, or at least it did for Rora. In proper dark, you could hear all the flavors of quiet. There was the waiting quiet, that wrapped itself up in a neat bundle and stayed calm as calm could be. There was the alert quiet, the one that half expected something to reach out in the dark and would be ready when it happened. There was the scared quiet, which was one breath away from a sob.

Etarro shook where he was wrapped up in her arms, and Rora was probably being generous if she said half of it was cold-shaking. The boy had the scared quiet on him so tight not even his teeth chattered, probably held together so tight they'd burst with just a little more pressure.

"Hey," she said, soft enough it wouldn't scare him. He still jumped. "It's not so bad. They'll come back for you."

"I know. But I hate the dark. I can't see anything."

Rora almost laughed at that, but was glad she didn't. Glad he couldn't see the bit of a smile on her face when she said, "Yeah, that's how the dark works. Comes with not having any light around."

An annoyed noise came out of the boy. "I know that. I'm not stupid." A big shiver rolled through him. "In the dark, I can't see *anything*."

"Oh." His special seeing, that he'd convinced himself he had. "So the dark turns you into a normal person."

"I . . . I suppose . . ."

"Isn't that what the Twins want? All dark and everyone's even, yeah?"

He was quiet, a surprised quiet, the sort of quiet that didn't know how to say a mean thing nice.

Smirking a little, Rora said, "I'm not stupid either."

He didn't say anything to that, and his surprised quiet faded back into the scared quiet. He seemed determined not to let his fear drift away.

"Hey," she said again, jostling his shoulder, hoping she could shake the fear off, "you ever hear the Song of Belora Blue-eye?"

"No . . ."

"It was one of my favorites as a kid. You wanna hear it?"

She knew this quiet—it was the quiet of a kid with one foot toward being a grown-up, the quiet of someone who thought they were supposed to be better than something. The dark had a way of peeling off masks, though.

"Please." He still tried to make it sound all dignified, like he was doing her a favor, but his shaking had already started to slow down some.

"Right. Well, Belora, she lived up at the top of a mountain— nothing so tall as this one, but still a mountain, and a mountain's nothing to suck your teeth at. Some people said her parents'd left her there to die and she'd been too stubborn to listen. Other people said she had no parents, that eagles had dropped her at the top of the mountain when she was a babe and she was too fearless to think there could be a better place to live. And then there were a few who said she wasn't human at all, that she'd clawed her way up from the mountain's heart and was too unnatural to join the rest of the world.

"No matter how she got there, Belora lived at the top of her mountain, and she stayed put. In all her life, she just sat there at the top of her mountain, still as death but as alive as can be, smirking on her perch as she dared the world to just try and move her. Winds blowed, but they couldn't knock her off the mountain. A great big bird who wanted the mountain for his own perch, he challenged her, but she beat him fair and ate good bird-meat for a week. The sun snuck up close to her, trying to drive her off with the heat, and her skin burned black and cracked like tree bark, but still she didn't move. The mountain itself tried to shake her loose, big rumbles that started in the ground and near cracked the mountain in half, but Belora, she just hung on and kept smiling.

"Now, with her skin all sun-black, the night turned Belora into a shadow, dark as the sky. Even if you knew where to look, at night, you couldn't see any trace of Belora on her mountain.

"But there was one night when Belora had a bad dream, and she woke up, and her eyes were like two bright stars in the dark. The moon saw, and from so far away, he was sure he'd found—"

"The moon's a 'he'?" Etarro interrupted.

"Yeah, the moon's a 'he,' now hush. Anyhow, the moon was chuffed at his luck, 'cause he was sure he was seeing not one but *two* other moons glowing in the night. The moon's a lonely thing, you see. The sun never wants to stay and have a talk with him, always running off soon as the moon gets close, and stars are no good at talking. So the moon, he was sure he'd finally found a friend, and he rushed on over to Belora.

"Now, you have to see it from Belora's eyes. She'd just got woke up by a bad dream, and her heart was still hammering with fear, and suddenly the moon had zipped right up next to her. She got scared, and can you blame her? She got so scared that she fell right off her mountain. She fell and she fell, a long way down, and she landed right on her face.

"The moon, he'd started holding his breath the second Belora started falling, hating that he'd scared away his new friends before he'd even got to introduce himself proper. But when Belora landed on the ground, the moon near burst with excitement. He'd been happy to see two little moons to be his friend, but this was even better . . .

"Y'see, sitting flat on her mountain, there'd been one spot of Belora that the sun hadn't burned black. And now, face-first on the ground with her white-as-milk arse sticking up into the air, the moon crowed with joy because now he'd found himself two nice big friends—"

A laugh burst out of Etarro—a good laugh, the kind that started in the belly and touched every other place on the way out. Rora grinned into the dark as the boy shook, but not with fear or cold now, just with laughing. He laughed for a long time, laughed so long his breath started gasping in, laughed longer than the story really deserved, but Rora knew that feeling. Sometimes you laughed too hard because it made the world feel a little less small and a little less dark.

"Why," Etarro finally asked, still gasping a bit for air, "is it called the Song of Belora Blue-eye?"

"I never did find out either." Rora chuckled. "My father, he used to tell us that one all the time when we were kids, and we always cracked harder'n you. I don't know how it ends."

He put his hand on her arm, his fingers damp from wiping away his laughing-tears. "I'm sorry," he said softly, his voice slipping back into serious tones.

"Thanks." She didn't ask how he guessed; with some stories, you could guess the ending even if it wasn't written out clear. Same way she didn't have to ask if his parents were wandering around inside the mountain. Some things were drawn so deep you could see 'em even in the dark.

"You know," the boy said, "I think that's the first story I've ever heard that wasn't about the Twins."

Rora snorted. "Yeah, well, that's what happens when you grow up around crazy folks."

"They're not crazy. They're just different than you."

"Everyone's crazy. We're all cracked a hundred different ways, some people are just better at tying knots to keep all the pieces together. From where I'm sitting, most everyone in this fecking mountain can't tie knots for shit."

"They're only—"

A sharp sound cut over Etarro's words, made the boy swallow his voice and shrink into Rora's side. If she'd had someone bigger to shrink into, she would've done the same. The noise was soft enough, but it seemed to come from everywhere, rushing down the tunnel, filling up the little chamber, snaking through the cell bars, and wrapping around Rora and Etarro. It was like grating stones, like dry leaves in a wind, like a body dragging along the ground. It didn't sound anything like the black-robes, didn't sound like anything she'd ever heard before. It swelled, growing louder, closer.

Rora pushed, shoved Etarro farther back from the bars, so they sat curled around each other at the back of the cell, and Rora was shaking just as much as the boy. When there was anything besides quiet filling a darkness, there wasn't space for much besides fear.

The sound got closer, clear enough she could hear it was *sounds*, more than one, all mashing together. Rasping breaths, something being dragged, the heavy slap of flesh. Etarro let out a little whimper, and Rora scrambled to cover his mouth. She held him tight and silent, wishing for a dagger, wishing for a sharp stick even, anything so she could feel less helpless.

She couldn't stop the yelp that jumped out of her mouth when something hit the cell bars. There was hard breathing, heavy and wet, and something hit the bars again. And again. And again. The dragging sound, so close she could feel it in her teeth, and her mind thought up all the monsters it could be, scaled arms sliding between the bars, claws bent toward her face, teeth like knives bared against the bars, and she couldn't see any of it, wouldn't know her death until it wrapped around her throat, tore through her flesh—

"Rora?" a voice rasped, hardly even sounding human, and it was a new kind of horror that it knew her name.

Etarro flailed in her arms, writhing like he was having a fit, and his mouth twisted out from under her hand. He hissed, "Anddyr?"

The wet sound that echoed around the cell was, Rora realized, supposed to be a laugh. "I did it," the voice said, and it
was faint but she could almost hear how it sounded like the
witch. "I did it."

If it really was him, well, that made things easy. Rora pulled
her arms out from around Etarro, and threw herself forward
until she hit the bars. She stuck both hands through and, guided
by his coughing, rasping breath, she found his throat.

Digging in her fingers, Rora pulled him closer, pulled him
till his face was pressed against the bars, pulled till his face
was pressed against hers, pulled till she could feel his panicky
breath wash over her cheeks and feel spit, or maybe blood,
splatter across her mouth as he wheezed for air. "You bastard,"
she snarled, and if there'd been enough space between the bars
to fit her face through, she might've sunk her teeth into him
just as another way to show how angry she was. She saw the
knives, her charges, good people—or as good as Scum got—
loyal and ready to follow her no matter how much Tare'd spat
and glared, all trusting in Rora to keep them safe, and now they
were dead because of the witch. "Fecking traitor." She wondered which'd come first, choking him to death or pushing
her fingers through his skin. Either way, it'd be a good start in
making up for all the knives he'd let die. "Murdering bastard."
There was something pulling on her arm, small fingers but a
stronger grip than she expected.

More spit or blood flew onto her face, and the witch gasped,
"I'm sorry."

"Liar." She squeezed her fingers in time with the word, feeling how weak his neck was.

"Rora." The boy's voice was quiet, much quieter'n the blood pounding in her ears, but somehow she heard it still. "Do you remember what I told you?"

She was never good at remembering the things people said, and what did it matter anyway, the only thing she cared about was making the witch pay for what he'd done to her and the other knives.

"I'm so sorry," the witch wheezed.

You won't die, so long as you hear the truth when it's given. That was what the boy'd said . . . And there was another thing, one she hadn't even remembered but it must've stuck in her brain somewhere, and it bubbled up to the surface: *You should listen to him, when he finds you.*

Her fingers slipped from flesh before she'd even decided to, before she could remind herself what he'd done and how much he deserved to die. She let him go, because just maybe the damned kid saw more than normal people and maybe he didn't, but sometimes, when her ears caught it right, his voice sounded just like someone else's, like the voice that kept her from tipping over into something less than she was, that kept her from becoming someone awful.

Rora sat back, away from the bars, heard the witch hit the floor, felt the boy at her side. There was the sound of gulping breaths. The sound of crying was louder, and really, between the three of them, she couldn't've said who made that louder sound.

"I'm so sorry," the witch finally whimpered.

Rora had to swallow hard before she could get out any words, still thinking of all the knives, all the people she'd led to die. "Why'd you do it?"

"I didn't mean to. I was weak. It won't ever happen again. I promise you, Rora. I'm . . . I'm learning how to fight."

She didn't want to hear any of his excuses or explanations, because those were just ways for a person to get around admitting they'd done wrong. But the boy's voice drifted back into her head: *You won't die, so long as you hear the truth when it's given.*

"Anddyr," she said, and she didn't growl it, though it was a hard thing. "Make a light."

There was rustling, the annoying mumbling she'd forgot about, and then a soft blue light swelled up near the ceiling of the little cavern. Etarro gave a sharp scream, and Rora almost joined him.

The witch was near as bad as all the shadow-monsters her mind'd thought up, like something that'd taken a step outside a nightmare. Half his face looked like it'd been scraped off, and most of what wasn't raw flesh was covered in blood. His eyes were mismatched, the pupils different sizes, and that was a bad sign. He was half lying on the floor, his hands holding on to the cell bars like they were the only things keeping him this side of death, and more than a few of his fingers looked twisted and bent like fingers shouldn't be. His shoulders and face were pressed against the bars so tight she almost thought he'd find a way to squeeze through the bars just from will alone. His clothes were ripped and bloody, and down along his leg, there was maybe a flash of white bone. Looking back, she could see where he'd dragged himself along the ground, faint blood-smears marking a line from the tunnel straight to the cell. Worse than any of that, though, was his smile, huger than any smile she'd ever seen, and all bloody teeth and broken lips.

"What in the hells happened to you?" she gasped. It was a close thing, but she stopped herself from moving farther away from the bars.

The witch grinned wider, though she wouldn't've thought it was possible. "I told you. I'm learning to fight." Rora could only gape, and when she looked over at Etarro, she gaped even more to see that the boy had a grin on his face, too.

Underneath all the blood, the witch went pale when his eyes settled on Etarro. He didn't say anything for a while, but the smile did a slow fall off his face. His voice was different, broken, when he asked real quiet, "Is it here?"

"No, Anddyr," the boy said, still smiling, though it was a softer thing now. "It's gone."

And the grin hopped right back onto the witch's face. "Good. That's good. I'll get you out—"

"Wait." Rora held up a hand, and the witch went quiet as fast as if her hands were around his throat again. It was one of the hardest things she'd ever said, but it needed saying—if she was going to learn to listen to the truth, she'd have to hear it first. "If you let me out now, I swear to any god you want that I'll just kill you. You look half-dead as it is, but I promise I'll finish the job because the way I see it, you deserve to die ten times." She met his eyes, the one with the pupil too big, and he stared right back, looking as serious and focused as she'd ever seen him. "Tell me why I shouldn't kill you. Give me any reason I shouldn't kill you for all the good people you killed."

He gave her a look like she'd punched him. "I didn't kill anyone."

"Let 'em die, then. We came in here with ten other people, Anddyr, but somehow we're the only ones left. So what I'm wondering—" she couldn't help it, she leaned forward some and her hands flexed like they were around a neck "—is if that was Joros's command, or something you decided to do all on your own."

His mouth dropped open, full of blood still. "I—God, no! It's nothing like that." A big shudder rolled through him, as if he felt the cold for the first time. "You think I betrayed you. No. I did, I mean, but not in the way you think . . . I was weak, I . . . I disobeyed the cappo's directions and I set the timing off, and I was . . . was too *stupid* to even think they'd have their own mages. They probably don't go anywhere without those swords-men and a mage to keep them hidden, just in case someone tries to . . . well. I . . . I wasn't myself, when I needed to be, and I couldn't save you . . . them . . ."

Much as she didn't want to believe him, that made more fecking sense than that he'd just decided to betray her or Joros wanted her dead. Damned hells, that made it harder to hate him—but he'd still let her people get killed by the black-robes' hidden protection. Something he'd said in there . . . "Weren't yourself?" she repeated.

The witch got that just-punched look again, and his eyes flicked down to Etarro. The boy shook his head and said, "Tell her."

Anddyr's body slipped slowly down the bars, his hands loosening, sliding down until he lay in a ball on the floor, not looking at them, not looking at anything. His voice was small, when it drifted up. "I'm dying, Rora. A slow thing, but I can feel it creeping closer with every beat of my heart. It's the price I have to pay, but . . . I've judged it worthwhile. It's a fair trade, for freedom."

"Tell her, Anddyr," the boy said again.

"I'm broken. I was broken here, years ago. A life ago. They enslaved me. You've seen it—the black paste the cappo made me take."

"A cure for your madness." That's what Joros'd told Aro, when he'd asked.

The witch shook his head. "No. And yes. It causes the madness, and gives me relief from it. It is both redemption and ruin. It will destroy me if I let it, but . . . I don't think I want to let it, anymore. I'm learning how to fight it. I . . . I want to be better than I was. I don't want to be a slave to it anymore. I'm learning how to be . . . free. But there's a price to that, too." He smiled, but it was like a bad carving of a smile, all wrong. "I'm a dead man either way—I can keep taking the skura and it will kill me, or I can stop taking it even though what's already in my system is enough to kill me early. That makes it easy, though, doesn't it? If I'm going to die a madman, why not die a free madman?"

There was so much in there she didn't really understand, like he was speaking a different language and she could only pick out every other word. "You . . . you don't seem too mad," Rora offered. He seemed more normal'n he usually was even after he took his medicine that apparently wasn't medicine—more weird and rambly, but still pretty damned normal, as far as he went. Take off all the blood and broken bones, and he could maybe be any regular person.

He just shook his head again. "With big storms, storms that shake the very sky, there's a center in the madness. A small circle of peace, quietude. I'm like that now, only there are a hundred storms, all swirling around me, in me . . . but every once in a while, a storm-center will drift over me, and I'll have a few moments of . . . me." He twisted his head up to look at her, and she could almost see the truth sitting there in his mismatched eyes, see the storms circling. "It's easier to be strong, when I'm me. I . . . I think it will be a lot harder, when the storms come. When I'm more like . . . like who I used to be." He made that bad-carved smile again. "I don't expect anything from you—I know I haven't earned it—but . . . it would be nice to have some help, when it gets bad. I'm trying to be better, but I don't know if I'm strong enough."

Rora shifted uncomfortably, looking away from his face. He was making it so much harder to keep hating him . . . "You still let them all die."

"I did. I'll spend the rest of my life apologizing to you for it. But . . . I'm trying to be better than I was."

Rora's fingers still itched for a neck under them, but truly, the fire'd gone out of her. The anger had slipped away and she just felt tired and cold and sad, sad for the dead knives, sad for herself, even a little sad for the witch. She closed her eyes, let out a sigh that clouded up the air in front of her face. "If you let us out," she said, "I won't kill you. Not right now anyway."

The witch dragged himself to his knees by the bars, swaying unsteadily, his face flickering back and forth from pale to green and back. Rora saw again how beat up he was, how much pain he must be in. She couldn't watch his fingers as they wove his spells, because they didn't move like fingers should, bent and twisted. She heard it, though, when the lock sprang open.

It looked like Anddyr maybe tried to tug the door open, but it ended up being him grabbing the bars and being too stupid to let go when he fell backward. Still, it got the door open. She pushed Etarro out the cell first, but once she was out, she came near to just dashing up the tunnel, the rest of 'em be damned. It'd be the smart thing to do. You took care of yourself first, always. You had to.

The witch was staring at her from the floor, eyes still all weird, and even weirder for how . . . simple he looked. Innocent, like a kid who'd never seen a hard day in his life. Maybe it was one of those storms passing over him, like he'd said, making him less than he was but still better'n he'd been.

And the boy was staring, too, looking like he'd gone and snatched all the years from Anddyr's eyes. He had that far-eye look but he didn't say anything, just stared at Rora like maybe the whole world'd stopped to hold its breath, waiting on what she'd do.

Rora knelt down, and she didn't touch the witch but she patted the air near his shoulder. "You look hurt. You . . . can't you fix yourself?"

The witch shook his head, paused, nodded. "I could." His voice sounded like it was moving through clouds, or water. "But I'll need all my power to get us out of here. And . . . I deserve this. I've earned it."

She couldn't really argue with that. "Right, then. So what d'we do now? You think that far ahead?"

The witch opened his mouth, got a panicked look, and snapped his mouth shut. He grabbed at his hair with his broken fingers. "No . . . I don't know . . ."

"I can help." Etarro said it with his kid-voice, the one he got back when his far-eyes went away. "I know all the ways out. And I know a way out even the Ventallo don't know about. I can show you."

That sounded damned promising. "Then you can finally see what the world's like outside this fecking mountain."

"I can't go with you."

"Why in all the hells not?"

Etarro gave her a sad smile, somewhere between kid and far-eye. "We all have our parts to play."

"The black-robes'll know you helped us. You'll get in trouble. Much worse trouble than giving me a blanket."

The sad smile didn't go away. "There's nothing they can do to me that scares me."

That wasn't really any kind of reassuring.

It took both Rora and Etarro to drag the witch up. He helped where he could, but it looked like at least one of his legs was broke, and there was wet blood on him mixed with all the dried, though she couldn't figure where it came from. They got him standing, but he was near to twice as tall as either of them, so they made for poor supports. They got about two steps forward before the witch collapsed. When something didn't work, it was stupid to keep trying it—ignoring her not giving up on the piss-rope lock picks, Rora'd always been pretty good at moving on to a new plan. She left the witch lying on the ground and hooked her arms under his, dragging him along. Etarro tried to lift his feet up, but even though the witch was thin as a stick and weighed about as much, Etarro didn't have much muscle to him. He still held on to the witch's feet to keep 'em from dragging along the ground, and Rora let him feel like that was helping. She paused on the way out, dropped the witch to go grab a bundle from against one of the walls. It was the cloak she'd worn into the mountain, that the swordsmen'd yanked off her shoulders before throwing her in the cell, and it was wrapped around her daggers, all of 'em, even the old broken-stone one that Neira'd held. There was still blood along its edge, dried and brown. There wasn't time to clean it, so Rora just hid the daggers away in their usual homes and threw the cloak around her shoulders before she went back to dragging the witch.

"No one will see us," the witch kept muttering as they went up the tunnel. He'd waved a hand and the little blue light'd gone out, leaving them in the dark again. "No one will see us."

"What about hear us?" Rora growled, and then muttered a curse as her back bumped hard into a wall. Apparently the tunnel wasn't too straight. "Way I see it, a piece of air that won't fecking shut up is more suspicious'n a bloody witch."

He got quiet for a while, and then she could feel his arm muscles moving under her hands. "No one will hear us. No one will see us."

"Fecking great." She'd been hoping he'd just stop talking instead, but she had to admit whatever magic he had was probably a better way, since dragging a witch across a stone floor wasn't exactly quiet business.

Light snuck up behind Rora, creeping down the tunnel, and she near dropped Anddyr when she saw it dancing around her feet. She'd known the black-robes would come back for Etarro, but of course, it was just fitting they'd come back right as they were about to escape . . . Twisting around, she felt a flood of relief not to see a group of black-robes and swordsmen coming down the tunnel. It was just the tunnel mouth, letting in light from the hall beyond.

The hall was empty, actually, she saw when she dragged

the witch out into it. Nothing but the one torch and, so far away she could barely see them, two more torches, one leading up and one down.

"Now what?" she asked, whispering even though she didn't have to. Part of it was maybe she still didn't trust the witch, no matter what he said about being someone different— it'd be stupid to forget who he'd been, or everything that'd come before. Even if she did trust him, it felt just as stupid to go shouting while you were sneaking around. She'd been trained for sneaking, and sneaking meant whispering. Sneaking usually meant not dragging bodies around, too, but she'd also been trained to readjust when she needed to.

"Up," Etarro said. Since Rora didn't want to find out what horrors the black-robes put below their dungeons, she was happy enough to drag the witch up the slow-curving tunnel.

The witch wasn't too heavy, but still, dragging a thing uphill had a way of wearing you down. Rora's breathing was so loud in her own ears she didn't hear it, not till Etarro tugged hard on one of the witch's legs to get her attention. That, and Anddyr's muffled scream, made her stop, and the look in Etarro's eyes made her listen hard. She heard the voices then. Low, but not too far off. The people coming down the hall might not see them, or hear them, but Rora had a feeling they'd sure as shit notice when they tripped over an invisible witch.

This stretch of the hall was empty, no doors or other tunnels—nowhere to hide. "Shit," Rora muttered. She tried to think back to how far it'd been since the last tunnel and couldn't remember it. Probably far enough that she couldn't get to it at body-dragging speed faster'n it took for black-robes to catch up to them. "Shit."

"Rora . . ." Etarro was looking at her with his wide eyes that looked young as they ever had, all innocence and fear.

"I know, I know." She shifted her grip on Anddyr's armpits, heaved him up, pressed his face and chest against the wall, and used that to get him upright. "If there's anything you can do to make yourself smaller," she hissed at the witch, "now'd be the time to do it." He just shook his head, eyes as big as the kid's and looking swirlier than usual. "Shit, shit, shit." She got the witch pressed flat to the wall, nudged at his broken leg so it stopped sticking out weird, ignored the pain-noises he made. Looking up the hall, she could see a circle of light getting closer, stretching around the hall's curve. She flattened herself against the wall, and Etarro pressed in on the witch's other side, each of them throwing an arm across Anddyr to keep him flat. If it'd been up to Rora, she would've picked a different way to test if the witch's spells were working, but life hadn't left 'em too many choices.

Rora didn't spend much time thinking about all the different hells the Parents'd crafted for dead people who hadn't been good enough to become stars, but she thought maybe she could guess what one of those hells was like, because there was something awful and helpless about just standing there while danger walked slowly toward you, like staring down a stalking wolf. Knowing you could run, but not doing it anyway. It was a deeper fear. If you were running, at least you were trying to get away, trying to save your own life even if it was hopeless. Standing still, waiting . . . there was nothing to do but think how your heart had about three beats left before it stopped beating forever.

The black-robes came around the corner, four of 'em and

just as many swordsmen. A big group, and with the way the walls curved, it was hard to tell how close any of 'em came to brushing against the walls. Everything in Rora shook with the need to run, to get as far away as fast as she could, but she stood frozen like a deer, watching as the wolf prowled closer. She could see the old man, the head black-robe, near the center of the group, his empty eyes fixed ahead as the others chattered around him.

They passed by, not quite close enough to touch, but close enough she held her breath so the swordsman closest to her wouldn't feel it on his neck.

And then they were past, going on down the hall, and Rora didn't know whether to cheer or sob.

A few seconds passed, and then Rora's mind started whirling again. Pretty soon, the black-robes would find the cell empty, and the whole mountain would probably burst in searching for Rora. They'd need to be a long ways away by then.

Rora'd stood still in front of danger, but now that it was out of sight, everything was screaming at her to move, and this time she wasn't going to ignore it. Dragging the witch was too slow, so she grabbed his arms, hauled them over her shoulders, and pulled his chest onto her back. It left his legs dragging on the ground, and put an awful ache between her shoulders, but it was the fastest she could think to move without leaving him behind. Not to say she didn't think about that, but she figured her chances of living were better with someone who could set a whole village afire without blinking.

She ran, best as she could, with Etarro keeping just ahead, ran from one circle of torchlight into near darkness until her feet found the edges of the next torch, trusting the kid knew where he was going. He swung down a side tunnel, Rora right on his heels, and she stopped dead inside the room—or, more like, she *was* stopped, by running headfirst into a carcass hanging from the ceiling.

The room was full of dead things, some whole, some carved up, some no more than bones piled against the walls. They all looked to be animals, far as she could tell standing there a little dazed from running into a froze-solid pig. Etarro dashed ahead of her, weaving around the hanging carcasses and the piles of meat or bones on the floor, and she followed after him slower, dragging the witch careful around the dead things.

The room was a dead end, but Etarro seemed pretty sure there was something against the back wall. Anddyr was starting to flail, and so she let go of him next to Etarro, leaving the two of them to scrape through the offal piled against the wall. Rora stepped back, wrapping her arms around herself. It was as cold in the storeroom as her cell'd been, and she took a second to moan over the fact that she was going to die half-froze.

The witch gave a breathless shout: "I remember!" He was pawing at the wall in a spot that looked no different from any other, far in a corner where the single light hardly touched. "It was here . . ." He waved his hands around, broken fingers twitching and twisting. A horrible sound shook the room, rattled the chains the carcasses hung from, knocked over piles of clattering bones, and the wall *broke*. A crack appeared out of nowhere, spread, and peeled back like the layers of an onion, rock melting away into nothing.

She didn't know how he'd done it, but the witch had made a tunnel through the wall of the very mountain, and sunlight spilled through it.

A crow of triumph burst out of Rora, and she lunged toward the tunnel. There was no feeling as good as escaping from death.

She had to go on hands and knees to fit into the tunnel, and she was already in it when she realized neither of the others was following her. "Come on!" she shouted. She could see the sun, smell the air. She hadn't realized how stale the air inside the mountain smelled. They still didn't move, and so she backed out of the tunnel, found the witch and the boy staring at each other—Etarro shaking with his arms wrapped around himself tight, Anddyr with tears freezing to his bloody cheeks. The witch was holding his stupid stuffed horse, holding it so tight it looked like his broken fingers might burst it. "What?" she demanded. "What is it?"

"The cappo sent you to kill the Ventallo," the witch said heavily. "He sent me to kill someone else, if I could." In a sudden rush of movement, he pushed the horse into the boy's arms, and Etarro held it just as tight.

Rora looked back and forth between them. It was hard to think of anything else with freedom so close. "You mean Etarro?"

"If you kill me—" the boy near whispered it "—the Fallen will have no twins." He reached out, his fingers touching against Anddyr's hand. "They'll have no hope. It . . . would be the smart thing to do." A shiver rolled through him, and Rora remembered how he'd shook in her arms back in that cell, colder'n she'd been. "So long as I live, they'll use me against you." She remembered how he'd laughed at the story of Belora Blue-eye, pure and happy. "There'll be peace, if you kill me." Maybe it was because she'd hit her head on the dead pig, but for just a second, Etarro's face twisted, changed, looked just like her own face mirrored back at her.

"Shit on that," Rora said, and she grabbed Anddyr's ankle. She hauled him into the tunnel, dragged him behind her, and through the choking noises he made, she thought maybe she heard him say, "Thank you."

She heard that horrible grinding noise again, and when she looked over her shoulder the wall was melting, the tunnel sealing back up just like it'd been before. Etarro was kneeling in front of the shrinking hole, his face pressed close, and his voice drifted down the tunnel over the shaking sound of moving stone: "You have to come back for her, Anddyr." He waved the stuffed horse like it was a flag. "I'll forgive you. Just come ba—"

And then the stone under Rora's hands turned to dead grass dusted with snow, and the sun stabbed into her eyes, and she was free.

CHAPTER TWENTY-FOUR

They should have been back already."

It was the fourth time that day Aro had said the same words, and each time they seeped out of his mouth, Joros grew closer to strangling the younger man.

"They'll be out soon," the merra sighed.

"That's what you said all yesterday." Aro was growing more restless with each hour that went by, pacing more often than not, and usually twitching when he wasn't pacing. "Something's gone wrong. We should go in after—"

"No," Joros said firmly.

"But something must have happened. They should have been back by now, and since they're not—"

"They're likely just being thorough." *Don't engage,* Joros told himself, but the twin had a tendency to work himself into a frenzy. "Or being *patient.* As you should be. Why don't you go back to throwing sticks at birds?"

"'Cause I can't hit 'em anyway," Aro muttered.

"Patience and practice fix any problem."

He huffed, dropped down next to Joros, nudged a few

stones with a few sticks, tried to talk to one of the silent fists who just shrugged back at him, then returned to his pacing.

Joros was keeping a careful eye on the fists. They were starting to become restless as well; they were just better at hiding it. Still, it probably wouldn't be long before they were demanding answers, too, answers he didn't have . . .

A crash from the surrounding forest had everyone on their feet. Hidden weapons suddenly flashed in the fists' hands, and Joros scrambled to pull out his own short sword. Vatri, the fool, moved to huddle behind Joros, and Aro was close to her heels. He could understand why the twin thought Joros would protect him, but if the merra thought he wouldn't sacrifice her first chance he got . . .

The crash came again, loud enough that the fists could determine its direction and spun that way, waiting. A few broke away, drifting into the trees, disappearing rather effectively, and Joros cursed them for cowards, though he was tempted to follow their lead.

The source of the crashing quickly revealed itself to be a rather disheveled Rora, dragging a very battered Anddyr. Relief flooded her face, and a high laugh escaped the mage.

One of the fists stepped forward, tension written in every line of his body. "Where's the others?" he demanded

Rora shook her head. "It was a trap. They didn't make it."

The fist's face twisted. "Tare was right." He turned toward Joros, raised a hand, and Joros saw the dagger after it had already been thrown.

Joros flung himself at the ground, heard Anddyr give a wordless screech as Rora cried out her brother's name, and then the dagger thumped to the ground near Joros's head.

"Kill him," the fist said, not loud, but there was no mistaking the authority in his voice.

Lifting his head, Joros saw the fist pointing, but he was pointing at Aro. *"If every last knife doesn't come out of that mountain,"* Tare had told the fists, told Joros, *"you kill the boy."*

Joros couldn't follow all the screaming—Rora and Aro, Anddyr, the fists, the merra. Everyone had lost their damned minds. He scrambled back as all the fists rushed forward, only to pause when they ran into the barrier of a mage-shield. They battered themselves against it, cudgels and hands, daggers and heavy bodies.

Joros smirked at them; they could throw themselves at the shield as long as they liked, Anddyr would hold until he died. He could certainly hold long enough for the fists to come to their senses so they could talk things through like they were better than mindless beasts.

He'd forgotten about the fists who'd melted into the trees.

Anddyr cried out, and Joros saw the mage twisting around a dagger planted in his back. Rora was busy grappling with one of the fists, both of her hands engaged so that she couldn't reach the daggers at her hip. Anddyr writhed and, horrifyingly, one of the fists stepped slowly closer to Joros, moved sluggishly *through* the shield.

"Parents preserve us," the merra whispered.

"Anddyr," Joros shouted over the rising fury of the fists, "hold!"

The fists pressed forward, moving like they were wading through deep water, but moving forward nonetheless. The air grew strangely heavy, charged, the hairs on Joros's arms standing straight.

"—have to keep them safe!" he heard Rora shouting. He didn't have a glance to spare for her or the mage, too fixed on shuffling backward, away from the approaching fists—who, abruptly, stopped as if their feet had fixed to the ground.

The merra was chanting behind his shoulder, an obnoxious litany. She paused when the fists did, as though prayers were no longer necessary if the fists weren't actively trying to kill them. That did seem to be her thinking, since she started the chanting again when one of the fists fought two steps forward. The air grew warmer, brighter somehow, and there was a metallic taste growing in Joros's mouth.

"Rora!" Aro shouted, and his voice was as thick as though he were speaking through mud, or tears.

Joros, edging slowly backward, bumped against legs, twisted to see the merra and the twin both with their backs to a thick tree, as though they planned on making some foolish stand. The fists were still advancing, slowly, but they didn't need to move fast if their quarry wasn't trying to escape. They reached with clawing hands, with sharp daggers and heavy cudgels and hard rocks.

"Rora!" Aro shouted it again like it was the last sound he'd make, shouted it like tearing the world in half. Heat burned against Joros's scalp, his vision filling with white, and there was only the sound of mindless screaming pain. And then there was silence, save for a weeping over Joros's shoulder.

When Joros's vision cleared, the fists were gone—no, not gone, just down, sprawled . . . burned, bloody, torn, a wreckage made of their forms. Joros stared at them, took in the pieces that had moments ago been attached to other pieces, all the blood that must have escaped when the various pieces broke free, the burned flesh and charred meat that had been left behind by whatever tearing had occurred. The four wagons were similarly torn and scattered, and what big pieces were left were busy burning. He couldn't see the donkeys, but maybe pieces of them were mixed in with everything else. Joros took it all in, but couldn't find any reactions with which to connect the sight. The best he could do was think of how he hadn't believed the merra, not the slightest bit, when she'd claimed she could call on the Parents and they'd answer her call; hadn't even entertained the thought that she could be speaking truth when she boasted of killing all the Northmen in that lonely pit. Simple lies to exaggerate her own importance, to keep Joros from chucking her into a fire when she annoyed him . . .

It seemed he had been very wrong.

The sobbing was replaced by retching. Aro dropped to the ground near Joros and emptied his stomach. Across the swathe of destruction, Rora stumbled forward, trying to run and slipping over pieces of the fists. She fell next to Aro, threw her arms around him as he vomited liquid. "I'm sorry," he wept between heaves. "I'm so sorry, Rora."

"Shh," she murmured, and when Joros looked at her, there was a deep terror written across her face. "Shh, it's okay, little bird. Shh."

"Monster," a voice croaked above Joros, and that seemed a mighty harsh judgment coming from the woman who'd just killed a handful of fists.

Handful of fists. That was funny.

"Shut up," Rora snarled.

"Monster!" The merra said it louder, with more feeling, and kept shouting it as she backed away.

A delirious laugh rose over the carnage, a terribly jarring sound, like a kick between the legs. "He's not a monster," Anddyr said between spasms of laughter. He blended in very well with the dead fists, the only thing to mark him apart being that all his pieces were still mostly attached. He seemed determined, though, to see what he could shake loose as laughter rolled through him. "He's a mage."

Aro had done this? Useless, sniveling Aro, who was the toll Joros paid for his competent sister? Joros looked around at the mess, at death in its most gruesome form. He marveled—as much as he could through the cotton in his brain—at the two points in the clearing that hadn't been torn into their component parts: one point centered where Rora had been over Anddyr, and the other point centered on . . . Aro, truly a mage?

Joros thought of the village where they'd first found the twins, where Anddyr had wrought a similar carnage. Anddyr had had years of training to turn him into such an efficient killer; gods only knew what Aro could do with some training . . .

"We've gotta get out of here," Rora said. "They . . . we're too close to the mountain, they'll come looking for us . . ."

"He's doubly cursed," the merra spat. "His blood runs foul."

"Shut up!" Rora said.

"Monster and murderer," the merra went on. "You two truly are the Twins made manifest. I do not know your plans, Joros . . . but if they involve these two, I cannot be a part of them. I *will* not."

Rora spat toward the priestess. "Then go! No one wants you here anyway."

The merra spat back at the twins. "Parents curse you, all of you. Whatever dark pursuits you're following . . . I'll not be a part of them."

Anddyr's laughter still rang, shivering out across the red clearing in the forest, beneath the shadow of the mountain. The sound of footsteps, leaving, was loud amid so much death.

"You said you'd help," Joros called after her. He'd spent so much time trying to get her to leave, but now, with the rest of his plans fallen to pieces, her leaving felt like dropping a spear before a charging boar. "All the Parents' power. That's what you said."

The footsteps stopped, leaving only the mage's hysteria to fill the space. "I would have paid the price," the merra finally said. "I would have paid all it cost and more, if your cause had proved worthy. But I was wrong about you. I didn't listen when I should have, closed my eyes and ears to reason. You are not worthy. There is nothing I will give to you." Footsteps again, and this time they did not stop. Joros didn't have any words to stop them.

For a long while, it was only the laughter, the high and wild sounds of the mage's madness. Even that sound died, after a time. Joros wondered, dimly, if Anddyr had died as well.

"We have to go," Rora said softly, but there was little conviction in her voice. She still sat wrapped around her brother, but his cheeks had gone dry, his eyes fixed resolutely at the treetops.

"Yes," Joros agreed, and used the tree at his back to pull himself to his feet.

Anddyr wasn't dead, or at least not *obviously* dead. He was certainly bleeding, and he'd stopped moving or laughing, but his breath wheezed out through his open mouth. That seemed a good sign. Rora grabbed the mage's wrists, and then stared back and forth between Joros and her brother. Joros stared back. Aro eventually took the mage's feet.

They made an awkward procession, bumping frequently into trees, stumbling and falling on occasion. Joros trailed after the other three, thoughts wandering around his mind like drunkards, crashing occasionally into each other and reeling away. It occurred to him that this was not his normal state, that there was some sort of distance between the world and his thoughts, some kind of fog. He could recognize that. Didn't have the bloodiest idea what to do about it, but he could recognize it. He could recognize, too, that the distance was probably a good thing. It made it easier, when a frightening sort of thought came crashing through his mind, to feel only a small twinge of panic.

He was growing steadily more fucked.

CHAPTER TWENTY-FIVE

"You're daft!" Berno shouted. The heavy flesh of his arms shook within his robes as his hands flew to the air.

"And you're fat." Zenora's voice was sharp as ever. Face pinched as though she tasted something sour.

"At least I've a reason for being fat. Food tastes good. You've no reason to be so stupid."

"You could stand to enjoy food a little less."

"After so many decades oozing across the earth, one would think you'd have managed to pick up a *little* common knowledge—"

Herrit's elbow tapped against Scal's. "What are they arguing about now?" the boy asked softly. He had a way of speaking so that his mentors would not hear him over their own heated voices. He had a skill, too, for reading as he walked. Most often, the boy had his nose pressed between the pages of a book. He let his ears guide him, following the sound of bickering as he read without looking from the words. Some days ago, with winks and broad smiles, Berno and Zenora had carefully argued their way off the road and let their arguing guide Herrit straight into a small pond. The boy had dropped his book into the water and still not forgiven them the wet pages, or their laughter. Still, it had not stopped him continuing to read as they walked.

Scal shook his head. "Zenora saw a bird."

"Ah," was all Herrit said, a small smile on his lips.

"What do you read?" Scal tapped a finger against the creased and faded leather that held together the pages of Herrit's newest book. He had three books, always. Each time they came to a town, the boy would go trade one of his books for a new one. Though most of the villages looked at the preachers with hard eyes, business was business. It helped that they only passed through, that they did not stop to preach.

Herrit glanced inside the pages as though he had forgotten. Scal could not imagine how he kept so many words in his head. "Banquero's treatise on peace." He looked up to Berno and Zenora, whose voices were growing steadily louder. "Ironic, isn't it?"

Scal nodded. He liked the boy, but Herrit was not always easy to talk to. He spent too much time inside his own head. He was kind, and gentle, but seemed most often to not be much like a boy. Older than the years on his skin.

"Have you decided yet where you're going?" Herrit asked.

There were times, too, when he seemed every one of his few years. "I have not," Scal said softly.

"It's only . . . well, we'll be to the Forest Voro soon . . ."

Together, their eyes lifted. They were days away, but the shape of Mount Raturo loomed above the shape of the land. A distant thing, but sharp. Dangerous. A thing to be feared.

"I know," Scal said softly, turning back to the road. Ahead,

Berno and Zenora had settled to grumbling. They would mutter for a time, until they found a new thing to argue about. After a moment, Herrit returned his nose into his book.

That day, as their feet pressed the road and the mountain swept closer, their path merged with another's. It was a woman, though Scal did not know it until she lowered her black hood. Long hair, and soft features, and smooth dents where eyes once had been long ago. "Greetings to you, sister!" Berno boomed, and the woman gave him a soft smile.

"You are returning, brother?" She had a voice like distant music. Her head swayed, ever so slightly, tipping and tilting as she searched for a response.

Zenora looped her arm through the younger woman's and said, "We are. And you?"

"Of course." She was lovely, somehow, when she smiled full. In spite of the eyes that were not there. Lovely, and broken. Her name was Anelle.

They walked together through the rest of the day. Feet following their shadows that stretched ahead in the moonlight. The great Forest Voro reached to meet them, scattered stands of trees growing closer, thicker, broader.

Herrit had told him in whispers that preachers were supposed to sleep in the day and travel through the night, but it was a hard thing to do. There was a silent agreement among the wandering preachers, he said, that it was a fine thing to hold to the ideals. But reality could not be ignored. As the sun set, light spreading like blood into snow, they stopped among the trees. Weaving, wending between trunks, to the heart of the copse. Anelle stumbled over a twisted root and nearly fell. Scal was not so far behind, and caught her arm, raised her up. She gave a nervous laugh, turning her eyeless face to him for the first time. "I'm sorry . . . I didn't see you." There was no joking to the words, only sincerity. Her head bobbed gently, twisting one ear toward him and then the other. "Are you always so quiet?"

Scal nodded. Realized. "Yes," he said, and his voice felt too loud, too deep. As though too many words might shake her to pieces.

Her hand touched his arm, gentle. Not fear, nor hesitation. The touch given to a wild thing that needed taming. Her head tilted. "Where are you bound?" She did not name him "brother." Sightless, she perhaps saw him for what he was. Still, there was no disapproval in her voice, no reproach. Only curiosity.

"I do not know," Scal said truthfully.

They sat in the shade of tall trees. Tired from walking, but none of them ready for sleep.

"Would you mind," Anelle asked, voice soft as falling snow, "if I told a story?"

Berno wrapped his arms around his big belly, and Zenora clasped her shaking hands beneath her chin, and Herrit gently closed his book. "Please," Zenora said. "None of these louts could tell a story to save their own lives."

"Oh ho," Berno said, "and you're always eager to tell a story, are you? At least I—"

"Hush," Herrit said, leaning toward Anelle. The surprise of being silenced by his apprentice closed Berno's mouth.

Anelle turned her face to the sky, and a smile turned her lips. "Long ago," she began, "in the time when Sororra and Fratarro still walked beside our ancestors, there was a young man named Birro. He was a walker, his feet and his heart full of restlessness. He walked all the corners of the world, and still he found no place that pleased him, no place that reached to his heart, no place to rest his feet.

"Do not feel sad for Birro, no—for he loved the walking, and he found joy in each wonder he saw, in each new place his feet took him, and the kindness of his fellow men touched his soul. Many doors opened to him, and countless hearths became his bed; he never hungered and never grew cold, for men would share their bread and women would spread cloaks over Birro's shoulders. He was welcomed in each place his feet touched. Yet, still, Birro would lie before a warm hearth wrapped in a borrowed blanket, belly full of freely given food, and he would see things that made his restless heart ache.

"A man brushing the hair from his wife's face. A mother rocking her child to sleep. A boy feeding his ailing father. A woman so old she couldn't move without shaking, caring for a flock of abandoned children. Strangers, all, with so much love in their hearts, and in their homes.

"Always, Birro would leave the warm hearth before the sun rose, before the kind strangers would wake. He would leave his borrowed blanket folded on the warm hearth, and atop it a small trinket, something picked up and carried from one corner of the world to another. A leaf or a rock, a bit of bone, or some gift that had been pressed into his hand by another kind stranger, in another kind place. Birro would leave his small offering, and walk through the door that had so readily opened to him, and he would walk again. Searching, always searching for a place where he could plant his roots, a place where he could grow, and flourish.

"In all his wandering, Birro came to a place of great beauty, where trees soared taller than twenty men and rivers sang with gentle voices and everything was painted with bright colors. For all that he loved the place, it did not pull at Birro's heart, did not grab at his feet. It was not home.

"Birro sat beside a broad lake that was a perfect blue, fed by a tumbling waterfall like a lullaby, and sadness touched on his soul. If this place, this paradise, could not grant him happiness, surely he was broken.

"A voice spoke to him then, in the same lilting voice as the water: *'A thing is not broken that has not found its proper place.'* Birro raised his eyes, and in the sweeping colors of paradise stood a piece of the night sky fallen and given breath.

"It was a *mravigi*, though Birro didn't know it; he saw only a winged creature every bit as magnificent as the land he had found, though in a darker way. Beautiful, for all the possibilities that swirled beneath its surface.

"*'Come with me,'* the *mravigi* said, *'and we shall find your place.'* It bent one great wing in invitation, and moving like a dream, Birro climbed upon the *mravigi's* back. Those great wings flexed and flapped, and Birro's feet left the ground, and his heart soared at his side.

"They flew, Birro and the *mravigi* named Iele, flew high as high, until they touched the very moon. Birro laughed, and wept, and grinned, and learned that his heart had simply been seeking out the sky, his feet searching for the moon.

"Birro has made the moon his home, and made of it a kind place, a place where he cooks and cleans and smiles. A place where roots can sink into the ground and grow deep. Yet, there's still a restless streak in him, and Iele loves to fly. They travel together to all the stars, a new one each night, resting in the warm fire and sharing stories, taking the simple joys there are to be taken.

"Always, when they leave, Birro leaves a gift—an old habit of his. He leaves something, picked up and carried from one end of the sky to the other: a piece of the moon, small and careful, laid gentle upon the fire of the star who hosted him. And so the moon shrinks as he travels, grows smaller as its pieces are scattered wide among the stars, dwindling slowly to nothing . . . until Birro returns, his hands full of small gifts brought from all across the sky, and builds the moon whole once more, a thing made of love, and joy, and a little bit of adventure."

The sun was well and truly gone when Anelle finished her tale, only moonlight twisting through the tree branches. Anelle sat, still, smiling into the light. If she felt their eyes on her, she did not show it.

"Well told, sister," Berno finally said. "I do not think I have heard that tale."

Anelle turned her smile down to him. "It's one of my favorites."

There was a deep sense of peace, laid over them each like a blanket by her words. They lay down upon the ground, wrapped in blankets and cloaks. Scal could not say if the others slept. He did not—or, at least, not right away. He lay staring to the sky, wondering if flying would make his heart sing. If his feet would thrill to touch the moon. If there was a place for him, anywhere, at all.

Two more preachers found them the next day. A man and a woman, passing a wailing child back and forth. They were welcomed as Anelle had been. Named "brother" and "sister."

Found more sets of hands willing to pass the wailing babe. They looked at Scal with curiosity, but with the same lack of judgment Anelle's voice had held. They let Scal hold their child for a time, but the baby grew no quieter in his big hands than it had in the others', and so he passed it along.

Scal nudged Herrit, and the boy raised his eyes from his book. "Are there always so many of you?" Scal asked.

Herrit's gaze flicked to Berno, to Zenora, to the others who had joined them and talked easily over the baby's squalling. His fingers touched a pendant hanging at his throat, dropped quickly. "It's . . . not for me to say. Ask Berno," he finally said, and quickly returned to his book.

Scal lengthened his legs to walk beside Berno. "A fine day, m'boy!" he boomed, hands clapping his round belly. "A fine day indeed, and those don't come often."

Voice low, much lower than Berno's, Scal asked, "Are there always so many of you?"

"There are scores and hundreds and thousands of preachers, m'boy! More than anyone thinks."

Scal waved his hand, fingers flicking to Anelle, the newcomers with their babe, Zenora, Berno himself. "So many at once?"

"Ahhhh," Berno rumbled. "That. Well, you see, you've found us at an interesting time." Berno looked to the mountain, visible still over the treetops, though the spreading pines had grown closer, taller, fuller. The fat man touched his fingers to his throat. A stone hung there, nearly identical to Herrit's. Scal, who was so conscious of the pendants hanging at his own throat, had not noticed the stones before. "We have been summoned," Berno said, "all of us. Every man, woman, and child, called home." He turned to Scal. "I don't know why, m'boy, and I can't say that I'd tell you even if I did—no offense, of course. But I do know there are likely to be important things happening. You'll be having some choices to make, m'boy, and sooner than not."

Scal looked to the mountain, and to his feet. Lifted his hand, dropped it before his fingers could touch the flamedisk and the snowbear claw beneath his shirt. "I know."

The trees grew thicker around them, branches reaching to block out the sun's light. The great mountain disappeared behind their screen, but a path was worn into the forest floor. The way made clear by countless feet through countless years. Shadows stretched and danced, and joy thrilled through the group. The baby, finally, stopped crying. They walked through the thick trees that spread without end, and though their feet crunched on needles and leaves untouched by snow, they did not seem to be moving at all. Each tree so like the others, and nothing but forest for the eye to see.

For that reason alone—the way time passed with no progress made, the stillness in movement—Scal felt once more as though he were walking through the swirling grayness of the far North. Walking, and going nowhere. Each step a meaningless thing, made against the vastness of the place. It was strange, but Scal felt as though he were waiting for the killing cold to reach out its hand. Fingers of ice wrapping around him. Pressing. Holding. A patient thing, for it did not have to devour. It had only to wait. He knew, truly knew, that it was not possible . . . and still. A shiver rolled through him, though his blood ran warm and the southern cold did not touch him.

The trees broke, fell away as though a god's hand had swept

them aside. Perhaps it had. The clearing was broad, and made larger by the rough stone that broke free from the earth. Mount Raturo. Raised by Fratarro, seat of a god, home of the Fallen. It seemed a sheer cliff, curving away to either side. They were still many lengths from the mountain, far enough that it would take minutes even running to press his hands to its face. Scal did not have the words to describe it. Perhaps Herrit, with all his books and all his words, could do it justice. The only thing Scal could do was stare.

A hand touched his shoulder. Berno's eyes were on him again, blue and honest. "It's time, m'boy. No point in dancing around it anymore. If you'd like to join us, I can show you where to start the climb. I don't doubt you'd make it to the top, and mayhap you'd give the Sentinels a good scare along the way. It'd be a fine thing." Berno reached with both hands, and Scal let the fat man turn him. Standing chest to chest, eye to eye. Hands firm around Scal's arms. "You're welcome here, Scal. If you'd like."

He could feel them staring. Berno's gaze heavy, for all the lightness that flowed through him. Zenora's sharp as claws, steady, though the rest of her might shake. Herrit's with the wisdom of a man and the hope of a child. Anelle, who had no eyes, and yet he felt her gaze still.

He did not know if the mountain was the place for him. But Birro had not known the moon was his true home until he set his feet upon it.

Scal opened his mouth to accept. To find his place at their sides, feet taking well-walked paths. To sit once again at the feet of a wise man, to learn, to be better than he was. To ask for the home they offered. "It is not the moon," his lips said instead.

They understood. Their lives were built of rejection, of dismissal. They clasped his arm, touched his shoulder, offered smiles that no longer reached their eyes. Anelle's touch lingered, and her smooth face seemed to stare. Yet she, too, left. Left him at the edge of the trees, the edge of a life.

There was a hollowness in him, and he had no name for it. The whispering, bear-deep voice in his mind—the only thing left of the red-robed priest with his gentle wise words—sighed, and fell silent. Something in him broke and fell away.

Scal turned his back to the mountain, to the black-robed men and women walking from him. Not his brothers, not his sisters. Just people, like any others. And he could not keep people. It was not a skill he had.

He walked once more into the deep trees. Turned his feet from the worn path, took them through the crunching undergrowth, where the ground was thick with hard, desperate life, fighting for sunlight. Did not know where his feet were walking. Did not care. There was no moon for his feet to touch, and so it did not matter where they went.

Words fluttered slow through his mind. Forgotten words, pushed away. Words he did not want to remember. The words of a woman who had worn a robe in a different color. *I need you.* He had made her leave, too. Had not wanted her to stay. She had grown too close, pieces of himself beginning to tie around pieces of her. Beginning to reshape him, to make him a different person. *Please, don't leave me*, she had said as she left. As Scal cut away the pieces of himself.

He had wanted this life to be a bloodless one. But there did not need to be blood for there to be pain.

"Scal?" a voice said, and it did not speak in his mind.

She stepped through the branches like a star, yellow robe glowing bright in the tight-treed gloom. He watched her come, not trusting his own eyes until she touched a hand to his chest.

Once, long ago, red-robed Parro Kerrus had given purpose to his second life, shaped him into a person that was strong and good and who knew his own path. He had wanted to be the man who the priest had tried to shape. Tried, and failed, and the priest's bear-rumble voice was gone from his mind. His words of guidance vanished, lost, and Scal felt adrift without them.

Perhaps the words could be replaced with another voice, and a new hand to guide him. A new hand, light and scar-seamed, to shape his life. A yellow-robed priestess, to give him purpose once more.

Scal did not know he moved, but his arms were wrapped around her, solid as hope. Maybe there was no moon for him. But a star, perhaps, would do.

CHAPTER TWENTY-SIX

Anddyr was fairly certain that he'd died. Everything felt like fire, and his God promised an eternal afterlife in the glow of His cleansing flames, so that was one point in favor of death. The problem, though, was that this fire *hurt*, and the whole point of cleansing flames was to wipe away all those silly mortal concerns like hurt and hunger and fear. That was a point against death, which left Anddyr no closer to knowing the truth.

Something nudged his ribs, hard. "He still breathing?"

"Don't do that," another voice snapped.

Anddyr turned his head and groaned, which had the effect of moving his eyes away from the dirt to which they'd been pressed. He saw that he was certainly not cradled in the gentle flames of a loving God, but was, in fact, lying facedown on a dirty patch of snow that was heavily colored by his own blood.

"Oh, good," a voice drawled. "He's alive."

A hand touched the side of his head, and Anddyr looked up. He allowed himself a wistful moment to think that perhaps he *had* died, considering the vision kneeling above him. God had never said anything about angels, but that meant he hadn't said there weren't angels either.

Rora patted his cheek quite forcefully—more two quick slaps than anything comforting. "You should probably get to healing yourself." She stood and walked away, going instead to sit at her brother's side, their backs to a thick tree.

"She's right," the cappo said mildly. "We'll have to move again soon, and I don't get the impression she'll drag you much farther."

"Where?" Anddyr croaked. It was the best he could manage, but he was already reaching out with mental fingers to inspect the damage to his body. It was . . . rather extensive. There were the lingering wounds from his mad race through Raturo, at least one leg broken and the other badly twisted at best, various scrapes and gashes, a throbbing lump on the side of his head. That was all before the two stabs to his back, which had somehow mercifully missed anything vital, and were already beginning to knit—that was the wonderful thing about the magic pulsing through his veins. Even unconscious, a mage was a hard thing to kill. He pulled on his stores of power, slowly refilling from his earlier, wanton use, and encouraged the healing along in his back, as well as in his legs—there was a terrifying undercurrent of truth to the cappo's claim that Rora wouldn't help carry him along anymore.

The cappo waved a lazy hand, and Anddyr had to twist his neck around to see what the cappo gestured to: the mountain, Raturo, always visible from a distance, but they weren't at a distance. They were still terrifyingly close, close enough that Raturo's shadow would likely swallow them when the sun sank. Anddyr gaped, his heart pounding erratically in his chest.

His head felt clear as it ever did, but still, specters of black-robed preachers swept down from the mountain's peak, shuddered through the surrounding trees, reached black-clawed hands out toward him . . .

"Anddyr," the cappo said, drawing back his eyes and mind. Joros held a little round-bellied jar in his palm. Anddyr's guts split in two at the sight of the jar, half twisting into knots as the other half flew up to lodge in his throat. "I couldn't find your skura on you, Anddyr."

"I . . . I lost it, cappo," Anddyr choked out. The storms were swirling at his margins, summoned by the sight of the jar, the thought of its sweet taste, the bright smell of it.

"Lost it," Joros repeated. His eyes bored into Anddyr.

Anddyr could only nod, his throat too heavy to speak. Still the cappo stared, and the truth hung on Anddyr's tongue—*I'm strong now, I'm free of you, I'm better*—but his mouth watered, and the storms of madness swung closer, and the words in his mouth began to taste more of false truths.

The cappo finally smiled one of those brittle smiles, and he gave a studied shrug. "Well, then." He leaned forward, hand twisting and turning, skin sloughing away and regrowing as leaves, fingers releasing the little jar on the cold, muddy, bloody ground before Anddyr's face. "I don't doubt you're overdue for your dosage. Go on."

Anddyr's hand shook, weak thing that it was, as he reached out to wrap his fingers around the smooth, turned clay. Touching it sent fire down his spine, made his wounds scream, his legs spasm, but it was a sweet sort of pain. *I'm free now*, he told himself, but the words fell like stones into an empty well, touching nothing, causing no ripples. Etarro had freed him from Joros, given him the chance to fight free of all of it. He had to *keep* fighting, for the rest of his short life, fighting the temptation, because even one dose would destroy everything. If he took this skura, he'd be lost again, trapped, enslaved, Joros's pet mage, no better than he had been—*worse* than he had been, because it meant knowing he had his freedom, knowing he could be better, and tossing it away because he really was too weak. *I have to be strong . . . be better . . .*

"Go on, Anddyr," the cappo said, his voice growing more sharp.

But he *was* weak, he always had been. Why had he ever thought otherwise? Anddyr twisted his other arm and it shook as badly. Half his forearm was bloodied and scraped, and he thought maybe that was a true thing, true seeing, but he couldn't be sure. He felt nothing but the jar in his hands, the throbbing pulse of it. He wrapped his palm over the lid, began to twist—

"Joros," Rora called out, and her voice set a spike into Anddyr's brow, the storms shattering over him. They fell in sharp, glass-edged pieces, raining around him as the cappo's thundercloud eyes turned away.

"What?" the cappo snapped.

"I met someone in the mountain. A woman named Neira . . ." Squinting through the storm-haze, Anddyr saw Rora wave her hand. Beckoning. That put iron in the cappo's spine—he wasn't one to be beckoned, and he stalked over to the twins likely to tell them so. Rora's eyes flickered, looked around the cappo, past him . . . and fixed on Anddyr. Her gaze was hard, and her mouth was set, and the jar in his hands grew heavy as a boulder.

Joros snapped at Rora, "I know her. The woman is full of lies and cheap tricks. I'm sure she spouted plenty of nonsense at you about shadows."

The storm sparked and spit around him, as Anddyr carefully set the jar on the ground before his face. *I am free*, he told himself, and this time the words rang like a bell through the storm. *I am better than this*. His hands still shook, though not so badly, as they began to weave sigils in the air.

"She knew things she shouldn't've," Rora said.

The cappo made a derisive noise, like a horse snorting. "She's an excellent manipulator of people, I'll give her that. She was one of my . . . subordinates, but she gathered a bit of a following of her own. Had them convinced they could bring back blood magic. But the secrets of blood magic fell with the Twins."

"Doesn't Anddyr's medicine work with blood?"

Quietly, softly, a fire burned through the jar. The smell of it lanced through Anddyr, making his stomach twist, a pathetic moan bursting from between his lips. His fingers twisted, and the fire burned brighter, hotter, consuming the black paste— and then Anddyr let his hands fall, fingers still. He could sense the remaining skura like a living thing, boiling and growling in the bottom of the jar, so little of it, just in case, just in case. His hands shook as he lifted up the jar, shook as he tucked it into his robe. *It's not there*, he told himself, hoping with his skura-madness that the belief would remain. *It's gone, all gone. I am free.*

And then the lowering storm dropped. The skura was gone, but the need wasn't.

Anddyr pressed his forehead to the ground, the snow hot

against his skin, and wrapped his arms over his head, pressing them around his ears. He couldn't see and couldn't hear, was safe from the storm, from everything it could throw at him . . .

Daggers tore into his body. They started at his legs, found the places his bones and tendons and flesh were beginning to knit, found the weak places and plunged. He could feel the hilts, the cold metal against his burning flesh. He had felt this before, this same thing, when the scar-faced merra had whispered to him that he was strong, that he could stop—and the daggers had torn into him then, too, ripping him apart, and they'd made him burn that village, all those people . . . *No, no, I can't, not again, please. I am free, please, not again.* The daggers dragged themselves up along his legs, slowly, steadily. He could feel them shifting, aiming higher, angling for his heart—

"Anddyr."

Braving the storm, facing the burned village, he lifted his head, focusing on her. She knelt in front of him, and even though her face was twisted, concern drifted around her eyes.

"We're leaving," she said. "Get up." Those were the words she spoke, but he could hear the words that lay under her voice, the words that spun on her face: *You're better than this.*

Anddyr got his aching knees under him, pressed his hands to the ground that his blood had frozen into, rocked onto his heels, and pushed up. He swayed, near falling, but didn't dare reach for her. Her hand caught him of its own volition, steady, warm, like her eyes. "Good," she said, her fingers lingering just a moment, and then she turned away.

The storm still raged around him, but he had a small shield

against it now, a shield that smelled like her, flowers and soft and dirt.

The cappo eyed him as they strung through the trees, four bodies together but so far apart. "You're acting strange," the cappo said.

Promptly, Anddyr offered, "I'm weak." *I'm healing. I'm growing strong.*

The cappo snorted, and said no more.

The silence stretched with the shadows, save for the storm that swirled around Anddyr, the storm that stuck his tongue to the roof of his mouth until he finally peeled it away and asked, "What now?"

The cappo glared and said nothing. Rora didn't look back at him. Aro finally took pity and said, "We don't know."

Anddyr reached within his robe, brushed his fingers against the smooth thing secreted away in one of his pockets. What he saw surprised him. Swallowing, Anddyr offered, "There were more preachers inside the mountain than ever before, and there was . . . even more mystery than usual. There were rumors that all the Fallen were leaving soon. I . . . I think something is happening, or they're planning something."

The cappo snorted. "Oh, you think so, do you?"

Anddyr felt a strange burning in his chest. He couldn't name what it was; it had been so long since he'd felt anything like it. "Rebellion" wasn't quite the word, but it touched at the edges. "I do," Anddyr said, drawing his fist from his robe. He held his hand out toward Joros, fingers up, and uncurled them to show the seekstone sitting on his palm. Frowning, the cappo held one hand up to halt Rora and Aro, who were watching with raised brows, and he reached his other hand out to pluck the stone from Anddyr. He saw the cappo's eyes narrow even as they went distant, drawn away by the seekstone's power. Anddyr kept the smile off his lips.

"Who is this?" the cappo demanded.

Anddyr hesitated, but decided there was no gain in lying. "Etarro."

Joros's eyes flickered away from the seekstone's pull, his glare resting on Anddyr. He could see the cappo's own storm gathering, waiting to drop. "The boy? You got this, but you couldn't—"

"It was the best I could do," Anddyr interrupted, and then nearly bit off his tongue as anger washed over the cappo's face. He never would have, *shouldn't* have, dared to interrupt the cappo. He flinched away from the cappo's palpable anger, and it was not entirely for show. "I couldn't reach the boy," he lied, "but I thought this would help . . ." He remembered Etarro's hand, resting atop his, as they knelt together before the sun-lit tunnel. He remembered how often Etarro had whispered of his sun-touched dreams. He remembered the boy's sad soft words—*"There'll be peace, if you kill me"*—even as his small hand had pressed the seekstone into Anddyr's. He couldn't look at Rora, for fear that she'd give voice to the lie in his words, that her accusing gaze would undo him. The words tasted like rotting meat, but Anddyr forced them past his teeth: "Did I . . . Cappo, did I do well?"

Joros glared a moment longer, and then his gaze slipped away, drawn once more by the second sight the seekstone offered.

A hand brushing his back startled Anddyr, and he twisted

painfully to see Rora standing there, her eyes strange. She kept her voice low when she asked, "Why aren't you ever who I think you are?"

"They're leaving," the cappo murmured. There was surprise in his voice, shock, and something almost like reverence. "All of them."

"Are they coming after us?" Rora asked. She had a hand on one of her daggers.

The cappo shook his head, face going set and grim. "They're hunting for a bigger prize."

"They know where to find the Twins," Anddyr whispered. "They know how to bring them back." He didn't have the seekstone anymore, so he couldn't see it . . . but it was almost like he could. They were, truly, not so far from the mountain; not so far away that he couldn't see the black-robed preachers boiling from Raturo's peak like ants from a hill, spilling down its sides, an angry mass collecting, gathering, waiting like a coiled serpent wound around the mountain, slowly tightening.

He'd watched through the seekstone as much as he could, concerned for Etarro, so he'd seen the boy wandering aimlessly through the mountain, waiting for Valrik and the others to find him. Anddyr hadn't heard the words of that confrontation, the seekstones didn't have that power, but he'd seen Valrik strike Etarro, and he'd seen the way Valrik's eyes held a touch of fear after. Whatever the boy said had sent the preachers scrambling, Valrik among them. Scrambling, no doubt, to mobilize the Fallen, to ready for their long journey. He'd watched Etarro go to one of the hidden doors, standing outside the mountain on the ridge that spiraled around its sides, and stare south. Waiting for the Fallen to ready themselves, waiting for the Fallen to take him to his godly counterpart. Anddyr wondered if, in those long staring moments, he had heard Fratarro's unending call: *Find me.* The desperate plea of a broken god, that had found its way through Anddyr's consciousness on occasion, but that seemed to pulse through Etarro like an irregular heartbeat. *Find me.*

"What now?" Aro asked, a higher echo of Anddyr's earlier words. The younger man wavered in shades of green, when Anddyr looked to him.

The cappo tucked the seekstone into one of his pockets, and his face was set like a man about to put his head through a noose. "We follow them," he said, and he turned, began walking through the trees the way they had come, walking toward the mountain, toward the rippling, black-scaled viper that waited there.

CHAPTER TWENTY-SEVEN

Vatri was silent as they walked through the thick trees, so close their arms brushed. Silence was strange on her, but she had changed since last he saw her. Thin-faced beneath the ridged scars, blue eyes grown dimmer. Pieces of herself, sheared off, stripped away, broken. But Scal, too, had changed since last he saw her face. Both of them torn like a wound and stitched closed as best as possible.

They found a glade. Free of the reaching trees, it was dusted with snow, marked by the feet of forest creatures. No boot prints, though. The sun winked at them over the treetops, slipping slowly away. They sat together at the clearing edge, backs to a tree broader than both of them. Their shoulders touched.

"I was wrong." Vatri spoke softly, and did not look at him. Watched her hands, folded against her knees. He watched them, too. Saw how they clenched, loosened, shook. "I still look into the fire every night, but it hasn't shown me anything in weeks. I thought maybe I'd offended the Parents somehow . . . and I suppose, in a way, I did. I took the wrong path, after they'd shown me the right one. I . . . thought I knew better than them."

One hand curled into a fist. "I thought Joros was the right path, but he's not. Or maybe he was, once, but he's taken a new path, and . . ." She stopped, and her face tilted, turned. Eyes finding his in the slowly dimming light. "The fires showed you to me. I should never have left you."

There was too much in her eyes. He looked away from them, said, "I should not have left you." An echo of her words, but it was all he could say. He could not look at her face, to see if they were enough.

The silence fell again. Shoulders touching, hands twitching restless. There had been a space between them, when first they had met. A space filled with Scal's distrust and his isolation, a space filled with habit and fear. She had reached to him across that space, and closed it. He had not seen it until she was gone, and the space was left empty. Now, joined again, the space between them was slim . . . but in the sinking light Scal could see it growing wider. The space between them stretching like an open mouth, and her hands stayed on her knees. Clenching, loosening, shaking. She would not reach across that space again.

"I was wrong," Scal said. Her words echoed, but they fit his mouth as well. "I thought that I should be something different. Something better. I have not ever been a good man. I wanted to be good." So many words came hard to him. They tumbled around in his mind, breaking away and re-forming, and they did not find their way easily to his tongue. "But I do not know how. I am as I was shaped, and I do not know how to change it. All my life, I have been shaped by the hands of others. I . . . wished to learn how to shape myself. Wished to be my own man." The trees swallowed the sun, shadows sinking deep.

Their shoulders touched, but the dark lay between them, and he could not tell if it was only shadow or the great wide maw. In the dusky light, he thrust out his hand, crossing the space between them. His fingers clutched at hers. "I do not know who I am, or how to be better. Once, you would have shaped me. Made me the man you wished me to be." He lifted his face, found her eyes, moon-wide in the seamed curves of her face. Meeting, across the shrinking space between them. "There are worse things than to be shaped by your hands."

She twined her fingers around his, and her eyes were soft. There was a sadness there, and a surety. She rose, fingers slipping from his. "We need firewood," she said.

Two fires she built. One small, fed with twigs and herb-pouches pulled from her belt, a fire that smelled like prayers against a clawing-cold night. A fire to hold back the darkness, to warm fingers and toes, to scare off predators and draw in friends. A gentle fire.

The second fire was like to swallow the whole forest. A fire great enough to swallow darkness itself.

Higher and higher she fed it, the flames dancing mad in her eyes, the heat making Scal's skin feel tight-stretched even where he stood at a safe distance. It bit at the trees' highest branches, leaves and needles curling, blackening. Falling gentle in a gray snow of ash. It drove back the night, making daylight in that small clearing. A sun in the night, that danced upon the snow-touched ground.

When the small fire died, deep in the night, Vatri told him to remove his clothes. "All of them," she added, looking to the side of him. Her ridged skin could not blush, but he thought that it would have, when she looked at him. Even the pendants she took from him, the flamedisk and the snowbear claw that hung always against his skin. She put the leather cord around her own neck, the pendants resting over her heart, one of fire and one of the ice.

She took a handful of ashes from the dead fire, and with deft fingers drew the ashes onto Scal's body. They were not any symbols he recognized, trailing over his flesh like leeches. If he looked at them too long, it seemed almost as though they moved. She drew a large symbol on each of his palms, designs that were like a mirror to each other. Her fingers brushed over the convict's cross in his cheek, and dragged heavy over the other cheek, as though she were trying to grind the ash into his skin.

In the depths of the night, bright as any day with the huge fire blazing, she stepped back from him. A small figure, between Scal and the fire. Her hands were black with ash, and shadows made pits of her eyes. "Do you trust me?" she asked.

"I do."

She did not touch him, did not risk smudging her long work, but she led him nonetheless. He would have followed, no matter where she went. Even to the edge of that great fire where his flesh felt as though it would melt from his bones. She held up one hand, finger pointing. Tongues of the fire, stretching to lick at that finger. Trying to pull her in.

With a breath, Scal stepped past her and into the heart of the fire.

The sun found him in a pile of ash. Bone-aching, bone-weary. Naked as the day of his birth, the cinder-drawn symbols faded from his flesh. It felt almost a dream. Perhaps it had been, for he remembered nothing after the flames had wrapped around his flesh, nothing but their whispering in his ears. Something like that, he surely could have dreamed.

Scal sat, ash rising in a cloud with his movement. It swirled around him, tugged by gentle breezes, a shifting shroud. His palms ached like they had been stabbed, but there was no mark on them. His head, too, ached so fiercely it hurt to think of it. His eyes flickered, hunting through the clearing. Vatri would tell him what had happened. What was real, and what was dream. Why he hurt. His eyes searched, but the glade was empty.

Empty, save for the dozens of boot prints that marred the scattered, ash-dusted snow. Large prints, marching and cross-ing, circling, circling. A handful of men, likely drawn by the fire.

Scal stood, aching palm to aching head, and the ash wrapped around his feet, trailing his steps. He went carefully around the boot prints, curled toes sure against the snow. His clothes were where he had left them, half-frozen. He did not feel their cold against his skin. He was of the North, and his blood ran warm.

The rising sun shone off something bright, near the clear-ing's edge. Leaning down, his fingers wrapped around the bright thing, drew it up. His pendants, the claw and the flamedisk. The leather cord broken, torn.

Scal closed his fingers around them, the edge of the disk bit-ing into his flesh, the claw's tip drawing blood. Cold from the snow, he held them over his heart. His eyes traced the path of the boot prints. He found where they had entered the clearing, and where they had left it. On their leaving, there was a smaller set of prints among the larger ones. Marched away, at the center of those who had found the clearing. Scal followed them, his feet covering the smaller set of prints. The pendants bit into his palm, and he felt nothing.

CHAPTER TWENTY-EIGHT

Keiro sat at the crest of a small hill, barely more than a wrinkle in the ground, but it gave him height enough to look out over the grasses that stretched endlessly away. In the fading light, they moved like water, rolled like the great ocean Keiro had found at the western edge of the world. Often, he had found peace in watching the grass sway, found patterns to the way the wind stirred the brown-green sea.

Watching now did not bring him any peace. Keiro was not sure he would ever find such a thing again.

One hand rested on the small form lying at his side, feeling the gentle rise and fall of even breaths. Cazi had fled through the tunnels, spurred by fear or anger or pain. Keiro had left more slowly, though no less alone, crawling the tunnels with his thoughts swirling. Cazi had hidden himself away in a little dell between the hills, covered by shrub and scree, but Keiro had found him nonetheless—walked straight to the Starborn, as though his feet had known the way. Cazi hadn't fought when Keiro had lifted him up, had let Keiro cradle him as he walked through the hills, making a shelter of his arms and his chest. He'd brought them to this place, the gentle hill that stood like a border between the rest of the hills and the endless Plains. It was a good place, a peaceful place. A place for resting.

Cazi nudged his nose against Keiro's fingers, and Keiro stroked his hand down Cazi's warm body, careful around the places where Cazi's wings had been. They didn't seem to pain the *mravigi*, but Keiro would rather not put that to the test. "I should have stopped it," he said, not for the first time. He could tell himself, again and again, that there was nothing he could have done, that his will was as nothing against a god's . . . but he should have *tried*. "I'm so sorry, little one."

Cazi trilled softly, his tongue snaking out to scrape against Keiro's finger. It only made Keiro feel more guilty, that the Starborn should feel compelled to comfort *him*.

Guilt is a useless emotion. Sterner words than would usually drift in his mind, but no less true for their harshness. *He should put aside guilt, and focus instead on retribution.* "But how?" he murmured aloud. It would need to be vengeance against the Parents, of course, but what more could he do? Saval's attendants would be returning to Raturo, would bring the power of the Fallen to bear, and Keiro was certain they would find some way to free the Twins.

If only they could have waited to remove Cazi's wings. It would not be so long before the Fallen arrived; once the Twins were free, there would be no reason for the *mravigis'* wings to be cut, no reason for Cazi's freedom to have been torn away. If only the Twins could have been patient . . .

But no. Even as he thought it, Keiro knew he was wrong. The Twins had to protect themselves, and young Cazi likely did not tend toward the circumspect. Should the Parents see him flying, the Twins' hopes would be destroyed before they could begin to grow. They had done what they had to do, and anger at the Twins would serve Keiro just as well as guilt. He should put both aside, and turn his eyes from the past to the future. There was still much to be done.

And yet. Keiro wondered again what he could possibly do. The Fallen would arrive soon enough, and nothing could be done without their aid. So where did that leave Keiro? Waiting, useless, unnecessary.

Over the waving grass, lengths and lengths away, a gentle wisp of smoke climbed into the sky. The tribehome, and the communal fire there. The whole tribe would be gathering, roasting groundbirds and berries, telling stories . . . no, begging *Saval* for stories. He'd be sitting there as the plainswalkers fawned over him, soaking in their kindness, his odd mage sitting apart.

A mage would be a useful thing indeed . . .

Keiro's fingers stilled atop Cazi's chest. He knew precious little about magic, but perhaps there was some spell that could help the Twins. Not restore them to their power, of course, that was beyond the ability of any mortal, but surely there was something the mage could do. And if Nerrin didn't know of any spells, the Twins themselves held the world's oldest knowledge, and magic had been a wild thing in the days they had walked upon the earth; they might know of something . . .

Cazi gave a soft chirrup as Keiro stood. "Rest, little one," Keiro said, but Cazi rose as well, lithe body stretching. Keiro forced himself to look at the smooth patches of scale where Cazi's wings had been, made himself watch the play of muscle beneath scale, the easy grace with which Cazi moved. He was not in pain. His eyes were bright and curious. The young were resilient, and Cazi was no exception. *There was no reason to feel such guilt, or worry*—he had to keep reminding himself of that. He lifted Cazi up to his shoulder, the Starborn's normal perch. As he began walking, he told himself it was in his imagination still: the way Cazi leaned forward, his muzzle stretched into the air that blew gently by, nostrils flared and eyes slivered. Or the way his claws tightened, his weight shifting, as though he were preparing to launch his body up, up . . .

"You're fine," he said aloud, sternly, and then looked at Cazi from the corners of his eyes. Softer, he asked, "Aren't you?"

Cazi's response was to bite gently at Keiro's ear, and that put a faint smile on his lips.

The tribehome was every bit as bustling as Keiro had guessed it would be. He approached it from a different direction than usual, leaving the worn path to walk instead through the grass stalks, through the thousand tiny cuts their waving blades left. He moved slowly, in time with the dancing shadows the fire cast, not wanting to be seen. All the plainswalkers had their eyes fixed on Saval, arms waving and voice booming, and so no one noticed Keiro when he stepped from the grass.

Nerrin sat alone, a distance from the others, rocking slowly and muttering to herself. She startled when Keiro touched her shoulder, but did not make a sound. "Come with me," Keiro said. Nerrin looked to Saval, and a shudder rolled through her body. "Come with me," Keiro said again, more firmly. He'd learned from his flock of followers—those who had now abandoned him for the new novelty of a Ventallo—that confidence and surety were powerful things, and so he spoke as though Nerrin following him were a foregone thing. Her eyes flickered to Saval again, but she rose and followed Keiro back into the enveloping grass. Saval's story followed them through the stalks, and Nerrin flinched near continually at the slow-fading sound of his voice.

Keiro took her far away, far enough that Saval's voice was swallowed by the grass. That stopped her flinching, but it made her muttering more apparent, a constant stream of barely audible nonsense. Keiro wondered, not for the first time, if she were truly mad—perhaps it was merely some astronomical coincidence that the last two mages he had seen had been mad. Perhaps nothing was being done to mages at all, and he was merely searching for meaning where there was none.

They stopped near where the Plains began to taper into hills, the grass only waist-high and sparser. Keiro stomped flat a portion of the grass and then sat; Nerrin remained standing, her eyes fixed into the distance, arms wrapped tightly around herself. It was warm in the grass-sea, and she must surely be warm wearing the thick black preacher's robes, but still she shook where she stood. She acted almost like she didn't know Keiro, like he was a stranger who had spirited her away. "Nerrin, why don't you sit?" Keiro said, and though he spoke gently, she flinched as though it was a blow. She did sit, though, legs folding beneath her and then drawing up to her chest, making herself as small as possible.

It was need—*and a questing for power*, there was that, too—that had led Keiro to bring her here. Now, though, those both began to pale by degrees as he watched her. She was so broken; broken, he feared, by his own people. He had known mages in his life, not well but well enough to know that they were no more prone to madness than any other group of people. It seemed too great a coincidence that he had met two mad mages in his life, and both had been in the company of a preacher. There was something deeper here, something sour, and an aching grew in him to set things aright. Perhaps it was worth hurting her, if it let him help her.

"Nerrin," he said softly, and gently touched the back of her hand. She cringed, but didn't move away from his touch. "I don't know what's been done to you . . . but I am sorry for it. I . . . I would help you, if you'll let me. Please, Nerrin. Tell me how to help you."

"I am the cappo's loyal servant," she said through chattering teeth.

"You don't have to be. You are *you*. Surely there is a better life for you than this."

"I am the cappo's loyal servant."

Cazi slipped down from Keiro's shoulder, trod slowly across the space between him and Nerrin. She gave a yelp when his small-clawed foot touched her leg, but stayed still as though roots had sunk her into the ground. Cazi climbed her leg, and Keiro saw how he was so careful with his claws, gripping with splayed toes and, when he did need to use his claws to pull himself higher, sinking them only into her breeches rather than the flesh of her legs. The young *mravigi* perched on her knees, and though his head blocked Keiro's sight of her face, he saw how Nerrin's eyes fixed on Cazi. Intense and intent, as though trying to convince herself he was real, even though she had seen Cazi before, had seen other *mravigi*. She watched him, and didn't flinch when he stretched out his slim body so he could press his nose to hers.

"Free."

It took Keiro a long moment to realize that the word, soft and high and sweet, had come from Cazi.

"Free," Cazi said again, and a wet, tearing sob burst from Nerrin's mouth. She rolled onto her side, curled around Cazi's small body, and wept like the world was shattering around her.

Keiro sat where he was, throat heavy, torn between giving her the privacy of her grief and wanting to comfort her. Her tears ran themselves out before he managed to make up his mind, and she pushed herself up to sitting, one hand cradling Cazi, the other reaching inside her robe. She set a jar on the ground between her and Keiro, the same jar he had seen before, the one full of the foul black stuff. Her hand shook, and stayed around the jar for a long while before she released it.

"There," she said, voice rough, and her eyes wouldn't look at Keiro or the jar.

"What is it?"

"It makes me his."

Those simple words made Keiro's guts clench with anger. He knew he had been right in hating Saval . . . "How can I help?"

"I don't know."

"How does it work?" Keiro leaned forward to pick up the jar, turning it in his hands, lifting the lid to watch the way the sludge moved when he tilted the jar. When he glanced up at Nerrin, the hunger he saw in her eyes was a frightening thing.

"Blood." The word fell heavy from her lips, and drew behind it a silence like death.

When the world was young, before the One God of the Highlands had woken and granted power to his followers, when gods had walked the earth beside men, there had been magic.

Not the shaping power of the gods, nor the gentler powers now commanded by mages—it had been magic born of blood, and those who could wield it had been the closest mankind had ever come to godhood. All preachers knew of blood magic, for its traces were woven through Mount Raturo, through the seekstones each preacher carried, through the Sentinels that guarded the mountain paths, through the secret things said to be kept away in the bowels of the mountain. Blood magic, though, was no more than a piece of a long history, no more real now than any of the old stories the preachers told.

The stories of the Twins, whom Keiro had seen and spoken to.

Keiro knew nothing of the power of blood, had no idea how any of the Fallen had unlocked its secrets, or how to undo its effects. But the Twins might know . . . *after all, Fratarro's blood had healed Cazi's wounds in an instant . . .*

"Cazi," Keiro called softly as an idea struck him, and the young *mravigi* wriggled obediently out of Nerrin's arms. She whimpered as he left, and Keiro felt a pang of guilt—*Put aside guilt. She could stand a moment of sadness.* "How does he do it?" he asked Nerrin as he ran a careful hand along the curve of Cazi's back.

"Three drops of his blood," she said, "mixed with each jar of skura. I . . . none of us have been able to figure how it works."

He was happy to hear the enslaved mages seemed to have formed some sort of confederation, even if it had proved fruitless for them—it told him there was hope yet, for the mages. Using the nail of his thumb, Keiro scraped at Cazi's scales, chipping away the blood that had dried there and sending the flakes of it into the jar. Most of the blood was Cazi's, but

Keiro remembered well how Sororra had smeared her brother's blood over the *mravigi*'s wounds. Perhaps there was enough of it remaining to do *something*, and gods' blood was certainly more powerful than a man's . . .

When Keiro had chipped away as much as he could, he stirred the black paste with his finger. He could feel Nerrin's intense regard, her eyes unwavering. When he lifted his finger, sticky with the muck, her mouth fell open, her tongue thrusting out. It turned Keiro's stomach, but it seemed a small thing to quail at, and so he pressed his finger against her tongue. She licked away the black paste, and then fell away as convulsions tore through her. Keiro sat, frozen again by indecision, watching as she shook and clawed at her stomach. A scream tore out of her, loud enough to echo through the wide plains, and then she went abruptly still.

Keiro's heart was pounding with something that felt close to panic, and he hurried to kneel at her side. She still breathed, raggedly, but that at least meant she wasn't dead. Why in all the hells had he thought that was a good idea? So foolish, and his own stupidity might have come close to killing her . . . He touched Nerrin's shoulder, and her eyes opened slowly. "Are you all right?" Keiro asked breathlessly.

Her gaze was distant, unfocused. "Bring him . . ." she murmured. She didn't even seem to realize Keiro was there.

"Nerrin?"

Finally her eyes fixed on him, and she let Keiro help her up to sitting. Cazi, with a concerned chirrup, fitted himself under one of her hands. The other hand she pressed to her forehead, as though she'd been hit, or was trying to press back a headache. "We'll have to get Saval," she said, voice faint. Not the muttering tone that was so common to her, for these words were clear and intentional, but it seemed almost as though she didn't realize she'd spoken them aloud.

"Why?" Keiro asked. "I . . . I don't think he'll approve of . . . what we've done."

Her eyes fixed on him again, sharp and sane, and then they slid away. "He is needed."

All the hard certainty had drained out of Keiro, replaced by a cold, creeping horror. *What have I done . . . ?* "Nerrin, you should rest. It's peaceful here by the hills. We can sleep and see what the morning brings. Sleep can give you a wondrous new—"

"There's no time." Her voice was sharp, her eyes hard, and he saw her fingers curl into fists. Cazi scampered away from her, disappeared through the grass. A shudder rolled through Nerrin's body, her jaw clenching so tight that Keiro could see the tendons stand out stark beneath her skin. Then her limbs relaxed once more, her face smoothing. She didn't look at Keiro as she stood. "If you will not help," she said, "we don't need you."

"'We'?" Keiro repeated, hurrying after her as she started through the grass, aimed toward the tribehome. He caught her up, pulled on her arm. "Nerrin, stop—listen to me! I don't know what that foul stuff did to you, but—" She ignored his grip on her arm, walking forward even as it twisted her arm behind her, Keiro's continued grip stretching her arm out until he swore he heard faint tearing, popping. He let her go and she carried on forward, unperturbed. "Twins' bones," Keiro breathed, "what have I done?"

He followed after her, dogging her steps and, like a dog,

yapping at her the whole way, trying to get her to stop or talk or pause or *anything* besides her rigid path and dead-eyed stare and pressed lips. He stood directly in her path, pressing his hands against her shoulders, using all his wiry strength to push against her, and both their feet put furrows into the ground as they pressed equally forward. Keiro was the one to break first, stumbling back and sideways as she moved inexorably forward.

Keiro raced ahead to block her path once more, and this time, when she reached him, he took a deep breath and brought his fist up from his hip. He had never hit another person, and the scrape of his knuckles against her face was a horrible feeling. Worse, was the way the soft part of her cheek, below the cheekbone, gave beneath his fingers. He hated himself for it, held his fist against his chest as though it were a live and rabid thing, but if it could break her from this strange trance . . . Her feet did halt, and her face lifted slowly from where his strike had cast it sideways. She blinked rapidly, confusion plain in her eyes, and relief flooded through Keiro so strongly that a half sob of joy burst out of him.

And then her eyes flickered, the fire rising in them once more, and the voice that came from her mouth hardly sounded like her own: "Oppose us again, Keiro *Godson*, and you will take Saval's place."

Keiro stood shaken, feet like leaden lumps as Nerrin stepped around him, her shoulder bulling against his as she passed. He did not try to stop her. He almost didn't follow her, wanting no more part in whatever strangeness, whatever *wrongness*, had taken her . . . but he had done this to her. It was his doing. Keiro was not a brave man, but he was no coward.

He would face what he had done, and he would try, to his dying breath, to fix it.

And so Keiro followed meekly in her path, watching and—he told himself—waiting for his moment. Watching, and wondering, and lamenting.

She walked confidently into the tribehome—*swaggered*, practically—and strolled right up to Saval, though he was in the midst of a story. She pressed her hand to his arm, and though her voice was not loud, she didn't bother to whisper when she said, "You must come."

The silence that fell was a heavy thing, made up of the broken spell woven by a story well told, and made up, too, by the mixture of curiosity and uncertainty of the tribe. They had likely not remembered that Nerrin existed, much less expected her to interrupt her master. They all watched with mouths agape, waiting to see what would happen.

Saval glared at his mage, clearly annoyed. "We'll speak later," he said, brushing her hand from his arm. He turned back to the plainswalkers, drew a breath to continue his story.

"You must come," Nerrin repeated, grabbing his arm once more. From where he lurked in the shelter of the tall grass, Keiro could see how tight her grip grew, how her fingers dug in. "*Now.*"

Saval's lips pressed into a thin line, and his eyes found Nerrin's with more scrutiny this time. Keiro could only see the back of her head, and so he could not guess what Saval saw there, but it caused the preacher to turn back and sweep a low bow to the plainswalkers. "Forgive me, my friends. There is pressing business I must attend to. Rest assured, I will return as soon as I am able."

There were protests, but they were small things. Even the plainswalkers, who knew so little of the culture among the Fallen, knew better than to argue with one of the Ventallo. Nerrin preceded him, walking into the grass once more, walking past Keiro without a glance. He saw the tightness in her jaw, the way her wide pupils seemed to shake ever so slightly, and then she was past him.

Saval startled to see Keiro there, and his eyes flickered between the man and the mage. He lowered his voice conspiratorially to ask, "What's going on? Did something happen?"

Made mute by guilt and uncertainty, Keiro could only spread his hands helplessly, shake his head. When he looked at Nerrin, she cast a look over her shoulder at him, a narrow-eyed glare, and her words echoed in his head. *Oppose us again, and you will take Saval's place.* "You'll have to see," Keiro said, hoping his voice did not sound as choked as he feared. "I . . . I cannot explain." It wasn't a lie, and it gave Saval enough surety that he followed after Nerrin. Keiro trailed behind, because he could think of naught else to do.

Nerrin led with confidence through the grass and over the hills, the head of their silent party, her path unerring. Occasionally Saval would glance to Keiro, but neither man strove to break the silence. For Keiro, it was fear of drawing any more of Nerrin's strange attention, worry of drawing her wrath, and, too, fear of facing again what it seemed he had done to her. He could not say what motivated Saval, but silence seemed a strange state for the man. Yet he held his words, his shoulders stiff and, when he would glance to Keiro, his face was suffused with concern. There were strange strands of kinship binding the two of them now, mutual confusion, shared unease, and

Keiro's earlier dislike of the man seemed a petty thing. He knew little more than Saval, but still, there was a growing knot of dread in Keiro's stomach, a dark and heavy thing. There was a certainty in him that, whatever was to happen, it was not going to end well.

They came to one of the *mravigi* entrances, the hole disguised but easy enough to see if one knew what they were looking for. Keiro had no idea how Nerrin would know of its existence, for it was one not even Keiro had ever used. Her eyes fixed on Saval, and she motioned expansively toward the hole. "Please," she said, her voice overly solicitous, tinged almost with the bite of sarcasm.

Saval hesitated, and for one mad moment, Keiro thought about grabbing the other man's arm and running, pulling him back through the tall grass, losing themselves in the waving sea. It seemed wiser, and safer. But then Saval climbed down into the tunnel and was gone from sight. Nerrin dropped down after him without a glance at Keiro, leaving him alone among the hills. He stood, his arms wrapped around himself, shivering, though the air was not cold. He could go still, run into the grass, disappear forever, and leave this all behind . . . Keiro sat on the ground, legs dangling into the open hole, and dropped.

He could hear the pulse of the earth as they crawled. Farther ahead, he knew, in the great cavern beneath the ground, the *mravigi* would be gathered, all of them, breathing and speaking and rustling; their very presence felt like the heavy beating of a heart against his palms. They would be waiting to bear witness to what was to come . . .

"Nerrin?" Saval said over his shoulder, his high whisper harsh in the tight tunnel. "Nerrin, what's happening?"

"You will see," Nerrin said firmly, pressing him forward, ever forward, deeper into the earth.

"I want to go back." He sounded almost a child, frightened and alone.

"There is no going back."

The dull glow of the chamber reached down the tunnel toward them, red eyes and *mravigi* starlight mixed. It reached to surround them, to draw them into the mighty cavern where they waited, all the Starborn and mighty Straz, Sororra and Fratarro. So many red eyes fixed to Saval as he crawled free of the tunnel and stood with shaking hands. Unnoticed, ignored, Keiro stood some ways away, in the faint shadow of a protruding rock, bound by his own vow to see but hoping not to be seen.

Fratarro's face was unwontedly solemn, and Sororra grinned broadly, white teeth shining through her burned face. "Welcome again!" she called. "Faithful Saval. Saval Tredeiro, Thirteenth among the Fallen. Did you know, Saval, that the first of the Fallen had no leaders? They knew our teachings well, knew that no men should be placed above another, that all were meant to be made equal. They wanted none to lead them—they only required faith and loyalty beyond reproach. Are you loyal, Saval?"

"Yes," Saval breathed, dropped to his knees, one fist pressed to his forehead. "Yes."

"That is good. Good! But how deep does your loyalty extend? How far can your faith stretch?"

From where he stood, Keiro could see the lump in Saval's throat bob rapidly. "As far as they need to, my lady."

Sororra turned her grin to Fratarro. "I like this one, brother."

The god inclined his head, but his eyes stayed tight on

Saval's face. "When we rise," he said softly, "all will be judged. We will see each man and each woman, and we will look into their hearts, and we will know them. Fears and dreams, loves and hates, every fiber that weaves the tapestry of their being. We know you, Saval. We have seen you. We have judged you. And now we must test you."

"I—yes, anything," Saval stammered. "My lord, my lady, revered Twins, I am your loyal servant. I will—"

"Bring him," Sororra said softly, but the deep thrum of command in her voice silenced all else. Nerrin stepped forward as though the order had been spoken to her, and she wrapped both hands around one of Saval's arms and pulled him to his feet, pulled him forward, closer to the Twins. He stumbled along at her side, looking torn between walking with her and running far, far away.

"Children," Fratarro said, and the word was hardly more than a whisper. His face was as hard as his sister's, but there was the deep sadness in his eyes where Sororra's were un-flinching. The *mravigi* surged forward at his call, four of them, huge beasts, and they swarmed around Saval. Nerrin stepped away and the *mravigi* took her place, their clawed feet reaching, pulling.

The whites shone huge around Saval's eyes as he cried out, struggling finally, fighting to break free, but there was no fighting against the Starborn. They were too strong and Saval disappeared from sight, the bodies of the *mravigi* writhing atop him as he screamed and begged. When they settled Saval lay on his back, a *mravigi* pinning each limb, holding firmly as he thrashed. It was too late, now, for him to fight. There was no going back.

Sororra, her low voice almost a purr, turned to Nerrin and said, "You have done well, mage. You are not one of ours . . . but there is so much potential in you. You could be great, grow mighty at our sides." Her eyes were full of dancing flames, of passion and power. Keiro could hardly breathe looking at them, and they weren't even fixed to his face. Yet Nerrin stood before the full intensity of the goddess's gaze, stood with her back rigid and her jaw tight. "Will you stand with us, Nerrin?" Sororra crooned.

Nerrin opened her mouth, worked her jaw as though the words would not come. The tightness in her back loosened, her shoulders curving forward, her eyes tilting down, fingers curling and uncurling. Keiro saw a slight narrowing of Sororra's eyes and then Nerrin's back snapped straight, a gasp bursting out of her before the single word, "Yes."

"Good." Sororra grinned again. "*Good!* You are wise, little mage. Isn't she, brother?"

Fratarro's eyes were beginning to droop. There wouldn't be much time left before sleep would drag them down once more . . . little enough time, perhaps, that this nightmare would finish before its end. "We should begin, sister. There is much yet to do."

"You worry too much, brother! We have our mage, we have our loyal Saval. There is naught to stop this." And then, unexpectedly, Sororra's eyes swung to meet Keiro's, and he quailed before their intensity. "Come, Keiro Godson. You need not hide in the shadows." A low laugh rolled through her body, charred flesh rippling, chains rattling. "Step forward, loyal Keiro, and bear witness to history."

He walked forward, for there was nothing else he could

do. Keiro stood before the gaze of his gods, half a dozen paces from where Nerrin stood rigid, from where Saval lay pinned and thrashing and pleading. He stood before them, and there was no thought in him of running, or of speaking against this. There was only the certainty that this was right, and necessary.

"Wise little Nerrin," Sororra said, turning her gaze once more to the mage, "listen to me now. Let your hands be my hands . . ."

Keiro stood wordless, watching, numb, as Nerrin stepped forward and, with Sororra's low voice whispering guidance, took the knife from Saval's belt. Took it, and cut open his robe and the shirt beneath, baring his pale chest. Took the knife, and began to slice into his skin, into muscle, into bone. The knife was not sharp enough, not by far, but Nerrin did not stop. Through it all the cavern was full of the murmuring *mravigi*, of Saval's screams, of Sororra's intonement. When finally Nerrin cracked back his ribs like an opening door, Saval's screaming had stopped. Keiro could not see, where he stood, if the man still breathed, if the blood that stained his body and the floor and Nerrin's arms still flowed from his chest. Nerrin made a few slices more with the knife, her face tight, and then her fingers opened around the hilt. The knife clattered to the floor, loud, jarring, but it did not break the copper-scented spell that had wrapped around the cavern. Nerrin reached both hands into the opening of Saval's chest, and when she pulled them free, they were filled with the red lump of his heart.

Keiro remembered how Nerrin had stood in a field of butterflies, their glowing shapes moving over her cupped hands, and how there had been such wonder and joy in her eyes.

"Quickly, now," Sororra crooned. "Let your voice be my

voice, your power my power. Speak with me . . ." She chanted, low and hypnotic, the words not any language Keiro had ever heard, and Nerrin repeated the sounds a moment behind her, sweet and discordant and eerie. In her cupped palms, Saval's heart began to beat once more, slow, erratic, beating in time with the chanting that wove through the cavern, and from the heart's tubes began to flow a black smoke, heavy and acrid. The smoke collected above the pulsing heart, swirling, writhing. Sororra's voice rose, louder, faster, and the fires burned in her eyes once more. Her last word came as a shout, and Nerrin's as a scream—the mage threw back her head, the shape of the word dissolving into a long cry of pain as more of the black smoke boiled from her throat, coalescing with the smoke surrounding the heart. The smoke surged forward in a cloud and flooded into the red opening of Fratarro's mouth. Nerrin's scream cut off and her body collapsed, limp and heavy, beside Saval. Fratarro closed his mouth, and Sororra grinned, and for three heartbeats, the very ground beneath Keiro's feet shook.

Fratarro raised his one arm, and where the rent flesh had dripped ichor, as though it had known of the destruction of his hand, now the flesh there was smooth and clean and new, and there was no blood. It looked an old amputation, that had had years and years to heal, that had had years and years to forget its pain.

Sororra lifted her own arm, reached until the chain between her wrist and the ground was stretched tight. The muscles beneath her charred skin bulged and flexed, and the strain showed clearly in her face, and for long minutes the only sounds were her sharp breaths and the low groan of metal. When she finally twisted her arm to the side, the chain's links shattered, and the manacle cracked from around her wrist like an egg, and Sororra laughed long and loud.

Keiro stood, his hands shaking, the taste of bile at the back of his mouth. He wanted to weep or to run, but the certainty had crept its way back into him, holding him: *This is right. This is necessary.*

Fratarro smiled, too, beneath the eternal sadness in his eyes. Beneath his sister's laughter he said, "We judge thee worthy, Saval. We judge thee worthy, Nerrin. Rest well among the stars."

"And now," Sororra said, "we may begin."

PART THREE

The Plains are long, but there is an ending to all things.

—A saying of the plainswalkers

It sat upon the snow like a fallen star. Soft and bright. A small thing, and fragile.

Scal bent his knees to touch his fingers gently to the scrap of fabric. Pale yellow, the color at the very edge of a flame. The color priestesses wore, to mark them as flame-sworn. In this part of the world, there would be few priestesses. There could, maybe, be just the one.

He had followed the boot prints, tracked them through the snow and the trees, followed the ever-walking tale they told until their steps joined with countless others. The snow churned to mud by so many feet. The trail of the great passage like a giant's body had been dragged across the earth.

He had to believe the dozen large boots, and Vatri's, had joined all the others. There was no other choice. No other hope.

He followed their path. His own steps small among so many, a single drop of water in a rushing river. He trailed the great moving beast through the day, and slept little that night, lying upon the bare snow. His blood was warm. He did not feel the cold, not even a part of it. Slept in the dark, with only the stars piercing fire-bright through the trees that reached above. He dreamed of the fire. The heat of it racing across his skin, the burning of it in his chest, the power of it. His cheek burned, not the scar-cross but his clean cheek, where Vatri's fingers had pressed ash hard into his skin.

It was still dark when he woke. His feet went once more to the path that wound careful through the trees but always, always skewed south. Like a pull, like a magic stone he had seen once that could call iron coins through the air and hold them fast. Straight as a summons. The burning in his cheek lingered from the dream, but it faded. Most things do.

He had seen no sign of Vatri. But neither had he seen anything to tell him she was *not* in the same group that had carved their path south. He could only follow.

And now he had found a piece of yellow. A piece of her robes, at the edge of the path. Damp and stepped-on, half-hidden, but the yellow color of hope.

Scal knotted the piece of fabric near his pendants. He had worked careful to fix the torn cord. It had felt wrong, to carry the pendants in his hand. They belonged on his chest, against his heart, warmer than flesh. He tied the scrap next to them—fire and ice and hope—and he walked once more on the trail. Pulled arrow-straight, pulled like a command.

After the second time he slept, after the second fire-dreams, he finally saw their backs. They paced like a line of shadows beneath the trees, but as he drew closer he saw they were not shadows, not at all. Some wore black, the color of dark and danger, but some wore plainclothes, no different than his own. Scal tucked his pendants beneath his shirt, the fire and the ice and the hope. He reached their backs, the end of the mighty churning press, and they did not remark as he passed into their ranks. Some nodded, murmured, "Brother." Scal kept his eyes ahead. Searching the ranks of dark and pale clothes for yellow. Searching, searching for a spot of light like a fallen star.

The night fell and still they pressed on. No torches, no lights. Just the dark and the bright-burning stars. For all that there were bodies beyond counting, it was quiet beneath the trees. The crunch of snow, the suck of ground churned to mud by so many feet, the snap of branch. But no voices, no speaking.

This was how they would shape the world, the followers of the Twins. Dark and quiet and even. In the dark, each dim shape could be a beggar or a king. In the dark, there were no better men, no worse men. No leaders, all following a single call. Moving together, working as one. A flock of birds, spinning through the night, one voice guiding them. There was a peace to it.

A few hours into the night, they stopped. It came like a silent command, rolling down the lines from the distant front. As with Berno and Zenora and Herrit, it seemed they were not willing or not able to only travel in the night, only sleep during the sunlight hours. There was relief at the call to stop. Some sat where they stood and slept as soon as they touched the ground. Others set to work. Here, at the back, were the bakers and cooks, the hunters and farmers, all those wearing the plainclothes, those who would support the ones wearing the black. They would not rest, not yet. Though the Fallen preached perfect equality, they seemed to have a harder time practicing it. Scal moved through the commoners, through the smells of bread baking in clever-made ovens hauled on carts, through the smells of roasting meat, the air full of smoke, of heat. He passed through the bustling, his steps careful and sure, his eyes searching, always searching. Moved forward, slowly, through the body of the great snake. Through the commoners, to the point where the plainclothes turned to black robes, the bustle and work changing to rest, to sleep. He did not stop, moving with assurance deeper into the nest of preachers.

He thought he saw, once, a fat man and an old woman and a young man sitting together. He walked wide around them, and did not look their way. Another time, he thought he heard a gentle voice telling the tale of wandering Birro, and he moved so the words no longer touched his ears. He heard murmurs, so many of them, that the ancient Twins would be freed, but he did not stop to listen. There was not room in him for anything else.

A man, black-robed, stood looking around, searching like Scal. He touched the man's arm, asked, "Have you seen a priestess?"

The man looked startled, and then he laughed. "If I'd seen a priestess, I'd've sent the blasted Parents a nice warm fire."

There was a woman in plainclothes, kind-faced, carrying a basket half her size full of warm bread. She went from person to person, the basket held out in offering, always a smile or a murmured word. Scal stopped her with a hand gentle upon her slim arm. "Have you seen a priestess?" he asked her, and her face changed. The smile falling into a frown, kind eyes looking him over with a deep suspicion, and he felt the muscles of her arm go tense. He moved away from her quickly, not knowing if he feared more her answer or the cry she might raise. He did not ask any others. He had only his own eyes, searching, always searching.

The silent call rolled down the ranks, bodies rising, feet

stepping. The rest was over. So much ground, still, to cover. The plainclothed fled to the back, and Scal was left amid a sea of black. He moved through it, like a stick floating atop the slow-moving tide, a part of yet separate. He did not pass unnoticed here. Some of the eyes were curious, some hard. Still, he passed untouched.

And then the black sea changed. There was a line of big men, as big almost as Scal, who did not wear robes. They wore black leather, black chain mail, armor dyed and painted, and their scabbards and shields were the same color. Fighters, all, but no less a part of the black sea. Scal stayed back from them, and watched. They questioned those who tried to pass through their line, turned away many. He did not think they would let him pass.

After night had fallen again and the column had stopped once more to rest, Scal stepped out of the sea. He went deeper into the trees, carving his own path beside theirs. It had been too long since he had slept, but a man could do much before his body would force him to sleep. Scal turned again to face the still black sea, and he did not leave the shelter of the trees, but his eyes searched.

Forward, ever forward, past three giant carts, past the ranks of Fallen thick as fur, past the scattered black-armored swordsmen. The sky lightened, stretched shadows across the carpet of breathing shadows. They did not see him, any of them.

Finally he saw. An uneven circle of red, dotted throughout with yellow like the heart of a flame. He knew the shape of her, even from so far away. Dim and dirty, but she was a single point of brightness amid the sea of black.

Scal sat among the trees, and he watched. There were more

swordsmen than he had thought. Working in shifts, taking turns to sleep. Spread, he imagined, in a broad circle surrounding the head of the great sea, the mighty of the Fallen. Guarding the Fallen leaders, guarding their captive parros and merras. There was no more than three lengths between any of the swordsmen, no unguarded gap through which he could slip. Even if he could, in his plain and dirty clothes, he would stand out. He could not get to her, not yet.

At length they all rose, the Fallen stretching, yawning, laughing. He watched Vatri pulled to her feet. Her scarred face was expressionless as a mask, but Scal knew the shape of it. Knew the small signs, the things that others would not see. He searched the curves and folds and ridges of her face for fear, for pain, for abuse. He saw none. Only calm. Only peace.

Scal stayed among the trees as they began to move once more. All the Fallen, the mighty rippling tide of the black sea. The three great carts, pulled by thirty men each, carrying strange-shaped things covered over with great pieces of black cloth. The stern line of black-clad swordsmen, marking where the head of the group ended and the milling body began.

Scal stood, but stayed still.

A black-robed man broke away from the sea, drifting into the trees to piss. Scal trailed after him, quiet as a breath.

The man stopped near a tree. Whistling to himself as he untied his breeches. Muttering curses against the cold. Scal stood behind him, silent, looming. He knew the odds were small, as small as finding one certain grain of sand on a beach, but perhaps this had been one of the men who had taken Vatri. He did not think it was true, but it would be easier if he was.

Scal did not have a sword or a knife. He had never needed

tools to kill. It was a thing of hands, blood against blood. Tools only made it easier. His hands rose silent, reaching to wrap around the man's neck.

He wondered, if the man were to turn then, if he would look like Herrit. If his eyes would squint to see anything that was not scribbles on the page of a book.

The man fell bonelessly. Scal knew the place to put his fist, to stun only. It was very near to the place a fist should hit, if a man wished to kill. When Scal rolled the man onto his back, his even breaths clouded the air. He did not look like Herrit.

Scal stripped away the man's black robe. It was too small, stretching tight across his shoulders, showing his wrists and his calves, but it would do.

Before he left, Scal stared down at the breathing man. Perhaps he had been one who had taken Vatri. There was no knowing. But his *people* had taken Vatri. The Fallen were the enemy. It would do the world no harm to have one less black drop among the sea.

When Scal left the trees, he did not look back. Did not look at the man, who sat propped with his back to the tree. The ground was cold, and Scal had taken his meager cover, and he would sleep for a good while. Not being left to lie entirely on the ground might keep him from freezing before he woke.

Scal pulled the black hood up over his head. Hiding his pale hair, hiding the scars that crossed his face. Hiding all the things that burned in his eyes. He stepped from the trees, stepped into the tide of the Fallen, and none noticed him. He was a drop, only, in the great black sea. He would watch, and he would wait.

CHAPTER THIRTY

It was warmer, at least, and that was about the best Rora could say.

She'd gotten good at sneaking in her years living in the Canals, and she'd gotten even better at it when she'd started learning from Tare and the other knives. She could pick the pockets of any of the city guard, and she could follow a man, step for step, through his own home and never be seen.

This was a different kind of sneaking, though, and it was a damned boring kind. The sort of sneaking where all they had to do was stay close enough to the column that they could hear the people, and far enough back that they wouldn't be seen. Apart from the "not being seen," the whole thing was a lot like walking through a forest with her brother and some people she didn't like.

She'd tried to convince them they needed more help, more bodies, more'n just her daggers to keep them safe—hoping, silently, that they could go back to Tare and Sharra, so she could explain everything that'd happened, and apologize till her tongue fell out. It was true, too, that there was probably fighting to come, and Rora didn't fancy her chances against all the black-robes. But Joros'd said there was no time, that for as long as it'd take to go get more fists and knives, the damage'd already be done. So it was just her to keep them safe, and wondering sometimes if she cared enough not to just let 'em get killed on their own. If it wasn't for her brother, maybe she would've— but even Aro was making her feel all kinds of stabby.

Every once in a while, just to do something different'n walking with the bastards, Rora would ghost up through the trees toward the long column, walking along at the edges, un- seen. She couldn't see far through the trees, but it wasn't hard to tell there was a whole shitload of people, stretching on ahead for forever. She climbed a tree once, tallest tree she could find, and got nearly all the way up to its swaying top, and even that high up she couldn't see where the column started. She did see, though, the three huge carts getting pulled real awkward through the trees, taking a whole lot of people even to pull 'em, not to mention what it took to get them through and around the trees.

She mentioned those carts to Joros, and his face got like a storm. "They found them," he said, like that was supposed to make any sense. She still hated talking to the witch, and he was usually busy with Aro anyway, but she dropped back to ask him about the carts, too, and his face got pale. "Fratarro," he whispered. "Or pieces of him. Flung to the far horizons . . ."

"I could burn them," she suggested to Joros later when they'd set up camp. "Sneak in and burn 'em just like we did that hand, and no one'd see me—"

"They would," Joros interrupted. "Their ranks will be crawling with mages, and even if, somehow, you managed to make it past them, the limbs will be too heavily guarded. They won't risk anything happening to them, and they'd kill you without a thought. I can't take that chance. Not now."

The man was looking more frazzled by the day, and it probably didn't help that his hair, which'd been half burned off before he'd found her and Aro, was starting to grow back but patchy, making him look crazier'n the witch acted. The merra leaving had, for some weird reason, made the cappo worried instead of acting like it was the thing he'd been hoping for ever since he'd met her. It didn't make any kind of sense, and Rora couldn't crack the puzzle since he spent most of his time quiet and brooding, ignoring the rest of the world. Maybe he was trying to figure a new plan, or maybe he was making up kids' rhymes—there wasn't any telling with him.

For all that Joros was silent, his witch'd taken up talking like it was his sacred duty. You couldn't get him to shut up, ever since they'd come out of that damned mountain. She guessed it had to do with the foul black stuff Joros still thought he was taking, but Rora'd watched him burn it, and burn the second jar Joros'd given him, too. Good for him and all, being a better person, but the bastard'd still got her people killed, and now he was trying to corrupt her brother on top of it.

It hadn't been more'n a day out, soon as the witch could walk without limping, when he'd turned to Aro and with his face all solemn, he'd said, "You'll have to learn."

Aro'd looked back at him with a mix of fear and excitement in his eyes, but Rora'd spoke before he could. "No. He's not a witch. Just leave him alone."

Anddyr had frowned at her like she was speaking a different tongue. "He *is* a mage, Rora. You saw what he did. His powers are manifesting—atypically, to be sure, and I'll admit I'm excited to study him more closely, but there's no doubting he's a mage. I think you've probably known that for a long—"

She'd slammed him against a tree at that, hoping she could rebreak some of the bones his magic had knitted back together. It took her standing on her toes but she got her forearm pressed across his throat, and not gently neither. He gaped at her like a bulge-eyed fish but she'd snarled at him, "He's *not* a *witch*." She'd dropped her arm, but only to punch him in the gut for good measure, and then she'd turned to her good-for-nothing brother and shoved him, hard, away from the witch. "You fecking stay away from him, hear?" she said to Aro, but really that was for both of 'em.

Joros'd watched it like they were just some weird-colored birds, different'n he expected but not all that interesting when it came to it.

They'd listened to her for a while, Aro sulking, the witch going back to talking only to himself and sinking into one of his crazy storms, crawling around between the trees like he was looking for something and laughing over every leaf he found. But she'd woken up one day to find them huddled together, and the second after her fist knocked the witch over, she'd seen the fire dancing in Aro's cupped palms.

It'd taken Aro and Joros both to pull her off the witch, because she was damned determined to kill him, and it'd taken Joros's fist on her own face to get her to stop fighting—Joros could throw a damn good punch, she'd give him that, one that'd made her body go to rags while her head spun.

"He has to learn," Anddyr'd said, spitting blood.

"Like hells he does," she'd said back, spitting spit.

"It will kill him if he doesn't."

And that'd given Rora a second of doubt. For all that the witch was a useless bastard, he usually wasn't a liar.

"It's a wonder it hasn't already. It needs to be controlled or locked away, or else it will consume him. Literally, Rora. He'll burn."

"Shut your mouth," she'd said, but without near as much of the confidence. Maybe it was because of the leftover spins from Joros's punch, but she didn't want to strangle the witch quite as much.

"It's true. I've seen it. They make us see it. It always happens somewhere, a child who tries to hide his fledgling powers, parents who don't want to lose their only child. The masters take us to see the results if we . . . if we try to run." He looked at her, but more like *through* her, like he was seeing some other person. "I was homesick. I wanted to see my parents, my sisters. I thought I could be gone and back before anyone noticed, but the masters always know. They took me the next day, to see what happens when a mage doesn't learn control." His eyes refocused, fixed back on her. "You've seen it, too. The night we found you. The whole village, destroyed . . ."

"And you," she said, "a trained witch, you did that."

"Trained, yes, but I was not in control of myself then. I . . . I was weak." His eyes were big and half-crazed, but he held her gaze like he usually didn't. "I am better now. Getting better. And Aro needs my help."

"We don't need anything from you."

"Who says you get to choose?" Aro burst out all sudden, and it was so unexpected Rora could only stare at him. "It's *my* life. I believe Anddyr when he says this could kill me because I can *feel* it, Rora. You don't know what it's like. I feel like water over a fire, and I could boil over any minute. How would you feel then, huh? If I died because you're too stubborn?"

"You're not dying!" She shouted it like saying it the loudest would make it truest, and Joros's fingers dug into her shoulder in warning. They were still sneaking, after all, still staying hidden, unknown to the column not so far ahead. She ground her teeth and then said quieter but just as fierce, "You're *not* dying."

"But what if I am?" Aro had his soft eyes on, the look like he was a sad little puppy that just needed saving and petting and love. "Isn't it worth learning a bit, just in case?"

"No," she'd said, and she'd stomped off and done some sulking of her own. She'd glared at them every time, over the next days, each time Aro and Anddyr huddled together, the witch teaching her brother how to flick his fingers and mutter. Rora would've never guessed she'd miss it, but she almost wished the merra was there to start screeching, "Abomination!"

Hard as it was to believe, those were actually the good times, when Aro and the witch put their heads together to mutter and flutter their fingers. Anddyr was changed since they'd come out of the mountain, and he was a lot like a normal person most of the time . . . but then one of his storms would hit, and he'd screech and rave and claw at his own skin, try to run away like he was being chased by monsters, fall to pieces if any of them tried to touch him. Sometimes the best they could do was sit and wait for it to pass, sitting in a loose circle around the witch, Aro with his hands up and his lips always moving and quiet tears on his cheeks as the witch pounded and clawed at the invisible bubble he'd taught Aro to make. "It should be the first thing you learn," Rora'd heard the witch say, all grim, "because you're going to need to use it." She hadn't really thought it was necessary at first—they could've pinned him down just as well with their own hands, and maybe kept him from hurting himself when he was at his maddest. But then he started trying to throw fire and lightning at them, and she was glad for the shield. She got to hoping her brother was learning well and learning fast, because there was no part of her that wanted to find out what'd happen if one of the witch's storms lasted longer'n her brother could hold up the shield. If Joros noticed the ways his witch was acting different, he didn't say anything—his eyes were always fixed ahead, or staring like he was trying to see through the trees, trying to see all the black-robes he'd turned against.

Rora took to doing even more scouting, mostly because if she didn't see her brother learning magic, she could pretend it wasn't happening. Not that there was much to scout, just the endless column of people trudging through the trees. The people near the back looked like common folk—farmers and cooks and craftsmen—and there were a good chunk of them not even wearing black robes. Just normal people caught up by a moving group, most like. This many black-robes, they'd need plenty of bodies just to keep 'em fed and clean and clothed. She ranged farther up, seeing how it got to be more black-robes the closer she got to the head of the column. She didn't know how far ahead the head was, but it had to end somewhere, and if the pattern held it'd probably be thick with black-robes like mayflies up front.

And then Rora near ran out of trees to hide in.

It wasn't that they ended all sudden, like the trees had

in the North—it was mostly that she'd stopped paying good enough attention, which was a fool thing to do and like to get her killed. She ghosted back a bit, into a nice thicket of trees, and then she shimmied on up one of 'em. From higher up, she could see the forest dribbling away to brush and tall grass, and the long column of black-robes winding through the grass like a snake. With the trees gone, though, she could finally see its head, far up but not as far as she might've guessed. There were still a bloody lot of the bastards, and it was going to be a lot harder to keep sneaking after 'em with only grass to hide in.

It took her a while to make it back to the others—she'd gotten farther up than she'd thought—but she got to interrupt one of the witch's lessons, so it wasn't all bad. Joros listened to her with his jaw getting tighter every word, until she thought for sure his teeth would pop.

"Couldn't we cloak us?" Aro asked the witch, looking hopeful and proud, and then like he'd been kicked when Anddyr shook his head.

"They have mages of their own, enough mages that *one* of them would likely see through any disguising we might do."

"So then what do we do?" Aro asked, looking between her and the witch and Joros, but no one had an answer for him. They made camp while they still had tree cover, and because there wasn't much point in going more without a plan.

Joros kept playing with the little seekstone, the one Anddyr'd given him, like he thought they'd somehow lose the column if he didn't keep an eye on them. Aro'd tried to poke the witch into a lesson, but Anddyr was in one of his storms, scratching shapes into the half-froze ground while he muttered. He was scraping his fingers bloody. Rora didn't start a fire, and since she was the one who usually did, they didn't have a fire. It was just warm enough they didn't need one.

It felt like a long time ago, but really it'd only been a few months—but there was a time when Rora would've been happy as coins, sitting with her brother and a few other people, relaxing and enjoying the winter melting away. That seemed like a different person. That was someone who hadn't abandoned her pack, who hadn't led a bunch of her pack to their deaths. That was someone who'd only known about the Twins as old stories that'd make people hate her, if they found out what she was. That was someone who'd known where she fit, who was as balanced as a good throwing dagger. It was hard to believe Rora'd been that person.

"You said the grass was tall?" Aro's voice was small and hesitant—someone who still didn't know how he fit. "Couldn't we hide in it? I know it wouldn't be as good as trees for cover, but . . ."

"Close as we'd have to be to keep on their path," Rora said, "they'd see us for sure. And if we got far enough away they wouldn't see us, we wouldn't be able to follow 'em."

"Oh." He stayed quiet after that, watching Anddyr scratch at the ground.

Rora didn't have any ideas better'n that, and Joros was just glaring south—maybe he was trying to think up an idea, but Rora didn't really think so.

That old Rora, the one she could remember like a hurting tooth, she would've been happy for a rest. She wouldn't've minded not doing anything important, would've told half-truth stories about all the things she'd done or pulled out some dice or maybe crossed daggers with one of the other knives.

She couldn't count the times that she and Aro, or she and some other knives, had gotten bored and gone sneaking through the Canals, knowing where some friend or half-enemy was headed and hiding there, waiting for the sounds of feet on stone or splashing water to tell them the target was near. It was a good day, when they could make the person piss themselves with fear—they'd laugh so hard they came near to pissing themselves, too, sometimes.

But that was a different person. This Rora, now-Rora, sitting still made her twitchy. She knew there were things she should be doing, important things. She knew enough to be scared, and was scared enough to worry she was making things worse by not doing anything. Maybe the old Rora'd had some good ideas, though. "Do you know where it is they're all going to?" she asked Joros.

He didn't look at her, still rolling the seekstone in his fingers, still staring south. "I have an idea."

"It's something like that hand, though, right? Another . . . piece?"

"Another limb, yes."

"Could the witch find it like he found the hand?"

Joros did look at her then, and there was something weird in his eyes. He left off the stone for a minute, putting his hand instead down to the pouch on his belt. The big pouch, where that ugly, awful toe was. "He could . . ."

"So what if we got there before the others?"

They left not too long after that, cutting a bit east before turning back south. They didn't even need the witch yet, which was good because he was a crying mess when they dragged him away from his scratchings. If they pushed hard, if they could get ahead of the column fast enough, then it was just a matter of *staying* ahead.

Rora kept her job as scout, jogging ahead for a while until she had a good lead on the others. It felt good, the wind in her face and the grass brushing her shoulders. It felt like being free, like not having any worries at all.

She turned after a while, heading toward where the column would be, and taking it slow. She didn't want to actually stumble over any of them, but sound traveled weird in the wide-open place. The other day, she would've guessed from the sound of it that the column was still a lot of lengths away, and then she'd near run into someone walking through the grass. That'd spooked her real bad, and maybe it was just someone drifting off to take a piss, but maybe the grass held on to sound tight as a lover. This time, soon as she heard any sound from the column, she turned back. She wouldn't get caught out again.

She went farther ahead, walking fast, air burning good in her lungs, and she hardly felt the little cuts of the grass stalks as they brushed past her. This wasn't proper sneaking, was more like a game of hide-and-chase than anything else, but it was loads better'n being in a freezing dungeon or the freezing North or a cramped room where one of her oldest friends'd just sawed off her ear. Maybe it was the best place she had left, and maybe that wasn't a bad thing.

Finally, on one of her turns toward the column, with her ears straining, she caught the sounds of chatter and footsteps and breaking grass, but the sounds weren't coming from ahead of her—they were coming from her right. She'd finally made it up ahead of the whole damned column.

She was grinning as she jogged back to Joros and Anddyr and Aro, grinning even broader because of a big fat bird she'd managed to kick up and put a dagger in, grinning right up until she smacked straight into a really fecking solid bit of air.

She muffled her cursing as she picked herself up off the ground, swatted at Aro's hands as he tried to help her up. "I'm so sorry, Rora," he babbled. "I couldn't dispel it fast enough—"

"*You* did that?" she demanded, and then she punched him on the shoulder. He didn't bother trying to keep his yelp quiet, so she punched him again.

The witch made him yelp a third time when he grabbed the shoulder Rora'd just punched. "You need to maintain your control." At least he had the sense to keep quiet, hissing into Aro's face. "Your edges were unstable, and if you had good control of it you could have dispelled it in seconds. You need to learn this, there's so little time—"

Rora grumbled and growled, any good feelings she'd had gone like a stomped-out fire. It seemed like Joros was in the same sort of mood, and she couldn't blame him—she'd probably be even madder if she was stuck around her brother and the witch for so many hours. Maybe the good news would make him happy at least. "We're close to the front," she told Joros while the witch kept babbling at her brother. "Another day of pushing, and we'll probably be pretty safely ahead of 'em."

"It's about damned time," Joros snapped, so it seemed like everyone was doomed to be pissed off.

Wasn't too hard of a choice to go back to ranging up ahead.

After a few days, being ahead of the column made Rora five kinds of twitchy. She had trouble falling asleep, sure that the column would catch up with them, and when she did manage to sleep she didn't get much, waking up at any sound, sure it was black-robes come sneaking through the grass.

She pushed her pack harder when they traveled, because the more distance they got, the longer it'd take the black-robes to catch 'em up. Rora herself moved in constant, big circles around their little group, making sure there was no danger ahead, swinging back to make sure the column wasn't in sight or sound. Made her damn exhausted when they set up camp, and no matter how many times she grabbed Joros's seekstone to make sure the column wasn't moving either, she was still sure they were taking a break instead of a full stop, that they'd keep pressing forward while Rora slept on blindly, and she'd wake up with a nasty knife planted in her neck.

Long and short, Rora was starting to feel like she looked as crazed and worn out as Joros did.

It got even worse when they reached the hills.

They were just small lumps at first, like the ground had burped a little, and those weren't any kind of problem. But the hills got bigger, and the grass got shorter. Creeping up to the top of one of the hills to scout, Rora felt like a big painted target standing there. She didn't see the column, from the quick look she took before she got too spooked, but that didn't mean much when you were looking out at nice tall grass that could hide anything. She stayed off the hills, instead winding her way through the valleys between them, and she made the others promise to do the same.

"I could cloak you," Aro told her once, with his big puppy eyes. "Anddyr says I'm starting to get good at it, and it'd keep you safe."

"No," she said, and made sure she didn't say anything more'n that. Aro just wanted her approval, he always had, but she couldn't give it to him, not for this. Still, that didn't mean she could bring herself to crush him like a bug. He was her brother—her stupid, headstrong, foolhardy brother—and she'd love him no matter the idiot choices he made. Didn't mean she had to approve of his showing off the thing she'd worked her whole life to keep hidden—well, one of the two things she'd been keeping hidden. She could hate him and love him at the same time. It was like that boy-twin in the mountain had said, *Without me, she'd tip.* He'd been talking about his own sister, but he might as well've been talking about Rora. *Without me . . . she'd mean nothing.*

Coming around the soft curve of a hill, a flicker of *something* caught Rora's eye, and instinct sent her stretched belly-flat to the ground. She could feel her heart thumping in her mouth as she finally fixed on what'd spooked her brain, and she wasn't sure if she should scream or cry or run until her legs couldn't take her any farther.

Somehow, the black-robes'd gotten back ahead of her, because one of them stood at the top of the biggest hill she'd seen so far.

He was still a ways away, far enough maybe he hadn't seen her yet, but she could tell by the way he moved that he was looking, looking out over the hills and the plains, searching for something. For her, maybe. Or for her brother and Joros and the witch . . .

She stayed on her belly, using knees and elbows to push herself backward, slow and easy, trying to pretend she was like the grass around her, just moving with the wind. Soon as she was back around the hill, soon as she couldn't see the black-robe anymore, she sat up and curled herself into a little ball, her back to where he was standing. She knew she should get back to the others and fast, warn them before they got to somewhere the black-robe might see them . . . but it was like she was back in the mountain cell, frozen so cold she couldn't get her body to do anything. All she could do was sit there and listen to the blood pound in her ears.

Rora squeezed her eyes shut and focused on that sound, focused on it and made herself take even breaths. Slowly, her heartbeat started to match the breaths, steady and not panicked—or not *so* panicked at least. It was a trick Tare had taught her, way back, after Rora'd made her first kill for the pack and realized that killing someone to save your life was a lot different from killing someone for money.

She got to her feet, and stayed low to the ground, and it was one of the few times she'd ever been happy she was so short. She snuck through the hills, careful to keep one at her back as often as she could, and always looking over her shoulder first if she ever had to cross into sight of that big bastard of a hill.

The witch was having one of his fits when she found them, which was good because it meant they weren't moving toward the hill, but bad because the witch usually wasn't quiet about his craziness. It looked like he was at the start of the storm, twitching and muttering and scratching at his arms like there was something under his skin. One time she'd heard him moan, "I can feel them, they're in my blood," and it'd turned her stomach so bad she'd nearly puked. She hadn't asked who "they" were, didn't want to know.

"Can you make him stay quiet?" she asked Aro, first thing she said to any of 'em. "Or make it so no one can hear him?"

Aro's eyes got wide, and maybe it was because he could guess why she'd ask something like that, or maybe she looked as scared as she felt, or maybe he was just surprised she'd ever ask him to do anything magic. "I . . . I think . . . maybe?"

"Do whatever you can," she said, and then she turned to Joros. "They got ahead of us, somehow. Saw a black-robe on a hill up ahead, keeping lookout. Didn't stick around to see how many of his friends were around."

Joros's face looked like thunder, and Rora had a mad moment of her own to think it was no wonder Anddyr had problems with storms, being slave to a living one. "Where?" he asked.

Rora looked over her shoulder, down the beating-heart path she'd come. Every part of her screamed not to go that way, fear pointing like an arrow. She lifted her hand to point the same way.

Joros ground his teeth. "*How?* How could they have gotten there ahead of us?"

"Tricky bastards," Rora said. "However they did it, plan's off. There's no way we can get to whatever limb's there first, don't know if there's any way we can get to it at all now."

Joros ground his teeth some more, and looked kind of like he wanted to hit her. She'd like to see him try—with the way her blood was running high, she figured she could take him, easy. He didn't hit her, though. Just stared the way her finger'd been pointing, the same way they'd been traveling the last few days, weeks, however fecking long it'd been.

"So what do we do?" Aro asked quietly, always the one to

ask that stupid question, to remind them they didn't have any plan, and not having a plan meant probably dying in some awful and foolish way.

"We go around," Joros finally said. "We come from the side, where they won't be looking. We watch." His eyes fixed back on Rora, and she didn't like what she saw there. "We do whatever we can."

CHAPTER THIRTY-ONE

Keiro stood atop the tallest hill, feeling the pulse of the Twins beneath his feet, and he watched the great serpent of the Fallen wind its way through the hills. He had known of their coming for a handful of days now, knew it by the way the grass murmured, by the scent carried on the wind, by the whispering certainty in his mind. He knew it because the Twins knew it.

The wind tugged at Saval's robe, making it dance around Keiro's legs. It felt strange to wear the black again, after so long naked, and so long in tatters before that. It was a *right* sort of strange, but still strange. He had washed the robe half a dozen times, turning a clear pool of water pink, and sewn closed the giant rents with a bone needle and grass-stalk thread. *Don't think of that.* He needed to look the part he was to play.

Keiro stood alone atop the hill. He was meant to be alone, knew that down to his bones. He was at peace with it. Saval and Nerrin were gone, buried, made two sad hills among all the others. *He'd wasted his time burying them.* The plainswalkers were together, back at their tribehome. Maybe they had a part in what was to come, but perhaps they'd already fulfilled their purpose. They'd stood guard and held their secrets close through the long centuries, but the time of hiding and secrets was gone. This was the time for revealing, and for shouting.

There was a rustle to his left, and Keiro's head turned instinctively, hopefully. He'd been doing the same for days now, but it was never Cazi. It still wasn't—only the wind, a warm breeze blowing at dry stalks. He hadn't seen Cazi since that day below the hill, the day that—*Don't think of it.*

The Fallen drew slowly closer. *Bring them all*, Sororra had said, and it looked as though Saval's attendants had listened well. Keiro had never known how many the Fallen numbered—he'd wondered, sometimes, if anyone had known. With so many of the preachers inclined to long wandering, it was hard to guess. He supposed the Ventallo would know, have some catalog, have shelves upon shelves of seekstones, one for each preacher, but it was beyond his knowing. He was not of the Ventallo, and the one he could have asked was gone.

He wondered why he, an apostate, had been spared over a Ventallo. He had asked Tseris, when she had found him sitting beside the two mounds of fresh-turned dirt. *"You hear what most do not,"* she'd told him. *"You see the world, and you see what lies beyond it."* His throat was too tight to ask for a better answer, and so he still wondered—and more, he wondered how he would explain it to the other Ventallo, that he lived while one of their number had been given to the gods.

They drew closer, step by steady step, and Keiro stood waiting. There was nothing else for him to do.

The first to reach the base of the hill weren't true preachers, though the clothes they wore were dyed black—they were fighters, mercenaries, faithless hired swords. They approached with their weapons drawn and, unexpectedly, Keiro felt a spark of anger flare in his heart. He stood straighter, and he looked down at the half dozen men.

"Hail, brother," one of the mercenaries called out. "We seek Essemo Noniro or Saval Tredeiro. Are they here?"

He would give them no more than what they asked. "They are not," Keiro said flatly.

The speaker hesitated, exchanging glances and whispers with his fellows. "Were you with them? One of their attendants?"

"I was not."

"Then . . . who are you?"

Keiro stared at the man, stared at each of them in turn, and he could see their hackles rising at his silence—not in true anger, but in fear. It was the usual response of strong-handed men faced with the unfamiliar. Finally he said, "I am Keiro Godson. I speak for these hills and all that lies in them. I will speak to the Ventallo."

More murmured conversation, and then one of the mercenaries broke off, loping through the curving valleys between the hills, heading for the long black snake. The Fallen had halted some distance away, sent these scouts ahead, no doubt, to question the strange man on the hill.

The other mercenaries tried to question Keiro more, but he stood with his back and his arms straight, looking high over their heads to watch the mass of the Fallen. Occasionally he would repeat, "I will speak to the Ventallo," in answer to their gruff questions, and finally the mercenaries fell silent. They did not sheathe their blades.

When a group of two dozen broke away from the snake, Keiro smiled. There was the elation soaring in him, but it fought with a grim, heavy dread that had settled in his belly.

Sixteen wearing black robes approached his hill, though only one of them had Sororra's Eyes sewn above his heart. There were others with them—a few extra mercenaries, and three in dark blue robes with the look of the Highlands about them, with the same mad eyes as Nerrin.

The mercenaries formed a line between Keiro and the preachers, a shield of their bodies, as though one man could do so much harm. Still, the preacher with the red-Eyed mark of the Ventallo stepped in front of their protection, and they let him. "You asked for the Ventallo," the man called out. He was old, white-haired, and eyeless. "I am Valrik, and I speak for the Fallen."

"I am Keiro Godson," he said. "I speak for these hills and all that lies in them. I speak for the Twins."

Valrik laughed. Keiro could respect that, a man who could laugh in such a situation—*he could respect it, but he would not stand for it.* "I know you, Keiro," Valrik said. "You are apostate. You are banished."

"These are not your lands. You hold no power over me here. And if I am apostate, you hold no power over me *anywhere*."

Keiro could see the tightness in Valrik's jaw, could see the anger boiling behind the empty pits of his eyes. "Stand aside, apostate. We have traveled long to reach this place. I will not have you corrupting it."

Keiro laughed now, though it sounded strange to his own ears, nothing like his usual laugh. "You traveled here, Valrik, because I asked it. I speak for the Twins, and by their command, I have brought you here."

A silence stretched out, and Keiro could see Valrik weighing his words—deciding whether they were madness or truth, deciding whether Keiro should be trusted or killed. Finally Valrik asked, "You claim to have seen the Twins?"

"I do not claim," Keiro said. "I state."

"You—"

"If you don't believe me," Keiro interrupted, "then come. I will take you to them." He turned, and walked down the far side of the hill, out of their sight. It took some time, and he could hear their murmuring if not the words, but finally they crested the hill, each of them, the mercenaries hale, the eldest among the preachers straggling. They all followed, and blind as most of them were, their steps were sure upon the ground. Keiro considered leading them to the nearest entrance, the most direct route to the Twins; but he decided a little waiting, a little anticipation, would not do them too much harm. He walked farther down the hill, gripped the low branches of a scrubby bush, and pulled them aside to reveal the *mravigi*-sized hole. "Hold this, will you?" he said to the nearest of the mercenaries, and after a moment of hesitation the man gripped the branches with one of his big hands. Keiro bowed to the Ventallo, and then disappeared as he stepped into the hole.

Again, he could hear them debating. A mercenary dropped down, bruised his shins, and then squinted suspiciously up and down the tunnel, his fingers wrapped around the hilt of his sword. Keiro smiled guilelessly when the mercenary's roving eyes passed his. "All clear," the mercenary called up the hole, and then he joined Keiro kneeling out of the way as the others dropped down, one by one.

Keiro began crawling after a few had entered the tunnels; he trusted they'd keep up with him well enough. The first mercenary followed immediately after him, and Keiro was again impressed to see Valrik right behind the mercenary. He seemed to be a leader who was not afraid to lead. Saval had been the same . . . *Do not think of it.*

Every so often, one of them would call ahead, "Where are we going?" or "How much farther is it?" Keiro answered them only with silence. Truly, it didn't take long to reach the cavern—the great, empty cavern. Keiro had never before seen it so, with all the *mravigi* gone away somewhere, likely hiding in their dens and burrows. It made the place dark without the false starlight, only a faint red glow from Straz's open eyes to guide his steps.

The first of the *mravigi* remained, of course, always lying faithful before his creator. Keiro couldn't claim to know what the preachers saw—his own missing eye showed him naught but all the drowned infant twins—but they must have seen Straz, somehow. They exclaimed over him, his great white form bathed in the light from his eyes—and then four more eyes opened, glowing brighter. Then they gasped out prayers, each of the sightless black-robed, as they saw their gods.

"Welcome, leaders of the Fallen," Sororra said, and ice touched the edges of her voice.

"Blessed gods," Valrik babbled from his knees, "mighty Twins, it is an honor . . ."

"Valrik," she said. "Valrik . . . Uniro, I believe. Are you not so called?"

Keiro, who was watching each of them carefully, but their

apparent leader most of all, saw Valrik's cheeks go pale. "I was so called," he said carefully. "No longer."

"No?" Sororra asked, and the arch of one brow was an elegant thing. "And why is that, Valrik Uniro?"

The man pressed his brow to the floor, and with his lips near brushing the ground, he said, "I am first among none. I am a faithful servant only, a guide . . . a shepherd tending to his flock. But I am no better than any one of my sheep."

Sororra's head tilted, her eyes blinking slowly as she regarded the prostrate man. "You truly do believe that, don't you?" she finally murmured, and then she smiled. "Good! Then rise, Valrik-first-among-none. I would see your face." He stood, though his old legs shook as he stood before the Twins. Sororra held him pinned beneath her gaze—even without eyes, Keiro imagined Valrik could feel the weight of her regard. "Tell me, Valrik, what of these others here? Your fellow shepherds, and your scythes, and these bright-burning candles?"

Valrik bowed his head, as though he couldn't bear to meet Sororra's eyes, though his voice was stronger, more sure. "Each of them I have chosen, O just Sororra. They are all faithful and true, and strong beyond measure."

"You chose," Fratarro said mildly, the first he had yet spoken.

Valrik's spine went stiff, and it took him a very long time to answer. "I chose," he finally repeated. "Sheep, sometimes, need a strong hand to guide them, else they will wander aimlessly." He looked up then, with the unseeing pits of his eyes. "All these years, I have shaped the Fallen into an arrow, strong and firm and true. But an arrow alone is nothing. An arrow must be aimed and shot. I am the hand that draws back the arrow."

"You claim to be many things, Valrik Uniro," Sororra said. "Shepherd, archer . . . and yet you do not lay claim to the one thing you seem most clearly to be. Keiro," she called out, pitching her voice slightly higher, though Keiro stood nearer to her than Valrik. "What would you name this man?"

He knew the answer Sororra wished to hear. "When I asked for the Ventallo," Keiro supplied, "he came forward first. He has spoken loudest, and most. He alone wears your Eyes upon his breast. I would name him the leader of the Fallen."

"As would I," Sororra agreed amiably, as though they discussed simple matters. "Let us see, Valrik, how well you learned your histories. Tell me, who was the first Uniro?"

"Abren Uniro," Valrik said, each syllable dragging past his reluctant lips.

"And tell me, Valrik—you must forgive me, I've been so long away from the world—how long after the Fallen were formed did Abren become Uniro?"

Valrik's swallow was audible in the quiet place. "Five hundred and twenty-five years, my lady."

"Five hundred and twenty-five years," Sororra repeated, and somehow a low whistle made it through her charred lips. "Tell me, Valrik, how do you think they managed without a leader for so long?"

In his long wandering life, there were many memories that stuck in Keiro's mind. In one forest, vast and damp so that the air beaded on his skin, he had sat in a tree and watched two strange creatures play below him. They had been almost like small furry humans, though with longer limbs and tails that curved behind them. Still, there had been something unsettlingly human about their faces, about the way their long fingers gripped. He had smiled to watch the mother-creature showing her child how to lift rocks and pick bugs from beneath them, and he had felt content.

He hadn't seen the greatcat until it had already wrapped its jaws around the mother's neck. She had enough time for a single, piercing screech. Keiro had covered his mouth and stayed very still in the shelter of his tree, and watched, paralyzed, as the greatcat had its feast. It hadn't noticed the baby until after it had eaten its fill, but the greatcat's long tail had lashed, and it had pounced—not on the baby, but right in front of it, close enough to make the small creature skitter away with a high, human scream. The greatcat had pounced after it, blocked its escape, sent it wheeling in one direction and then another— toying with it. Surely it was too full to be hungry, and it could have killed the baby creature easily.

Keiro had watched helplessly, until the small creature had been unable to run any more, collapsing, shaking with terror and exhaustion. It had seemed to Keiro that the baby creature's eyes found his, somehow, through the shielding branches— begging, pleading. The greatcat had nudged at its body a few times, prowled around its still form, picked it up and gave it a quick shake, sending its body flying two lengths away. The greatcat had tried a few more times to get its toy moving, but the creature had lain still as death save for the heaving of its tiny chest, and the greatcat tired of its game. It prowled away, swallowed by the forest.

Keiro had fled down his tree as soon as he deemed it safe, sooner than he probably should have, and he'd run to the little creature's side. He'd scooped the baby up, cradled its panting body in his arms. Red blood, human blood, trickled down his arms from the small wounds where the greatcat's teeth and swiping claws had pierced skin, and the baby had looked up at him with so much sadness and confusion in its huge eyes. Its hand had wrapped tightly around one of Keiro's fingers, holding tight as the sun fell beyond the tops of the trees. Keiro had whispered prayers and songs, the creature's fur growing damp with his tears as its breathing grew more labored. The light fled from its eyes along with the sun, and its fingers had slipped gently from Keiro's.

Keiro wondered how long Sororra, catlike, would toy with Valrik.

To his surprise, though, Valrik did not fold in on himself as the baby had, didn't give in. His back straightened, and his chin jutted out, and the empty sockets of his eyes pointed directly at Sororra. "I *have* learned my history well, my lady, O wise Sororra. Edello Blackfist was the first to name himself Fallen, and it was he who gathered together all those brave enough to say they followed you still. It was Edello who led the Fallen in their first years, Edello's hands that shaped the small group into something good and strong. It was Edello who, dying, begged his most trusted advisor to guide the Fallen as he had done. As they did even until Abren named himself Uniro." The smile that stretched across Valrik's face was a surprising thing, toothy and proud. "The Fallen have always been led, my lady, even if the leader was not named so."

Silence followed his words, a brooding, burning thing, Sororra's bright eyes fixed on Valrik's sightless ones. Perhaps Valrik wasn't a small, helpless creature, but Sororra held no less resemblance to the greatcat.

A low chuckle broke the silence—Fratarro, who chose his words so carefully, content to let his sister play leader. A smile further creased his burned cheeks as he looked down at Valrik. "This one has fire, sister."

"He does," Sororra agreed, though she made it sound less a compliment. Fire was, after all, the tool of the Father. "Embrace who you are, Valrik Uniro. We see the things that lie in your heart and your mind—what use, then, in hiding them from us? You lead the Fallen."

Valrik's jaw worked, and then his chin tipped just a little higher. "I lead the Fallen," he said, his voice strong and steady.

"Good, then!" A great *boom* echoed through the cavern as Sororra's palms smacked together, and Keiro was not the only one to startle. Her remaining chains rattled louder than the clap. "The Fallen will need guidance as we begin this new and exciting chapter. But you are only one man, Valrik Uniro. You cannot do everything. Keiro." Obedient, Keiro turned to face her, bowed low. "Keiro Godson. You found us here, the first of the Fallen to come searching. We will never forget that. There is so much potential in you. You will be great, Keiro Godson, and you will grow mighty at our sides. Do you stand with us still?"

Keiro bowed again, even lower. Facing the floor, gazing down at the dark-stained patch where Saval's blood had pooled, those words felt very much like what Sororra had said to Nerrin. *Do not think of it.* "I stand with you always, my lady, my lord."

"My brother's creatures named you well, Godson. You will be our voice, and our eye, and our hands. Your word is as our word, and silence shall fall at your speaking. Your actions are as our actions, and none shall doubt you. You are our feet upon the earth, and the world shall bend before you." Her eyes bored into him, merciless. "Do you stand with us still?"

"I stand with you always," he said again, for there was naught else he could say.

"Hear this, Valrik Uniro. You will lead the Fallen, but you will heed the voice and the hands and the eye of Keiro Godson. Will you abide by this?"

Valrik pressed his fist against his brow in salute. "Of course, my lady. If it be your will, it shall be so."

"Good," Sororra said, and her grin was broad. She turned her gaze to Fratarro. "What say you, brother? Have you seen all that you need?"

Fratarro nodded once, slowly.

Sororra looked back to Keiro and raised one hand, chains jangling, to point unerringly at one of the black-clothed mercenaries. "Take up his sword, Keiro." Keiro's hands shook as he accepted the blade from the reluctant man—he noted idly, distantly, that it was the same mercenary who had been the first to follow him into the tunnels. He forced his hands to still, wrapping them both around the hilt, though it was meant to be held with one hand. He did not want to look to Sororra, did not want to learn what she would have him do with it.

But he was loyal, the most faithful of the Fallen. Godson.

He lifted his eyes, and she smiled at him almost gently. "All who stand before the Twins shall be judged. So it has been said since the time we first walked the earth. You are our hands, Keiro Godson. Pass our judgment."

With his heart heavy in his throat, Keiro turned from the

Twins to face the two dozen who stood arrayed before him. He held the sword before him, its tip wavering before his eyes. Slowly he stepped forward, and stood before the mercenary who had given up his blade.

Blades for the darkness, they were called. When the sun fell, when all the world changed, their blades would be useful. The whispering certainty was there once more: *they will have a place in the new world.*

He turned from the mercenary, and in the tally of judgment that swam behind his missing eye, he marked the rest of the black-armored men as worthy also. The first Ventallo he stood before was an old man, shaking under the weight of his years, but he stood as straight as he could when Keiro stopped before him. *Weak, but he will serve.* The next was a woman, old but motionless, elegant, and she lifted her chin high, baring her neck to him, and it felt as though a hand squeezed around Keiro's own neck. *She is brave.* The man next to her stood tall, the sockets of his eyes staring ahead, fearless. He, too, lifted his chin, the thick expanse of his neck bared. *This one is false. This one lies in his heart.*

Keiro's hands shook again as he slowly lifted the sword, turning its blade sideways, shook so badly its tip nearly pierced the man's neck. Keiro tried to breathe around the tightness in his throat, to breathe around the sickness boiling in his stomach. *I am the hands of the Twins,* he told himself, but it was not the whispering certainty, and it felt weak and ineffectual. *I am not my own hands.* Softly he pressed the blade against the man's throat, feeling how his skin would give way with so little pressure . . .

He is false. He has been judged. Gritting his teeth, biting back bile, Keiro pressed the blade forward, and the judgment of the Twins washed over him.

I am not my own hands. The next two were judged as well, their souls cast to the skies, their bodies to the cold ground. Others were spared, found worthy, deemed useful. Keiro's hands grew steadier as the judgments went on, though his arms turned to lead with the weight of the sword. *I am not my own hands.* A young man, barely more than a boy, and he shook as Keiro pressed the blade to his neck. *I am not my own hands.* Keiro could not close his eye, could not hide from it, but he could stare beyond—look through his other eye instead, the missing eye, where all the wide and innocent babes stared back, never accusing, never angry. Only sad, so, so sad.

Valrik was the last. He met Keiro's eye in that empty place, calm and sure as Keiro pressed the blade against his old neck. He stood still for a long while, the blade leveled between them, waiting for Valrik to breathe.

He will serve.

The sword fell from Keiro's heavy hand, from his wet red fingers, to clatter against the stone floor. *I am not my own hands. You did well.*

"Leave us," Sororra said in her booming voice, sleep touching its edges. They could wake for longer now, but still they were pulled to the hard embrace of sleep. "Choose your faithful well, Valrik Uniro, and listen wisely. Go."

Keiro staggered forward, exhaustion falling upon him like the weight of all the dirt above his head. He hadn't noticed the pressure until it was gone, as though an enormous hand clasped around his chest had finally released him. Air burned in his throat, and the sight of his good eye blurred and flickered as he swayed. He felt, unexpectedly, empty. Fratarro's eyes closed, and then Sororra's, and the cavern was left in near darkness. *I am not my own.*

Keiro followed the others from the cavern, those who remained—Valrik and the mages and the mercenaries and the few preachers left. He stumbled in their wake like a drunkard, one red-coated arm wrapped around his stomach, one sticky-red palm pressed to his forehead.

He left them, somewhere along the tunnel, and found himself kneeling in a small chamber, a closed space with nowhere to go but back, and he wrapped both arms around himself, bent in two as he gasped for air, and his tears were hot where they fell upon his arms.

I am not my own.

There was a twisting in his mind, like a serpent coiling to sleep, like a beast pulling back its fangs. A releasing of something held tight, a cornered mouse, a caged bird, allowed to live because it would be there waiting when the serpent woke, when the beast hungered.

Keiro's hands, red and awful, smacked against the floor. He vomited between them, and it felt like something inside him tore away. The murmuring certainty was gone like a closing eye, his mind clear of the whispering he hadn't even known wasn't his own. He felt both more himself, and less. A caught thing, helpless and shaking and paralyzed by fear.

I am not . . .

Somewhere, sometime, a small piece of warmth pressed against his side. A hand-sized scaled head nudged at his bloodied fingers, and Keiro opened his arms. Cazi curled into them, curled around him, long tail wrapping his waist like an embrace and the *mravigi*'s heavy head leaning against his own. *"I am sorry,"* Cazi said in his soft new voice.

Keiro could not find any words, not yet. In the darkness, he could see only the eyes, all the eyes, wide and staring, and the smooth empty pits where eyes had once been.

I am not.

CHAPTER THIRTY-TWO

Joros stood at the top of the hill he had chosen for them to make their stand. It was just as unremarkable as any of the other hills, and he had chosen it mostly because it was as far away from the largest hill as he could get while still having a decent chance of seeing what the Fallen bastards were doing over there. He'd ordered Anddyr to make the hill hidden, unfindable, and safe, and the mage had used it as a teachable moment, showing Aro the proper finger-waves and mutters. Aro had repeated everything, and the air surrounding them had gone dark and heavy—too heavy to breathe. Panic had registered in Anddyr's eyes a second before it did in Aro's, and they'd frantically scrabbled at each other's hands. The pressure had built in Joros's chest, and if he'd been able to draw breath, he would have shouted at them to fix whatever stupid thing Aro had done. Luckily Anddyr's twitching hands swept everything away in moments, so at least one of them wasn't entirely useless. Aro had pouted for a good long while, sitting with his arms around his knees and watching Anddyr with sad eyes, until the mage had Aro start practicing his barriers within the shelter of Anddyr's reliable protective shield.

And then there was little else to do but sit upon their hill, and stare at the shadows walking across the far hill, and wait.

Rora had grown more restless—she wasn't one inclined to inactivity, and this was inactivity incarnate. She paced constantly, circling the hill again and again. She'd tried to walk out of the circle of protection, and Joros had snorted laughter as she'd run face-first into one of Aro's clumsy barriers. He'd needed that laughter, but it had been days ago now. Just the other day she'd thrown herself at the barrier with fists and feet, pounding and screeching like a cornered cat, until she'd noticed her brother flinching with each blow, as though she were hitting *him*. She'd been more docile since then, contenting herself with pacing and staring at the distant hill.

Across the rolling hills, the Fallen had been digging into their hill, straight down from its crown. Joros had Anddyr cast his seeking again, holding the blackened toe between his shaking hands, and the mage had been cloud-white when he'd opened his eyes. Joros had known before he'd even said, "It's not a limb there, cappo." He could feel it in the air, reaching across the hills. The Twins were so very near, and their call was powerful. Joros had begun idly digging down into his hill with his short sword in foolish, ineffectual imitation.

In a twisting sort of way, Joros had brought the Fallen here—with Anddyr, he'd given them the tools to find the Twins. He'd brought them here, and now he sat near helpless as he tried to think how to stop them. It was his doing, his responsibility if the Twins were unbound—and it was starting to feel as though that was a heavy responsibility he'd have to shoulder for the rest of his likely-to-be-short life.

Joros wondered briefly how different things would have been if he'd stayed with the Fallen. He would have been squarely under Valrik's heel, true, a powerless lackey, stripped of purpose and meaning . . . but at least he would have been on the right side. He would have been one of the multitudes surrounding the hill, waiting for their greatest hopes to come true. He wouldn't have been *here*, a single stalk of wheat standing against a whirlwind, with no hope and everything to lose. He would have, perhaps, been standing beside a fiery-haired woman . . .

He'd made his choice, though, made all his choices—wrong as they'd turned out to be. His singularity of purpose—to ruin the Fallen in general and Valrik in particular—had lined up so nicely with the Parents' cause. Joros wanted with a violent passion to keep the Twins bound, wanted it as badly as any follower of the Parents, and so he'd placed his hopes in them, sure the Parents' devotees would stop their fears from being realized, sure they would keep the Twins bound. With their sheer numbers and Joros's quick mind, he'd been sure of a resounding victory. They would sunder the Ventallo, set Patharro's cleansing fire to Raturo, and Joros himself would kill Valrik, whisper a single name in the man's ear at the height of his vengeance. And when it was over, he would go his separate way from the Parents' followers, a mutual truce, and he'd gather up the sad, lost remnants of the Fallen, who would need a new name and a new leader and a new purpose . . .

But he hadn't counted on being the only one who knew

there was a problem that needed to be stopped. He hadn't counted on being the only one fighting for this cause.

Regret served no purpose. The past was as it was, and all he could do now was pray that the Parents cared enough about their world and their people to grant him a miracle.

Anddyr was standing at the barrier, his hands splayed flat against the solid air, muttering as ever. Joros watched him idly, checking occasionally to make sure his fingers weren't twitching—so long as he wasn't trying to cast any spells, he could be as foolish as he pleased. He noticed Aro watching the mage, too. Aro had grown very skilled at sensing when the mage was taking a sour turn, and containing him before he became a danger.

Anddyr's bouts were coming more and more frequently, he was sinking deeper into his madness. Multiple times, Joros had ordered the mage to tell him what was happening, why he was acting so strangely, but each time—mad or sane—Anddyr had stared at him with eyes that were at once distant yet clear as the sky. Years and years ago, another life ago, Dirrakara had given him a jar and a mage and named them both his. His, for as long as the mage's mind could withstand the madness. "He likely won't live long," she'd whispered, her lips tickling his ear, the scent of her strong in his nostrils. He pushed the memory away, vicious and uncompromising. He wondered instead if Anddyr was nearing the very end of his sanity, and hoped the mage could keep his mind together long enough to do one last useful thing.

Occasionally some of Anddyr's muttering came out clear and loud enough for them to hear: "I should go over there," or "I need to get her back, I promised," and then over and over, "Etarro, Etarro, Etarro."

"There's something coming," Rora said, as faithful a guard dog as he'd ever met.

Joros lifted his eyes from his dirt-scratching and looked where she looked—not toward the large hill but south, beyond the hills and beyond the Plains, south where death lurked like a specter in the shape of shimmering sand. And there was indeed something coming from the dead-lands.

From this distance, it was little more than a smudge, a blur against the horizon, but there was no denying that it was moving, and moving steadily closer. Joros watched for a time until he realized whatever-it-was was moving as slow as mud, and he went back to his irritated scratching. Rora could stand watch for the both of them.

Anddyr slunk to Joros's side, his eyes down and his hands shaking. "Please, cappo," he whispered, and then dropped onto his face, prostrating himself like a supplicant before a god. "I need to be there. I need to go."

Joros aimed a halfhearted kick at the mage. "Shut up."

"But Etarro . . . he'll . . . I promised . . ."

Joros ignored him.

"It's people," Rora said after a time.

Joros grunted—of course it was people. Nothing lived in the Eremori Desert, and only people would be stupid enough to walk willingly into its hot maw. More minutes passed, the tip of Joros's sword digging deeper into the ground, biting and burying. Maybe turning up the smooth surface of the hill would turn his thoughts over in a similar way, jumbling them up like throwing a deck of cards into the air. Nothing could be organized if it wasn't already disorganized.

"They're pulling something."

That got Joros to lift his head, and he stood once more, using the sword to lever himself to his feet. He went to Rora's side, and after a moment her brother stood to her other side. He was looking more haggard by the day, doing well over half the work in keeping them hidden and silent, his newfound powers pushed immediately to their limits. That sparked a bit of worry in Joros—he couldn't afford to lose either of the twins. There was little enough to be done yet, perhaps they could retreat to the lee of the hill and leave Rora to watch, let Aro drop his shields . . .

"What is that?"

Joros blinked, focused on the smudge that had resolved itself into actual shapes. There were people, no more than a handful, and they were indeed pulling something . . . something long and black and bent that his eyes and mind couldn't make any sense of. He squinted, tilted his head, but still it looked like nothing natural, nothing he could place . . .

A laugh wheezed out near his feet, startling him so that he nearly stomped on Anddyr, who was gazing up crazy-eyed and twist-necked from his stomach. "Arm," Anddyr gasped, and flapped his own arm, the long limb thumping against the ground, sending up a cloud of dust that made the mage choke and cough and laugh.

Joros kicked the mage away, and when he looked back at the slow-moving procession, they did indeed seem to be pulling a monstrous arm, three times the size of any human arm.

Joros felt very cold, though the sun beat heavily against his back on its way down the sky, and then a fever-bright heat twisted through his gut. His fingers were tight around the hilt of his short sword, his other hand curled into a fist so tight he thought his nails might draw blood from his palm. Quietly, he asked, "How many is that, Anddyr?"

The mage gurgled, spat out, "Four," and then screamed as he beat himself around the head with his own fist.

"Four what?" Aro asked. His sister stayed silent; she'd likely already put together the pieces.

"Four limbs of a god," Joros said. "Four pieces to make Fratarro whole."

"How many are there supposed to be?"

"Anddyr was able to track six, counting the hand we burned."

Aro's fingers twitched at his side and his lips moved, as though he were weaving some spell—though Joros rather guessed that was how he counted. "So they're still missing one, yeah?"

"No," Anddyr moaned from the ground, "no, no, no . . ."

"If I had to hazard a guess," Joros said grimly, "I would say the missing one is already under that hill."

That shut Aro up well enough.

They stood together—save Anddyr, who writhed at their feet, caught up in his private madness—and watched the newcomers with their arm approach the hill. They were greeted warmly by the main column, welcomed with cheers. As the sun stretched shadows long across the hills, countless hands pulled the arm up the side of the great hill, to the very top where, he saw now, the digging had halted. They worked together, smooth as water turning a wheel, and soon they were lowering the arm into the hill itself, dropping it down the great hole they had dug, perhaps dropping it down to the very center of the earth.

"So what now?" Rora asked, the question she never stopped asking.

The moon already hung in the sky before him, pale against the bright streaking colors of the setting sun. It was a full moon, perfectly round, and it would color the night like a second sun. He nudged Anddyr with his foot, and when the mage blinked up at him with watering eyes, Joros turned his hand in a certain way. "Now," Joros said heavily, the tip of his sword biting into the hill, "now it begins."

Rora barked out a curse as Anddyr's arms flailed against her legs, buckling her knees, knocking her to the ground; she continued cursing steadily as Anddyr drew stilling designs in the air, weeping next to her immobile form. Aro stared hang-jawed, his hands half-raised, and it was simple fear—cowardice, perhaps—that held him still. Joros pressed his foot to the back of Aro's knee and the man fell easily, crumpling so that Joros could grab a handful of his hair. His other hand lifted his sword to rest against Aro's throat.

Rora lay with her limbs splayed and held by the power of Anddyr's spell, but he hadn't stilled her tongue. She swore at him, all the vile words known to humanity and more he guessed she made up on the spot, and she glared at him with a pure and burning hatred that he hoped would be enough.

"Truly," he said over her cursing, and it was one of the rare times the words that followed were indeed true, "I am sorry."

CHAPTER THIRTY-THREE

Keiro stood at the crest of the large hill, at the edge of the open shaft that had been dug straight to the beating heart—*hearts*—of the hill. He gazed up, at the stars poking through the darkening sky, at the heavy moon watching like an enormous eye, at Sororra's Eyes shining their red light over the earth. Looking up was easier, far easier, than looking down.

He no longer had the luxury of avoidance, though. There was so much to be done. So much ending, so much beginning.

Keiro looked from the sky down to the hole into the hill, his dirty toes nearly touching its edge. In a moment of complete mundanity, he thought how strange he must seem, walking black-robed and barefoot among the Fallen, but Saval's boots hadn't fit him, and anyway, they'd needed too much cleaning . . .

Better, by far, to think of his own hardened feet.

There was no stopping this, and only so long he could delay the inevitable. He didn't need the whispering certainty to tell him that, though it had—though *Sororra* had. He understood, now, that there was no avoiding those not-quite-his-own thoughts, just as there was no avoiding what he must do now. Dragging his dirty feet would not help them—there was nothing, anymore, that he could do to help them.

Keiro made himself look at them again, one last time. The young twins, their faces a perfect match, bound to either side of the great pit. They lay on their backs, with their legs and arms spread wide, lashed to stakes driven deep into the earth. They hadn't struggled when the ropes had been brought out—they'd gone to their fates willingly, as though they'd known this was coming.

"Avorra," Keiro said softly. "Etarro." His voice was heavy, but his purpose was firm. *There was no other way.*

Keiro had fallen to his knees when he saw them—he'd been sure, at first, that his good eye was lying to him, or that it was some trick of his missing eye. But no, they were real, real as life. The girl's brows had shot up and the boy had taken a surprised step back, and Keiro had pressed his face to the ground before them. In that moment, after everything that had come before, they were the perfect thing to lift his heart.

The young twins had grown so much since he'd last seen them. Then, they'd been small children, hardly more than babes. Now, they stood almost as high as Keiro's shoulder, and their eyes and faces were full of more years than had gone by. In all his walking days after being banished from Mount Raturo, Keiro had almost convinced himself he'd seen false, that there hadn't been living twins inside the mountain, that he'd thrown his life away on a pain-born hallucination . . . but no. They were real and true, and they made everything—all of it, every step and every drop of blood—worth it.

They'd both looked at him curiously when he'd lifted his

head from the ground, and when he'd held out his hands toward them, they'd willingly pressed their palms to his, the girl a fraction of a moment after her brother. "Please," Keiro had said, sure he was weeping like a fool and not caring, "I have wondered for so long. What are your names?"

"I'm Avorra," the girl had said, and if her eyes had held any uncertainty looking at him, her voice showed none of it. "He's Etarro."

"Avorra," Keiro repeated, savoring each syllable. "Etarro. By the gods, it is good to know you."

"And you are?" Avorra had prompted with stiff formality, beginning to tug her hand from his.

"I am Keiro."

"Keiro Godson," the boy had said softly. When Keiro had looked at him in surprise, he'd seen how pale the boy's eyes were, and how wide. Keiro had had no idea how he'd known the moniker, but the knowing had seemed to draw his face down, add more years to his eyes.

Cazi had chosen that moment to appear—for as big as he had grown, he was still excellent at hiding and sneaking. Avorra had recoiled, but the boy's eyes had gone wider, this time with wonder. "Is that . . . ?"

Keiro had hefted the Starborn, a grin stretching his face. "This is Cazi." It had felt good to smile, and it had hurt that the smile felt so strange on his cheeks.

Etarro had reached out, fingers gently tracing the curve of Cazi's nose, the ridge between his eyes, the spines that fanned around the base of his skull. The joy that had suffused his face had done much to smooth the deep-etched sadness, and the years had peeled back as Cazi had leaned into his touch.

They had that one moment at least. And then there was no more time for joy.

The wonder was gone from the boy's face as he lay staring up at the stars, and his sister's apprehension was gone, too. Such perfect little offerings, Valrik's pride, waiting so patiently to fulfill the purpose for which they'd been groomed from birth. Keiro felt sick.

It was his doing, all of it orchestrated by his command. *You will be our voice, and our eye, and our hands.* He had seen, and spoken, and done, and it had all come to this.

"Be well, children," he said softly, though the words sounded hollow even to his own ears. They gave no answer, just stared silently upward. He couldn't begin to imagine what thoughts lay behind their too-old eyes.

Keiro turned away from them, left them for the second time in his life, in their short lives, and it was no easier this second time. His steps were slow, his feet never more reluctant to walk. He stood at the edge of the pit, the earth's gaping maw, the darkness within touched by red. A rope ladder hung over the edge and he took it down, his eye flickering between the bound twins until the ground took him from their sight. Down and down, his hands shaking, and his throat tight. His feet touched the floor of the cavern, and he made sure his hands were steady before he released the rope ladder.

Preparations had begun here, too. The limbs had been laid out, stretched like corpses upon the floor—an arm, a foot, two legs. All the pieces to make Fratarro whole once more—all save the one hand that was lost, truly lost, though the Twins had come as close as they could to restoring it with blood and magic.

They stood waiting, the few he had chosen. *The most useful.*

Valrik, with smooth skin where his eyes had been, and yet he seemed to follow every movement made. Yaket, so old and sad, who held a heavy bundle near as big as she was, held it tight against her body. A mage named Berico, who seemed to shake and rave less than the other thrall-mages Keiro had met.

There were others, of course. Scores of people pressed against the shadows, and that many and more *mravigi* were giving their glow to the cavern. They waited, watching, and they had their parts to play, true enough, but Keiro had not chosen them. If it had all been his doing, without the whispering certainty in his ear, he would have sent them away, each and every one. *And yet it had been his choice*, of course, all him. His was the voice, and his were the hands.

Keiro stood with the other three, the chosen, and together they watched the sky through the hole in the ground above. When the edge of the moon peeked around the mouth of the pit, Keiro lowered his eye, met the gaze of each of the others. He had already spoken the words that needed saying, spoken until his throat was raw. All that was left now was the doing.

Keiro raised one arm, and the shadowy forms surged forward. Hands gripping, scaled bodies pressing, man and *mravigi* together moving the great limbs rapidly across the floor. The Twins watched them come, Sororra cradling her brother's head against her shoulder with both hands. There was triumph in her eyes, and joy. Beneath the burned crags, Keiro could see fear written into Fratarro's face. As they arranged the limbs before Fratarro, pressing end to ichorous end, Yaket opened the bundle she held. Her armful seemed to glow and shimmer in the faint light.

Four long needles the plainswalkers had made, one for

each of the chosen, and four long threads of grass-fiber woven through each needle's eye. It was the most Yaket had let her people do, though they had begged to help more, though they had hated her for her refusal.

Keiro had visited the tribehome days ago, the only time he had left the hills since the Fallen had swarmed over them. He was eye and hands, and he had needed to go. The plainswalkers had looked peaceful, seated in two broad circles, the men in one circle with their knives working steadily, and the women in the other with stalks of grass stretched between them. Their brows had shone with sweat, and their fingers had moved a frantic pace. Over it all Yaket's voice had woven, the powerful cadence of a story.

"The whole tribe carved the boar's tusks until they were slim and sharp and as long as a man's arm, and they carved a hole in the base of each. These they took to the Twins, along with the woven grass rope that was thinner than a blade's edge..."

She had never told this story to her people before, never told it to any but him. They listened intently, faces glowing with fervor. Yaket had met Keiro's eye over the distance between them, single eye to single eye, and he had not been able to bear her look for long.

This, too, he had done.

Keiro gripped his needle hard enough that his hands would not shake, and he led the others forward. He would take the arm, which had arrived only hours earlier. He'd been worried it wouldn't arrive in time, but Valrik had promised Essemo Noniro was on his way, that he would not fail them. He had not been wrong, and so the arm was left to Keiro.

The preachers had worked quickly, tearing apart the great carts they had used to haul Fratarro's limbs from the mountain, cannibalizing them to build a hasty platform tower. There was little enough building material in the Plains, so they'd had to make do with what they'd brought, but the first slats held Keiro's weight as he climbed carefully up the side of it. He held the needle with one hand, its death-sharp tip swinging near his gut each time his hand reached higher.

There were some preachers already at the top of the tower, holding the arm in place, supported by *mravigi* and more preachers below. They made space for Keiro, their faces solemn. He stepped close, hands near to shaking once more. He almost reached out to rest his hand on Fratarro's broad shoulder, but he stopped himself. Instead he asked softly, "Are you ready, my lord?"

Fratarro did not look at him, eyes staring, unfixed. Above, atop the ground, in the bathing light of the full moon, the Starborn began to sing, their high voices rising and dancing. Fratarro's eyes squeezed shut, and when they opened once more, they seemed clearer, calmer. He gave a terse nod and said, "Do it. Let it begin."

We are ready.

Keiro took a deep breath, glanced once more through the hole where the heartbreakingly beautiful Starborn song drifted down, and then he fixed his eye upon his task. The needle steady in his hand, Keiro drove its tip through the cracked flesh of Fratarro's shoulder. A heartbeat later, the other three did the same in their respective places, four needles driving into him, the tips appearing once more from the burned flesh of his missing limbs. Ichor flowed steady from each tear in his flesh, from each tiny hole pierced into him. Keiro pulled on the needle, on the long grass-fiber thread, until the knot at its end caught and held. And then he drove the needle down once more.

Fratarro didn't scream, not at first. With Sororra's hands holding him, her voice whispering low words of comfort, he sat stiff and still, held in place by the shard through his chest. But after the needles were driven through again and again, the thread tugged tight as could be . . . finally his mouth opened in a cry of pain. Once the screaming had begun, it did not stop. No matter how Sororra spoke to him, how her hands moved to calm him, he screamed and screamed, and blood flowed from him, and his eyes wept hot tears as they screwed shut with pain. Keiro felt himself weeping, too, his sight blurring as his hands drove the needle down again and again. Tight stitches to seal the god together, to make him whole once more. Keiro wept, and still his hands moved, steady and sure.

Under the screaming, under the raw pain, under the slight sound—somehow, so loud—of thread pulling through flesh and skin, under it all soared the singing of the Starborn. He had always thought the sound so beautiful. It sounded obscene, beneath the screaming of a god.

Keiro's hands were wet with ichor when finally the needle came through where it had begun. Carefully he knotted the thread, and one of the preachers came silently forward to cut the remainder free. Keiro stepped back, the needle suddenly unbearably heavy in his now-shaking hands. He fell to his knees, thought he might be sick, but he made himself look. The stitching was well done, strong and sure, sealing Fratarro's arm to his body once more. Though he could see the ragged edges where the limb had been torn away, the blood had ceased to flow there. Finally, finally, Fratarro's screaming fell away, leaving only the high song of the *mravigi* above.

He was the last to finish. Valrik and Yaket and Berico stood to the side, waiting, the bone needles still clutched in their hands. Keiro knew he should join them, but he did not have the strength.

Fratarro's head lifted from his sister's shoulder, and though he didn't smile, some of the haunted look had fled from his eyes. Sororra smiled wide enough for both of them. As one, they looked up, up through the wide-gaping hole, to the bright moon that stared down at them. Together they reached, chains jangling from Sororra's wrist, Fratarro's fingers moving slow and wondering as they stretched toward the sky.

Together, their hands fell back to the ground with a sound like falling stone, and the red light faded from their eyes fast as blinking.

CHAPTER THIRTY-FOUR

Anddyr couldn't bring himself to look at Rora. Her screaming and swearing were bad enough, but he'd made the mistake of trying to explain himself to her. The hatred in her eyes had nearly made his will crumble like ancient stone. His magic was enough to keep her pinned, and he didn't need to look at her for that; so long as she stayed still, she could hate him all she wanted. He told himself it didn't matter whether she liked him, because repeating a lie often enough made him feel somewhat better. He kept himself busy with Aro instead, working quickly to get the younger man similarly pinned, trying to use as little of his magic as possible—he'd need it for later. For soon, rather. The end of all things was rushing closer, all the storms coalescing and swirling above him, and he needed to be ready.

His power held Aro pinned to the ground, still silent in his shock, not understanding. He had been such a quick learner, so eager to embrace new knowledge . . . but he didn't *think*. He grabbed the lesson but not the concept, not the meaning behind the motions his fingers made, and that was a dangerous thing. There was a deep well of power in Aro, so much that it must have taken an incredible amount of willpower for him to keep the magic from devouring him all these years—but he couldn't seem to bring that willpower to bear now. His power was a trickle or a flood, nothing in between, and combined with his lack of thought . . . Anddyr supposed that was a good thing, or else Aro might have seen this coming.

Anddyr squeezed his eyes shut as he reached into his robe, fingers finding the pocket easily. He touched the familiar earthenware jar, and even now, his mouth watered and his stomach twisted at the touch. He almost couldn't grab it, his hand was shaking so badly. But he had to do this still. No matter how hopeless it all looked, no matter he knew it would fail and the storms would fall and the ground would swallow him—he had to, still.

In the ice-place, where he'd been set free for the storms to swarm around him, a small voice echoed in his ears. *When the time comes . . . you still have to try.* He couldn't understand why— surely Etarro, with his sight that reached farther than it should, knew how hopeless it was. The cappo's last desperate plan was doomed, no chance of it succeeding. Now, at the crux of it all, when Anddyr wanted only to curl into a ball and die quietly, he was instead bound—*commanded*, by the traces of skura running sluggish through his veins—to see this useless plan through to its end.

Anddyr opened his eyes and he looked down at the little earthenware jar in his hand, lighter than a stone but not quite as light as it could be. It was not empty; he'd made sure to leave some of it, just enough. He could feel its contents calling to him even now, black tendrils that snuck beneath the lid to reach for him . . .

His other hand came up, shaking, and with a twist he set it free.

The smell of the skura washed over him, pulling a groan from his mouth, from his stomach, from his core. He squeezed his eyes shut once more, trying to block out its pull. He had burned all of the skura Joros had given to him, burned every last bit . . . except for this. He had saved it and carried it with him each day, feeling its sickly warmth against his skin and its call vibrating through him, twisting his gut. Just enough for one dose, one final dose. But not for him.

Long ago, the night after Joros and Anddyr had fled quietly from Mount Raturo with their secrets and their stolen goods and the cappo's fury burning brighter than fire, they had walked through the great Forest Voro—quickly, putting as much distance as they could between themselves and the mountain. Joros had growled his plans aloud, every possibility, every contingency, all the various ways he could destroy the Fallen. He'd growled his plans like commands, and those words had seeped into Anddyr's skin, flowed along the skura in his blood, and lodged themselves into his brain. All of his orders for every possible plan, ingrained into the core of his being.

All the plans had failed, save this one. Every possibility, every contingency—narrowed to this one last hopeless, horrid plan.

Anddyr opened his eyes and the storms were swirling around him. He didn't want to—*he didn't want to!*—but there was still old skura flowing in him like poison, and the command thrummed through him, inescapable. Cradling the skura jar, Anddyr leaned forward over Aro, held to the ground by an invisible hand, his eyes growing slowly wide with understanding.

"Don't you dare," Rora snarled, but even she was a dim and distant thing. "Don't you fecking dare—"

He lowered the jar, held Aro's mouth open with his other hand. For a moment, his face was Etarro's, but then it wasn't.

No matter what happens, no matter how it looks. You still have to try.

"I thought you were better than this!"

Anddyr paused, the jar just above Aro's mouth, the skura making its slow slimy way toward the lip of the jar. *I am trying to be better than I was.* He moved his hand, and the skura fell between Aro's open lips.

He threw the jar away from him when it was done, threw it so far he would never see it again, and then he curled himself into the smallest shape he could. He couldn't watch it roll through Aro, watch it stream through his mage's blood, turning his insides sludgy and black. It was bad enough to hear Aro's screaming. He screamed with two voices, from two mouths, Rora's cry tying around her brother's, and they wrapped around Anddyr like a thunderstorm. *I had to, I had to!* A desperate plan, a foolish plan, all but doomed to fail . . . and yet he was bound to follow it, bound by Joros, who had been his master, and bound by Etarro, who had claimed to free him. It was a terrible sort of freedom the boy had given him: the strength to fight for a better future for himself, but no power to fight against what the past had put into motion. No power to stop this wheel from turning, and crushing them all.

"We have to move quickly, now," the cappo said, his voice tight and angry and scared. "Leave him. See what they're doing."

Anddyr dragged his eyes open, but avoided looking at Rora, whose fury scorched the air between them. He looked to the far hill, to the swarming hive of the Fallen, and with a murmured word he sent his mind soaring over the hills.

He could look down on them like a bird, see how they moved quickly over the hill as the light fell from the sky. There were so many of them, on the hill itself and scores and scores and scores more surrounding the hill, trailing between the hills, all gathered to bear witness. The sheer number of them made his head hurt.

Diving closer, he could see that they had staked two people to the ground atop their hill. Two small people. Children. Etarro and Avorra, their small faces serene. They had known their own purpose since the day of their birth. They had never doubted what they were. *You have to try.* Between them was a giant hole, gaping mouthlike, and it put a twisting in Anddyr's stomach as bad as the skura. He fled away from it, back to his body, and kept his eyes away from the cappo as he described what he had seen.

He didn't need to be told. The cappo had suspected, and prepared. Anddyr fetched his pack, pulled out the rope and the long wooden stakes he had brought, and he set to work.

If Etarro and Avorra were bound beside that hole, it could only mean that the cappo had been right: the Fallen had found their banished gods, and were preparing to free them. When the ancient Twins rose, when the Fallen freed them from their bound bodies, they would go seeking new hosts. The Fallen had brought a set of twins, but Joros had his own set now, an older pair, a stronger pair, a more enticing prize . . . and his hope was that the Twins wouldn't see the trap until it had already closed around them.

Destroy one, the cappo had said, *and you destroy them both.* If Fratarro chose Aro, if the skura burning through Aro's blood could overpower even a god, if, if, *if* . . . The cappo's final plan, and it relied so much on luck, on conjecture, on hope.

Aro didn't twitch as Anddyr worked, moved so little that Anddyr kept checking to make sure he was breathing. "Keep your hands off him," Rora said as Anddyr splayed his limbs, stretched the ropes, but the threat had fallen out of her voice. It sounded more, now, like despair.

When he had finished with Aro, he planted the other stakes, pounding them into the earth with his own fists. It made them bruise and bleed, his skin cracking over the heads of the stakes, his bones splintering, but it didn't matter. He deserved this. He would always deserve it.

When Anddyr was done, rope tied to each of the stakes, he heard Joros say softly, "This will go easier, if you don't fight." He heard, too, the sound of spitting.

Together they muscled her over to the stakes, tying her at the wrist and ankle, tied like her brother, tied like the young twins on the far hill. It was a relief to let his power fall away from her, to let her be held by simple rope rather than by his own shame. He had plenty of the shame, but he would need all his power for what was to come. When he turned away from her, fled from her screaming, he heard the singing.

It was unlike anything he had heard before. There were no words, but the song didn't need words. It was the sound of a heart, a dozen hearts, a hundred hearts, all pulled free and laid bare. Hope and pain, joy and despair, fear and dreams, and fear of the dreams. It was, he thought, the song his own heart might sing, if it had known how.

Joros came to stand at his side, and his hand rested heavily on Anddyr's shoulder. "Be ready. It will be soon, I can feel it. We only have one chance." And then he left Anddyr, going back to stand between Rora's head and Aro's, and his short sword hung from his fingers.

Anddyr closed his eyes, closed his ears to Rora's swearing and the heartsong, closed away everything, and set his mind adrift in the lowering storm.

No matter how it looks. You have to try.

He thought of Etarro, poor Etarro, how scared he must be. Etarro, who he knew as well as he knew himself, the kind boy with the sad face and too-old eyes. He could save the boy from his fate, give him a life like he'd never known, let him be a child, let him *smile* just once . . . he could do it. He *would.*

He felt it, when the Twins left their bodies and let their consciousnesses rise through the hole on the hill. He could almost *see* them reaching through the dark sky. They were reaching for Etarro and Avorra, but Anddyr reached back first. Reached for them with his power, but his hands reached, too, grasping at the air, grasping hard, and he could *feel* them, writhing and wriggling in his fingers. He dragged them, let his power flow through his fingers to burn through them, weakening them as he pulled, toward himself and toward Aro and Rora, who were unwillingly waiting . . .

He thought of her face. Rora, beautiful Rora, hard-edged and unbending. He thought of her face, how if he succeeded in this it would twist, change, turn to stone, to the horrible carved face of Sororra in the archway—gone . . .

A moment of fear, of skip-heart panic—*Rora!*—and that was all it took. Anddyr's grip loosened convulsively, and the Twins fought him. They sensed the trap, or perhaps Sororra riffled through his thoughts as all the old tales said she could, or perhaps they simply wished to spite him for his moment of weakness. Either way, they fought. There had been some hope when they were newly freed, weak and uncertain—but now that they knew, Anddyr alone could not hope to outmatch two gods. They rid themselves of his grip effortlessly, like a child flicking a beetle, and he would swear later that he heard laughter. As he had sent his power burning through them, so, too, did they send their own to burn through him.

Anddyr fell back screaming, convulsing, the skin of his palms burning, blistering, cracking. There was shouting over his own screaming, swearing over Rora's swearing, and then something hit the side of his head. "You've doomed us all!" Joros screamed. Another kick, and another.

"I tried," he whispered to the air, whispered to the storms falling around him like ash. He curled into the smallest shape he could, and he whispered across the hills, "I'm sorry." He couldn't see it, wouldn't want to, but in his bones he knew it was happening: Etarro, his young face twisting, changing, turning to the stone-carved face of a god. Anddyr had come so close to sparing him that. Could have spared him, if not for his own weakness . . . . "I'm so sorry."

CHAPTER THIRTY-FIVE

S cal stood amid the black sea, watching its waves surge around him, its currents pass him by. Steady as a rock in sea-spray. He stood near the base of the tall hill—not too near, for the swordsmen stood there. Vigilant, watching just as Scal watched, though they looked out instead of in. Scal stood and stared up and watched all the shapes moving atop the hill. Most wore black robes. Some a deep blue, and they shook as badly as Joros's witch-man had. He wondered, briefly, if Joros and his witch-man were atop the hill as well. Then he stopped wondering, for he could see at last there were others on the hill, a handful of others who wore red robes and yellow robes, and nothing else mattered.

Priests and priestesses, and among them, one with a scarred face.

He had watched her carefully through the long nights and longer days. Watched for any sign of cruelty, of abuse. If he had seen any, he knew his caution would have vanished. But she had not been mistreated. Had been treated well, in fact. Fed and cleaned, given a blanket to sleep on, others to speak with.

She had even smiled, once. He did not think she had seen him, in the long journey through the woods and the plains and the hills. If she had seen him, she had given no sign of it. Yet he had watched, vigilant as the stars at night, and he had waited for his moment.

Now, it felt as though time was rushing forward. As though there was so little of it left. As though his moment would pass by, and he would be left standing in the spinning breeze of it.

There were great happenings upon the hill. Rushing and shouting, cheering, laughing. Vatri sat on one slope with the others, ringed by two swordsmen and two bored-seeming preachers, their eyes constantly wandering to the crown of the hill. They would rather be elsewhere, and that was good. Distracted men were easy to move through, to knock down. He would need only to pass through the ring of blades around the hill, and he could manage the others . . .

Still he stood, waiting and watching, and his legs would not move.

Shape me, he had asked Vatri. It felt a dream. She had drawn on his flesh and told him to step into a fire, and when he had woken he had been no different, save that she was gone again. She had not made of him anything better than he was, and he did not know if he was good enough.

The sun fell and the moon rose high into its place. A full moon, shining sun-bright, wearing the night sky like a cloak. In its light he watched two preachers and two swordsmen harry the priests and priestesses to their feet, prod them farther up the hill, near to its crown. In the moonlight, he could just see Vatri, the edge of her face lined in moonfire. Blue eyes bright, and waiting, and watching.

The moon rose triumphant, and the black sea stilled, and there began a noise from the top of the hill. He did not understand it, at first. He had not heard much singing in his life. But singing it was, many voices raised together. He had never heard a song dance. Never heard before how a voice could sing the things that lay hidden in his heart.

There was fear in him, strong as the ocean-tide, heavy as all the snow in the North, blacker than death. But there was the singing, the soft and low fear-song rising over the high hill, and it sang to him of other things as well. It sang of making a weapon of fear. Of honing the fear to a sharp and deadly thing. The song spoke to him of what he had been, the hands that had shaped him, and the song spoke of what he could be. Perhaps Vatri had not shaped him as he had wished. Perhaps she had not shaped him at all.

But there was one true thing. He had asked her to shape him, and she would not be able to shape him if he did not get her back.

Scal had not held a weapon since leaving the North. He had thought he would be better for it. He gathered his fear together, and he shaped it, and he cast it ahead of himself. Following the fear, and following the song, Scal stepped forward through the black sea. One step, and another, his heart pounding in time with the song. The fear was gone from him, and it hung over the tall hill, over the head of a yellow-robed priestess, calling like a star. Three steps, four, and then he was running.

The black sea parted around him, fell before him. He ran, and he did not stop when he reached the ring of swordsmen. They saw him, but the song did not sing in their blood as it did in Scal's. They moved too slow. The one before him, the one whose eyes looked wide into his own, did not get his sword more than half-drawn. Scal lowered his shoulder and slammed it into the man's neck. Sent him falling, flying, choking. In the same moment, Scal wrapped his fingers over the hilt of the man's half-drawn sword. Pulled it free as the man fell away.

When his hand closed around the hilt, thumb-tip touching fingertips, fire kindled along the blade of the sword. True fire, sunfire, licking at the cold steel. Surprise rippled through Scal, and his fingers came loose, the sword falling, fire dying. He stood, stunned, heart loud in his ears as the singing ended. Staring down at the sword, only a simple sword. When he looked up, there were eyes on him. Two swordsmen, advancing. There was no time. Scal leaned down and grabbed the sword, and when fire lit along its blade once more, he did not drop it. There was a warmth on his palm, but it did not burn, did not hurt.

Scal ran forward through the silence, faster than the swordsmen, faster than the preachers turning slowly, too slowly, to look at him. The fire in his hand led him, up the side of the hill and to the moon-glowing priestess at its crest.

The ground shook beneath his running feet, but he held his balance. His heart still beat the time of the now-silent song, and he would not be stopped. His sword flashed, trailing flame, and any who drew too near, any who blocked his path, felt its bite. He was almost to her. The swordsmen there saw him coming, had the time to draw their blades, to face him. Ready. But their fear shone in the light of his sword. Its cut left behind blood and scorched flesh. A blade slashed along his arm, but he did not feel it. He turned the sword and swung again, felt it sink and slice and burn its way through.

The swing twisted his body, and when he looked up he saw

two children—twins. Old children, near-grown, but they did not seem like children at all. He had not cared to listen to the plans of the Fallen, had not wanted to know how they thought to free their gods. It seemed, though, that they had succeeded. The Twins, given life, given freedom. They were bound to the ground, but as he watched, the ropes around their wrists turned to ash, and they sat slowly up. A loud cry tore from their throats, loud and long, pain and joy and anger and love. One cry with two voices. As their shout died away, slowly the pain faded, and the love, and the joy. The ground trembled again.

Then Scal looked to Vatri, and she was looking to him as well, her surprise written clear, and her creased face was bent into the saddest smile he had ever seen.

Scal's fingers wrapped around hers, his other hand still around the fire-lit blade, and she ran with him from the hill. Only once did he look back. The Twins stood together at the hill's tallest point, their hands clasped, their heads tilted to the sky. They screamed together, and dark smoke boiled from their mouths, and a shuddering wave rolled through the sea of black-robed preachers. Bodies collapsed, untouched by any mortal hand, as the wave rippled outward. They fell, and they did not rise again.

A great white creature burst from the hill like an arrow shot into the sky, bellowing a scream to match that of the children, and great white wings snapped open. The wings flapped, bearing the great body into the sky, bearing the Twins upon its back, and the night swallowed them. Vanished.

Through the darkness Scal raced, Vatri tight in his wake, and the sword led them like a streaking star.

CHAPTER THIRTY-SIX

K eiro's ears were still ringing as he clambered over the lip of the hole, ringing with the screaming that had echoed through the cavern, echoed through the world. He could hardly think clear over the ringing, but he knew he should be above-ground, needed to see . . .

Keiro climbed from the hole, and stepped into chaos.

By the light of the moon and stars, he could see bodies racing frantically over the hills. Dimly, he heard their screaming, too, though it was a low echo of the ringing in his head. In the faint moonlight glow, he could see, too, all the bodies that were not moving. All those who lay perfectly still, sprawled upon the ground like cast-aside dolls.

Keiro tipped back his head. There was a spot of white disappearing into the dark sky, smaller, star-sized, gone. Straz. Below the hill, when the ancient *mravigi* had risen, the flapping of his wings had knocked Keiro to the ground, and the wind of it had stolen his breath away. Straz had flown, for perhaps the first time in centuries.

And, it seemed, he had taken Etarro and Avorra—Fratarro and Sorrora—with him.

The ground was faintly scorched where they had lain, the ropes gone as though they had never been, the stakes skewed guiltily.

A hand grabbed at Keiro's arm, but beneath the ringing, Yaket's voice was too distant for him to hear. Her eyes, one brown and one milky white, were wide with fear. Her own hand pointed, finger shaking, and he followed its line. There was a space on the horizon, a place where always, even on the cloudiest of nights, two red points had cast their glow over the world. That space was empty now. Sororra's Eyes had fallen from the sky.

Keiro pressed his hands to the sides of his face, trying to force his thoughts into order, to squash the ringing from his ears. He couldn't . . . *I am not* . . .

Keiro turned, and nearly fell through the hole in the earth in his haste. His toes found the ladder, and his fingers, and he scrambled down into the darkness. There were important things to be done beneath the hill, he told himself. He was not running. Not fleeing.

It was quiet in the great empty cavern—and empty it was. When the Twins had left their bodies, the preachers had left, too, raced up the ladders to see what was happening above. The *mravigi* . . . he searched the shadows for any sign of them, for any starlight glimmer, but they were gone. They had not gone aboveground, but perhaps they had retreated into their tunnels and caves, though he could not think why. There was nothing in the cavern save Keiro, nothing living . . . nothing save the slumped bodies of the Twins, shed like an insect's husk.

Keiro knelt before them, not quite believing, not daring to. They were gone, gone as surely as . . . as what? There was nothing sure in the world anymore. Even until the final moment, the final stitch he had placed through Fratarro's arm, he had doubted. Deep in his heart, he had not thought it would work, not thought that the Twins could ever truly flee their bonds. But now he knelt before their empty bodies, and it seemed as though he had been wrong about everything.

A hand touched his arm, and this time when he looked up at Yaket, lined in the dim moonlight still filtering through the hole, he could hear her soft voice clearly. "It is done, Godson."

"It is done, Elder," he echoed, and his voice sounded unspeakably tired to his own ears.

"I didn't think . . ."

"I know."

Quietly she knelt at his side, and together they stared up at the mighty bodies of the Twins, burned and lifeless. Their eyes were empty, their limbs loose, their heads tilted together as if in sudden sleep. A very soft *plop* startled Keiro, for the ichor had stopped dripping when Fratarro's wounds had been sealed . . . Ah, but not all his wounds had closed. There was still the ebon shard, pierced through the center of him, holding him as surely as the chains that held Sororra. The ichor flowed slow and steady from that ancient wound, carved dark trails along the burned flesh of his chest and stomach, and dripped onto the floor, to the glistening pool that gathered beneath him. If the ichor still flowed, that meant the Twins' bodies still lived, that only their minds had left . . . gone to the young twins above, who were gone now, too, though in body rather than mind. The Twins had taken their bodies, and he couldn't imagine how their own young minds were faring in the shared space . . .

"What will happen now?" Yaket asked, jarring Keiro from his thoughts.

"I do not know," he said, giving himself a small shake before turning to meet her eye. "If they have truly risen, they will usher in the Long Night. The sun will fall, and the Twins shall walk the earth once more, passing their judgment on all whom they meet, and making all men and all women equal. But I don't know how much of that is truth, and how much is merely the hope of centuries."

"Many preachers were struck down. They are saying it was the Twins' judgment."

"Perhaps it was." A thought struck him, brought him half to his feet. "The tribe. Yaket, they will be wondering, scared . . ." He couldn't bring himself to finish, to say that he didn't know how far the Twins' judgment might have stretched.

Yaket didn't move to stand, merely looked down at her hands. It seemed as though the same thoughts had crossed her mind. "I am frightened, Keiro." It was the first time she had used his name, in all the long months they had spent together.

Keiro swallowed the fear in his own throat. He thought of Poret, Keten, all the bright-eyed younglings who had listened so eagerly to Keiro, and all the steadfast folk who had stayed always by Yaket's side. He thought of them, and he didn't think of them as anything but living. He reached his hand down to Yaket. "We'll go together." She pressed her fingers into his, and it was too dark to tell if it was moonlight or tears on her cheeks.

The tall grass swallowed them, took them far away from the gentle hills and the still forms that sprawled upon them.

Some of the living had begun to organize, arranging those who the Twins' first judgment had struck down into neat rows. Keiro could not look at them too long, the dead and the living both, or it set off the deep ache within his chest. So he turned to the grass, and his hand was tight around Yaket's. He wondered, dimly, if the grip hurt her, until he realized she was holding his hand just as hard.

Night stretched over the Plains, bright stars above, heavy moon at their backs, and their steps were like lead. Never before had Keiro less wanted to walk somewhere, never had to force his feet forward so much as he did now. But this was a thing that must be done.

In the hours before light touched the sky, the tribehome was quiet. In that way, it was very much not like the hills with their screaming and their frantic pace. In another way, though, it was very like the hills—in the way that mattered, in the way that hurt.

In Fiatera, deceased were given to the flames or given to the ground, depending on which set of gods one followed. In his walking, Keiro had seen groups who gave their dead to the water, or to the animals, or to the sun. In the quiet Plains, the peaceful grass-sea, he learned that they gave their dead back to the grass.

There were more lying than there were kneeling, but the living had not been idle. Keiro watched, numb, as Yaket's hand slipped from his, as the elder went to join her grieving people. They wove grass stalks, their fingers deft, weaving a cocoon of grass for each still form.

Keiro wandered through them as if in a dream. He saw their faces, all those he had grown to know so well: Temon, who had a high and silly laugh that rang out often; Relat, who had the best way of cooking groundbirds but wouldn't share her secret with any others; Pakel, who could kick her leg up higher than any of the men; Kamat, who could throw a spear farther than anyone; so many more, all laid out with their glassy eyes reflecting the stars.

Somehow, Keiro had known he would find Poret. There had been a certainty in him. She lay staring at the stars, a faint look of surprise painted forever on her still face. He knelt beside her, or perhaps he fell, and touched her cheek with shaking fingers. He remembered all the times she had sat with that cheek pressed against his shoulder. How her laugh had fluttered from her lips across his skin. How she had smiled so soft and sweet.

He laid her out gently, smoothing her legs, crossing her hands above her heart. Then his hands reached, and pulled grass from the earth—long strands of grass, tall as a man, strong grass good for weaving. Keiro began to weave the grass around her, wrapping and tucking and tying, a cocoon to take her to her rest. He would have buried her, given her to the earth as the preachers did, but she was of the Plains. She should rest as they rested.

He had told her, it felt like long ago, how wondrous her life would be under the Twins' rule. That they would rise, and she would rise with them, a mighty hunter with a Starborn at her side. A certainty had whispered those words to him, another voice speaking with his own lips. He knew, now, the shape of the hand that had touched his mind.

Was any of it me? He worried that he had been entirely taken from himself, that he had been nothing more than a quiet dream these last months, that he had only just woken up to himself. *I am not . . .*

He worried more that he hadn't been.

The sky was going to gray when he finished, and Keiro rose without sound. The weavers were near done, a long line of green shapes bisecting the tribehome. He didn't know what they would do with the bodies next. He didn't want to know. Instead he walked, the long walk back through the grass, over the hills where more lines of bodies stretched. Something caught his eye upon the grass, a knife that someone had dropped. Its weight felt strange in his hand. He walked until his feet found the ladder, and then he was kneeling again, in the dark again, gazing at the empty shells of the Twins. The knife was still in his hand, and there was in him a dark urge to use it.

"Why?" he asked aloud, and he gave them a very long time to give answer. Waited for the whispering certainty, the insidious voice in his mind, but it did not come. Keiro stood, and the knife felt so heavy he could hardly hold it, but he stepped forward, toward Fratarro's body. His right foot had been stitched into place, long, sure stitches made of fine-woven grass. Grass was easy enough to break, easier with an edge. He wondered what would happen, if he cut away the thread.

He lifted the knife, and though it was heavy as death, his hand was his own. There was no whisper, no touch, nothing in his mind save himself.

As he raised the knife higher, its tip burned with sudden brightness.

The sun had found him, stretching its fingers over the lip of the hole. The Parents' sun, that they had loved more than their children. The Twins were gone, freed or lost, and still the sun rose. Nothing had changed, and so much had been lost for it. He watched the sunlight reach across the floor of the cavern, watched it crawl up Fratarro's restored limbs to the hole in his chest, the ichor-dripping eternal wound. They were gone, as good as dead, and they had no power here.

Keiro lifted the knife again, just before all the new light fell abruptly from the sky.

CHAPTER THIRTY-SEVEN

I'll kill you."

Rora'd lost count of how many times she'd said the words. She'd screamed them at first, screamed 'em until her throat went raw. Then she'd growled them, low and hard. Now she just said them flat and dead, like there wasn't anything left to her except those words, and maybe there wasn't.

"I'll kill you."

It'd been a few hours since they'd untied Aro, not too long after Joros had quit kicking the witch. They'd left Rora tied up. She couldn't really blame 'em; she'd kill them if they let her go. Now her brother and the witch sat with their heads bent together, both of 'em with too-wide eyes as they whispered at each other. She couldn't believe that Aro could be so stupid—no, that wasn't true; she *could* believe it because he'd always been a damnfool idiot, and he would've died five dozen times over if she hadn't been around to do his thinking for him.

And the witch . . . It hadn't been too long ago that she'd had her hands wrapped around his neck, squeezing the life out of him. Now, she wished she hadn't stopped. She hated the kid for making her stop.

"I'll kill you," she told Anddyr, even though he wouldn't look at her anymore. He had his big sad eyes on, black with bruises, like she should feel sorry for him, feel sorry that he'd failed to do whatever his master'd ordered, which probably involved killing her. And she was supposed to feel bad about that.

"What are they doing?" Joros asked the witch. Joros'd been staring over at the hill for hours, as the moon trailed down the sky, as the dim screaming finally faded away. The sky was turning gray in front of him, and he still hadn't done anything besides stare.

Anddyr crawled to his side, pathetic thing that he was.

"I'll kill you," she told him as he crawled by her, and she tried to kick at him even though she couldn't move her legs at all, but he flinched away like she could. He huddled at Joros's feet and did some magic thing. Rora was happy to see how his hands looked burned and blistered, like he'd grabbed a cook pot straight from the fire and not let go. It looked like it hurt him to do his spells, too, and that was good because it meant maybe he couldn't corrupt her brother anymore.

"They're tending to the dead," the witch said quietly.

"How many?"

"Too many to count."

"Try."

The witch flinched again and was silent for a long time, fingers twitching and lips moving. "A third? Half? It's hard to tell . . . some may be sleeping, or in shock . . ." Joros waved his words away and they both sank into silence.

A hand touched her arm, and Rora twisted around to see her

brother crouched near her, his eyes wide and sad and scared. "Rora," he whispered, and his voice broke like the world was falling to pieces around him, and even with how much she hated him, all she wanted to do was reach out to him. But her wrists were tied fast, and the best she could do was twist her fingers toward him.

He lay down next to her, curling up at her side like a baby, his head making her shoulder wet. He was always crying, was Aro. She leaned her head against his as best she could, squeezing her eyes shut. "I'll kill you," she whispered soft, because they were the only words she had in her.

"We should leave," Joros said, but he didn't do anything besides keep staring. "They'll organize soon enough, and the gods only know what—" He stopped himself, seemed to think about the words he'd just said. "There's no telling what they'll do once they've recovered and organized, and I don't want to be around to find out. We should be far away by then." Finally he tore his eyes away from the hill, and when he came to stand over Rora, he looked like he'd aged two decades in the night. "Will you cooperate if we release you?"

"I'll kill you."

"Rora," Aro said again, still blubbering on her shoulder, "you can't." He sat up so she could see his eyes, which was his best defense. "I need Anddyr. He . . . he's the only one who can help me now."

Over the hours lying there, Rora's anger had burned down to a coal, dull and soft-edged. But Aro's words set a spark to it and it flared up just as bright as it'd been when the witch had first knocked her over. It burned away the numb hate, and she spat out, "He's the one who *did* this to you."

"Yeah." Aro didn't argue; he was either smart enough to know it wouldn't do any good or dumb enough to not even try. "But it's been done. It's over. There's no changing what happened, so all we can do is make it right. Make *me* right." He sniffled, and if she looked close enough, she could almost maybe see storms swirling behind his big eyes, the same storms that swarmed over the witch. "I know we can do it, Rora, but we need Anddyr, and Joros, too. We need them, Rora."

It felt like it'd been someone else's life, but there'd been a time not so long ago when she and Aro'd been cornered in a village, and she'd stared out at the angry faces knowing she was about to die, and Aro, too, and there wasn't a thing she could do to stop it. Aro'd fallen to the ground, clutched her leg, grabbed her shirt, and she hadn't blamed him for crying, not then. "I'll do it, Rora," he'd said soft, but somehow she'd heard him clear over the villagers' screaming. "Ask me. I'll do it if you tell me to." She'd looked down and seen the blood in his eyes, the terrible tearing thing they never talked about. She'd seen all the people he'd killed without meaning to do it—Kala, some bullies who'd attacked Rora, and once a group of Blackhands thugs. She'd seen how he'd do it again, for her. "You have to ask me."

It'd near broken her, trying to decide—if it'd been her doing it, she could've killed that many people without much worry, without hating herself after, but Aro? He still had nightmares about Kala, who'd got to know them too well, figured out that they were twins, so Aro'd had to stop her. He couldn't kill one woman without it haunting him his whole life, so how much would it haunt him to kill a whole village? How much would it haunt her, to put that much hurt in him?

She hadn't had to decide, when it'd come down to it—Joros and his witch'd taken care of the problem for them—but she still remembered the look in Aro's eyes when he'd said, "You have to ask me."

Rora looked up at her brother now, and the words tasted like mud in her mouth. "Ask me. I'll do it if you tell me to." She saw how the words hit him like a punch, saw how he remembered that night as bright and sharp as she did. *I didn't make you kill all those people*, she shouted at him with her eyes, *so don't tell me I can't kill these ones. It's the same thing.* "You have to ask me."

Aro's head hung down and he got real small, like the words'd made him small. He didn't say anything for a long time, and she could see Joros getting angry. Probably seemed like an easy thing to him, because he was a heartless bastard who only cared about himself. Finally Aro lifted his head, and his cheeks were more wet, and he said, "I need them. I need their help."

"You have to ask me," she said again, not caring how it was like twisting a knife in his gut. Not caring how she felt herself tipping, just a little bit.

"Please, Rora." He grabbed her arm, and if she'd been able to, she would've twisted away from his touch. She just looked up at him with hard eyes and sharp edges until a wet sound burst out of him and he whispered, "You have to let them live. I'm telling you. You can't kill them."

She ground her teeth and looked away, looked up at the sky that was going from black to gray to yellow, the stars fading away like they were dying. "Then untie me," she spat up at them, and it didn't matter whose hands were at her wrists.

She spent a few minutes rubbing feeling back into her ankles and wrists, rubbing hard enough she wouldn't've been surprised if she scraped some skin off. Soon as she could feel the blood flowing again, she stood up and she started walking north. They followed, all three of 'em, but she didn't much care.

The sun was bright on her face as it rose, and it made her want to shout back at them how they'd been so stupid, how none of it mattered because if the damned Twins were free, then there wouldn't be any sun, so it'd all been for nothing. They'd broke Aro all for nothing, twisted him into someone different, and if he wasn't Aro anymore, then where'd that leave her? But she kept her teeth pressed together, and her eyes ahead, and the sun on her cheek, until it started to get dark.

It started slow, no different'n sunset, except the sun was still to the east and hadn't been up for more'n an hour. When she stopped and turned to look, it was like something was stretching in front of the sun, pulling away pieces of it, like a washerwoman snapping a long sheet and letting it settle slow. Bit by bit the sun went away, and the sky went from blue to gray to black, and one by one the stars came back to life in the sky.

And then there wasn't a sun anymore. Just like that.

The others were standing near her, but no one said anything. What could you say to something like that? It wasn't cold, not any more cold than it'd been any night on the hills, but a shiver rolled through Rora.

A light streaked across the sky, big and white, glowing like a star . . . and *growing*. Streaking through the sky, and looking like it was heading straight at the hills.

A hand grabbed Rora's arm and near yanked her off her feet, and then they were running, and there was only room for a fear that blocked up her ears with the thump of her heart. She didn't dare look over her shoulder, didn't want to know where the falling star was or how close. She wasn't brave enough to stare death in the face.

The ground shook so hard it sent them all sprawling, Rora landing half on top of the witch with Aro tangled in her legs. The ground kept on shaking as she scrambled to her knees and tried to stand, shook like it was cracking in half and would shake itself to pieces. They started running again as best they could, stumbling and falling and always getting back up, until finally the world settled down under their feet and they could just run.

A sound rolled across the hills and the grass, the same way the shaking had rolled through the earth. Only the sound was laughter, two voices laughing, and it seemed like it followed them no matter how fast they ran.

Rora didn't stop running until her side ached so bad she couldn't breathe through the pain. She tried to stay on her feet at least, bent over and panting, but it still hurt like hells so she gave up on it and fell onto the ground. The dark grass surrounded her, swaying, hiding and showing the stars in the sky above.

Aro fell next to her, and the witch, too, though he stayed farther away. That was smart, because even exhausted and hurting, she still hated him. Joros stayed standing, breathing hard as any of 'em, but probably feeling like he was too good to fall over. That was good, too, because it let her keep hating him. Soon as he got his breath back, Joros started swearing. Rora could appreciate them for being good swears, but she didn't care enough beyond that.

There was something that'd kept sneaking into her thoughts as she was running, sneaking in under the fear: something from a long, long time ago. Her father's face was something she could remember, clear and shining, a sharp memory of green eyes and a big smile and a tickling beard. But that memory was like a stone—if you held it too often, you'd wear it down so it was dull and smooth, nothing more'n a smiling smear of green. That was one of the worst things she could think of, so she kept his face tucked away, safe and bright. But in all the running, his face'd come into her mind even though she hadn't called it up, and she'd heard his voice, deep and sure, a rumble like stones settling into place. Whenever she and Aro'd got in trouble, the smile'd fallen off his face and he'd always asked, "Is this how you want to be remembered, after the world ends?"

All the time she'd been running, she'd heard him asking that, over and over, each word timed with the beating of her heart. *Is this how you want to be remembered, after the world ends?*

And it wasn't.

Rora stood up, and she started walking. She was done with running—it didn't do any good, when it came down to it.

"Where do you think you're going?" Joros shouted after her.

"Home," she said over her shoulder, not stopping. She'd been running too long. If the world was ending, she didn't want Whitedog Pack, the second-best family she had, to remember her as a traitor and a murderer. If the world was ending, it was better if it ended while she was surrounded by her pack, even if they still hated her. That had to be better'n running.

But she did look back, at fuming Joros and the witch staring back south. You could choose your pack, but you couldn't choose who was in it. Much as she hated it, these bastards were part of her pack, too. And Aro . . . her sweet fool of a brother, tugging at Anddyr's sleeve, loyal to the point of being stupid. *Home* sounded like Sharra and Tare, but it sounded like Aro, too. "Come on," she growled at them. "There's nothing left here."

Joros came after her, stomping and swearing and pulling at his hair, no better'n a kid. Aro followed after a second, after another few tugs at Anddyr's sleeve. The witch didn't move.

"Witch," she snapped at him, and then spit his name like poison, "Anddyr."

He finally turned, and his cow's eyes had ghosts in them. He just said one thing: "Etarro."

The name felt like a punch, but sometimes you had to turn with a hit, let it spin you around. Some punches would take you down if you let them. "There's nothing you can do for him."

"I made a choice," the witch said, and the ghosts in his eyes were telling her that should mean something. Maybe it would, if she let the hit land, but she was already turning with it. "Etarro . . . I chose . . ."

"Then go," she snarled. Anyone in a pack was only useful so long as they kept doing what they were needed for. When they stopped . . . "I don't care. You're useless anyway." She started walking again, Joros behind her, Aro trailing. After a while, she heard the witch still muttering about his choice, and since the muttering wasn't getting any quieter, she knew he was following, too. She didn't care.

If the world was ending, she didn't have time to make everything right—maybe didn't have time to make *anything* right. Some things mattered more'n others, and those she'd do everything she could to fix. If she couldn't fix 'em, there were worse things than dying next to old friends. There were worse things than old friends killing you, too, and that was a strange kind of comfort. Rora reached up as she walked, touched the wrinkle where she used to have an ear. She'd go back to her pack, her real pack, the pack that mattered, and she'd try to make things right before all the world ended.

CHAPTER THIRTY-EIGHT

They stopped when the sun fell out of the sky. Vatri's loose fingers tugging on Scal's, halting his churning legs. Her fingers were tight around his, painful, as they watched the sun swallowed piece by piece. Watched, helpless, as the world went dark around them.

He glanced at her face, and her jaw was hard. Her eyes fierce and bright. There was no fear in her face as the sunlight left it. Grief, yes, but only faint traces of it. Mostly, there was determination.

The sun left, piece by piece, but Scal and Vatri were left standing in a pool of light.

She held his fingers tightly, but the fingers of his other hand were wrapped just as tight around his sword, pointed downward. He did not want to look down. Did not want to have to face, finally, the thing he could not understand. He made himself look, to see his fingers clinging tight to the leather-bound hilt. To see the long blade, slightly curved, with fire licking along the blade. Its light a steady crackle, not devouring, not consuming. It simply *was*, and the longer he stared, the more a song seemed to glow at its heart. A song of justice and of revenge, a song of retribution, and of fear, too . . . a song of blood . . .

Scal's fingers came open slow, stiff. The sword fell, and the fire faded from its blade sudden as waking from a nightmare. His hand felt heavy and cold where he had held it. He flexed his fingers, open and closed and open, and his skin was not burned. Was callused and rough as old leather, no different than it had ever looked.

Vatri's fingers loosed from his other hand. He turned and found her facing him, head tilted back to meet his eyes, shoulders tight. There, in the sudden daylight dark, with only the faint-ember stars to shine upon her face, she said, "Ask." Her jaw was tight, and her eyes were fierce, but beyond the fierceness he thought he saw the whisper-light touches of fear.

He closed his fingers, felt the dull distant bite of his nails into his palm. She had drawn sigils on his palms with fire-ash, and she had pointed him into the roaring fire. He turned to face her, his fists held between their still bodies. "You did this?"

She shook her head. "I don't have that sort of power. You know that."

"You made this happen," he tried instead.

"You asked me." There was a sharp note in her voice. A low-lurking anger. Defensiveness. "You asked me to shape you. You said you trusted me."

"I did. I do." Scal opened both palms to her, perfectly matched, though the one had held a sword of fire for long hours. "But I do not understand."

She bent down, hands sure in the darkness. When she stood, she held the sword between them, hilt loose in her fingers, held toward him. In her hand, it was a simple sword, hard steel and bright with starlight glow, but there was no fire to it. She looked away, to the dark empty place where the sun had hung only moments ago. "Take it," she said softly, without meeting his eyes.

It made him uneasy, but Scal did. His fingers brushed hers, touched leather, and the fire sprang between them, shining along the blade like rippling water. On the other side of the blade, the fire echoed bright in her eyes. Her face was a sudden mask, and an awful thing to see. Inhuman, with fires in her eyes.

Her fingers slipped from under his, and it left his hand cold, though the fire burned bright above it.

"Now with the left hand," she said. Scal passed the sword into his other hand, and the fire quenched—replaced, just as sudden, with a sheen of ice and spines like crystals, short but sharp as knives themselves.

Scal dropped the sword, and the ice was gone before it touched the ground. He stared again at his palms. They looked no different. Skin over flesh over bones. He closed his fingers over them. "I do not understand," he said again.

"You saw the swordsmen the Fallen have. 'Blades for the darkness,' they're called. Not quite enough of them to be a true army, but they have a good fighting force, and now that the Long Night has come, they'll be passing their own judgments alongside the Twins'. I think the Parents deserve at least one sword."

Scal clenched his fists tighter, stared at his bared wrists. His jaw was tight when he looked up at Vatri. He could see, almost, why Joros had grown so frustrated with her. "Speak plainly."

She made a sharp sigh, and spread her own hands. "How

can I? This is . . ." She ran a hand through her hair, brought it down to thump against her leg. Stared into the dark sky once more. Her eyes now were less fiery, more troubled. More human. "I told you before that I was godmarked. Called at birth to serve the Parents, and I always have. Everything I do is to serve them. My life is a clear path, my choices drawn like a map. I know to my bones who I am." She looked up to his eyes, and hers were at once sad and fierce. "But you. It's like you were put together by a blind man at a loom. You're a dozen different colors of thread, and none of them match, and there are big empty spaces of nothing with no clue how to blend the mismatching pieces together. You asked me to shape you." Tears gathered in the corners of her eyes, bright and distant as stars. "I'm not a weaver, or a shaper. All I know is doing what I'm told. This—" she gestured at Scal in a way that covered the sum of who he was "—is what I was told to do."

He had been many things in his many lives. Each of them had had a name, a purpose. A reason. They had all fit poorly as a small glove, but at least he had known what to name himself. "What am I, then?"

"You are fire. You are ice. You are a blade for the light. A sword to fight back the Long Night."

Scal opened his fingers, closed them again. He could not think of the right words. He could only ask, "Why?"

Vatri made an impatient noise. "Why what?"

"Why . . ." He showed her his palms, waved one at the sword lying in the grass. "Why . . . me? Why was I chosen for this?"

She shook her head at him. "No one is ever chosen. You merely are, and all the things that make you *you* have shaped you into a tool that fits within the hand of a god. You asked me to shape you, but . . . that's not something I can do. Not something *anyone* can do. You shape you. You are nothing more than what you've made yourself, and nothing less."

There was a place in Scal that had been empty for most of his lives. An aching hollow, filled by slow drops, and they leaked away as easily as a pierced waterskin. The empty echo rang through him, full of a priest's smile and a snowbear's smile, an everflame and an ice-shelf, lonely steps and lonely sleeps, and blood, always blood.

He had wanted to be more than he had been. Wanted to be better.

"Scal."

She drew his eyes back up. Her face was still tight, tense, closed and dark as the sky. The tears touched her eyes, but the fire did, too, the distant fire that glowed within her. Her lips trembled, and then they flattened. "You're not alone," she said. "I'm not leaving you this time." She did not reach out to him, did not reach across the yawning distance of the space between them. Her eyes were sad and they were fierce, and she stood straight and still as a mountain peak.

He wanted to reach across that space, to touch her and make the distance between them vanish. But there was fire in his hands, and there was ice, and the familiar peaks and valleys of her face had become a mask.

Shape me, he had asked her. She had only done what she could. Nothing more, and nothing less. It had not been how he would have wanted . . . but then, it never was.

He bent down, and in the darkness his fingers found the leather-wrapped hilt. Raised the sword, fire-flickering, to his side. Though it touched the grass, brushed against countless stalks as he raised it, the grass did not burn. The blade sang to him again, its song of glory and retribution and blood, and he let the song hold him. It lit the world around them, made a new small sun upon the earth, and he stared at Vatri in its dancing light. She stared back, and the fire was in her eyes. There was more in her, beyond the singing flames. Words that would fill the space between them, words like a rock slide that would make a bridge, a path. So many things she could have said. Held back, or trapped. Words unspoken, lost among the plains and the fire.

Scal walked forward, and Vatri walked at his side, but the space stretched between their swinging arms. The sword led them, its fire-glow piercing through the Long Night, and its blood-song sang sad and steady through his veins.

About the Author

Living in the cold reaches of the upper Midwest with her beast of a dog, Rachel Dunne has developed a great fondness for indoor activities. *In the Shadow of the Gods*, her first novel, was a semifinalist for the 2014 Amazon Breakthrough Novel Award before being picked up for publishing. For as long as snow continues falling in Wisconsin, she promises to keep writing.